R.C.
BRIDGESTOCK
CONDEMNED

CANELO

First published in the United Kingdom in 2021 by

Canelo
31 Helen Road
Oxford OX2 0DF
United Kingdom

A CIP catalogue record for this book is available from the British Library.

Print ISBN 978 1 80032 430 5
Ebook ISBN 978 1 80032 323 0

Look for more great books at www.canelo.co

Printed and bound in Great Britain by Clays Ltd, Elcograf S.p.A.

At this time, amid the current pandemic of Covid-19 the emergency services across the country are being pressed to their limit. Morale is tanking and the stresses of the job are ever increasing...

We would like to dedicate this book to the countless doctors, nurses and healthcare workers treating coronavirus patients, for their selfless commitment and diligence as they undertake vitally important roles to protect and improve the health of people in these testing times, and to all these who have lost their lives fighting the virus.

&

To our police family who put themselves in harm's way every day in the pursuit of justice and to make the world a safer place, by bringing to justice those individuals who seek to inflict pain, injury and suffering. For this they are rarely shown gratitude - in fact they are frequently ridiculed for their virtuous acts. Your commitment is laudable and necessary work.

'Blessed are the peacekeepers, for they shall be called the children of God.' Matthew 5.9

Chapter 1

Cold air, peppered with icy rain, smacked Charley's face the minute she opened her front door, temporarily blinding her. Immediately she put her chin to her chest and pulled her hood over her head. She turned her back on the snowstorm and stepped down onto the gritted pathway as she put the key in the door, and locked it. On doing so, she stole a glance up at her bedroom window, and a shiver came from deep within. The yearning for the warm bed she'd abandoned was overwhelming, but duvet days were seldom come by for a Senior Investigating Officer in charge of serious crime. Aristotle's words hovered on her quivering lips; 'To appreciate a snowflake, you have to stand out in the snow.' Yorkshire weather was rarely predictable.

Ghostly, freezing fog hovered above the thin layer of snow, every inch of the path ahead covered with the white powder. Teeth chattering, Charley cautiously put one foot in front of the other, fearing with every step that she might slip on the ice lurking beneath. With shaking hands, she rummaged in her coat pocket for the car keys. Relieved to be out of the worst of it, once safe inside the vehicle she sat patiently waiting for the windows to defrost, letting the engine idle for a few moments. There was no rush about her. The dead body was going nowhere until the SIO arrived, suspicious circumstances or not.

Tuning in to the local radio station, Charley listened with interest to the forecast as she considered her route out of the village of Marsden, coming quickly to the conclusion that it would be best to avoid her preferred route to the Calder Valley over the Packhorse bridge, via the scenic valleys, rugged peaks and crags, and head for the more reliable A62.

As if in response to her thinking, the radio presenter announced, 'Take care if you're driving on the A62 between Marsden and Diggle, it's allegedly the fourth most dangerous road in Britain.' Charley raised an eyebrow. How come she had lived in Huddersfield all her life, yet she didn't know that? The following news distressed her: a report of the fire brigade attending a house fire at the local property known as Crownest.

Rubbing her palms over her face, she groaned. There had long been accounts of strange events reportedly taking place, and numerous mysteries associated with the family who owned the property. Charley wondered if these would now cease? The last she'd heard was that the house had been put up for sale, and that plans for its demolition were imminent, and for some reason that news had made her extremely sad.

When the windscreen cleared, she saw that her neighbours' curtains remained firmly closed, shutting out the outside world. 'You must be wrong in t'head to have sought the position of a regional Head of Crime in the fourth largest police force in the land. Especially in winter.' she said to her reflection in the rearview mirror.

As she spoke her breath formed plumes of vapour, and as it rose, she saw what looked like the blurred image of two black eyes looking back at her. Adjusting the direction of the car's airflow vents made them vanish. She chuckled, she *was* definitely 'wrong in t'head'.

–

On the approach to Marsden Moor Charley was delighted to see the ghostly outline of the orange flashing lights on a gritter wagon on the road ahead. Once the road surface was treated, it was left to the traffic to do the rest; to wear ruts into the ploughed snow that would turn to slush and eventually clear. She knew that following the gritter slowly was her best chance of making progress to the scene of the body that Control at Headquarters had requested she attend. The crime's location wasn't her normal patch. Although, she conceded, if the formidable, legendary Detective Inspector Jack Dylan doubted his ability to get there, God only knew what made them think she could! Harrowfield was his domain, and he was closer than she was to the cadaver. She weighed up the HQ controller's thought pattern – maybe given the conditions, it was likely wise having two officers attempting to get to the scene, to determine if it was foul play or not?

Born and bred on the Marsden moors, she was aware more than most, that the four seasons brought dramatic changes to the land across which she travelled, but thanks to her folk whose ancestors were all farmers, she knew the moors like the back of her hand. Today the going was slow. The patchy low cloud made sure of that. In fact, so dense was the fog, that at times Charley felt as if she was in a spaceship on its way to an unknown universe. The prevailing fog meant that the journey offered up surprising corners and sweeping curves, but when the veil was lifted, Charley relaxed a little, as she could see long stretches of road, way ahead of her. She turned up the radio and hummed along to the music. When she knew the words she sang, and when she didn't, she made them up.

Suddenly blue flashing lights on the receding horizon in her rearview mirror, grabbed her attention. Charley put her foot slowly on her brake and steered the car as far into the side of the road as she dared, without fear of getting stuck in a snow drift. She let the fire engine pass. Radio now off, she looked at her watch. Becoming increasingly warm, she turned down the heater. The windscreen began to mist over, just slightly, but it was enough to make her wind down her window only to be confronted with a confusion of cawing. She looked up. A murder of crows circled their roost in a well-protected copse of trees, which hugged the rocky base of Millstone Edge. 'It's an omen…' she could hear granny's caution. She remembered how her younger self, puzzled by her granny's discomfort, had questioned the remark. Charley was an inquisitive child. 'It's the harbinger that guides souls from the realm of the living into the afterlife, lass.'

'What a load of old codswallop,' Charley could hear her mother Ada retort, quite clearly. Turning to Charley, Ada's voice had softened to a whisper in her ear. 'Your granny is ruled by the moon. Another day she'll tell you a crow is a sign of a spiritual blessing. Whatever suits. Isn't that right, Mother?' Charley's mother had no time for the old lady's fables, but Charley loved spending time with her granny. Unkindly regarded as 'loopy' by some, Granny was hugely entertaining. Never short of telling a good story, Granny had been the youngster's favourite playmate.

When the fire crew had passed, Charley nudged the accelerator with her foot, and very slowly the car crept forward on the packed ice. Looking ahead at the darkening sky, she found herself transfixed by the number of large birds diving, lunging and cawing in singles, and in pairs, as they flew around above her vehicle in a circle, before they began to break apart. The car then plunged into another wall of dense fog, and the birds were lost to her. Concentrating hard in order to see ahead, Charley carefully navigated her way around a hairpin bend, and then another, until all of a sudden, the fog snapped away again and she was upon Eastergate, as if the car had found its way all by itself.

Below her, the hill peaks reared up into the low clouds, and in front she saw the shadow of an impressive detached, period property smouldering in the distance; Crownest. Locally, the house was of huge interest, rumoured as it was to be haunted, with its extensive grounds used by witches in days gone by, for dark, satanic rituals. Or, at least that's what Granny said. What couldn't be mistaken was the hive of activity that now surrounded the property, just as Charley envisaged after hearing the earlier radio announcement concerning the fire.

At that moment her phone rang. It made her jump, such was her focus on the house. She steered the car off the road, and into the gateway to Crownest; the only place that was free from snow.

Detective Constable Annie Glover didn't give her boss time to speak. 'Have you been stood down?'

'No, why?' Charley was slightly confused.

'I've just been reading the Chief's log. Dylan's just pronounced the body as not suspicious, so I guess you will be stood down soon.'

'Good,' Charley said, her eyes seeking out the extent of the fire damage at the house. Then it came to her. 'Wait on, what are you doing at work?'

Annie grimaced. 'Err… I've been called in.'

Charley frowned. 'What for?'

'Ricky-Lee asked me to cover for him, apparently the Force's rugby team has had several cry off, and it's an important match.'

'I bet.' Charley mumbled under her breath. 'Where's the nearest race meeting?'

The line went deathly quiet. 'Wetherby, I guess. He's circled the runners and riders in the paper on his desk.'

–

Realising she'd potentially dropped Detective Constable Ricky-Lee Lewis in it, Annie quickly ended the call, but she needn't have worried, as Charley's attention had been drawn to the name on the demolition company's vans parked in the driveway. *NEVERMORE* adorned the vehicles' rear and side which were tucked in tightly against the dry-stone wall boundary of the property, which had long since seen a reduction in height since it was built.

A lanky young lad with a hard hat, and an oversized, threadbare donkey jacket that had seen better days, came alongside the fire engines towards Charley's car. He saw her looking at the faded, battered 'For Sale' sign hanging on the gateway.

'Howya! You're a bit late if you were thinking of buying it.'

Charley smiled. 'Oh, no, I'm not in the market for buying a house, especially one with such a ghastly history – or thrilling – depending on your position on the macabre.'

'Well, while you're here, crack on and help yourself to some of that lovely dry-stone walling,' he smiled with twinkling Irish eyes. 'It makes a nice rockery, so me oul' fella says, and he should know; he's a real cute hoor!' When he saw Charley's questioning look, he continued in a whisper, 'Don't worry, no one's going to notice a few stones missing now, are they, the wall's banjaxed, and I'm not about to tell.' With his mind very obviously on more important things the young man looked this way and that, as if anticipating someone's imminent arrival.

Charley nodded her head, and made no attempt to move. 'Indeed. I bet that's what they all say – those that have taken just a few stones, that is.'

He watched Charley's eyes continue to study the building and called out to her, 'the stories about this place, they'll no doubt go on.'

She was surprised by his interest. 'I guess so,' said Charley, knowing that soon the formidable property which had been part of the scenery of her childhood would be reduced to a pile of rubble, making it impossible to find the facts to disprove the legends associated with it. From here on, the only proof of the house's existence and occupation by the Alderman family would be the tales passed down by word of mouth.

Shoulders hunched, and with his hands deep in his jacket pockets the young man hopped from foot to foot. His face pinched and grey, his lips held a blue cast. 'I wish they'd hurry up,' he said, his voice quivering. The noise his metal toe-caps made on the tarmac made her look down at his work boots – very obviously secondhand, or borrowed.

'Who?' Charley furrowed her brow. Her phone rang. 'Excuse me,' she said. She took the call but her eyes remained on the young man who now stood under the entrance to St Anne's Church across the road from

Crownest, which provided him a little shelter from the icy wind.

'Ma'am, since you're already out and about, Control are asking CID to attend at a property called Crownest. The Fire Brigade in attendance suggest circumstances could be suspicious. I wonder if you'd mind calling on your way back?' Charley's eyes raised to meet the workman's watching her from over the road.

'Tell Control I'm already at the scene, although I'm not sure what I can do, the fire is still going, but I'll liaise.'

Much to the young man's surprise, Charley turned off her car engine and got out of the car. He eyed her quizzically.

'What's your name?'

'Finn, why?' Without waiting for an answer, he carried on impatiently. 'Where are t'Old Bill when you need 'em? I'll tell you where they are, they're all over mi' oul' fella like flies on cow shit. Once a wrong 'un always a wrong 'un in the Old Bill's eyes.' Finn looked back at the house with concern in his eyes. 'He swears he's done nowt wrong this time. Holy Joe!'

Charley frowned. 'Holy Joe?'

'The gaffer, he's doing his nut. Truth is, if the plod don't come soon, he'll have no choice but to send us off site, and that can't 'appen. I need the money to give to mi Ma for the young 'un's Christmas party.'

'Why's that then?'

Finn's face fell. 'The old fella, he's been sent down this morning by the Magistrates which is why I'm 'ere instead of at college.'

Charley's look was a wry one. 'Come on. I guess, right now I'm the answer to your prayers.'

The young man looked at her once, then twice. The silence of the early morning was only broken by the scrape of a snowplough on the road coming towards them. He closed his eyes momentarily. His pale face became suddenly flushed as her revelation hit him.

Finn lowered his head. 'What an eejit! I'm sorry, Missus. I didn't mean to be disrespectful.'

A smile escaped Charley's lips. 'Better show me the way if we're gonna try keep this site open, eh?'

–

She followed Finn. The high security fencing erected around the building's perimeter displayed danger signs as she approached. For her safety, she was taken down the side of the left wing of the building which was mostly a shell, blackened and still smoking. Moving slowly and carefully over debris, Charley took a moment to glance up at the beautiful, high, ornate, carved stone arches that without a roof, reached up towards the sky. Charley's heart felt heavy, distraught for the sorry state of the property which was rich in history, and once so grand.

The pair picked their way through rubble, which combined with the water from the fire hoses was now a sloppy, wet mess. They managed to avoid the worst of the mud and the deepest puddles, but had to keep an eye out to negotiate where there was fallen debris. As she moved slowly over the site to the front of the house, Charley got a glimpse of a number of yellow hard-hatted heads, huddled together in conversation at the far side of the overgrown bowling green, beyond which was an extensive garden that wrapped itself around the house. The glistening white branches of the leafless trees in the wood beyond looked as if they were frozen in time, and space.

9

Finn guided her carefully past two site containers. A bulldozer stood next to a cherry-picker.

The idle demolition workers were facing away from Charley, but could be heard joking with the fire crew for putting out the house fire that had been keeping them warm. As the fire crew continued to clean up, the banter made it obvious, quite quickly, that the fire was nothing but a hindrance to the demolition team, as they couldn't get on with their work. No wonder Finn's boss was 'doing his nut' if he was paying them just to stand around. Charley could see that left to the elements, Crownest had taken a battering from the inclement weather. Ferocious gale force winds, torrential rain and snow had savaged it on all sides for over a hundred years, but yet it had survived – until the unexplained fires had started. Not the first a few weeks ago, but the second had finally destroyed it beyond repair, and now another today, even though this time the house was already in the hands of the demolition services.

Finn touched her arm gently. 'You wait here,' he said. 'I'll go find Mr Greenwood.'

–

Charley stood with her back to the men, who were beginning to show interest in her. She studied the house frontage which appeared on the face of it barely touched by the fires. That is until her eyes reached up as far as the roof. The skeletal roof was silhouetted against the now darkening grey skies. If God were looking down on her, he would send rain instead of more snow. She shivered as large snowflakes began to fall.

'Miraculously, the pair of chimneys at either side of the grand building remained erect, like two proud soldiers, don't you think?'

Charley turned to see the rugged face of Nevermore's owner, Mr Greenwood. The demolition company director sported a thick woollen hat.

'Joe,' he said shaking her hand.

'Detective Inspector Charley Mann, Huddersfield CID.'

Joe Greenwood took her to one side conspiratorially. 'Look, this building is no doubt going to implode soon. With the west wing gone, the damaged walls won't be able to take the strain much longer. From a health-and-safety point of view, it's causing me a great deal of concern. Which is why we need to get it dropped as soon as possible,' he said. There was a certain amount of frustration in his voice, as well as desperation, and for the first time Charley felt certain that not all was as it should be.

Charley shook her head. 'I'm sorry, I do have a great deal of sympathy for you, but there are procedures that I have to adhere to. Like it or not, it's my job to determine whether it's arson and that means first I must speak to the leader of the fire crew, to get their take on the situation before I do anything else.'

Joe Greenwood scowled. 'For goodness sake, does it matter how the fire started when the place is in such disrepair? You and I know it was probably local kids that have nowt better to do than cause mischief. Come on, give me a break; the lads are on site and I can have what's left of this eyesore dropped...' He took a look at his watch, '... in precisely two hours.'

Charley raised her eyes at Mr Greenwood. 'I seem to remember that I saw the property up for sale at Raglan's Estate Agents in the High Street not that long ago and they didn't call it an "eyesore". According to them it was quite a desirable family residence!'

Out of the corner of her eye, Charley could see a firefighter walking towards them, and as he did so, he removed his gloves and helmet. 'Definitely a smell of accelerant,' he said, wiping his dirty face with a piece of rag.

Charley saw Joe's shoulders drop, and a heavy sigh emerged from his lips. It was evident that the firefighter saw it too.

'It could be from the machinery you're using.'

'Still, it could be suspicious?' asked Charley.

'I'm saying there are a couple of seats of fire which suggests to me that it's no accident, but let's face it, which person of any significance would bother setting fire to a house that is about to be demolished?'

'Who indeed,' said Charley. 'However, just as important to me, is *why*? But, Mr Greenwood is right, it's insecure and needs making safe. There's no likelihood of securing any evidence from that water-soaked debris.' Charley turned to face Mr Greenwood. 'Do what you need to do.'

Chapter 2

Crownest was the title on the deeds, and the name that had been hand-carved into the naturally weathered grand Yorkshire stone pillars, which, despite having had a knock or two over the years, had remained standing as monuments of the past at the gateway to the house.

Owing to her interest in the property, mostly fuelled by her grandmother's tales, Charley was aware that the house had been home to a number of generations of the locally renowned Alderman family, so the results of Annie's enquiries with the estate agent surprised her somewhat.

'The occupants of Crownest had apparently been renting the property from the owners, prior to the completion of the sale.'

As she stood at her filing cabinet, Charley acknowledged the hot drink the young detective constable had put on her desk with a 'thank you'. The SIO paused, reminiscent of another time. 'I recall Danny Ray, my ex, once wrote an article for *The Chronicle* about Crownest.'

'You mean the ex that is looking at a minimum of twenty five years in jail, for murder?.'

Charley breathed in deeply, and with a file in her hand swiftly slammed the drawer shut. 'Yes, that's the one! And, the reason why I'm single and more than happy to stay that way,' she said with a cynical smile. She walked past Annie to her desk, and sat.

Four years her junior, with significantly less service and life experience, that Annie put down to being schooled by nuns, Detective Constable Glover slid into the visitors chair opposite. Thoughtfully, she ran her tongue over her tongue stud. 'Me too. Life's complicated enough without men!'

Charley looked at her quizzically, 'The thing with the new, young, fit, Chief Inspector didn't last long.'

Annie pulled a face, 'He might be young, fit and extremely good looking, but would you go out with a man who farts in front of your friends and then rates it by sound and smell?'

Charley giggled. 'Oh, I'm sorry, it's not funny.'

'No, it's not,' Annie said sulkily.

Charley picked up her mug of coffee.

'Whilst doing the research for the article Danny said that solicitors had been searching for a relative of Adam Alderman's, to claim his estate, for donkey's years – hence I guess why Crownest had been empty for so long. Adam, Felix's bastard son died at a ripe old age in the 1950s. It's news to me that anyone had been found, but maybe it happened when I was seconded to the Met for those years. According to local gossip, Catherine Alderman, the sister of Felix and Seth, was banished to Australia by Seth, who was reported to be insanely jealous of her relationship with his wife. Catherine was never heard of again. Some say Seth killed her in one of his drunken rages and she never actually left the country.' Charley paused, her eyebrows creasing together in a frown. 'Don't you think it odd for the buyers Mister and Missus Bradley Dixon to be renting first? Why not wait until the sale goes through to live there?'

Annie shrugged her shoulders, and stuffed a chocolate bar in her mouth.

Charley took off her suit jacket and reached behind her to hang it on the end of the radiator. She paused. 'Maybe something was holding up the sale, and the sellers, presumably the benefactors of Adam Alderman's estate, didn't want to lose their buyers?'

Annie chewed the chocolate-covered toffee bar, her eyes rolling back into her head, her expression indicating she was chewing as fast as she possibly could so she could carry on the conversation.

Charley leaned forward, put her elbows on her desk and her chin in her hands and looked at Annie, expectantly, 'In your own time.'

Annie swallowed hard. 'Apparently, according to Miss Finch at the estate agents, the buyers claimed to be chasing references, and it was taking forever! When the estate agent pushed the buyers for a completion date, at the seller's insistence, it was suggested by the buyers that they rent the property in the meantime to show their commitment.'

Annie slid the estate agent's brochure for Crownest across the desk. Charley picked it up. It was obvious to her that the cover photograph had purposely been taken from an angle that would not capture the masses of colourful graffiti on the boarded-up windows, or the crumbling ruins which had proved to be such an irresistible attraction to the unidentified youths, whom it was believed had caused the fires and the subsequent damage.

Charley's whistle was long and low. 'It's no wonder the sellers were willing to do whatever it took to avoid the sale falling through if the buyers offered them anything near that asking price!'

'My thoughts exactly! Sadly, it also appears that the sellers were extremely eager to raise as much money as possible from the sale, as a deal with a local property mogul had collapsed due to a planning application being refused, which would have seen the demolition of the building to build several houses on the plot. It was against the advice of the estate agent to allow the Dixons to move in, they say. I guess the sellers thought the deal with the Dixons would go through, eventually.' Annie paused for a moment and took a sip of her coffee. 'Of course, they'd have the added bonus of the rent money.'

'But you'd have thought that alarm bells would have rung for all concerned when no references were forthcoming from the Dixons, wouldn't you? The sellers must be very trusting.'

Annie nodded. 'Or stupid! Especially as the agent told me that when she met with the Dixons at the property, when she returned to the office she discovered that her purse and mobile phone had mysteriously disappeared from her jacket pocket.'

Charley cocked her head. 'Really? Did she report it?'

Annie shook her head. 'She claims she didn't put two and two together until it became obvious that the Dixons had fled.'

Charley ran her fingers through her hair. 'Good Lord...' she drawled. 'What do we know about the Dixons?'

'Intel tells us that Brittany and baby-faced Brad, as he is known, are actively being sought by the police for a string of undetected armed robberies across the country, where firearms have been discharged. They are a would-be modern-day Bonnie and Clyde.'

'They sound delightful! Do we know this for sure?'

'Yes, absolutely, thanks to Forensics who have provided indisputable evidence to prove that these two are indeed the culprits of these crimes.'

'Is there anything else our intelligence can enlighten us with?'

Annie thumbed through her paperwork ready to discuss the pair's modus operandi. 'Brittany is the elder of the two by seven years,' she read. 'Her criminal record is relatively unremarkable compared to her husband's.' Annie held up a piece of paper between her forefinger and thumb and passed it to Charley. 'According to this précis, we know they have carried out a string of robberies together, whilst both being in possession of firearms and discharging them during the raids, apparently to scare people.' Annie lifted her head up from the next document she was reading. 'Whilst they haven't actually shot anyone, one shop owner in our area is known to have died of a heart attack six weeks after being confronted by the pair.'

'Can we attribute the shop owner's death to the robbery?'

Annie's lips formed a straight line, and she shook her head. 'Sadly, no. Not according to the report anyway.'

Briefly Charley closed her eyes. 'Go on.'

'They've both served a prison sentence since, but it doesn't look like that has changed their outlook, or broken the strong bond between them either.'

'How d'ya know?'

Annie took a sip of her coffee and coughed out a laugh. 'Well, last time they appeared in court, the prosecution is said to have described them as 'takers' who preyed on others, simply to finance their own lifestyle.'

'Disputed by the pair, I imagine?'

'No, quite the contrary!'

'Then why would they slum it renting at Crownest? It hardly looks like a comfortable residence without some serious renovation work.'

'I don't know. Perhaps because it's out of the way?'

'Maybe. What troubles me is that they have discharged their firearms. If they had no intention of using them, then why not brandish an imitation gun? Just as effective in scaring people, I would imagine.'

'Dunno. Maybe they wanted to make sure that people knew they were serious?'

'Well I'm sure they achieved that.'

–

Charley sat for a moment in silence, alone with her thoughts. It felt warm and cosy in her office, and as day turned to night, the snow started to fall steadily again. Researching Crownest on the net had stirred a passion to discover more about the house which had intrigued her since she was a child. It was all–consuming, and extremely interesting. According to the writer and local historian, an elderly lady by the name of Josie Cartwright, the house, she read, had never managed to become the loving family home it was originally intended to be by its creator, the wealthy mill owner and landowner, Jeremiah Alderman.

At six foot, Jeremiah was said to be a giant of a man in comparison to those around him, who were less able to afford the luxury of a comfortable home, and food aplenty. Charley discovered that Jeremiah had been born in 1819 in Halifax, on Beacon Hill. He was the eldest of five children, of which only he survived childhood. His mother died in childbirth. His father was a struggling tailor. Jeremiah, it was said, had a fascination for fabrics, and an attraction to wealth. The local farmer's wife, a God-fearing woman, taught him to read and write, and he laboured on the farm to pay his way. On his father's death, Jeremiah was determined to escape poverty. The farmer agreed to take him under his wing, and Jeremiah worked long hours, turning his hand to carding, the process of preparing wool fibre for spinning by separating all the fibres and removing impurities. Alderman made various modifications to the carding machine, thereby improving its ability to disentangle, clean and intermix fibres.

With the help of the farmer, his invention was patented. When the farmer's wife died, the farmer decided to put Jeremiah in charge of the yarn side of the business. At work he became desperate to make a name for himself, and such was his ambition that he became increasingly competitive, which upset several businessmen, including neighbouring mill owner Sir George Pickles, who accused Alderman of stealing and implementing Pickles's ideas.

Weekly, a pair of shire horses pulled the farmer's cart to The Piece Hall in Halifax, where Alderman quickly became well-known for selling to the international buyers owing to his amiability. However, Jeremiah was fortunate that the animals knew their own way home without the need of their master's ministration, as it was understood that Jeremiah couldn't resist a jug of ale or two with his fellow yarn makers after the dealing had been done, which is when it was said further ideas were discussed for him to steal and pass off as his own.

It was reported that, when the farmer died childless, he left the farm to his young protégé. Jeremiah Alderman's fortunes continued to rise. And when the sixteenth-century farm croft later burnt down, reputedly by an unfortunate strike of lightning, Jeremiah gave instructions for Crownest to be built.

It had long been the boast of the elder businessman, Sir George Pickles, that no one could see into his private grounds, owing to its high walls and impenetrable gated access. However, so ambitious and competitive did Jeremiah Alderman become that he decided to combat this, ensuring that in the building of Crownest above on the hillside, he could see all the toing and froing of his rival's workers in the valley, no matter what time of day or night.

Charley sat back in her chair, rubbed her eyes, and blessed the fact that the feud between the two men had become legendary, resulting in a plethora of information being to hand. By now, her piqued curiosity was so keen that she read on.

Charley learnt that in middle age Jeremiah suffered terribly with gout, triggered it was thought by obesity and heavy drinking. Jeremiah's long-suffering wife, Roselyn, gave him three children, but in his drunken rages, he was reported to have become increasingly violent.

In quick succession Alderman patented more machine adaptations. His greed was such that his workers laboured thirteen hours a day, as young as some were, from six in the morning to seven at night. With the workforce becoming unsettled and fearing for their jobs, Jeremiah became more suspicious of others – even his own family. Alderman's physician was reported to have said at the time that his lifestyle was affecting his mental state. It was only money, and the local power he wielded it seemed, that had kept him out of an institution.

As time passed, Jeremiah's health deteriorated, and he began to upset more people, leading to a series of court cases challenging Alderman's patents as copies of others' work, namely that of his rival, Pickles. Other yarn manufacturers jumped on the bandwagon and more lawsuits were pursued by others, who claimed that Alderman had stolen their ideas.

Eventually, despite his considerable wealth, Jeremiah Alderman could not prevent himself being sent to the gallows in 1868, for the murder of his wife Roselyn, by decapitation. It was said by the judge presiding over the murder case that Crownest had become a macabre place of torment.

Charley let out a long sigh. She was so tired. She kneaded her cheeks with her fingers. Her neck and shoulders pained her, but she felt compelled to continue tracing the family history.

After the relatively early deaths of both their parents, the Alderman children continued to live at Crownest, the eldest son Felix who was four years the senior of sister Catherine, and nine years to Seth, proclaimed himself master of the house and owner of the prosperous mill. Like his father before him, he ruled the roost with an iron will, and he too, took to drinking heavily. Similarly, he was sentenced to death in 1872, this time by the way of the gibbet.

The office's central heating had begun pumping out, and Charley's eyes felt dry and increasingly heavy, but still she felt compelled to continue. She read that a well-known poacher by the name of John Ackroyd was initially arrested for the murder of Felix Alderman's maid, Mary

Shire, after giving himself up to a member of the local militia, Matthew Cragg. The intense brutal questioning and incarceration did nothing, Cragg said, to gain a confession from Ackroyd, who reportedly told him only that that he had 'sin her off'. However, Cragg was not to be fooled into believing that Ackroyd had killed her. Ackroyd had more money in his pocket when arrested than Cragg earned in a year. Instead of charging the prisoner, Cragg decided to enlist Ackroyd as the main prosecution witness, and after he'd been given that role, Ackroyd talked. Ackroyd finally confessed that whilst checking his traps in the woods, he had seen Felix with Mary, and told of the vicious assault Felix had inflicted upon her. When Ackroyd had tried to flee the scene, 'Master' had given him money to 'keep his mouth shut'.

With the militia befriending him, Ackroyd became very important, and took Cragg to the alleged site of the attack, where a hammer and an axe were found. Both had the initials F.A. embossed on them.

Felix Alderman eventually confessed to the murder of Mary Shire, and was subsequently charged to a public execution.

Although this local history was gruesome, more shocking to Charley was finding out that Felix had, unbeknown to him, fathered a child to his maid Mary, a boy called Adam. After Mary's mother, who had continued to look after Adam after her daughter's death, lost her husband to tuberculosis, it was reported that she went to see Catherine Alderman, Felix's unmarried sister, who agreed to take Adam into the Alderman home and raise him. Adam was reported to be a sickly child, yet he went on to live until he was at least 92 years old, according to the census that Charley checked against. That made Adam

Alderman the last known family member, and resident, of Crownest. There were no known living relatives on his death.

'You really couldn't make this up!' gasped Charley, as she leaned forward to click into another thread on Google which told Charley that, after Felix's death, Seth and Catherine remained at Crownest, with the little boy. The family, although still wealthy, had become somewhat reclusive. According to local midwife Agnes Pritchard, incest was reported amongst brother and sister. She, it was noted, had been paid handsomely for her silence about helping to deliver a stillborn to Catherine who later went on to emigrate to Australia. However, before Agnes Pritchard went to meet her maker, she fully confessed her sins in order to cleanse her soul, and admitted to the burning of the body.

Charley was riveted by the knowledge she had gleaned, some of it confirmation of what she had already heard from her granny and local rumour. She paused from her research to stand and she went to look out at the window on to the darkened night sky, with numerous questions swimming around in her head. 'Why would Catherine not take Adam with her to Australia, rather than leave him, a little boy she had sworn to look after, with her brother Seth?

Down on the ground, from her office window, Charley saw the thickness of the snowfall. How long she had been reading she did not know, but her stomach was rumbling, and it was apparent to her that she would be better off staying where she was for the rest of the night rather than attempting to cross the seven miles of open country roads, and moorland to get home. Compelled to read on, but alone in the office, she made herself a coffee, and after searching her handbag, she retrieved a packet of peanuts in a crumpled packet.

On researching further, she discovered that Seth had married a Lucinda, the daughter of the sexton at the nearby church of St Anne's. However, as much as she tried, Charley could not find any more information about the life and times of Lucinda Alderman. She knew from local tales that Seth had blamed Catherine for coming between him and Lucinda, but reading between the lines, Charley surmised that Seth's growing dependency on opiates and alcohol were the problem, not his sister.

After Catherine's exile shortly after, Seth was reported to develop depression, or the 'black dog'. A report from his doctor brought home to Charley his depths of despair: 'He didn't sleep, he rarely ate, and became a veritable recluse, drinking himself into a stupor most days. Huge mounds of dirt were found in piles in the back yard, and on the odd occasion he was seen, he would have a shovel in his hand. There was talk at that time that Seth Alderman had lost his mind.'

Not twelve months from Catherine's departure, he was found dead.

–

The Alderman's family history consumed her thoughts, night and day. Three days later, as Charley sat at her desk waiting for her team's morning briefing, she came across the document that had been placed on her desk. *Full report into the most recent fire at Crownest. For the attention of Detective Inspector Charley Mann.* Charley, eager to read more, picked up the papers.

The information provided suggested that the recent fire at Crownest had been started deliberately and had been reported to the police by Joe Greenwood, the owner of Nevermore Demolition. The only evidence to support this claim was extremely limited and based on the fact that a piece of timber used for boarding up a lower floor window had been forced off, giving access to the lower floor of the unoccupied house. Further to that, the fire officers in attendance had suggested that there was the possibility of accelerants being involved, due to the fire's ferocity, and two seats of fire had been found. The building itself was said to be structurally unsound, the danger of which Charley had witnessed herself, hence the decision to demolish it now as soon as possible.

Following the disappearance of the Dixons, JT Developments, the original local developer who had shown interest in the property, until the council had refused its original plans, was now back on the scene with approval gained for five detached dwellings on the land. They were eager to move things forward swiftly due to their financial investment, but could shed no further light as to who might want to damage the property or why. After all, the only people to gain from its speedy demolition would be them, wouldn't it, and the fire had in fact caused a delay. It made no sense for them to be involved.

The report reinforced that an investigation was a non-starter, reasons being:

1. Isolated location.
2. No CCTV.
3. No witnesses.
4. No positive lines of enquiry to pursue.

This was nothing more than a paper exercise, requiring Charley's signature as head of CID, plus any additional observations to be noted before it was filed.

In her bold, neat handwriting she wrote:

NO FURTHER ACTION REQUIRED.
NO POSITIVE LINES OF ENQUIRY.
PLEASE FILE.

All she needed to do now was sign and date the report, and staple the paper to the file. Thereafter, it would be filed away to gather dust. Charley's pen hovered over the paper. As she screwed off the lid to her fountain pen and was completing the first swirl of her signature which hadn't changed over the years, her phone rang, and distracted her.

'Force Control, boss, sorry to disturb you, but your attendance is being requested at Crownest. Mr Greenwood, the owner has informed us that work has ceased owing to two bodies, one more skeletal than the other apparently, being found entombed in the building.'

Charley's eyebrows rose. 'That sounds interesting, show me as attending,' she said screwing the half-signed report into a ball and deftly binning it in the waste basket by the door. 'GOAL!' she declared, with feeling.

Thoughts flashed through her mind, as she picked up her coat. 'Are the bodies the reason that Crownest was set alight? Are they the remains of the allusive Dixons?'

Chapter 3

'Detective Constable Glover get y'coat, you're coming with me,' Charley shouted from behind her desk, loud enough to be overheard in the outer office where her team worked, despite the chit-chatter.

She scooped up her keys on the way out.

Annie was waiting for the computer programme that she had been working on to close, when she heard the sound of hurried footsteps coming her way. She turned to see Charley's attention focused solely on her. 'Today would be good, Glover!'

Sliding her feet into her plimsolls, Annie stumbled to her feet and grabbed her bag, whilst watching her boss's coat billow out behind her with every step she took towards the exit; the way it snapped in the blast of air when she opened the door appeared to accentuate her urgency, as did her swift disappearance.

DC Wilkie Connor stopped typing. The bandage around his head was the first thing Annie saw as he peered from behind his screen on the desk opposite hers. Just a few months on from the Chronicle journalist Danny Ray's attempt on his life in a hit and run traffic accident, which rendered the detective on a life support machine, no relapse had occurred. His fingers reached over and whipped a piece of toast from Annie's plate on her desk. Annie raised an eyebrow, Wilkie grinned waiting for her retort. When she failed to react, he pushed her patience further. 'Waste not want not! Choppity chop!'

'Shut it Chrome Dome!' she snapped as she grabbed the remaining piece of toast off the plate.

Wilkie's tittering followed her as she darted from the room. As second in command to Charley, Detective Sergeant Mike Blake shook his head at Wilkie. 'Why do you have to wind her up?'

'She loves it really,' Wilkie chuckled, licking the butter off his fingers one at a time.

Mike's eyes were suddenly glued to his computer screen. 'Whatever, looks like we might have a job on.'

The remainder of Annie's breakfast dangled from her teeth, which enabled her to throw on her coat. She dashed along the corridor, rushing down the steps two at a time and at the bottom she slammed her hand on the door pad to release it, before breaking into a run across the backyard in Charley's wake.

Nearing her car, Charley clicked the keys, and the lock disengaged. She looked up at the dark clouds overhead, then over the car roof towards the noise of the police station's rear door closing behind Annie, who was hurrying towards her.

'Where're we off, ma'am?' Annie asked breathlessly, tumbling into the passenger seat beside Charley.

'Crownest.'

Annie, hand still on her seat belt, looked up at Charley somewhat puzzled. 'You mean they haven't dropped that yet?'

Charley shook her head, reversed out of her parking spot — a bespoke slot came with the privilege of rank — and tore out through the large metal gates. 'Nope, and neither is it likely to be abandoned any time soon.'

Annie's eyes were like saucers. 'Why, what's happened?'

'They've found two bodies, human remains.' Charley glanced across at Annie. 'You don't happen to have any experience with bones, do you?' she asked.

Annie considered the question. 'I'm partial to a barbe-cued spare rib, dipped in a chive sauce. Does that count?'

Charley cocked her eyebrow. 'Not unless you've taken up cannibalism it doesn't. Looks like this is going to be a learning curve for us both.'

'Plastic skeletons scare the shit out of me. Are you sure these are real?' Annie said, lunging forward at Charley's sharp braking, at the temporary roadworks.

With her foot hard on the accelerator, Charley's car left the others standing behind them at the traffic lights. 'Better be, or somebody will get a rocket up their arse for calling me out.'

'The last time I saw a skeleton was on the ghost train at Clacton Pier.' Annie shuddered, and held tightly onto her seat. 'Those spiders' webs! Mind you, I was only fourteen, but I've never been on a ghost train since.'

'It's only bits of string and wool hanging down from the roof, you idiot!' said Charley. Her eyes checked her mirrors, the last thing she needed was the traffic cops on her tail.

Sensing Charley's need to process her thoughts, Annie stayed silent whilst Charley navigated the route through the busy town centre.

—

Out on the open road, Charley relaxed a little. She caught Annie smiling to herself. 'Penny for them?' she said.

'I was thinking how good it is to have Wilkie back in the office. He's come a long way in such a short time.'

'I think maybe the job's given him something to focus on since the accident. He tells me that he is hopeful the dressing will be off for good later this week. I'm in no doubt he'll be on full duties before long. He's a tough old codger to be able to take the full impact of a car being driven at him at speed, and survive it. He's getting there.'

'Wherever there is,' said Annie.

Charley nodded. 'Yes, wherever there is,' she muttered, slowing down as they approached Crownest. At the sight of the owner, Joe Greenwood, standing by the gate, she pulled over, and stopped the car in front of him.

The appearance of the demolition site immediately told the Detective Inspector that the contractors had been very busy since her last visit. However, she was pleased to see everyone standing away from the building, presumably at the request of the police operator after the three nines call.

Young Finn was standing with his hands in his pockets. He kicked the ground with the metal toecap on his work boots, but as occupied and solemn as he looked, he managed to raise a tight smile and a hand in greeting to her from where he stood, with the rest of the bemused-looking workers, behind the perimeter fence.

Joe Greenwood's face was the pale colour of the Yorkshire stone as he shook Charley's hand. Was it the cold that made him shake, she wondered. Perhaps shock, or was it something else that had unnerved him?

'I'm ever so glad you're here. Mr Thomas is on his way, and he's mad. In fact…' Joe Greenwood looked up and down the road. He turned his back on the workers so he could continue unheard. 'If he carries out his threat, we'll be off site today, and the rest…'

Charley frowned. 'Who?'

'Mr Thomas, the owner of JT Developments. The owner of this place... James.'

'Why would he sack you, Mr Greenwood?'

'Ah well, he suggested I get rid of the bones. According to him nobody would be any the wiser, but I told him I couldn't do that, and now all hell's been let loose because I ignored him and called you lot out.'

At that moment Charley heard the roar of an approaching vehicle. The thrum told her it had a powerful engine. When a white Lamborghini pulled alongside the outer dry-stone wall, she wasn't especially surprised to see an angry-looking man in the driving seat. However, what did startle her was the marked police car that pulled up directly behind him – she hadn't requested back-up.

If the traffic police had wanted to speak to the driver of the Lamborghini when the red-faced driver jumped out of the car, they took their time to follow. There was no doubt in Charley's mind that they were admiring the sports car. That was until threats began to be made from an irate Mr Thomas towards Joe Greenwood, which resulted in their quick attendance.

Despite his gesticulating, Charley's focus was immediately taken with Mr Thomas's clothes. He was dressed in a three-piece, well-cut suit.

'Are you in charge of this circus?' Mr Thomas spat at Charley, who was desperately trying hard not to bring his attention to the muddy puddle that he was standing in, and that was about to ruin his expensive-looking leather shoes.

When Mr Thomas got no immediate reaction from the Detective Inspector, he ran his fingers through his hair, lowered his voice, and flapped his hands at her patronizingly, 'I'm sure it would be of benefit to us all if he just gets rid. Do you get my drift, darling? You probably don't realise this, but for every hour these clowns are standing still, it costs me and my business thousands. Thousands.' He brushed aside his floppy blonde fringe again. Charley was just about to introduce herself and Annie, when he started again. 'What with the snow, and now this, it'll be spring before we know it.' James lowered his voice for a second time, and turned away from the crowd. 'I've been there, I come from working stock, I grew up hand to mouth, and I know some of these guys desperately need the money.' James turned to Joe. 'You know me, I'm a generous man, you got a good deal for the contract, enabling you to give your men a good day's pay for a good day's work; tell her, Joe?'

As one of the uniformed traffic officers reached to lay his hand on Mr Thomas's elbow, Charley stepped forward. 'I understand you've been informed that human remains have been discovered, Mr Thomas. Mr Greenwood made the right decision to call us, and now, in my capacity as head of CID, I have a duty to investigate. That's what will be of benefit to us all, which is I'm sure what you meant to say.'

The owner of JT Developments looked as if he was about to burst. 'Tell me. How long is this, this nonsense going to take?'

Charley found herself bristling. 'How long is a piece of string?'

Thomas clenched his fists. His face twisted, ugly in anger. 'Oh, come on, give me a break.'

'Once I know what I'm dealing with, I promise that you'll be the first to know. Now, if you'll allow me to get on with my job, the quicker I get started, the quicker I'll be able to make a decision as to the way forward.'

Charley took a step towards the house. Thomas huffed and puffed. 'Then I'm coming with you. As the owner, I have my rights!'

'You may own the place, but it's a potential crime scene, and, as I'm sure you will understand, the best chance of solving this mystery is to keep the place as sterile as humanly possible. For now, everyone is required to stay off site,' she said, indicating to the workers looking on, 'and that, of course, includes you.'

With that, Charley dismissed Mr Thomas by turning her head towards Joe Greenwood. Together they walked with Annie towards the big house's imposing front door. 'I assume it's structurally safe to go in?' Charley asked.

Hands on his hips, Joe stopped and craned his head to look up to the tallest of the burnt rafters above. 'For now,' as he offered Charley and Annie a hard hat each. 'Health and safety requires you to wear these.'

'How on earth did we ever manage to do anything before Health and Safety regulations, I wonder?'

Joe allowed himself a chuckle. 'Used common sense, and got on with the job.'

—

Charley was taken aback when she stepped through the grand doorway. Something about the atmosphere changed. She chided herself silently for being silly, but the sense of freedom and space that the outside afforded was now overshadowed by a feeling of dread and foreboding.

The large entrance hall was dark and smelled badly of mould and cat pee. There was an underlying odour of rotting cabbage. Charley put her hand to her mouth and Annie held her nose, but the smell didn't seem to bother Joe Greenwood. He forged ahead, sweeping his work boots from side to side, to clear any fallen debris from the detectives' path. 'Be careful where you tread,' he warned.

On hearing an altercation outside, Charley frowned, looked over her shoulder and saw James Thomas running towards her. A uniformed police officer was directly behind him, calling out his name.

'No, I insist,' Thomas was shouting. 'I absolutely insist!'

Charley retraced her steps and blocked his way into the house. 'You can insist all you like, Mr Thomas, but it won't get you anywhere. Now, are you going to leave the site of your own free will, or do you want to be arrested for obstruction, and escorted back to the nick to wait for me in a cell?'

James Thomas's body language told her he was far from happy. It appeared he wasn't finished. Angrily he jabbed an outstretched finger towards the Joe Greenwood, but the question was directed at Charley, 'What gives him the right?'

Annie cringed as she waited for Charley's reaction. Anyone who knew her boss knew he was making a big mistake by antagonising her. Annie was a relative newbie to CID, but she had been told by the team about her superior just before Charley's imminent arrival at Peel Street Station. Physically fit, and as tough as her bare-knuckle-fighting father before her, Charley's right-hand punch was one that any professional fighter would have been proud of.

Charley's voice was quiet, and devoid of emotion. 'Mr Greenwood was the one to make the discovery. He's already been into the scene. Now, will you please calm down? I won't stand here being shouted at.' Her voice rose, but was steely. 'Do I make myself clear?'

Thomas's eyes resembled those of a raccoon, so black were the circles around them. 'Don't you tell me what to do, this is my land you're standing on!'

Charley stared Thomas straight in the eye, and lowered her voice to a threatening whisper. 'Do as you're told or I will personally throw you out, and I'm sure you don't want the others to see you squealing like a stuck pig, do you?'

As she readied herself for his response, she didn't anticipate seeing the quivering of his lower lip, as he took a step backwards and pointed a finger in her direction. 'You don't know who you're dealing with, Sherlock. I'll be having words with your boss, you mark my words.'

'Good, it'll save my updating him,' Charley shouted to his retreating figure. Annie wasn't the only one to see the expression on Charley's face as she indicated that the uniformed officer should follow him.

After their departure, Charley stood for a moment, quietly soaking up her surroundings. She turned to the others. 'Right, now where were we?' she said.

Although she had never been inside the property before, she could see why Crownest had long held the interest of so many historians down the generations. There was a lot to take in even where the walls, now lifeless and cold, had crumbled; in their place stood beams of wood, blackened and charred where the flames had licked them. The odour of smoke and ash filled Charley's mouth, nostril and lungs and she began to cough.

'You okay?' Asked Joe.

Charley nodded. The glass littering the floor where the remains of the once beautiful stained-glass window had fallen crunched under the sole of her shoes, and the metal base of the hall chandelier lay blacked and twisted at her feet. After a moment or two Joe Greenwood moved slowly and quietly towards one of the doors leading off the ornate grand entrance hall to the dining room. When he reached it, he cast a look over his shoulder with eyes that invited her to follow him. When Charley joined him, he spoke to her in a reserved tone. 'I can't think what's got into James. I've known him a long time. We grew up on the same estate, Irish Catholic workers. He went to Rome to become a priest, but he didn't qualify in the end.'

'Don't worry about me,' she said flatly. 'I'm not here to be liked, I'm here to do my job.'

Chapter 4

Joe automatically reached down for the handle on the door. Realising it had already been removed in preparation for the demolition he looked down at the round hole through the old door that showed them the thickness of the wood, and finding Charley's face, his lips turned up at the corner. 'Habit,' he said, 'the handles are of value, the doors, not.'

The dining room was dark, with a minimum of light, more so because of the outer branches of the dense tree just outside, which had forced themselves through gaps in the broken boarded-up windows.

'Just tell me this, how could any decent human being want to move the bones of another found in suspicious circumstances, without trying to find out who they belong to, how they got there, and why?' Joe said.

There was no answer Charley could give that would satisfy Joe Greenwood, because she couldn't decipher it herself. 'I've spent most of my life trying to understand people,' she said in response.

Free from any furniture, the floor space in this room was littered with bricks, smaller stones, rubble, wood, and debris of all shapes and sizes. Adjacent to the door lay the would-be crime scene, concealed somewhere behind the walk-in fireplace.

'Wow,' said Annie, on seeing the grand feature. She gagged and pulled her rollneck jumper up over her mouth. 'The smell! What is it? It reminds me of the recycling centre on a hot day.'

Joe grinned. 'It's at times like these that I definitely don't miss my sense of smell.'

Their feet tapped on the stone floor as they proceeded towards the source of the strange odour, and the sound echoed loudly. Despite the smell Charley found herself swallowing deep breaths to fight off a sudden feeling of nausea. The smell was not only putrid, but the atmosphere was heavy, as if all the energy had been drained from it, leaving behind a bitter taste of… what? Hate, anger, death? Again, Charley checked her emotions.

Joe removed the plans for the original building from a pocket inside his jacket, and studied them closely.

'Could I have a copy of those by any chance?' Charley asked, grateful for the distraction.

Joe nodded. 'Aye, 'course, I've got some in the cabin, outside. I'll grab you a copy when we've finished here.'

Annie was preoccupied surveying the room. She came to a stop at the fireplace. 'Can you just imagine the heat that it gave off? Look at the size of it.'

'Hot enough to burn anything, and everything in them days, but that's another story.' Joe stepped to the back of the fireplace, and squatted on his heels. 'It's quite valuable, given its age. We were trying to figure out a way of taking it out without damaging it when we found the corpse.'

'So, where is it?' Annie asked.

The two detectives watched and waited in anticipation of seeing the final resting place of the decaying body. Joe pointed to the stone to the side of him.

'Well, if you look closely, there is a lack of mortar surrounding this particular slab of stone. This suggested to me that it's removable, and since I'm wondering about that, I'm also thinking that if there was a big fire roaring away in here the concealed opening, that led to who knows what could be hidden by a roaring fire in this old grate,' he stopped to steady himself by putting his hand on the iron basket. It was a good job he did, for in the next moment there came a blast of wind down the chimney and he rocked precariously back on his heels. A shower of soot floated down, blackening Joe and the floor surrounding him. Using his sleeve to wipe the coal dust from his face, he held his breath. After a moment or two he looked tentatively up the chimney, but no more black powder was forthcoming. Unfazed, Joe continued. 'Finn and I decided to take a jemmy to the stone. It wasn't easy to open, let me tell you, given its size.'

Joe grunted with the effort, but he sought shallow fingerholds around the edge of the big piece of stonework at the back of the fire. As Joe cursed, the stone shifted slowly, eventually exposing a sort of doorway in the fire-place, just as Joe had suggested. As Joe worked away at the stone, the feeling came to Charley of something searching for a way to escape, after the torment of being trapped within. She shivered.

Sticking her neck out to peer into the black abyss, Annie had an idea. 'Maybe it's an old priest hole, and the priest got forgotten about?'

'What makes you think that?' asked Charley.

'I went to a convent school, remember?' Annie nodded towards the window. 'The church on the opposite side of the road, it's the nearest building, isn't it? Churches have long been known to have tunnels to connect them to another building, haven't they?' A smile crossed her face. 'A priest hole is nothing more than a modern-day panic room really, isn't it?'

'A lot less comfy though,' said Charley.

The pair didn't realise that Joe was listening to their conversation as his head was stuck inside the cavity, which he was searching with his head torchlight. He spoke up, 'Don't think so.' His voice sounded strained, 'this house was rebuilt on the site of a sixteenth-century farmhouse, around the time of the Industrial Revolution,' he said. His body then disappeared further into the doorway and his boots could be heard making faint scraping sounds on the tunnel's uneven surface as he inched himself forward in the darkness. There was a moment's pause. His words sounded garbled and echoed in the enclosed space. 'This tunnel – it appears to go on for ever. Your guess is as good as mine as to where it leads,' he called out.

The two detectives looked at each other.

Joe appeared back at the opening of the cavern. He stretched out his hand and beckoned to them. Once they were directly behind him he pointed just inside the passageway. A metal bar attached to the stonework provided a simplified lock that, when dropped, would ensure that the door couldn't be opened from outside.

'Now, this suggests to me that there is another way out for whoever was coming to and fro, don't you think?'

'Maybe it was a servants' passage?' said Annie, in nothing more than a whisper. 'They're quite common in grand houses and palaces, I hear, to enable the servants to go about their duty undetected, without disturbing anyone or causing offence to the nobility.'

Joe shook his head. 'The door to a servants' passage wouldn't likely be in the fireplace. It's usually in a wall which is often covered in a highly patterned wallpaper so as to hide its position.'

'Plus, the number of servants required in a house of this size would be minimal. They wouldn't require servants' passageways,' replied Charley.

Joe scratched his head. 'I've certainly never seen nowt like this 'afore.'

Joe stepped back inside the dining room, and offered Charley the chance to step forward. As she did so, cold air rushed towards her. Her blood chilled. Feeling aimless and adrift, she stumbled ahead. Placing her feet on the increasingly uneven ground, she put her trembling sweaty palms against the walls of the tunnel, and twisted her head around to scan the impenetrable blackness. Her breath was coming rapidly, the strain of the day no doubt taking its toll. Another strong odour reached her nostrils, similar to rotting meat or sour milk. Joe switched on his torch and shone the ultra-bright light over her shoulder, where its beam reached way deep inside the long, narrow tunnel until it hit a wall of darkness. Slowly he pulled the torchlight back, counting the tunnels support which reminded Charley of a tunnel in a mine, as he did so. He stopped to concentrate on one wooden beam in particular. 'Corpse number one,' he announced. Seconds later he flipped the beam to Charley's immediate right. Charley jumped to see the darkness open up with light. In front of her lay a corpse in a discarded heap, in a bundle of dried-blood-soaked clothes.

Charley's own knowledge told her that within a year, the remains of a body are only the skeleton and teeth, unless the body is frozen. She could see flesh on these bones, and that smell – of course, it was that of a rotting corpse. A smell that stayed with you. The head or partial bloodied skull was positioned nearest to her.

'Can I?' asked Charley as she put her hand up to reach the torch Joe held above her shoulder. Taking hold of the torch she directed the beam up and down the remains that were covered with possible ash, or rubble. She could be wrong, but her first impression was that this body had been put there quite recently.

'What do the plans tell us about the tunnel?' she asked.

'There is no depiction of a tunnel on the drawings, but then you wouldn't mention it, would you, if it was something you wanted to keep a secret?'

'Mmm… point taken.'

'Obviously, when we came across the tunnel, we were eager to investigate its final destination, but once we saw the dead body, we decided not to go any further. We didn't want to disturb anything.'

Charley swung the torch round and her eyes found Joe's face close behind her. 'You did the right thing.'

Moving the beam of light here and there, Charley sought clues in silence.

'I think you could be right, Annie. St Anne's Church opposite is definitely a line of enquiry we should pursue.'

As she walked out of this incredible tunnel, that someone had taken time to excavate, and back into the spacious fireplace, her mind was exploring all sorts of possibilities.

'I read that the Alderman family had links to the church, but how much of what I read is fact or fiction is yet to be seen.'

Charley passed the torch back to Joe.

'Okay, where's body number two?' Charley asked, impatient to move on before she called the experts out.

'It's in the cellar,' Joe said.

'Lead on. We're right behind you.'

Chapter 5

Joe gave the cellar door a hearty kick and it swiftly fell away from the woodworm-infested frame with a satisfying ripping sound. He switched on his torch again and peered down the steps. It was completely silent and dark as a grave.

'Do be careful, let your eyes adjust to the darkness,' he called over his shoulder. The sound of his jacket scuffing against the walls of the staircase indicated just how narrow it was.

Suddenly he halted, and there was a catch in his breath.

'It's slippery in parts,' he warned, inching himself forward with a great deal of caution. Dust billowed around, making him cough; he stopped again for a moment, but the crunch of the debris beneath his foot on the next step told Charley he had pressed on regardless.

Charley prepared to follow. She gripped the hand-rail tightly in anticipation of her steep descent, the paint crusty, cold and damp to the touch, but no matter how abhorrent it was to her, she wouldn't be letting go for man nor beast – not until she reached the bottom.

'Can you imagine having to carry yer washing up 'ere, through the kitchen and out into the yard just to dry yer clothes?' said Annie, mocking the Yorkshire accent in her typically Southern drawl.

'Or worse, coming down into this pit for a bath?' said Joe, whose voice echoed beneath the low granite roof. At the same moment as they reached the bottom of the stairs, a black cat scrambled hastily up the low cellar wall towards the coal chute situated on an external way. When it reached its destination, it turned round, showing its gleaming green eyes briefly before making its escape.

Charley heard Joe anxiously draw in his breath.

A little nervous chuckle escaped Annie's lips. 'For fuck's sake!' she squealed. 'I did not expect that!'

Heart beating wildly in her chest, Charley felt the temperature plummet, and goosebumps rose on her arms. The darkness played tricks with her mind. With each tentative step she found the musty smell all-consuming; it took her back to her six-year-old self, dodging cobwebs that licked her bare skin and stuck like candy floss to her hair in her granny's cellar. Now, she jumped instinctively as a spider fell onto her face, and she raised a hand and silently screamed as she batted it away in haste.

Now, in her mind's eye, Charley pictured this cellar as a mirror to her granny's. The floor, made of flagstones, had held a coal bucket always filled with wood and coal taken from the coal 'ole, ready for the fire to heat the water in the 'Copper' for wash days and bath water. The tin bath situated farthest away from the coal 'ole, had a flowery, plastic curtain drawn across the front for privacy. As Charley now stood in Crownest's cellar, her grandpa's words rang in her ears, 'See behind there, that's where the bones are kept.' He was jesting, of course, he was always joking, but there were some seriously bad vibes in Granny's cellar that gave her nightmares as a youngster and it put her on edge now.

The light from Joe's torch began to flicker, before turning off completely, leaving the three of them trapped in the pitch darkness. Charley's six-year-old self was more than ready to flee and scramble back up the steps, had it not been for Annie's hand clamped firmly to her arm, encouraging her to go on. For Charley knew, such was the influence of an SIO, that if she ran away screaming, so would her credibility.

The darkness remained for what seemed like an age, but the sound of the tap, tap of the torch being hit on the wall was followed by light once more, and the beating of Charley's heart returned to a less erratic beat.

Immediately Charley eyes swept the room, lit only by the moving beam of light. She caught sight of a mangle, and on the shelf above, flaked washing soap and a scrub board. It was as if her childhood nightmare had returned.

When Joe turned sharply to the left, the light from his torch shifted with him, and it felt like a curtain had fallen on wash day.

'Over here.' His voice echoed, and its urgency startled her. 'We discovered a false wall.'

Charley swallowed hard.

'Why, I ask myself, would anyone build a false wall in a cellar?' Joe continued, 'That was until we found more human remains.'

Charley crept across the dark shadows to gaze into the hole in the wall that had been partially demolished, with what looked like the swing of a hefty hammer. Joe shone his torch through the hole. Charley felt Annie's fingers curl round her arm again. A muffled cry escaped her lips. 'Holy Mother of God!'

A body lay spread-eagled in the centre of the hidden room, the ribs glistening, in the torchlight. Joe flicked the beam up and down the skeletal remains. This corpse, it was plain to see, had been laid out carefully, as if this was its final resting place, unlike the one behind the fireplace. The torchlight caught something else that shone, between the ribs, in the darkness. Whatever it was they'd have to wait until the body was removed to find out.

Careful scrutiny of what was visible of the skeleton showed them that, from where they were standing, the body appeared complete. There was no flesh on the bones which bore a yellow tinge, and what looked like coins were placed in the eye sockets. From Charley's experience, she knew that these bones had been *in situ* for some considerable time. Just how old the skeleton was she had no idea, but one thing she did know was that this corpse had been here far longer than the one behind the fireplace.

She scrutinised the remains with expert eyes for a moment longer, and could see what looked like the remnants of cloth. She wondered if they might be the remains of a shroud.

'Crownest is certainly living up to the reputation it has long held locally,' she whispered through dry lips.

'"Munster Mansion", by any chance?' said Annie.

'Close… "Murder House",' said Charley straining to see Joe's face. 'I'm open-minded, but neither gossip, hearsay, rumour, nor folklore will stand up in court. I read that since the day the soil was first broken, it has been documented that countless people involved with the building of Crownest, on the site of the old farm, have experienced strange activity, that paranormal investigators have gone on to describe as demonic. We know that even recently, unexplained fires have, it appears, spontaneously manifested, and we also know that there have been a number of deaths, both recorded, and as suggested now, non-recorded, which have occurred within its walls.'

'I think I heard all them stories when I was about to undertake its demolition,' said Joe.

'You did,' said Annie, 'and you didn't run a mile? I would've.'

'A building foreman apparently drowned himself, so affected was he by the shadowy figures devoid of human features he was said to have encountered. I don't know who spread that particular rumour. Probably my opposition for the contract, to see it dropped to the ground.' Joe chuckled.

'You're not superstitious?' said Annie.

'I'm not superstitious at all,' he replied.

'Good job,' said Charley.

'Well, theories might be varied, but one thing that I do agree with, is that there are some seriously bad vibes here. And come on, why else would you conceal a body unless something sinister had gone on?' asked Annie.

Joe raised his brows. 'Exactly!'

Charley pursed her lips. 'Well, that's our job to find out,' she said. 'Could you, and a couple of your fellas make yourselves available to help us a hand if required?' Her request felt more like an order to Joe. Without waiting for a reply from Nevermore's owner, she turned back to Annie.

'We need Forensics at the scene as soon as possible. Call Senior Crime Scene Investigator Neal Rylatt will you? I think his expertise is required. As quickly as he can, before we lose the light. The recovery is going to take days, rather than hours.' The words tumbled from her lips, expecting disappointment.

Joe's reply was far from expected, 'I don't have a problem with that.'

Did Charley detect lightheartedness in Joe's voice? 'You don't? What about the contract with Thomas?'

'I don't have any time restraints for completion. I made damn sure of that before I signed anything. If he didn't read the amendment, that's his problem. I'm too long in the tooth to take chances with the unpredictable Yorkshire weather.' There was a hint of one-upmanship in his tone. 'Anyway,' he continued, 'he can hardly refuse to pay us, or try to wriggle out of a contract with a police investigation to be solved, can he?' He paused for a moment. 'Do you think we're likely to discover more bodies?' Joe sounded intrigued, and even excited to be party to the enquiry.

'Hopefully not, two human skeletons are enough, don't you agree?'

Chapter 6

Joe threw log after log, followed by branch after branch on the fire, but the garden waste didn't appear to be receding. However, this didn't appear to have dampened his spirits. His ultimatum to the workforce was, work in the garden or go home without pay. The fire seemed to burn more brightly as the cloak of darkness fell at four o'clock on the winter's night. The others had left. In a low and hushed voice he was singing a tune.

'It's a marshmallow world in the winter
When the snow comes to cover the ground
It's time for play, it's a whipped cream day
I wait for it the whole year 'round.'

Joe caught Charley and Annie staring at him. 'I don't know where that come from,' he grinned. His face was red, and glowing from the fire.

The fire created some warmth for their chilled bodies as they waited with anticipation for the arrival of the on-call pathologist, Davis Chevelle. The air around the fire was hot, but the wind was building, and it swept the red-hot embers away, thankfully in the opposite direction.

'My mother would've rejoiced to see the back of this place. She'd often warn us off when we were kids. "Don't run to me when you've scared yourself witless," she'd say.'

Joe made a pretty good attempt at mimicking a woman's voice. It made Annie chuckle. 'She was a believer in the paranormal, my mother.' Laughter lines crinkled at the side of his tired eyes. 'Worst thing she could have done though. It was like throwing down a gauntlet to a group of bored kids!'

Charley smiled. 'Maybe it was an era thing, the folklore passing through their generation. My granny told me tales passed down from our ancestors, which I guess was all they could do, since many wouldn't be able to read or write. My late grandpa was a farmer who regularly spoke of the dire consequences we would face, should we upset or offend the mischievous, hairy little man he called the Hob that apparently came with the farm.'

'Believers, I guess, would also say that this is evidence that ghosts are real?' said Joe.

'Sceptics see it as the continuation of belief, each ghost the echo of its antecedents,' replied Charley.

Annie's eyes, sore from the smoke looked mesmer-ised by the content of the conversation she was party to. 'Whatever, she's has got me putting a jug of milk out for the Hob every night, rather than witness his wrath!' she told Joe.

Charley looked back at the house and sighed, 'I must admit that as I've grown older I've become more interested in the paranormal, but I think it's the detective in me. Always trying to get to the crux of the matter.'

'Apparently, the idea of ghosts are hard to shift from our psyche; it's too deeply rooted,' said Annie.

'I guess you could call them the equivalent of Japanese Knotweed then!' said Joe wrapping his hand around a wayward bunch of greenery, pulling it out of the ground and tossing it onto the fire.

'I read somewhere only recently that, due to modern-day technological advances there are those who want to consign ghosts to the scrapheap of redundant beliefs, but yet more people are said to believe in ghosts than they do God these days,' said Annie.

'I bet that's true, and I bet there are probably still more people who don't believe in ghosts but won't spend a night in a haunted house, because deep down they do believe in ghosts, at least just enough to get scared,' said Joe.

'Who's to know what's true, and what's not true?' said Charley.

'We all know how Chinese whispers can get twisted, don't we?' Annie said. 'The rumours are enough for me though. I wouldn't want to spend a night inside there.'

'Well hopefully, if the pathologist gets a shifty on, you won't have to!'

Annie pulled a face. 'On a positive note, there's one thing we aren't waiting for, and that's a paramedic to pronounce that they're dead.'

Annie's mobile rang. Ear to the phone, she relayed the message to Charley. 'Mike Blake and Ricky-Lee are on their way,' she said.

'Good, we need a separate exhibits officer for each body.'

'Why?' said Annie.

'We need to treat them as separate crime scenes, so that there is no confusion, or contamination.'

They looked up as Senior CSI Neal Rylatt made his way through the garden to join them near the fire. 'Well, I guess you'll be pleased to hear that Professor Davis Chevelle's ETA is ten minutes,' he said.

Chapter 7

Davis Chevelle was clever, and had a reputation for having a loud mouth, but that wasn't the first thing that people noticed about him. Presently he was insisting that he did not have a Napoleon complex, when he came into Charley's earshot, accompanied by Mike Blake.

'That bastard was five-foot six, what did he 'ave to complain about?' bellowed Davis. 'I was born yelling, and I guarantee it'll be the thing people will remember about me.' He laughed, showing an overly large set of pearly white teeth, in an exceedingly wide smile. 'I have to do something to make sure I'm not swept underfoot,' he said, stepping forward and offering Charley an extended hand. His demeanour changed immediately as he spoke to the SIO and he became serious-looking. 'Well, hello, I'm Davis Chevelle,' he said, in an unexpected deep, rich, velvet voice. 'I do believe you have been waiting for me?'

At four-foot one, Davis stood out in a crowd. He was stocky, muscular, and generally misunderstood, or so he said. He had a mass of wispy brown hair, goatee beard, small, dark, round spectacles, and with his colourful mismatched clothes, he could have been mistaken for a court jester. Standing between the lean, smart, clean-shaven DS Mike Blake, and the ever-suntanned DC Ricky-Lee, he looked like a French bulldog in drag.

Davis's unique way of working, and his inordinately loud mouth preceded him, but no matter, as Charley needed him, as she desperately required his expertise on the two separate scenes, with the two skeletons at differing stages of decomposition.

Davis carried a pair of lightweight, brightly coloured, plastic folding ladders with him as Charley led the way back into the house and down into the cellar. She saw the look on Mike Blake's face, and his mischievous eye caught hers. 'Don't you dare!' they said, as she felt the corners of her mouth twitch, and a chuckle catch in her throat.

With protective suits on to protect both the scene and their clothing, the group stood quietly, allowing each other to visualise the skeleton that lay before them behind the wall, amongst the dusty debris in the cellar. The additional lighting that had been brought in flooded the area, making it much easier to see the burial site in more detail. Towards the outside wall which was next to where the skeleton lay, tree roots clung together to form one giant mass, reaching out eerily towards the bones.

Davis secured his size four shoes on the third step of his ladder. He pulled two rubber gloves from a box that Ricky-Lee offered him, and blew them up like a balloon to enable him to put them on more easily.

'Fascinating Inspector, absolutely fascinating,' he muttered, his eyes remaining focused on the scene as he adjusted the volume of his recording device.

That may be, thought Charley to herself, *but as I have the remains of two bodies in this house, just tell me how they died, and better still, who killed them.*

The professor appeared to be in his element. Humming away, he picked a few white stones from several that lay scattered on top of the skeleton. 'Pure quartz,' he said, with glee.

'Believed to ease the passage to the afterlife,' said Charley.

'I believe you're right,' said Davis with a hint of admiration in his tone. 'You are well read,' he declared. His eyes remained on the quartz that he was placing in an evidence bag.

'My granny's family were Irish, apparently they were used by her forefathers for burials.' Charley paused, her expression turning thoughtful. 'Funny how the brain retains little nuggets of information to recall years later.'

With featherlight strokes Davis carefully brushed the skull back and forth, until the soft bristles snagged. Charley found herself holding her breath, closely watching the goings-on in the illuminated search area.

'This skeleton has age to it,' Davis said, as he tentatively fiddled in the debris to shift the obstruction.

DS Mike Blake flicked his eyelids at Charley. She knew what he was thinking. *Don't all skeletons have some age to them?*

'Seems to be some evidence of cloth, possibly remnants of a shroud?' Davis said, confirming Charley's earlier suspicions. Gently, he eased a stone from between the skeleton's jaw. Ricky-Lee held open an exhibits bag for him to place the stone in, sealed it tight and commenced to write upon a label. 'In the past they believed that putting something in between the jaws would stop the dead from chewing through the shroud,' he said. Annie looked intrigued.

Davis made a show of checking for vampire fangs, in a light-hearted way. He drew back and mopped his brow with his forearm. 'There is still potential for it to rise at some point.'

Charley's impatience to get on with the investigation was now also felt by Annie. 'The only time it will rise is when you've finished and we lift it out of there,' she whispered. Annie's voice grew louder and she emitted a gasp. 'You actually think it could be a vampire, Professor?'

'I think, whoever buried her – it's a woman by the way, I can tell that from the size of her pelvic bone – thought she needed to be pinned down to stop her from rising again.'

'What makes you think that?' said Charley.

Davis measured the length of the skeleton, and he asked for further photographs to be taken by Neal in his role as CSI before he continued, 'See this iron rod through her shoulder blade?' Annie nodded eagerly. 'That shows me that whoever buried her believed she had the capabilities to leave her grave, and terrorise the living. This pagan custom spread throughout European countries, and the practice was continued as far as the early 1900s.' Davis paused. 'They must have thought this person was a terrible threat as she also has spikes through her ankles,' he said, pointing to her feet. 'A bit over the top even for a pagan burial I admit, but they believed they could prevent the deceased from rising up and attacking the locals.'

'Or, maybe the person who killed her?' mumbled Annie. He raised his eyebrows. 'Maybe… I've read plenty about this type of burial, but I believe there have been only a few found in the UK.'

'You said, "over the top",' said Charley. 'Is there some-thing else?'

Davis pointed to the rib cage. 'See this?' The professor lifted a disc shaped, pendant carefully in his gloved hand from the corpse. 'It's a pagan pentacle necklace.' He brushed the necklace carefully, as he spoke. His eyes were quickly averted. 'Now,' he said, peering further into the cavity. He pointed a straight finger, as he raised an eyebrow at Charley. 'That is very interesting. Do you see what I see? A bone-handled dagger, which suggests to me it was a ritual killing.'

'Makes a difference from it being from a knife taken from the kitchen block, the cause of many a domestic murder these days,' Mike Blake commented.

'She has two broken ribs, clearly visible, perhaps they were caused by the force used when she was stabbed. Closer inspection at the lab will confirm.'

'How old do you think the skeleton is?' asked Charley.

'If you pressed me, I'd make a guess at around seventy to a hundred years, but we'll do some carbon dating, and that'll tell me how accurate I am.'

Annie whistled through her teeth.

'Remember that skeletons are not only the remnant of a life once lived, they are also a lasting blueprint of that life. She has wisdom teeth, so we can confirm that she was over eighteen years of age. Looking at her skull and bone development, I'd make a guess that she was not much older when she died. What I'm seeing suggests to me that there was third-party involvement in her death.'

'Murder?' said Annie.

'Murder,' echoed Davis.

The professor looked above and around him. 'Once we have removed the skeleton from where she's been entombed, then we can examine the surrounding area. My first thoughts are that for whatever reason she was killed, she was then placed here by someone who cared deeply about her and what had happened to her, and then the wall was bricked up, maybe at the time, maybe sometime later, who knows?'

'A tomb?' whispered Annie.

'A tomb, yes.' Davis gave a little moan as he stood upright and stretched his spine. 'Time for a break and to discuss whether we arrange the movement of this skeleton before examining the next.'

'Makes sense. It would save changing our protective clothing, which we will need to do before moving on to the next body,' said Charley. 'Last thing we want to do is contaminate that scene.'

Pre-packed food bags and hot drinks had been delivered to the site at Annie's request, and not only was Charley grateful for the food and drink, but she was impressed by the younger detective's foresight. Fifteen minutes later, guided by the professor's experience, the skeleton was removed, almost intact. The dagger was easily accessible, and was removed with little effort, photo-graphed, and placed in an evidence tube. Once the scene was free of the bones, the wider search of the area began.

The concrete tomb was relatively clean, surprisingly. Sifting through the rubble, dirt, and other debris, no doubt caused by the current demolition work, was their main hurdle. Nevertheless their patience gave them rewards, as a mirror, a tube, and coins were found. Possible reasons for the mirror and tube being in the tomb was explained away by the professor as safety devices, as they allowed others to look into the tomb for signs of life; pennies were used to seal the eyes shut, or if you believed a practice associated with the north of England regarding the latter in the 17th Century, to 'give to St Steve'.

'But why?' asked Annie. 'Whoever killed her obviously wanted her dead, and a pagan burial suggests that she didn't believe in God.'

Amongst the debris they also found a small ring. 'Did it come off her finger?'

With no more to do at the present on scene one, they took a brief break to discuss the body and their findings.

'I think it's time we called it a day,' said Charley. 'After all, the body behind the fireplace isn't going anywhere, and we can start refreshed tomorrow with new coveralls for the second crime scene.'

–

It was 8.30 a.m. the following morning when the team regrouped at the site. Davis was protective of his ladders, and although assured that he would not need them to get behind the fireplace, where his small frame would prove an advantage in the restricted tunnel, he nevertheless took them with him.

'The decomposition of this corpse makes me think it has probably been here a matter of weeks, months at the most,' said Charley above the loud grinding noise the fireplace stone made when it was turned to reveal the tunnel beyond. Bowing his head, Davis walked into the tunnel with apparent ease. Hunched over, Charley followed. Was that a soft glow of light she saw down the tunnel? She blinked and when she opened her eyes, the light was gone. Maybe it was her vivid imagination, or tiredness that was playing tricks with her mind, as she had slept but a little. Whilst Davis continued his visual examination of the body, she listened intently and when he turned and spoke to her, his thoughts were not unexpected. 'I wouldn't want to make an enemy of his killer. This man appears to have been executed!'

Charley blew air out between her lips, straightened up best she could, and found herself looking at Davis in the eye. 'Another execution, you think?'

'Most certainly, but this time with a modern-day weapon. I can see he has a remarkably clear circular bullet hole in the back of his head. This has been done, I suggest, at close quarters. The barrel of the gun would have been touching his head. I'm many things, but not a ballistic expert, although I do think that this sort of wound would have been inflicted with a small calibre handgun of sorts.'

'Who was he, and who had he upset enough to shoot him in this barbaric way?'

Davis turned to her, his eyebrows raised. 'You're the detective! However, I am thinking that perhaps Crownest was torched to conceal these human remains? People need to realise that house fires don't get as hot as a crematorium fire. Human remains will always be found at the scene of a fire, if there are any to find. Time will tell us if the fire was started in an attempt to do just that, and to make sure that any evidence appertaining to a crime was destroyed in the act.

'Whoever started the fire may have not known about the corpse in the cellar, but you've got two for the price of one, Inspector, that's modern-day science for you.'

Davis was a clever man. He wasn't wrong, but the only thing that connected these two bodies was Crownest. Two murders committed years apart, yet both concealed in the same house.

Chapter 8

The chill in the empty dining room had already cooled
Annie's body considerably, and it was only midday. What
she would give to feel the heat of the sun, however weak,
upon her skin. Her task, this winter's day, was to wait with
the pathologist until he finished his examination of the
body *in situ*.

Fascinated as she was by the plethora of changing
shadows the artificial lighting created in the tunnel, Annie
was equally intrigued by the dining-room's beautiful
woodland mural on the wall, albeit somewhat faded by
age and damaged by smoke and water. She slid her back
down the rough stone mantel of the fireplace, pulling
her wool coat underneath her posterior as she did so, to
enable her to sit a little more comfortably on a cold slate
of the hearth, where she began to fantasise that the ghostly
shadows were, in fact, the souls trapped in the house, not
caused by Davis surveying the corpse in the opening at
the back of the fireplace.

All of a sudden Annie noticed a change in the air that
felt threatening, and it unnerved her, more so when she
began to hear eerie, unidentified sounds coming from the
chimney. When she closed her eyes, and hummed a tune
in an attempt to shut them out, she swore that she could
feel the vibration of the noises floating around her, boun-
cing back off the walls, and into the tunnel. The sound

of Davis swearing indiscriminately at his recording device brought her to her senses, and she told herself sternly that she should refrain from letting her imagination run wild.

'How'd you know for certain it's murder, Mr Chevelle?' she called out towards the tunnel. There was no instant reply, and she shuffled closer to the tunnel where Davis was working, for comfort. Head back to the wall she closed her eyes again, and sighed deeply. 'Relax,' she told herself. 'Just relax.'

'Like I told the Inspector earlier, it's not rocket science when the bullet's in the back of the head,' the pathologist said, popping his head out to obtain a tool from his rucksack.

Annie chuckled to herself, reassured by his voice, even though his tone mocked her.

With not enough light in the dining room to do anything but continue to wait, she assumed her position with her head against the wall. Closing her eyes she concentrated on controlling her breathing, and on the rise and fall of her chest. 'Relax,' she repeated. 'Just relax…'

Focusing her mind on the ambience of her surroundings, although a bit spooky, her mind once again wandered. She was convinced that if there was a ghost in the vicinity, she would get a sign.

After a few moments of nothing, she opened her eyes. 'Don't be stupid,' she berated herself. 'You know perfectly well there are no such things as ghosts!'

In that moment, she heard a noise coming from inside the chimney breast. Inquisitive, she moved quickly to peer up the flue, half-expecting to see the sky full of ominous grey clouds rushing past in the howling wind. Peering into the gloom she saw nothing but darkness. Then, with a rush of stones that came rattling down the chimney, a bird appeared, flapping its wings frantically. Instinctively Annie screamed, and covered her head with her hands. Small fragments of debris flew in the young detective's direction, and she flung herself into the opening of the tunnel to prevent being smothered by the descending cloud of soot. Hearing the commotion Davis backed out of the hole in haste, and then fumbled to help her sprawled figure up from the floor.

With two hands gripping her upper arms tightly, and concern in his eyes, he shook Annie slightly. 'What in God's name? Are you okay?' Convulsed with shock, and fear, with her eyes still screwed-up tightly, Annie found herself nodding her head vigorously, and trying very hard not to cry. When Davis heard a loud screeching he automatically cowered. As its wings flapping violently, the jackdaw flew so close to his face that Davis imagined he felt its feathers brush his cheek. Unsuccessfully, the dark bird tried to land on several unsuitable surfaces, its claws too large to grip anything, before it perched on the top of the door. Its horrible black eyes searched for something unknown.

'I think the sooner we are done here the better, don't you?' Davis said, thrusting a bottle of water in her hand. 'Trust me, I'm a doctor; sip this, you'll be fine. I'll try not to be much longer.' When he vanished into the tunnel, the bird took flight once more, this time into the hallway.

Eyes on the door, Annie settled with her back against the stone wall. Her nose began to itch, and she blew it violently, in an attempt to rid it of some of the dust. 'With some luck you'll uncover the cartridge shell, eh?' she said to Davis feebly, shoving the blackened tissue deep into her trouser pocket, with a shaking hand.

'I hope so. Nothing yet although, unbeknown to us, it could well be sitting quite happily inside the skull.'

Annie rubbed her chest. Breathing was uncomfortable, and with each intake of breath panic seemed to rise within her – she coughed, and coughed again harder. A few minutes passed. 'Can you breathe in there?' she called out to Davis.

'Don't fret, I promise you, a little dust never killed anyone,' he replied instantly. The tone of his voice told her he was concentrating.

'If you say so,' she coughed again, and again. Annie's throat felt as if a boa constrictor was wrapped around her neck, squeezing her airway shut.

'Will you do as you're told, and sip the water I gave you!' Davis hollered, impatiently.

On hearing the front door close, and the sound of debris in the hallway cracking underfoot, Annie anticipated that the bird would once again soon be making an appearance. But instead of a bird swooping in, the dining room door was slammed shut with a loud BANG! 'Yikes!' Annie cried, jumping backwards like a surprised rabbit. Tears blocked her eyelashes, and out of habit, growing up with a mischievous younger brother, she held her breath to keep them from flowing.

'What the hell?' she heard Charley shout, as she kicked the door open with force, and a size-six boot. Seeing a dishevelled, cowering Annie, she quickly made her way to her side. 'What happened?'

Annie's face turned from the wall to look at her, her shoulders shaking. 'A bird flew down the chimney and dislodged some debris, no doubt including its nest,' she said, as she struggled to get to her feet. 'It unnerved me a bit, then the door slammed! Was that you?'

Charley shook her head. 'What kind of bird?'

'A big, dark one.'

A strange tingling sensation dispersed from the top of Charley's scalp. It ran along the sides of her skull in prickly tendrils, and she watched as the blood slowly drained from Annie's face. She heard a hollow laugh escape from her throat. 'It's a sign of death,' she said in a whisper.

'What is?' said Annie.

'A jackdaw coming down a chimney.'

Annie looked about her. 'Stop it!'

Charley forced a smile. 'Go grab a coffee. You're hungry, and no doubt tired.'

Annie walked towards the door, and Charley gasped when she thought she felt a featherlight touch on her cheek.

Annie turned 'What's wrong?' she demanded.

'Nothing, I just thought I felt something touch my face.' Charley rubbed her fingers across her cheek to convince herself there was nothing there.

Annie's lip trembled. 'I can't see anything.' She smiled. 'You're probably tired and hungry too.' The colour had come back to her face, and Charley was glad, but, hearing a loud cawing they were both startled. They both looked up, and then burst out laughing.

'I think I prefer a mischievous Hobgoblin, to bloody jackdaw nonsense,' Annie said.

Davis Chevelle seemingly oblivious to the drama, could be heard speaking into his recording device. 'Attached to his left tibia is a metal plate which tells me that he has been subject to an operation; he is still in possession of teeth, which gives us two immediate stabs at possible early identification.' Charley sat down next to

Annie, put her head back and shut her eyes. She concentrated on the drone of Davis's voice. 'The right arm is tangled in the ribcage, and the left arm outstretched on the floor.' Then with his head slightly bent, Davis walked out of the confines of the cavern. 'Who'd have thought we'd have two concealed bodies, yards apart, and both murdered, in the same house…?' he said before he saw their faces. 'What's up with you two, you look as if you've seen a ghost!' He laughed at his own joke and turned his head in the direction of the body. 'There's no doubt in my mind it's a dump site, Inspector,' he said. 'I'm all finished here.' Davis moved swiftly to gather his belongings together. 'It's all yours.'

Annie looked pensive. 'I've been thinking… How did anyone know the tunnel existed, if it's not on the plans?' said Annie. 'Let's face it, it was more by luck than management that it was found by Joe and Finn, wasn't it?'

Charley shuddered, a goose having just walked over her grave, as her granny would have said. 'Maybe that's how it was found by those who dumped the body there too – just by accident.'

'Mmm…' Annie didn't sound convinced.

Davis picked up his stepladders and walked towards them.

Annie was still in questioning mode. 'I know we have a full skeleton here, but say we just discovered one human bone. What can that actually tell you?' she asked as they removed their coveralls at the door.

'What do you mean?' he said, rubbing his face with a crumpled handkerchief that he'd extracted from his shirt pocket.

'Well, can it tell you how tall the person was, for instance?' she said.

'Depends what bone you found. Say for argument's sake it was a femur, that's the thighbone, which makes up about a quarter of the length of the human body. From this I would be able to calculate the approximate height of the person that it belonged to.'

'Wow! I already know you can tell if an injury was caused before or after death, but how?'

'Trauma seen in skeletal remains falls basically into three categories. Antemortem trauma includes injuries during life, and in death, the evidence of healing still exists.'

'Like the operation to insert the metal plate you just mentioned?'

Davis nodded. 'Perimortem traumas are injuries sustained at or around the time of death. As in this case, the skull shows evidence of a gunshot wound, and here I can say with certainty that this injury was the cause of death.'

'Could it be possible that the guy shot himself?' she asked.

Davis shook his head, 'Not in this case. The point of entry is directly into the back of his head. Now, if the wound had been at the temple, or if he had put the barrel into his mouth and fired the gun, then that's a different kettle of fish. That injury could possibly be self-inflicted.'

Annie frowned. 'Possibly?'

'Never assume!' chanted Charley.

'How come not certainly?' said Annie.

'Although a wound to the side of the head, or via the mouth suggests suicide, I have known perpetrators grip their victim's hand on the murder weapon, and, shall we say, assist in pulling the trigger?'

'There wouldn't be anything left above the jaw if he had shot himself in the mouth. I went to one such incident which resulted in our scraping an eye off the ceiling!' Charley interjected.

Annie's face blanched.

'All wounds help us understand when, how and with what they were caused,' Davis paused for effect. 'Of course, what they can't tell us is *why*. That's your job to find out,' said Davis.

'Dead people really do talk,' said Annie.

'They certainly do,' said Davis, eager it seemed to get the body to the lab for further scrutiny.

'As a matter of interest, when you were in the tunnel, Mr Chevelle, could you make a guess as to where it ends?' asked Charley.

'No, that tunnel must run for some distance.' He arched his eyebrows. 'No doubt the tunnel will now be the subject of a further search once we extract our man?'

'That's right,' said Charley. She looked Annie up and down. Annie shook her head, a look of horror on her face. 'Oh no, NO! There is no way I'm going down there!'

Charley's face was pensive. Unable to keep up the act, she winked at the younger detective and her face broke out into a grin. 'Don't worry, kid, I wasn't thinking of sending you. Lucky for you, you don't annoy me enough! We'll be calling on the experts.'

–

With a vast amount of work to do, Charley was more than aware that the media would get wind of something afoot at Crownest very soon, if they hadn't already done so. An interim statement to appease them would need to be released. This story would shortly be in print, heard over the airwaves and seen on the screen everywhere. Sadly, every journalist wanted a story, *the* story, and this sort of gruesome headline would no doubt catch people's attention, and that's what the journos wanted, because it sold newspapers. Legend, folklore, whatever you called it – these tales intrigued people. Just thinking that some of the stories about this house that had been told throughout three generations could be about to be proved correct, made the hairs stand up on Charley's arms.

It would be unprofessional, and slapdash of her, not to order an extensive search of the tunnel, and for this, once the body was removed, she would require the help of the local Mount Rescue Team. God forbid if they found more human remains, but it was a possibility that she couldn't rule out.

Chapter 9

Amongst the team of volunteers on the mountain rescue team, Charley knew there would be people with the necessary experience for searching underground cavities. They needed to be aware that there was a possibility that they could be crawling into a crime scene, although the house may already have yielded all that it had. No matter what, it needed to be searched as a matter of urgency. Ted 'Gently' Bentley, she was aware, was the leader of the group.

Ted was a grey-haired, wily old character with ruddy cheeks and a great sense of humour. Charley had worked with him and his team of volunteers before, in her role as a police constable, searching for missing people on the desolate, unforgiving and dangerous Marsden Moor, whose beauty belied its hostile nature.

Whilst Annie was tasked with co-ordinating the scenes where the bodies were found, Charley's next immediate priority was to try and identify them. 'Who are you?' she whispered as she waited on the drive for Ted to arrive.

From the most recently murdered corpse, DNA and dental records would be a strong line of enquiry, along with possible identification through the metal plate that had been fitted to his leg. Charley was confident that the male skeleton would be the easier of the two to identify. Weirdly, she was just as intrigued about finding out the identity of the woman's skeletal remains, even though the body had been buried a generation before.

It was dark when Ted Bentley arrived, and obvious that he had just been walking the English springer spaniels. Nell and Wynn lay in the back of his old-style Land Rover, panting heavily.

Ted's grey hair was tied in a ponytail at the nape of his head, his wax jacket covered his waterproof trousers, and on his feet he had well-worn walking boots. This, she knew, was his daily garb. He lifted his hand in a friendly greeting, smiling as he approached the DI. She guessed that he must be now in his seventies, but the firmness of his handshake, his agility and his mannerisms were those of a man twenty years his junior.

'Ey up, a young lass like you ought to be out and about with the living, not dealing with the dead and buried. That father of yours would be turning in his grave if he knew you were here.'

Charley smiled, 'He'd have trouble turning in his grave, he was cremated, but I don't have to tell you about being addicted to your job, do I Ted? How long have you been retired?'

'Touché, but the trick is not to let your addiction become destructive. You look tired, lass.'

'Nothing a strong coffee won't put right,' she said, turning away to walk with him to the front door.

'How do you think I can help you?' Ted said. 'You seemed pretty desperate on the phone.'

Before they entered the house, he looked up at the gargoyles that topped the stone pillars above them, and shuddered. Charley could see his breath in the lamp light. 'I hate this bloody place. Allus 'ave. Some people don't believe in witchcraft, but I've seen stuff in my time, that if

I repeated they'd have me locked up, and throw away the key,' Ted said.

Inside the house Charley poured Ted a coffee from her flask, and offered it to him. It was true something was troubling him; his hands were all of a dither. She shared with him the details of the gruesome finds, and her concern that there could be more undiscovered; Ted listened intently as she unwrapped the scene. She saw the professional mask appear on his face, as the adrenaline kicked in.

'I get your drift,' he said eventually. 'Let me get Nell on the lead.'

'What, now?'

'No time like the present.'

'Are your two body dogs?'

Ted nodded. 'Aye, and I'll tell you something for nothing, if there are bodies, alive or dead, secreted in that tunnel, mark my words, Nell'll find 'em f'ya.'

With a plan, and Nell on the lead, Ted appeared to be more confident. Charley felt less fearful than she had done earlier, but the anticipation of what might be found was making her stomach churn. But was it that or more the fact that she had missed breakfast and lunch, with the prospect of teatime looking like it would become supper?

Nell appeared a little over-excited as the two walked towards the fireplace in the dining room. 'Recently removed?' asked Ted.

'Yes, the body was only removed about an hour ago.'

'That could be the reason she's so eager.'

Ted stuck his head in the tunnel. 'Jesus, that's some tunnel,' he said as he saw the length stretch into the darkness. Ted encouraged Nell to start searching, keeping a tight hold on her leash for the moment. The walking was made more difficult owing to the flickering torchlight, the only operating source of light inside the chamber. After a few minutes he turned to speak to Charley who was following pensively in his footsteps. His face was aghast as he started to release her leash. 'You can see by how much rope she's taking, this tunnel goes on forever!' he shouted.

After treading through several turns of the tunnel passage, over and around boulder-sized rocks strewn across their path, Ted turned once more. Eventually, all became quiet and still. 'She's stopped. She's barking. Can you hear her?'

Charley nodded. Her face pensive. 'At what though?'

'I have no idea lass, but I think we're going to have to find out aren't we?'

—

Ted hollered down the tunnel, then whistled for the dog to return. 'Nell is trained to locate and follow the scent of decomposing human remains, even if the remains have been buried for years, or are deep underground, or have been lying at the bottom of a body of water for some time.'

Nell started to bark incessantly. 'Hear that still?' said Ted.

Charley nodded.

'That bark tells me she's found something and she wants me to go to her.' Ted commenced to pull Nell's leash back in. 'I'll contact the rest of the team members tonight when I get home, and we'll be back here tomorrow morning, with the proper kit and do the necessary.'

It was ten past nine when Ted exited the tunnel. His fingers touched the walls slightly, his eyes searching intently for any sign of instability.

'I've been told that there's a few reasons why tunnels connect buildings,' said Charley. 'One being that the building is associated with religion.'

Ted bent down to pat a panting Nell, as before, the springer spaniel now sitting obediently by his side, nose in the air, panting and sniffing.

'The tunnel does appear to go in the direction of St Anne's Church,' her voice quickened. 'Do you think it could have been built as a concealed entrance to the church?'

'The only other reason I can think of is that it may have been used for the movement of black-market goods. That was the case in the caves under New Brighton, and apparently connects old houses beneath the streets of Rottingdean in Sussex,' answered Ted.

'You think that the tunnel is long enough to reach other buildings further afield?'

'Who knows as we've not reached the end yet. Don't underestimate our predecessors. Look at York, there's a whole network of tunnels and passageways beneath the city's surface. A whole series of Roman roads built over and forgotten after the ancient empire fell. Have you never heard of that famous ghost story?'

Charley shook her head. Politely, Ted stood aside to let Charley go through the stone door. He halted, and turned.

'As the story goes, in 1953, a local apprentice plumber had been working at the Treasurer's house, on Church Street, York when he heard some strange music, followed by apparitions of Roman soldiers appearing out of one wall and walking straight through another. The plumber reported that the soldiers were cut off at the knee, and sure enough, when the cellar was later excavated, archeologists discovered a Roman road around eighteen inches beneath the ground.' Ted stopped. Charley turned to see a puzzled look on his face. 'Wait a minute though. Crownest isn't as old as Roman times. If my memory serves me right this house was built in the nineteenth century by the infamous Jeremiah Alderman.'

'Ah, but what you obviously don't know is that Crownest was built on the site of a sixteenth-century farm croft, that was also subjected to a fire when Jeremiah inherited it on the owner's death.'

–

Before Ted's Land Rover had disappeared over the horizon, Charley had left a message on the answering machine of St Anne's Church, with a request to view the premises in the hope of finding out if there was anything known about the old site where Crownest was built, and how the two buildings could possibly be linked.

Leaving the scene protected overnight by uniform personnel, she ensured that the perimeter was secure.

It had been a long day. Charley headed back into the office. A quick de-brief at ten o'clock for those still working brought them up to date with her meeting with Ted, and she requested that they reassemble for a briefing at seven o'clock the next morning, when she would update them, and the rest of the team fully. Still, as the others took their leave, she was aware that her working day was not yet done. Sitting at her desk, with nothing more than a desk light for company, she composed a message to Connie Seabourne, the Press Officer. It was brief, but to the point.

During the planned demolition of the unsafe property locally known as Crownest, Stoney Lane, Marsden, and after an unexplained fire, the skeletal remains of two humans have been discovered. The enquiry has only just begun, but it appears that one may have been there for a number of years, whilst the other, only months. Neither of these deaths was accidental, and murder investigations are underway, led by Detective Inspector Charley Mann.

—

It was midnight when Charley found herself driving out of Huddersfield, onto the open country roads and she struggled to stay awake. She turned on the car radio as loud as she could handle, and wound down her window to let the cold air blow through her loosened hair. She forced her eyes open wide and focused on the cats' eyes that guided her on the dark road ahead. Once or twice she considered pulling into a lay-by as she felt herself falling asleep, but instead she pushed on, swaying to the music, tapping the steering wheel to its beat, in the hope it would help.

When she finally reached home, and turned off the car engine, the silence in the car was all-consuming. Once out of the car, she walked briskly to her door. The beeping of the car alarm rang out into the night air and she looked up to a cloudless sky. The stars were bright, and one in particular twinkled strongly, the North star, the one that Granny had told her was really Grandpa watching down on them. But even that beautiful sight didn't sway

Charley from thinking of the enquiry and the days ahead. She shook her head as she turned her key in her front door and let herself into the dark, cold house lit only by the moonlight through her undrawn curtains. She had eaten very little, but felt too tired to prepare anything now. Getting her clothes ready for the next day was a normal routine for Charley, after all, she was on-call senior detective and could still be required to attend another major incident, but hopefully not tonight, she prayed; she already had enough on her plate.

The weather, it appeared, was being kind in the morning when she woke. Seeing it dry and bright, Charley's mind was active the minute she opened her eyes.

Today's priority at the station was to get the Incident Room established. The investigation, as always, had been named by Headquarters as Operation Angus. This meant that no other operation, either in this Force's area or countrywide, would be known by the same name, to avoid any confusion. The Incident Room intelligence cell under Charley's command were digging into the history of the house and its occupants. The Operational Support team was on standby to search, or even sieve, the dirt from the area where the body had been discovered behind the fireplace. In addition, a small team was set to do a fingertip search of the basement. Nothing would be left to chance, every eventuality being covered, in the hope that there was some evidence yet to be discovered.

The owner of Nevermore was waiting for Charley when she and Annie arrived back at the house.

'I'm intrigued to know more,' Joe said, enthusiastically.

'Aren't we all,' said Charley, watching on as Ted and three of his colleagues prepared to go into the house, and then the tunnel. Dressed in protective clothing, they were making final safety checks which included ensuring that their lights were in good working order. In turn, Charley was preparing to leave the site, to make enquiries of her own at the church.

'I'm contactable by mobile,' Charley reminded them.

'Say a prayer for us lass,' Ted called above the noise of the team's banter. A little mischievous smile tugged at his aged lips.

'If the stories my dad told me about what you two got up to as kids are true, Ted, I better say a couple, or three.'

With a smile on her face, and a happy gut feeling, Charley called out for Annie to meet her at the front door. 'People to see, places to go.'

The church was still in use, but sadly by the few rather than the many. Charley and Annie walked in silence through the partially neglected graveyard, past dark, weathered headstones blackened by the passage of time, and mostly illegible now, depending very much on how sheltered their location. In some respects, it appeared to Charley that they were walking through time, as the elaborate headstones changed to an assortment of single crosses and statues, possibly the preferred mark of respect for a particular era, the taller of them peeking above the wild grasses of the graveyard. Annie halted Charley by grabbing her arm, and with a finger to her lips, she pointed out a little fat robin being fed a worm by a larger slimmer bird, who appeared more alert to the surroundings. When the exchange of food was over, they conversed with one another, seemingly unaware, but Charley saw that they weren't the only ones interested in the birds' antics.

Under a nearby memorial bench, edged by a mass of brambles on the periphery of an expanse of grass with white marble grave markers, sat a cat. It was the cat that Charley had seen before in the cellar at Crownest, and who was now, to all intent and purpose, waiting for the right time to pounce. Charley clapped her hands, and the loudness of her actions in the quiet of the graveyard made the birds startle, look up, and then fly into a big oak tree.

'Just look how disgusted that cat is with me,' said Charley. 'Well, serves you right for frightening me the other day.'

They walked onwards and it seemed as if the two robins followed them, flying from one bush to another, until they flew up into the tangle of ivy that hung from the Yew tree which half-blocked the path. Charley bent down, pushed the ivy out of the way and squeezed through. She walked in front of Annie towards the arched, double doors of St Anne's Church, with locks that reminded her of a fortress. Charley reached for the large black iron door knocker and it was only as she did so, that she noticed the shape of an ugly-looking half-man, half-creature resting in the palm of her hand.

'The Hob?' asked Annie.

Charley shrugged her shoulders as she slammed the knocker hard against the wooden door, to hear the echo coming from within. A drop of water fell directly on her forehead and, brushing it aside, she looked upwards to see large stone gargoyles staring back at her.

Annie followed her line of sight. 'Most probably they were put there for drainage. I do love Catholic Renaissance art, don't you?'

Charley pulled a face. 'Yes, but symbolically I don't think they're appropriate for a church, do you? Why do

79

you think they used figures of demonic creatures instead of angels on a house of God?'

It was Annie's turn to shrug her shoulders. 'Dunno, I do think they are rather cool to look at though.'

When no one was forthcoming in answering the door, Charley lifted the door knocker once more and rapped it harder against the wooden door three times in succession. 'I read somewhere that the Catholic Church is pagan, perhaps that's why,' she said.

Annie laughed. 'I've heard that too, but if that is so, tell me, where do Protestants come from? Before the sixteenth century, there were no Protestants, so if you're calling the Catholic Church pagan, which by the way, consists of both Orthodox Eastern and Roman Catholics, then you are calling the Twelve Apostles pagan, because they are the original leaders of the church of which Jesus Christ was the head.'

Charley appeared to be considering Annie's words, and the feasibility of the breaking the lock on the door which was blocking their entrance. 'Doors have never got in the way of police enquires before, and this one, no matter how old, will not stop us now.' Charley raised the knocker again.

'Have you tried the handle?' suggested Annie.

'Why didn't I think of that? Golden rule of policing; nothing more embarrassing on a police raid than using the door ram to force entry, only to find the door is already unlocked.'

'Mmm… Never assume springs to mind,' mocked Annie.

'Okay, smart arse.' Charley turned the metal-ringed door handle and the door opened with a long moaning creak. The SIO pushed it open wide. A shiver ran down

Charley's spine as she turned and closed the door behind them. In the semi-dark interior, two pillar candles could be seen burning at either side of the altar table. They offered a welcoming glow amidst the dark wood and stone statues. The only natural light was through some of the most beautiful stained-glass windows, which depicted glorious Biblical scenes, that Charley had ever seen. For a moment she was mesmerised by their beauty.

'I feel like I'm walking into some forgotten place, where time has stood still for donkey's years,' murmured Annie.

'Heaven on Earth.' The words were spoken by a female, but neither Charley nor Annie could see who was speaking. Then suddenly a hunchbacked, grey-haired lady appeared from behind a curtain. 'Come on in,' she said.

Charley produced her warrant card and introduced themselves.

The old lady eyed them with curiosity, 'N'er mind. God welcomes everyone into His House.' She held out her hand. 'Lily Pritchard,' she said. 'Parish Sexton. How can I help you?'

Chapter 10

Over the years, St Anne's Church had gradually become the solace in Lily Pritchard's tragic existence, which made the haggard-faced old lady a soothsayer and prophetess to some, somewhat of a curiosity to others, and the butt of jokes amongst many of the locals.

The sexton's age and career in the church were somewhat of a mystery to the parishioners, of which there were now but few. No one it seemed dare question the formidable woman, not even the diocese who paid her wages. 'Best just wait now till something 'appens to her,' they said. 'Then we'll decide what to do with it.'

However, her store of anecdotes and folklore tales, both mysterious and terrifying, were renowned locally as 'gripping yarns'.

Lily's profession, interest and beliefs had familiarised her with the graves and local stories of goblins, and what was evident was that the 'crazy' old woman was held in awe by the locals. On the bright side, Lily's reputation of being a witch who reportedly flew round on a broomstick cackling at the moon and turning people into toads, kept the morbidly curious away, and the truants, who would otherwise play leapfrog over gravestones and climb the ivy in search of bats' or birds' nests, as in other graveyards, gave St Anne's a wide berth.

'Do you get any help to maintain this place?' said Charley, following Lily into a smaller, brighter room at the back of the altar.

Daylight streamed through the small round window on the outer wall; its bright light bestowing a new atmosphere around the place.

'Isn't it obvious?' Lily said, her eyes sweeping over the massive stack of dust-laden boxes at her side. She lifted a lid and wafted the dust from it directly into the air in front of the detectives' faces. The dust swirled back and forth, and Charley sneezed several times in quick succession. Unperturbed, Lily wiped her dusty fingers on the heavy wool blanket that doubled as a cape around her rounded shoulders, then looking down at it, she sneered at the ashy smears she'd made. Sitting down in the comfy-looking but old chair, a loud groan escaped from her lips, and a wince appeared briefly on her frosty face. The chair's cushions were saggy, flat, faded and riddled with holes that showed filthy straw stuffing poking through like the organs of a bloated corpse. The room had a smell that was hard to define, a mixture between sulphur and a stagnant pond, which was odd because the church was miles from anything larger than a puddle, although who knew what horrors lurked beneath the flagstones.

Once settled, Lily's suspicious grey eyes looked up at Charley, in her smart navy suit and brilliant white shirt. All indications pointed to the old woman's general frailty, but the detective's intuition told her something different.

'The money pot,' Lily said, as if the weight of responsibility had all become too much for her, 'it's gone, and truth is, I thought I'd be dead long before that 'appened.'

'The church's money pot?' said Charley, looking about her for the 'pot', but all she could see were bottles, bottles of all types, containing liquids and items only known to Lily Pritchard. 'Is that a metaphor?'

Lily Pritchard frowned. 'I don't know what you mean.'

Charley shook her head. 'Never mind, tell me, Lily, where did the money in the pot actually come from?'

The old lady sighed heavily, tossing her head in the direction of a church pew that stood against the wall. 'It's a long story, so you'd better sit down. Who's died or can't you tell me?'

Charley looked taken aback. 'Well we could tell you, if we knew who 'they' were, but we don't.'

Lily Pritchard looked puzzled.

Charley pushed aside a stack of hymn books and indicated to Annie that she should sit down too. Charley made herself at home amongst the rest of the rubbish, sitting down where the music sheets used to be stacked. An old electric heater spewed hot air up into her face.

'And you think I might know who they are?'

'We thought you might be able to shed light on the history of Crownest, and maybe you could tell us about the recent occupiers.'

The sexton's eyes left Charley's face. 'I'd offer you a cup of tea, but the kettle went bang, and it hasn't worked since.'

Annie's wide eyes invited Charley to look at the straggly bare wires leading out of the plug.

Charley raised her eyebrows. 'May I suggest you call an electrician?'

'Oh, I did call an electrician. In fact, I called all the electricians in the Yellow Pages, but everyone was surprisingly busy.' Lily paused for a moment, before turning her head towards Annie.

'You could always go into the crypt and boil a pan on the gas stove m'love,' she said. Was that a spot of mischief Charley saw flash in the old woman's eyes? When Annie looked at Charley for her reaction, Lily pulled a face.

'Odd that, people always decline. Probably the prospect of going down into the black hole where coffins gape horribly amongst tattered shrouds, bones and dust which time and mortality have strewn!' she hissed. A single light bulb with a dust-coated red shade hung on a strand of wire above a table at her side, upon which there was a bottle and two upturned glasses.

Tittering, Lily poured herself a glass of blood-red port, swirled the beverage in her glass, and held it up to the light. Dramatically she sniffed it once, took a taste, and savoured the nectar, before looking towards the detectives with a wicked smile upon her face. 'I'm jesting.' She paused and smacked her lips together. 'There is electricity down in the cellar. Will you join me in a drink?'

Charley politely declined.

Annie shook her head, produced a notepad from her bag, and sat with legs crossed and her pen hovering above the paper.

'I'll start from the beginning, shall I?' said Ms Pritchard.

Charley nodded. 'Please. In your own time.'

'Crownest House stands on the site of a former farmhouse, but there was a fire back then when the lightning struck. A long way back. A man known as Jeremiah Alderman was the beneficiary of the farmhouse in the will and he built Crownest using the ruins of the original house. It was a bad idea. He should have demolished the lot, but wasn't allowed to as the will had certain conditions attached. The farmhouse had been long been cursed, you see, by the farmer's wife who, losing the only child she'd borne, had renounced her faith, and turned to witchcraft for her vengeance.'

At that moment the sun must have been crossed by a cloud, and the light shifted. 'Go on, what else do you know?' said Charley, in a hushed tone.

The old woman raised her arms in the air. 'Jeremiah Alderman donated money to help rebuild the church buildings, including the place where I grew up, God's house, bless him.'

'Would you know if there is a tunnel leading from here through to Crownest, by any chance?' Charley asked.

For a moment it felt like the unthinkable had been spoken, to Lily. She appeared guarded. 'There are lots of stories about all sorts of ridiculous things that supposedly relate to the Aldermans and to the church. Comes with the territory when you have a murderer or two in the family's history, I suppose, but that one is true.'

Annie couldn't disguise the excitement in her voice. 'So, you know about the tunnel?'

The nod of Lily's head was confirmation. Lily's demeanour had changed. 'Oh, don't you go getting yourself all excited. It's bricked up, on Master Seth Alderman's instructions. He was Jeremiah's youngest son, and Lucinda's husband. She grew up here, daughter of the caretaker.' Lily dipped her head to place her hand to her brow. When she raised her hand, she looked uncomfortable.

'Are you okay, Ms Pritchard?' asked Charley.

'I will be,' she replied. 'You see, I shouldn't be telling you this because Seth Alderman forbade anyone to mention the tunnel ever again.'

Charley was puzzled. 'Why?'

But Lily sat staring up at a photograph of a priest hanging on the wall. When she lowered her eyes to face the detectives, she briefly closed them, and shook her head.

'Seth was only nineteen years of age when he was left in charge of the family business after his elder brother Felix was executed, but he secretly loathed it, so much so that he turned to drink and to drugs.' Lily sighed heavily.

'I read that,' said Charley.

Lily's eyes were downcast. 'They said he was a selfish, selfish man,' she said, quietly, but with feeling.

'I read that he had an older sister. What became of her, do you know?'

Lily frowned. 'Catherine; I was told she went to Australia.'

'Do you know why Seth Alderman didn't go with her?'

'They say Lucinda was carrying his child,' said the old lady.

'What else do you know about what happened after Catherine left?' asked Charley, gently. Without knowing why, she sensed that she needed to tread carefully, but she had two sets of human remains to identify, and she suspected that the earlier murder would be the most difficult to solve.

'It is said that Seth beat Lucinda. One night, the pregnant teenager is said to have fled through the tunnel to take sanctuary in the church, afraid of what he might do to her, or so the story goes. Seth was apparently heartbroken when he sobered up, but fearing that he might actually kill Lucinda in one of his drunken stupors, he ordered the door to be bricked up and, and the gates to Crownest barred. Reportedly, he never saw Lucinda again.'

'What happened to Lucinda and the baby?'

Lily shrugged her shoulders. 'No one knows.'

The silence in the room was such that Charley could hear the pen scratching the paper on which Annie was writing.

'Moving forward, do you know anything about the latest occupiers of Crownest? We are led to believe that they were called Dixon.'

Lily's glum face brightened up the instant the Dixons were mentioned. She leaned conspiratorially towards Charley.

'They were bad 'uns,' she growled. 'I heard they had guns. I saw the estate agent, old man Raglan, waiting for them one day. He's a bad 'un too, truth be known. He has a gun, so rumour has it.'

'An estate agent with a gun; business must be bad,' said Charley.

Lily's face was serious. 'You might mock young lady, but that's what I heard,' she said.

'Sorry,' said Charley. 'I didn't mean to joke, but why would an estate agent have a gun?'

'I don't know the answer to that, but he might if he's mixing in violent circles.' The old woman pulled herself to the edge of her seat. 'Now, I suppose you won't be leaving until you have taken a look at this bricked-up door, will you?'

'Indeed,' said Charley, 'but before we do, are the church documents archived here? There may be something amongst them that will help our investigation.'

'All there is, is stored in the attic,' she said.

'Excellent!' said Charley. 'Maybe I could send a couple of my officers round to have a look?'

Lily looked pensive. 'Of course. I haven't been able to get up there for years. Can I be nosey and ask if you can tell me any more about the bodies you have found in the house?'

'It's no secret. We've found the remains of a female that we are advised may be around eighty to a hundred years old. We think there may be some pagan history owing to the way she was laid to rest. The other is a male whom the pathologist thinks may have been in the house for a few weeks, months at the most.'

Lily's face drained. She fell back onto the cushion. Charley and Annie rushed to her aid.

'It must be all the excitement,' she said when she came round from her faint.

'Well there is going to be a lot of activity around for a while, and a lot of media interest. Maybe you would like to take a break from your duties for a while?'

Lily looked shocked. 'Where would I go? This is my home. I've lived here all my life, and my mother, and father before me. I don't think so.'

Chapter 11

Behind the red–and–gold, heavy brocade curtain there was nothing for the women to see but a blank wall. Although in knowing that there was once an opening that led into a secret passage, Charley fancied she could make out the shape of the porthole. She laid the palm of her hand on the cold stone, and imagined that the masonry would reveal what was hidden. 'I wonder who bricked it up?'

'What does it matter?' asked Annie.

'The wall's not rough, the plaster is perfectly smooth; whoever did this was concerned about how the final results looked.'

Lily scowled. 'The artisans of yesteryear had pride in their work, not like today.' She turned and walked away, stopped at the tabernacle that doubled up as the altar and appeared to be searching for something in her deep pocket. Three keys were produced, and then she held them up to the stream of jewel–toned rays of light pouring from the stained–glass window.

Annie lifted a brow. 'She's got a point.'

With a nod of her head to indicate to Annie that she should observe the old woman, Charley lowered her voice.

'I was thinking it was more to hide any trace of the door's existence.' Her attention swiftly moved from Lily to Annie's face. Charley frowned. 'Don't you see why it would it matter? Let's face it, a rough bulging wall would have served just as well as a smooth one, if the intention to stop Seth having access to the cluster of church buildings from the tunnel, was only to keep Lucinda safe from her husband's alcoholic episodes.'

'Mmm,' Annie looked thoughtful, 'you're right, but wouldn't a lock and key serve the same purpose? Plus, if it's true what Ms Pritchard says, and Seth instructed it to be done, then why didn't he wall up the fireplace entrance instead, or both for that matter?'

Charley shook her head. 'It doesn't make sense, does it, or am I just thinking too deeply?'

All of a sudden Annie's eyes dimmed. 'If only we could speak to the brickies?'

Lily Pritchard was kneeling on the floor, her arm on the recessed cupboard door, her head inside the ambry. 'You'll 'ave a job on. They'll be long dead and buried.'

'Nothing wrong with the hearing,' said Annie cocking her head. The two detectives walked slowly towards Lily. Looking over her shoulder, they could see that the ambry was lined with purple silk, and appeared to contain a variety of highly decorated, precious metal chalices amongst other fine objects. Charley turned to see the silent Annie's mouth was wide open, as she focused on the bejewelled antiques. She nudged the younger detective. 'Shut it. You'll catch flies!'

Lily clung to the tabernacle. On one knee she made an attempt to stand, and puffed and panted. Annie stepped forward and put a helping hand on the old woman's elbow. 'Let me help you find whatever you're looking for,' she said, peering further into the cupboard as she did so.

'I need to find the donation boxes. They were in here, if my memory serves me right.'

'Why?' Annie mouthed to Charley. 'You expecting visitors?' she said to Lily.

Lily opened the drawer beneath, and immediately stopped rummaging when she had found what she was looking for. One by one she took out several dark wooden boxes and laid them on the faded carpet. 'You, more than most, should know what folk round 'ere are like. They're nosey, they are. When they hear about this palaver on the news they'll be like bees around a pot 'o jam. We'll have visitors all right, mark my words.'

'I don't understand. Why would you need donation boxes?'

Lily looked from Annie's face to Charley's. 'Are you sure she's smart enough to be a detective?' Charley found herself unable to suppress the laugh that rose in her throat. Annie scowled.

Lily pushed tendrils of stray hair from her forehead, damp from the exertion, with a crooked finger. 'Do they pay for interviews these days? Tell 'em, there'll be a charge for filming 'ere, too.' Standing, with Annie's assistance, Lily looked towards the figure of Christ, which stood next to one of the burning altar candles. She put her head on one side and her face softened. 'One way or another, you'll find He always provides.'

With the donation boxes, which would have benefited from a coat of varnish, in their arms, the three women walked through the arched chapel in a slow procession. Turning to walk up the aisle was like heading into a wind tunnel. By the time Charley had reached the outer door of St Anne's, she could feel that the chill had reached her bones. Maybe the old woman was a witch of some kind, for how else had she survived on these moors in winter, alone for so many years?

Charley was glad to put the boxes down at the top of the aisle. In an attempt to feel the benefit of her jacket, she grabbed its lapels and pulled them together with one hand. With the other hand on the door handle, she stopped and turned to face Lily. 'Is there anything else you'd like to share with us? Anything that you think might help us with our investigations?'

Charley followed the direction of Lily's eyes and, for a moment, was distracted by the dramatically beautiful design on the ceiling. The shiver that ran down her spine broke her reverie. 'For instance, have you seen anyone acting suspicious around here, recently?'

Lily pondered for a moment, paused, and then a thought struck her. 'A young man knocked at the church door, I wouldn't say recently, it must be at least a couple of months ago now.'

'Is that unusual in a church?' said Annie.

'As it 'appens clever clogs it is, especially when he wasn't from around here,' she said with a smirk on her face.

'What did he want?' Charley asked.

'He wanted to know if I knew the Dixons, and what was the best time to catch 'em in.'

'He didn't say why he was looking for them by any chance did he?'

'No, and contrary to Mr Raglan's beliefs, I'm not a mind reader,' Lily said, with a flash of impatience in her eyes.

Charley was not to be distracted from the job in hand. 'What did this chap look like?'

Again, Lily's eyes rose to the ceiling. 'Smart. In fact, I thought he might 'ave 'bin a police officer. Although, come to think of it his English wasn't too good.'

Charley frowned. 'Where did he come from?'

'How do I know?' Lily paused. 'I suggested he speak to the estate agents, and he thanked me and went on his way.'

'So apart from looking smart, is there anything else that you can tell us about him? His name?'

'I don't think he told me his name, if he did, I don't remember. He was polite. He had a strange accent. He wasn't from round 'ere.'

Annie opened her mouth to speak. 'Do you know if he saw the estate agents?' said Charley, before Annie could get the words out of her mouth. Lily's facial expression, and the rolling of her eyes, told Annie the question she was about to ask was another stupid one. 'No!'

'Would you recognise him if you saw him again?'

'I don't know.'

Lily Pritchard stood at the door watching the two detectives walk down the church path. Purposely, Charley chose to avoid the graveyard, and chose to walk down the path and along the road. They now had Lily Pritchard's contact details and new leads to follow up. Charley strode out like a woman on a mission, and Annie found herself running to keep up with her.

'Tell me, if the church is in such a bad way, why don't they sell some of that gold?'

'How should I know?' said Charley.

Annie fell silent. A few steps later she spoke again, her breathing heavier and harder as she walked at Charley's side. 'According to Lily,' she said, 'the tunnel is bricked up...' Annie turned and her eyes fixed once more on the church door, in the distance. 'Did you see the jug of milk outside?' she said, with a giggle.

Charley nodded.

'A woman of God, and yet she believes in the Hobgoblin?'

Charley shrugged her shoulders, a smile on her face. 'I suspect most of her generation wouldn't dare upset the Hob!'

'Bet that cat has a field day,' the younger woman sniggered.

Charley stopped and spun round on the ball of her foot. 'You're daring to doubt the existence of the Hob, my girl?'

It was Annie's turn to shiver. She stopped. 'Oh, no! I wouldn't! I do believe, I do believe, I do believe,' she called into the wind.

When the detectives reached the main road with Crownest in their sight opposite, Charley couldn't mistake Annie's sigh of relief.

'You okay?'

Annie nodded. 'Pretty damn surreal this. Working here feels like I'm taking part in a reality show,' her voice took on a hint of excitement. 'Have you ever watched any of those Most Haunted programmes on the TV?'

'Most Haunted?' Charley shook her head. 'You mean you actually believe in that sort of rubbish?'

'Methinks you protest too much!'

Charley stopped to face her.

Annie swallowed the lump that had suddenly appeared in her throat. Had she overstepped the mark? 'Ma'am,' she said quietly.

Charley walked on.

'You mean you've never seen any of them?' Annie hurried to walk at Charley's side. 'Frightened myself half to death watching it on a Friday night when I was younger, and the folks were out.'

'Well, all I can say is that if you like that sort of thing, maybe you'd like to be the one to volunteer to go back and sift through the church records with Lily?'

Annie stopped. Her face paled, 'On my own?' Seeing Charley nod her head, she hurried to catch her up.

'You wouldn't do that to me, would you?'

Chapter 12

Walking always enabled Charley to think; not as much as when she was horse riding, but it was the next best thing when time was scarce.

'I've decided to link the two investigations on the HOLMES computer system,' Charley said to Annie over her shoulder.

Annie's eyes were to the ground as she navigated her way across the grass verge. 'Can I ask your reasoning?'

Charley held her head high, her focus on the big house. 'The background information on the Crownest and its occupants is the same.'

Annie's nod was slight. 'Makes sense.'

'The last thing I want to do is waste time by duplicating enquiries.' Charley fell silent.

'What's next then?' asked Annie.

'I need to allocate a few from the team to look at the enquiries into the older skeleton; an experienced detective sergeant, plus two others should suffice. The majority of our resources will be required to concentrate on the latest murder victim, in the hope that we will find those responsible alive, to be put before the Court. Let's not forget, we still have a cold-blooded murderer on the loose.'

At the narrowing of the pathway, Annie stepped back to follow in Charley's footsteps. There was no doubting her SIO's determination to solve both enquiries. In order to do so Charley needed to think hard about what she knew of the individuals in her team, their strengths and weaknesses, and who would be best placed in specific roles. Experience would help her to solve the crimes in an efficient fashion.

'First though, I have to update the Divisional Commander,' she said. The new Divisional Commander, Bobbie Stokes, was a breath of fresh air in the Division, after his predecessor, the despot Brian Roper, had retired before his disreputable past caught up with him, and he faced getting the sack. When Charley called through to the station, Ruth, Stokes's secretary, told her that Bobbie was in a meeting, but that she would update him on his return.

Two hours had passed since Charley and Annie had left Crownest to visit Lily Pritchard, and neither of them had heard from Ted and his team, nor Detective Sergeant Mike Blake, whom they'd left behind to monitor the mountain rescue team's exploration of the tunnel. As she approached the house, Charley wondered if the quickening of her heartbeat was caused by anxiety or by excitement.

At the outer police cordon near the gateway, there were a handful of people taking pictures of the coming and goings. Annie glanced at the uniformed police officer at the gate as the two detectives passed. Neither knew if the photographers were from the press, freelance or other. Not one of them approached the officers, nor did they appear to know the SIO, or she them. It spoke volumes about the reorganisation of the newspaper industry in recent years that the photographers seemed more focused on getting their work used as digital content nowadays, rather than on the printed page. The local paper, the *Chronicle* was no different, switching as it had to a weekly publication. Journalists that Charley had known for years, including those who had supported her through the incident with Danny Ray, had either jumped ship shortly after the switch to weekly publication had broken, or had been made redundant owing to the restructuring. If her ex hadn't landed himself in jail, then he would have without doubt been a victim himself.

Even though it was not particularly bright outside, it took Charley's eyes a while to adjust to the inside when the detectives reached the house. When her vision returned, she saw the search team, emerging one by one from the porthole behind the dining room fireplace, like time travellers returning from a mission. Spilling into the room, the explorers immediately loosened the chinstraps under their helmets, and turned off the lamps. They huddled together in muted conversation. Charley knew instinctively to stay clear when a debrief was taking place. From where she stood observing with Annie, the team's bright orange overalls appeared to be dry and their boots relatively clean. It pleased her as it indicated that the tunnel was dry.

'Their eyes looked red and sore. I expect it's the strain of searching in the darkness,' whispered Mike. Hardly able to stand still with anticipation, he ran his hand through his hair, his eagerness to hear what the mountain rescue team had to say was tangible. 'Let's hope there are no more bodies…'

'That would be a nightmare, but we'd just get on and deal with it like we always do, Mike.'

A few minutes later Ted Bentley walked towards the detectives. As he did so, he put a bottle of water to his lips and eagerly drained the contents before he spoke.

'Well lass,' he said, on the back of a long breath, grimacing as the cold appeared to find a nerve in his tooth. 'No wonder we couldn't see the end of the tunnel, it follows a downward slope and divides into two, at approximately what I would say is about twelve foot from the church.'

Charley's eyes were wide 'There are two exits?'

Ted nodded. 'There are. For ease let's call the tunnel that leads to the church tunnel A, and the other that I believe will exit into the graveyard, B.'

'You're confirming to me that one of the tunnels does lead to the church?'

'It's without doubt. A bricked-up Gothic-style doorway in the south-east corner, and we heard talking, or should I say we heard something like garbled voices, female ones. At a guess I'd say it was probably you guys making your enquiries?'

Charley's eyes were wide. 'You think so?'

Ted nodded, and as he did so, his eyes crinkled at the corners when he smiled. 'Who else could it have been? There are no more dwellings in that area.'

Charley was eager to share her news with the Ted, 'I can confirm that our enquiries at St Anne's revealed the place where local rumour suggests there was a doorway, which leads to Crownest's tunnel, according to Lily Pritchard who has spent her life there. Knowing where it is located, it's easy to see where the door would have been, although it is a solid stone wall now. It's concealed behind a curtain. Lily, it appears, is a fount of knowledge about the church and Crownest's heritage, and is, I suspect, going to be very useful to us with our enquiries.'

'Maybe she could enlighten us as to why we might find a heap of candle remnants and a ton of old bottles piled up at the foot of the door then?' Ted paused, 'and there are two inscriptions, amongst a plethora of scribblings on the walls.'

Charley frowned. 'What do they say?'

'They are in Latin,' Ted said, leaning towards her conspiringly. 'I only know it's Latin because Fred over there is a total geek; he allus has been, even at school.'

'You went to school together?'

'We did.' On hearing his name one of the volunteers, a red-faced, rotund, jolly-looking character raised a hand, and Ted beckoned him to join them. Fred dabbed the beads of sweat on his forehead with his handkerchief.

'Tell 'em what the motto said in English, will you,' said Ted.

The phrase '*facilis descensus Averno*,' rolled easily off the bearded man's tongue. 'Basically, it means the descent to Hell is easy.'

'I suspect that Tunnel B to the graveyard is a later edition.' Ted paused for a moment as if in thought. 'Although why the hell you'd want two tunnels going to nearly the same place only Him upstairs knows.'

Fred lifted a shoulder, and hunching his back, he leaned towards Annie, with one eye tightly shut. He gave her an icy stare with the other, his voice nothing short of that of a chilling demon, 'With ghostly looking caches, suggestive of ancient castles in the days of the Knighthood, connecting this house to a tomb!'

Annie's stared at Fred, her eyes large and unbelieving.

'Ignore him. He's got a sick sense of humour. The translation of the other inscription, please?' said Ted, nodding at Fred to do his bit.

Fred pulled a face at Ted. '*Sed revocare gradum superasque evadere ad auras, hoc opus, hic labor est.*'

'What does that translate as?' asked Charley, matter-of-factly.

'It's from Virgil, and it means something like, to get out of Hell, that's where the hard work lies.'

For the moment it seemed as if the world stood still for the SIO. Why would anyone inscribe such things? And who was supposed to read it?

Ted lifted his boot, and stamped it down. Annie jumped, such was her reverie. 'The tunnel's floor is hard-packed clay. The walls are uniform and solid. It's an absolute credit to the workmanship of those who created it.'

'Who do you think might have done?' said Charley.

'Rumour has it that it was dug by Seth, Jeremiah Alderman's youngest son. I heard that his mental instability was caused by schizophrenia,' said Fred.

'A type of psychosis,' said Mike. 'Which might explain his dependency on drink and drugs if he was feeling upset or anxious, or even angry and suspicious of those around him; all traits of schizophrenia, I believe.'

Charley's eyes were thoughtful as she absorbed what Mike had said. 'Schizophrenia tends to run in families too, doesn't it? Which might explain the murderous actions of his father and brother, Felix, before him.'

Fred was sombre. 'I was disappointed we couldn't leave the second tunnel B by its intended exit. It would have been satisfying to see where that led.'

'What was stopping you?' asked Mike.

'We think that the soil, beyond a wooden door that appeared to be an entrance to where we do not know, has collapsed, probably due to the lack of beams placed at specific points like in the church tunnel A, which was obviously designed and built to stand the pressure,' said Ted.

'There were no other bodies or bones in the tunnels then?' asked Annie, disappointment written all over her face.

'Not that we could see,' Ted's smile was wide. 'As far as underground ventures go, this one proved to be quite uneventful for us. The ground beneath our feet was relatively even, it was dry, just dark, and not half as intimidating with the right equipment and me mates alongside me. Like I said afore, a credit to them that built it.'

'Now we may never know where the second tunnel leads,' mused Mike.

Ted's eyes lit up. 'Now, I didn't say that, did I? What I haven't told you is that we managed to push a metal rod up through the tunnel roof to the ground above, which, we suspect, if my calculations are right, should appear, like I said before somewhere in the graveyard, we just don't know where exactly.'

Charley's stomach did several back-flips. 'What are we waiting for?' she said, beckoning them forward with a wave of her hand. 'The more sets of eyes looking for the rod, the better! We need confirmation about that tunnel's final destination.'

The investigative team which crossed the main road in haste didn't go unnoticed by those gathered outside, whose sole interest was in what the coppers were doing at Crownest. Annie followed Charley in single file, where the overgrown pathway that led to the graveyard from the main road narrowed. Ted and Fred's booted feet could be heard, as they walked with a purpose, crunching the frozen leaves fifty yards behind.

When Charley turned she could see a couple of hangers-on from the press in their wake, but the landscape and proximity of the church graveyard meant that they were unable to conceal themselves.

Charley and Annie stood at the gate to the graveyard waiting for the others to catch up, and for Annie to catch her breath. Charley offered Annie a mint from her coat pocket. Annie spoke up as she took one, 'I wonder if it's true, that people were employed to hang about in graveyards, waiting for "the dead" to ring their bell should they wake?'

Charley nearly choked on her sweet. 'How does your mind work, Annie Glover?' she scoffed.

Annie's cheeks were red from exertion, and the cold. 'It's true, I read that in the olden days they thought the dead might be just "sleeping", so they put a bell above the ground, near the coffin, attached to a piece of string so that if the person awoke, they could ring it and be rescued.'

Even though it was daylight, the graveyard still contained a certain blanket of darkness, mostly owing to the overgrown trees which bordered the plot and the dense low-hanging cloud which had thickened since their earlier visit. Rain threatened, but it was cold enough to fall as snow. Charley quickly looked back to see the men heading towards them.

From a few feet away, Ted hollered at the women. 'Don't wait for us! We'll catch you up! Go find Seth Alderman's headstone! It seems as good a place as any to start, don't you think?' She lifted the heavy metal bar and walked through the wooden gate. She looked around at the church whilst Annie followed, with the search and rescue team not far behind.

'I wonder why the birds don't sing in this graveyard?' said Annie.

Charley could feel the hairs on her arms raise. Goose-bumps prickled her skin.

'Given the location of tunnel A to the secret doorway inside the church, I think if we pace out, it should give me...' murmured Ted, as he joined them and began walking to and fro between the dull, grey gravestones, with long, purposeful steps. '...which should give me a rough idea.' Suddenly he came to a halt in the overgrown jungle, and searched around with his eyes. No words were necessary. With small steps the others joined him to search for the rod.

'It's got to be somewhere amongst this overgrowth,' he said. Ted appeared to be holding his breath, as did the others, their attention on the grass beneath their feet as they walked in a line, searching.

Charley's eye was drawn to a dismal-looking head-stone where a robin sat. As if the robin's work had been done, it flew. This was not a bit like the one she had seen in the history books. Roots of a fallen tree had broken it into many pieces whilst freeing it from the earth. She went down on her haunches, straining to read the weather-worn inscription, when she was made aware of someone behind her. 'If you'd asked, I would have shown you where Seth Alderman is buried,' Lily Pritchard said, appearing as if from nowhere.

Chapter 13

Annie eyed a rectangular-shaped stone nearby, raised from the ground. It had a stone lid upon it.

'Don't!' shouted Lily, but it was too late. Annie had already sat down.

The younger detective put her hand to her chest, jumped swiftly to her feet, stumbled, and fell flat on her face. She gasped and tried to sit up, holding her stinging right cheek. When Annie withdrew her hand, she could see blood. Charley saw the anxiety in Annie's eyes.

'Are you okay?'

'I'm fine,' Annie replied, with a forced cheerfulness. 'It was her tone,' she said, nodding towards Lily. Annie was about to get up.

'Stay where you are for a moment,' said Charley. 'You've had a shock.'

'It's an altar tomb...' Charley could hear Lily talking to the men. She offered no apology for alarming Annie.

Seth Alderman's broken gravestone was in the corner of the graveyard that was isolated and concealed from view by a large felled yew tree. Their eyes explored the fallen trunk. When upright, the tree had been growing beside part of the cemetery wall which had tumbled down, when the tree had become uprooted.

'Could it have been that the tree was planted purposely to conceal the exit to the tunnel, by giving the exit a canopy of foliage to protect it from view?' The thought crossed Charley's mind.

'Did you know yew trees were planted in graveyards because they thrive on corpses?' said Ted.

'Druids regarded yew trees as sacred plants,' said Lily.

'Altar tomb?' said Annie. 'What's an altar tomb?'

Fred walked the few steps to where she sat.

'They were often placed over the vaults or burial place, sometimes they have supporting leaning statues or memorial brasses on top,' said Fred. Head down he continued to searched the surrounding area by sight. He offered Annie his hand to help her get to her feet.

The young detective took it with one hand and put her other to the ground as she made to stand. A sharp pain ran up her arm and she squealed. 'Ouch! What the—' Instantly Charley knew it had to be Ted's indicator from the tunnel. The Detective Inspector's heart picked up a beat.

Ted's eyes found Charley's. 'I reckon we'll find exactly what we're looking for under this tombstone,' he said, with a certain degree of satisfaction.

A minute later Fred was down on all fours, frantically pushing fallen branches of the tree away to reveal more of the buried tomb. Ted dropped to one knee to help. Panic appeared to have set in, such was their desperation to uncover the metal spike, which would announce the location of the exit to tunnel B, before they lost the light for the day.

Annie was rubbing the palm of her hand where the spike had pricked her. 'You're not gonna go *in* that tomb, are you? Who knows what's waiting for you beneath? Holy Mother of God!' she said, crossing her chest as the nuns had taught her.

'It's a fair question. What is in that tomb? Maybe Ms Pritchard can answer it for us?' said Fred.

Lily Pritchard's face was free from emotion. In fact she appeared to be in shock.

'There's a saying, "Leave no stone unturned",' said Charley, 'and that's what we're going to do.'

'Is it legal for us to go on in without any authority?' asked Annie.

But Charley's attention remained on Lily's face.

'What will the church records tell us about this particular plot? Do you know, Ms Pritchard?'

Still the sexton remained mute.

–

Charley needed to find a common thread that ran through the evidence gathered in the investigations so far to be able to proceed, now the probe had been found. As darkness approached, the team returned to Crownest, to find the others were still painstakingly sifting through the dirt taken from beneath where the male corpse had been found behind the fireplace. If there had been something to be found, they would have done so by now, of that she was certain.

Neal Rylatt the CSI supervisor caught Charley's questioning gaze. He shook his head. 'There's nothing. Not a scrap of evidence to suggest who he is.'

'This lack of evidence, does it suggest to you that this was not done by accident?' Charley asked.

'Killed, dumped in a tunnel, left to rot? It suggests to me that whoever killed him didn't want him to be found, or identified, wouldn't you agree?'

Charley considered that with both murders, there were resources available to aid them in determining identification and in dating the evidence. Several burial artefacts found upon and around the skeleton of the female in the cellar were significant finds. However, this information was also confusing, as it appeared to the SIO that every pagan burial symbol known to man had been buried with the unidentified corpse.

Perhaps they were put there in the hope it would aid the woman in her passage to the hereafter. Which suggested to Charley that, when she was buried, there may have been some confusion, as if the person who buried her didn't know enough about her chosen pagan religion. However, what this act of kindness did seem to endorse was that the person, whoever she may be, had been well loved, and that she had been buried with whatever was thought necessary to take her safely to the next life. Putting coins over the eyes, Charley did know, was thought to pay the ferryman who was believed to take her there. 'She must have links to Crownest to be buried here,' Charley reasoned, holding on to the thought that the well-documented history of the house, genealogists, and forensic archaeologists would all serve to help her in the mysteries surrounding the investigation.

Unfortunately, in the case of the male, there were no similar signs to suggest he was thought well of, but what Charley did have at her disposal were experts who could, with the DNA evidence available, use modern-day technology to try and trace the man through dental and hospital records and other national Force databases.

Joe Greenwood approached Charley as she watched the team work. He was searching for his handkerchief inside his pocket. When he found it, he took it out and blew his nose, glowing red from the cold. 'I hope you'll have something for me soon. I'm gonna catch my death if I have to hang around here much longer without doing proper work,' he said.

Charley nodded towards the team. 'Once their work is done, I'll be able to hand the site back over to you for the demolition to continue.'

'Really?' Joe's surprise was genuine.

His joyful expression raised a smile. 'Really. I've got everything I need now.'

Neal Rylatt raised his hand to catch her attention. 'I'll be off now to take footage of the church,' he said.

'Photograph the graveyard, Seth Alderman's grave-stone and the altar tomb which is adjacent to it, please.' The SIO nodded her head in Annie's direction. 'Take her with you, it'll be quicker in the dark, if she shows you,where to go.' Annie turned and Charley spoke directly to her. 'I'll wait for you outside in the car and take you back to the office. Quick as you like,' Charley called after the pair.

Joe waited patiently at Charley's side, his relief apparent. 'No more human remains then?'

Charley shook her head, as a brief smile crossed her lips. 'No, thank the Lord.'

–

Charley sat waiting for Annie, the car heater blowing hot air in her face. She had learnt long ago that time at a crime scene was time well spent, and the use of any expert was essential to understand something that is not commonly known. She began to recall the most bizarre details from her days at training school. South East Texas Forensic Science Laboratory that she had visited, had buried partially decayed human bodies in different soil types, so that they could study every stage of the natural decomposition process. Such was her interest, and the impact it had made on her, that she could recall their findings and recite them verbatim. A body buried six feet in the ground, without a coffin, takes between eight to ten years to decompose. Also, fingerprints were one of the last things to disappear from a human body.

Warmed up now from her time outside, Charley switched the car engine off, lowered her window and rested her elbow on the driver's door, idly stroking the top of her pinned-back blonde hair. Eyes drooping, she watched Annie walk around the front of the car before she opened the door, and slipped into the passenger seat next to her boss. It was obvious she had been running by her shortness of breath. The younger detective fastened her seatbelt. Charley started the engine, looked in her rearview mirror and pulled away.

'What's next?' said Annie, when they had left the unlit, country roads behind them and had pulled up at a red light in the town centre.

'Full briefing with the team to ensure that enquiries into each of the human remains are not duplicated, but instead complement each other – that's the most important thing to remind everyone right now. But first I must go and see the Divisional Commander to let him know what's happening.'

–

Back at the station Charley took the stairs two at a time to the management suite. Flora, Ruth's guide dog was the first to greet her, in her owner's office. Ruth indicated that the Divisional Commander, Bobbie Stokes, was in.

Charley knocked on the office door, opened it slightly, and put her head inside. 'Come on in, Charley Mann,' he said warmly.

'I know it's a little late to update you on the discoveries, but I wanted to be sure of what we were dealing with before I spoke to you.'

'Forget the bullshit. I know how busy you've been, and appreciate the good work you've done. Mike Blake speaks very highly of you.'

'Yeah, but he lies a lot,' Charley joked.

'I don't think so, I've known Mike for a long number of years; he's loyal, he's good at his job and he's no liar...'

–

Meanwhile whilst the investigative team had been on location at Crownest, and Charley had been updating the Divisional Commander, the additional support staff who had been called upon to be attached to the mounting enquiry had been arriving in the Incident Room. Now, late as it was in the day, it was time for the first briefing.

Charley introduced herself, then her deputy, DS Mike Blake, who sat beside her, before outlining the grim discoveries. 'Ladies and gents,' she said, 'our enquiries are focused on the crime scene, a detached house, called Crownest, that, as many of you will know, has a notorious, bleak past. It was being prepared for demolition prior to the investigation, ultimately to be replaced by several new homes. The house, and land, is owned by JT Developments, and has been sold by Raglan Estate Agents. Several unexplained fires over recent months, including this latest, have been reported at the property.

'The semi-derelict property was put up for sale by the owners. There was interest from property developers JT

Developments – but their plans to demolish the house and build five detached houses was turned down by the council. In recent times it was rented by a husband and wife, Brad and Brittany Dixon, with a view to purchase. I will return to them shortly. And, finally it was bought by Mr James Thomas the owner of JT Developments who were in the process of having the house demolished, by Nevermore Demolition.

'The fire brigade were called out a few days' ago to attend a blaze at Crownest. The house and its grounds were secured; Nevermore workmen had been on site the previous day. This fire appears to be a deliberate attempt to burn down the house, as there were several seats of fire confirmed by the fire crew in attendance. I attended the scene, and some time later, the incident was released in order for the demolition work to commence again. The owner of Nevermore is a Mr Joe Greenwood. However, shortly after, and to the annoyance of James Thomas, the owner of the property, work was forced to cease when two sets of human remains were found. Footage taken at the scene, and of the recovery of the human remains, will follow.

'The human remains were found in two separate parts of the building. The female skeleton is thought to be over 75 years old. The evidence shows that this woman was murdered, and it is our duty to investigate her death, although it is now historical. Her remains were discovered behind a bricked-up wall in the cellar. The second body was found in a concealed tunnel, which was discovered behind the large stone fireplace in the main dining room. The tunnel is not included on the plans of the building. This male corpse, we are led to believe by pathologist reports, has only been there a matter of weeks or months at the most. We found a gunshot wound to the back of his head.

'The majority of our enquiries will now focus on the murder of the male, for obvious reasons. However, because both bodies were discovered in the same house, we will be conducting our enquiries from the same Incident Room. The tunnel I mentioned has been found to lead to the graveyard at the nearby St Anne's Church. So, we have at least one murderer at large with access to a firearm. Our priority is to identify who this is, and take the necessary action.

'In respect of both corpses, we have no information as yet to their identities, and nothing was left at the scene to assist identification, so, further priority enquiries will be to establish who our victims are.

'I mentioned the Dixons previously as the couple who were the last-known occupants of the building. My question here being, why would you rent rooms in a semi-derelict house, with a view to buying it? However, after reading the intelligence on both Brad and Brittany Dixon, it appears they are known to us for committing armed robberies and discharging firearms, so maybe they had an ulterior motive.

'It will also be a priority to trace the pair as soon as possible. When we do, I don't want anyone taking chances. They are known to be a violent couple who have previously spent time in prison. Firearms officers will be brought in if, and when, required to detain these two individuals.' Charley took a deep breath.

'That's a summary, but let's talk more about the human remains. The female body discovered in the cellar is a full skeleton. There are artefacts in her tomb which suggests a pagan burial. Including this…' Charley turned to Mike who, held up a piece of paper between his finger and thumb. 'This pagan dagger.'

'Did it kill her?' piped up Annie.

Mike Blake shrugged his shoulders. 'I doubt we will ever know exactly what killed her, but the dagger stuck in her ribcage is a good start. Her remains are yet to be examined by the experts. Work is underway to ascertain how long she's been there; the dates of the coins that covered her eyes will be of some help.'

Charley continued. 'Pagan, for those of you who are unaware, is an umbrella term relating to people who hold religious beliefs other than those of the main world religions, and worship several gods of the Earth.' The SIO's tone changed. Her eyes were specifically on Wilkie Connor half-expecting his usual prejudiced remarks that she'd had cause to speak to him about recently, half-hoping he had taken heed of her warning. 'What I don't want anyone to do is wear blinkers on this enquiry. We will, as usual, let the evidence speak for itself, understood?'

Wilkie Connor's mouth turned up at the corner. 'Indeed we will, ma'am,' he said under his breath.

'Okay, for those who have been notified that they will be working on this enquiry, your desks are situated at the far end of the Incident Room.'

With no interruptions or other questions forthcoming, Charley carried on, 'The second body, the male, has been dead possibly only weeks. A bullet hole found in the back of his head made the pathologist suggest that the cause of death was nothing short of an execution. If we're lucky, the shell might be rolling about inside his skull like a marble when he's opened up. The location of this corpse is relevant to the enquiry, and you'll see why.' Charley's nod was to Neal Rylatt who ran through the footage from the outer scene, and the graveyard in his capacity as senior CSI, and then concluded with the inner scene, a close-up of the body, followed by pictures of inside the tunnels.

Charley went on, 'Crownest has, for as long as I've known, been called Murder House because of its infamous past. A brief of its nefarious history compiled from research so far, for those interested, is available from Ellen Tate, Office Manager.' Charley beckoned the middle-aged woman, known as Tattie to her friends, to stand up from her chair at the desk she had chosen by the window, where she had placed her beloved green plants on the windowsill. Ms Tate was easily identifiable owing to her nest of frizzy sandy-coloured hair. She then sat as quickly as she had stood.

Wilkie Connor mimicked the tipping of a hat in her direction. 'Good egg, that one,' he said, nudging the detective sitting next to him. 'She's always got a stash of goodies in her drawer,' he said with a wink, before reaching for a handful of biscuits from the plate in the middle of the briefing table.

'All relevant information will be on display boards around the room for easy reference very shortly,' continued Charley.

Charley looked towards the door. 'We were supposed to be joined by two members of the cold-case team who are looking at the Dixons for various unsolved crimes.' She sounded a little annoyed. 'They must have got delayed.'

Wilkie chuckled to himself. Old-timers Ben and Terry from the cold-case team had never been ones for rushing to a job, but were well known for letting others go before them.

On that note, Charley closed the briefing. 'Every line of enquiry you are given to investigate is a priority. Don't hesitate to ask, or to share anything with me or Mike.'

The briefing over, it was nine o'clock. A tired, but adrenaline-charged Charley retreated to her office with Mike, to allow the identified team leaders to further instruct their teams on specific tasks. 'Where the hell are Ben and Terry? You'd think this would be a priority for them, too, given what we suspect about the Dixons.'

Chapter 14

The next morning Charley was standing at her office window next to her door, a mug of steaming coffee in her hand. The window looked immediately into the main office, part of which now formed the Incident Room. With the initial briefing over, there was a lull in activity. This was because the majority of the team, with the exception of Wilkie Connor, who was still doing administration on light, part-time duties following his convalescence, and Tattie, who was based in the building as the office manager, were out and about to trace, interview and eliminate people from enquires. Interestingly, Ricky-Lee Lewis was also still in the office.

Transfixed, Charley watched the younger, tanned, athletic-looking detective constable frantically search his locker, then his desk drawer. Her eyes widened to see him crouch down and crawl right under the four desks in the central reservation. Charley giggled to herself for she knew exactly what he was looking for – and she knew that his search was futile. The tightly-rolled, well-thumbed, heavily-marked *Racing Post* newspaper was in her waste bin.

Next, not surprisingly, came the teasing and jeering from Wilkie. Then Tattie, who patience was finally lost, stood squealing at Wilkie for silence. How could she possibly prepare the budgets with such a din?

The arrival of the cold-case team officers soon after couldn't be mistaken. Jovially, they pushed and shoved each other to enter the Incident Room doorway at the same time. Taken by surprise by the noise, Ricky-Lee lifted his head quickly and accidentally slammed his face into the steel filing cabinet.

Two pairs of strong arms swiftly lifted the dazed-looking Ricky-Lee off all fours, to his feet. However, the agonising pain appeared to be short-lived when he recognised the men. Charley continued to observe as Ben and Terry stopped briefly at Ricky-Lee's desk. With a slap on the back and a ruffle of the detective's hair, Ben counted notes from his wallet into the palm of Ricky-Lee's hand. There was no mistaking the face of a gambler.

Again, Charley's eyes found the racing paper protruding from her rubbish bin, the newspaper that she had plucked from Ricky-Lee's jacket pocket this morning when he was making a brew.

When she glanced back in the direction of the Incident Room, she saw Ricky-Lee shaking Terry's hand with vigour, then he grabbed Ben's face in his hands and kissed him forcefully, on the lips. When Ricky-Lee sat, Ben clipped him round the back of his head and the pair left him counting his money, to walk the short distance to her office. There was a loud, confident rat-a-tat-tat at her door.

'Morning gents,' she said, on opening the door for them to enter. 'Better late than never.' Wilkie Connor followed them to the door. Overhearing her curt welcome, he withdrew grimacing. He knew that tone, and being greeted by the boss in that way had never ended well.

His hand rested on the door handle. 'Can I get anyone drinks?' he said. Charley nodded. 'I don't think there are any biscuits left.' His eyes flew backwards to the empty tin on his desk, 'but maybe Tattie might have some in her drawer,' he said, looking for Tattie's confirmation, but his unspoken plea was met with a slow shaking of her head. Charley's expressionless face told him to get on with it, and she closed the door firmly behind him.

'Sorry we missed the briefing ma'am. We'd a bit of business to take care of.' Ben's eyes were bright, his round face sporting shiny, red, chubby cheeks. He groaned as he made himself comfortable in a visitor's chair next to Terry. 'Cold weather does nothing for my knackered knee,' he said, rubbing it hard. He had a rasp to his voice, but his face carried a charismatic smirk that could have given any would-be Don Juan a run for his money.

Straight-faced, Charley leant down to retrieve the *Racing Post* from her bin, unwound it, and opened it up on the desk in front of her. Her eyes moved from the marked pages to the men's faces, then to the clock on the wall behind them. She cocked her head to one side, purposefully. 'That wouldn't have anything to do with the 2.30 at Wolverhampton, or the 8.10 at Leicester last night would it?'

The seconds ticked away loudly as she waited for an answer. Ben and Terry turned to each other for back-up, their bodies tense. Charley's remark had caught the old-timers off guard. The men stared blankly at each other for a moment. Once upon a time, a challenge by the ex-army supervisors of the day would have resulted in the threat of violence. Nowadays, retired from the Force and back working as civilian employees they were mostly left to their own devices. With no pressure to run around, break into places, find out the big secret or catch the villains, they were never properly challenged. Which could be why they were no nearer catching the Dixons than they had been in the beginning.

'Okay, gents. I don't want to fall out, but let's get one thing straight. I won't tolerate anything other than professionalism in my team. I don't have time to play games. This Incident Room isn't a betting office. What you do in your own time is up to you, but if it starts affecting any of my team, or casts a shadow over the murder enquiry, then beware. Understood?'

'I can explain…' Ben started.

'Don't bother. I expect a hundred per cent commitment from you, while we work together, as I do from any of my team. And the only form that I want Ricky-Lee studying right now, is that of suspects.'

Charley's smile was fixed. 'Right, let's start over, shall we? No further tossing it off and testing my patience in future, and we'll get along just fine. Oh, and don't ever be late for a briefing again. Agreed?'

The two detectives appeared to have the sense to accept the reprimand gracefully, and were no doubt thankful that that was all it was.

The hot drinks that Wilkie brought into the office at that moment helped Ben and Terry to compose themselves. Charley felt the glance that came her way from Wilkie as she took her hot drink from the detective's hand, and she proffered a softly spoken thank-you to him, with a gentle smile. She knew she had to gain the old-timers' respect if she was going to get them on side, and she hoped that she had at least given them food for thought. 'You can't fool them who've fooled others,' her Dad used to say, and she knew that was undeniably true.

With that, Charley dropped her reprimanding tone. Her change of attitude didn't go unnoticed by her companions. 'I'll get straight to the point. I need your help to put Brad and Brittany Dixon in, or out, of the murder enquiry as quickly as possible. I understand that they are wanted, and that your team has evidence in respect of outstanding, unsolved armed robberies?'

Guilt and relief were written all over the faces that looked back at her from across the desk. They knew she had them on the back foot. They knew she meant business. Playing it with a straight bat was the best way forward Ben decided, and then he hoped she'd let sleeping dogs lie.

'The two are wanted for interview in respect of two cold-case armed robberies, ma'am. Brad Dixon has been caught on CCTV on both occasions. Once, when he lifted his balaclava in a shop raid, and on another occasion he is seen discarding a tab-end prior to going into a store which they raided. We managed to get DNA from that cigarette butt. These two crimes are part of a series of six robberies that the Dixons are thought to be linked to by the identification of clothing, and also from words spoken, but, as yet, the pair haven't admitted responsibility.'

'Have they been previously interviewed about these crimes?'

Ben nodded. 'Yes, they were questioned in prison when serving time for the other offences and they were having none of it, but back then we didn't have the evidence that we have now. That's why we are presently trying to locate them.'

'So, you don't know where they are?' Charley asked.

Ben dropped his eyes to the floor. 'No, we don't know.'

Charley heard herself tut and corrected herself immediately.

Terry went on hurriedly, speaking for the first time.
'The suggestion is they are in Spain.' He lowered his voice,
and nudged his partner. 'Glad they've gone somewhere
warm. Me and him are hoping to get a trip out there
once they're traced and detained,' he grinned.

Ben appeared more subdued. 'They're circulated as
wanted with all the necessary precautions, ma'am.' he said.

Charley sat back. 'Tell me, what enquiries have we
done in the UK?'

'What do you mean?' said Terry.

'Well, for starters, do we know for certain that they've
left the UK?'

The men looked at each other. 'Well, er, the suggestion
is yes, but we don't know for certain, we've only just had
the case allocated to us,' said Terry.

His words were met with a frown from Charley. 'Three
months to be exact, according to my notes.' Charley
paused. Both men studiously avoided eye contact with the
SIO. 'With a view to tracing them, what lines of enquiry
have you exhausted so far?'

Ben looked up; he tapped the palm of his hand with his
index finger. 'We've liaised with National Crime Agency,
and in turn we've been told that they have liaised with
their colleagues in Spain.'

Sitting upright Charley took a deep breath, followed
by a sigh.

When no more information appeared to be forthcoming, Charley continued. 'Okay. Look, I'm concerned
that my team don't waste time making lines of enquiry
that have already been completed. Is there anything on
file linking the pair to Crownest, do you know?'

Ben shook his head. 'No, to our knowledge there isn't.'

There was a pause, and Charley appeared to be thinking. 'Can you let the HOLMES sergeant have all the relevant documents concerning the Dixons, so that we can at least link them to our database?'

Ben nodded. 'Not a problem, when do you want them?'

Charley picked up the *Racing Post* between her finger and thumb and placed it in her tray. Collecting the rest of the paperwork on her desk into a pile, she looked at the men, with a tight-lipped smile. 'No rush, this afternoon will do. By tomorrow, I want to know more about Brittany and baby-faced Brad than their own mothers do.'

Wilkie Connor was waiting for Ben and Terry in the main office. Ricky-Lee was nowhere to be seen. The detective leaned back and spoke to them out of the corner of his mouth as they passed. 'How did it go?' he said. 'At least the boss can't send you back to uniform any more.'

Ben's face was paler than when he arrived. 'Still a sackable offence, going out of the Force area without permission, to go to the races, or not, in works' time, especially with exhibits in the boot of the car.'

Wilkie cringed. 'You didn't? You idiots!'

Terry frowned. 'I'd like to know how she knew where we were, Ricky-Lee was hardly likely to tell her.'

'Hey, don't look at me. I didn't know he'd had a bet on the horses until he told me this morning that he thought he was in for a windfall.' Wilkie's eyes looked towards the SIO's office. 'He saw her clock him with his ear piece in during the briefing, and he apparently missed the last race of his "Round Robin", but there is no way she could've known for sure what he was listening to.'

Ben was defiant. 'I don't care how she knew. Some bosses would have wiped the floor with us. Fair play to her. We deserved a kick up the backside, and that's what we got. Let's get going and get the information she wants before she changes her mind.'

–

Rumours that the Dixons had absconded to Spain weren't enough for Charley. A bullet found in the male victim's skull, matched by the ballistics team with those left at the scene of other robberies that the pair had been linked to would be a great result and a positive step forward. She could only hope that this sort of information was forthcoming soon.

With the appearance of DS Mike Blake in the Incident Room, she plucked her car keys from her drawer, grabbed her jacket from the back of her chair and marched out of the office. 'Don't take y'coat off, we're off to Raglan's Estate Agency to see if they can shed some light on the Dixons and Crownest.'

'What, right now?' Mike's voice was unbelieving, but Charley's command was not up for discussion.

'That's what I said didn't I?' Charley briskly entered the corridor. Mike dodged the closing door and followed closely behind.

The SIO thought out loud as she walked, 'They must have something that will assist us with the investigation, contact details, last known address, bank details etcetera, and by the way, Mike, let me know in the future if you talk to the Divisional Commander about an ongoing murder investigation, will you?'

'Sorry boss, I passed Bobbie in the corridor and he asked what the rush was about. I didn't... I wouldn't...'

'Understood. Oh, and please don't use Divisional Commander Stokes's first name; you might have known him a long time, but remember the chain of command. It's there for a reason.'

It wasn't often that Charley used the front of the police station, with its great glass doors headed by the Force's crest, to access or exit the building. She preferred the back entrance, which was nearer the car park. At the officers' approach the front doors glided silently open and, before she knew it, she was on the pavement outside and heading towards the town centre.

Marty, the desk sergeant in charge of manning Reception, watched their exit on the monitor in the back office, his colleague Marie-Clare at his side. By her stance Charley looked to him like she was on a mission. 'What did I tell her? Keep yer head down, but no. She's a law unto herself our Charley,' he said, with a slight shake of his head and a worried look upon his face. 'Just like our Kristine, once she's got the bit between her teeth there's no stopping 'em. Allus been the same, even as kids.'

–

There was no need for a ride in a car, as Raglan's Estate Agents was a small, local, family-run business on the corner of the High Street at its junction with Peel Street, less than a hundred yards from the police station. How the estate agents had survived several recessions was a mystery to some.

Miss Finch, the receptionist was a small young woman with long dark hair, a sunny complexion and manner to match. 'Is there any particular property that you might be interested in?' she said, sweetly as the officers stepped inside the offices.

Silently Charley showed her warrant card which didn't seem to impress. 'Crownest,' Charley said. 'I'm DI Charley Mann, and this is Detective Sergeant Mike Blake, Peel Street, CID.'

'I'm sorry that property is sold,' the young woman said in a dismissive tone. 'Any others that I can interest you in?'

Seconds later an elderly gentleman appeared in the doorway at the back of the office. Small in stature with a slight stoop, he was dressed in a dog-eared suit, an ill-fitting shirt and paisley tie. Charley had a thing about shirts and ties. She liked to see a crisp collar fit properly, but the man's shirt looked old and frayed. It was a few sizes too big, making his long, thin neck look scraggy. He addressed the detectives as he offered his hand. 'Jonathan Raglan, proprietor of this establishment,' he said. 'How can I help you?'

'How about you tell us all you know about Crownest and the Dixons?' said Charley, noting that his hand was trembling in hers as she reached out to grasp it.

Chapter 15

The estate agent's file on Crownest sat on the corner of a dusty mahogany desk which was covered with well-worn red leather and positioned in the centre of Mr Raglan's small office, with the visitors' seating arrangements to one side. Raglan shuffled around his desk, sat down heavily in his chair, put his round spectacles on his vein-threaded bulbous nose, and peered sternly across the desk at the detectives. 'Sit,' he said curtly, as he pointed to two ladder-backed chairs.

The faded, reused file with curled edges that he slid across the desk appeared to have been subjected to strong, direct sunlight at one time. One thing that was certain was that it was a large file and Raglan was frugal. After briefly flicking through the dossier, Raglan settled to study the handwritten note at the top. Charley's eyes wandered to the dust motes that could be seen dancing in the grey light pouring through the yellowed window. The old transistor radio in the corner of the room played quiet, classical music. Raglan repeatedly took deep breaths, and sighed heavily.

As if someone had flicked a switch, the winter sun was suddenly gone, and Charley's attention turned to the dark wooden shelves that lined the office walls, while the room took on a different mood. The bookshelves held old leather-bound volumes. She turned towards Mr Raglan and wondered if the estate agent had read them all. He probably hadn't had the time, despite his years, considering how long it was taking him to read the summary on the file.

As Charley proceeded to further explain the reason for their visit, leaving out the extraneous material not related to the estate agent's need-to-know status. The lifting of Raglan's head revealed a slight tic on the right side of his neck, which not only disturbed Charley, but which she also found distracting. A moment later, as if he wasn't able to keep it in a normal position, his head dropped, as if a puppeteer had loosened a string.

Charley raised her shoulders at Mike's questioning gaze.

'I've met Mr Thomas from JT Developments,' she said, after a moment or two.

Raglan's eyes turned upwards to meet hers, over the top of his glasses.

'And?' he said, in a drawl.

'He was upset about the delay of the demolition. Due to our ongoing investigations.'

Raglan raised his bushy eyebrows. 'Is it any wonder that he's frustrated, really?' he said gruffly. 'The delay of a building project would test the most agreeable businessman, time's money y'know.' The estate agent grunted and continued to stare in Charley's direction. 'What else do you want to know?' Confusion flickered in his eyes. 'That Raglans will be selling the new homes?'

The insight into the background of the angry man that owned JT Developments was interesting to Charley.

'What of the people who took up residence at Crownest before JT Developments took ownership?' Charley said calmly, making herself more comfortable in the uncomfortable chair by crossing her legs at the knees, letting Raglan know she was in no rush to leave.

Mr Raglan looked uncomfortable. 'A man and his wife were renting it, but it didn't work out.'

'We're talking about a Brad and Brittany Dixon,' said Charley, aware of his discomfort.

Raglan looked surprised. 'Yes,' he said curtly. 'I see that those are the names that are recorded in this file.' There was a pause. The detectives took a breath. This was the extra beat which the seasoned interviewer uses, to see if it brings further revelations from the interviewee. 'It was rather awkward, if not somewhat embarrassing,' Raglan continued quietly. 'The Dixons, to all intents and purposes, were supposed to be buying the property before JT Developments took over the ownership. However, references were not forthcoming in a reasonable time, so at the request of the owner to "hurry the sale along", and indeed try to secure the sale, they agreed to rent the property to the would-be buyers, Brad and Brittany Dixon. The couple signed a rental agreement, paid a bond, and at the same time submitted a further cheque for the rental of the property, whilst the sale was ongoing.'

'Could you give us the name of the owners?'

Mr Raglan appeared flustered. He sifted through the papers to find the owners details in the file, to no avail. 'I can't bring their name to mind… It'll come to me,' he said, eventually.

'Was the house habitable?' said Mike.

Mr Raglan gave a slow closing of the eyes, and a slight nod of the head. 'They told us that they weren't bothered about the state of the place. They intended to live in a couple of the rooms, and when the purchase of the house had been completed, they intended to start renovating it back to its former glory. We had no reason to disbelieve them.' He took a deep breath and a sigh escaped his lips. 'After a few weeks however, I was surprised to learn that their cheques had been returned to us from the bank.'

'The cheques bounced?' said Mike.

Raglan raised a shoulder, silent and slightly sullen. 'Yes. That's what happened.'

The two detectives looked at each other, both with the same thought, how could the seasoned estate agent really be so naive?

Mike was the first to ask the question on both their lips, 'What did you do?'

'Miss Finch tried to contact them – she had been dealing with them. Unsuccessful, I personally visited the house. I was quite determined to get the matter sorted as soon as possible.' Raglan's head bobbed up and down, and quickly he placed his hand on his neck to stop the uncontrollable tic, 'but they didn't answer the door.'

'Didn't you contact the police?'

Raglan's head swung from side to side. 'No, no, it wasn't a matter for your officers. However, a bad business decision on our part, and I promise you we didn't give up easily.' With a clenched fist he weakly banged on the desk. 'I wasn't going to be beaten by those two scoundrels.'

'What happened?' said Charley, clearly unimpressed.

'I eventually caught up with them one evening. I saw a light in the house one night as I was driving home. I stopped. Knocked on the door, and when no one answered, I looked through the one of the windows at the back and I could see them sitting together, watching the TV. I banged on the door again and when they didn't answer, I rapped on the window. Mr Dixon came to the door eventually. He didn't invite me in, instead he kept me on the doorstep. He told me that they intended to leave the next morning, and to be perfectly honest, I was glad to hear it. The last thing the owners wanted was squatters. They want the house sold, gone.'

'What of all the money they owed? The owners of the property must have been expectant?' said Charley.

'Mr Dixon told me that if I wanted money, we would have to sue him because he didn't have it. He became aggressive, and well—' Raglan rubbed his neck, the tic was obviously disturbing him, too, '—he didn't come across as the sort of man you'd want to argue with, if you know what I mean. Especially late at night. I told him that I would be back the next morning with a locksmith to change the locks, and they'd better be gone, and that's how I left it.'

'Where are the cheques now?' asked Charley, holding his gaze.

Raglan screwed up his face. 'I wouldn't know.' His eyes dropped to the file, and with what appeared to be shaking hands, he rummaged through the paperwork, but the cheques were nowhere to be seen.

Mike's eyes narrowed. 'I can't believe that without further hassle they left, just like that,' he said, 'and you just let them?'

'Well, they did.' Mr Raglan mopped his forehead with the neatly-folded handkerchief which he had extracted from his shirt pocket.

'Without any further arguments the Dixons left, just like that?' repeated Mike. 'Doesn't that seem odd to you? Given Mr Dixon's previous aggression and their evasive-ness.'

'Well it did, but then they'd had free accommodation for the time they were here, and lucky for us we had a new interest in Crownest from James Thomas, at JT Developments, who had heard that the planning permission that they had sought, and had previously been declined, had now been passed in principle. And, although the Dixons had done some damage inside the property, this didn't matter to him because JT Developments had only one thing on their mind, and that was its demolition.'

'How coincidental,' said Charley.

'You didn't think to report the crime then?' asked Mike.

Raglan looked Mike straight in the eye. 'What was the point? It would hardly be top priority for the police, would it? I didn't want adverse publicity, and this time the purchase went through very quickly because it was a cash sale. I've learnt that sometimes it's better to put certain things down to experience, move on, and learn from it. I'm sure you'll learn that too, given time.'

Charley ignored the remark, although she conceded it to be true. 'The evening before the Dixons left, was this the last time you visited the house?'

'Yes. I've had no reason to go to the house since. I have people who do the day-to-day stuff.' Jonathan Raglan closed the file, sat back in his chair, took a deep breath, and sighed deeply again. 'Now, is that all?'

Mike shuffled to the edge of his chair, scratching his head. 'There's just one thing that is bugging me,' he said.

Raglan frowned.

'I've heard you're a shrewd businessman. You've been here for what, two decades?'

Raglan nodded as he held himself stiffly.

'When I've looked at Brad Dixon's convictions, I can see that he was charged with burglary at these very business premises some years back, and yet you didn't feel the need to mention this to us either?'

Chapter 16

Raglan straightened up and frowned. 'I might be old, but I'm not senile yet. I can't recall that incident. Are you certain?'

Charley nodded her head, something akin to suspicion in her eyes. 'Yes, we are. It's strange that you can't remember. You haven't had a burglary since, have you? Or, if you have, it hasn't been reported to the police.'

The old man's jaw clenched, emotion flared behind his eyes, he let out a long puff of air, and opened his eyes, blinking hard purposely it seemed, to clear his mind. Now, falling back heavily in his chair he appeared to be somewhat breathless. 'No, no we haven't. Well I must say, you've taken the wind right out of my sails. I didn't make the connection. Who'd have thought it? There you go!' He paused.

At Mike's look, he continued. 'As you can appreciate, I have the reputation of the business to think of,' he said, more quietly.

'Yes, and you will appreciate, Mr Raglan, we have two murders to investigate at a property for which you are the sole agents. It goes without saying that we too have a reputation, but ours is for ascertaining the truth.' Charley's tone shifted. 'If people deliberately lie to us, then that may be classed as an obstruction, and that's extremely unhelpful in any enquiry, let alone something as serious as murder.'

Raglan had the grace to look suitably ashamed. 'I understand.' The tic on his neck pulsed frantically. However, it didn't appear to impair his speech, which was now stronger than the detective had expected, and he appeared to have no problem venting his feelings as he slapped a hand on his neck in what seemed like frustration, in an attempt to lessen his body's reaction to the upset. With his other hand he made a balled fist and slammed it on the desk again.

'What else are you not telling us, Mr Raglan?' Charley asked.

'I'm telling you what I do know,' he said, picking up the property file and waving it fleetingly in the air. 'Everything is duly, meticulously recorded here. The previous owners inherited Crownest. A property they neither needed nor desired to keep. Our instruction was to sell it, for as much as possible.' Mr Raglan paused. In that moment his eyes lit up. 'Ah, the Hayfields, that's what I've been trying think of. The owners, I recall that they live on the south coast, in a little village called Milford-On-Sea, in Hampshire. I've never met them, but I have spoken from time to time over the years, to the gentleman on the telephone. He was happy to leave the sale in our hands, knowing it isn't easy to market this type of property, especially one with such a lurid past.'

Charley stood, and Mike followed her lead. She thanked Raglan for his time, told him not to get up, and reminded him that the missing cheques might play an important part in the investigation, and that she would await his response. And if there was an issue with obtaining the records of the bounced cheques from the bank, which she also wanted to see, then she would be happy to contact them direct. Mike Blake leaned across the desk to shake the old man's hand. Swiftly, he picked up the empty cups and saucers, proffering a smile. 'I used to be in the hospitality business,' he said by way of explanation. 'Hate to see dirty pots lying around.'

Charley waited for Mike to go through the office door that she held open for him. 'By the way,' she said, turning around, 'We will need a copy of the Crownest file for our records.'

Raglan looked taken aback. 'It contains personal data.'

'That's okay. We will treat it as such. Unless you have a problem with that, and you would like us to obtain a warrant?'

Raglan shook his head.

'Good, I was hoping that you would want to co-operate.'

Miss Finch accepted the crockery from Mike with a soft thank you and a weak smile. He had placed his calling card on the saucer. She eyed it suspiciously for a moment or two, but as Charley stopped at the glass front door on to the High Street, and opened it, she saw the receptionist spinning the card between her fingers, before she slipped it into her handbag, which was positioned at her feet near her desk.

The main street seemed extra busy as they walked back to the Incident Room; everyone it seemed was heading in the opposite direction. Mike struggled to keep up with Charley's long determined stride and dodge the crowd at the same time.

'What did you think?' asked Charley.

'To be honest, I wondered if, off the record JT has bunged Raglan a wedge to be able to buy the property, with the prospect of advertising the new builds for him?'

'Mmm… You're probably right. We'll see if Raglan manages to produce the cheques. If the bank had returned them, you'd have thought they'd have been attached to the file. I reckon he might've also done a cash-in-hand deal with the Dixons to stay in the property, judging by his reaction to our questions. I'm going to get the intelligence unit to do some digging into his background and into the financial state of the company.'

Mike looked amused. 'The Dixons don't sound to me like the type of people who would have a bank account, never mind a cheque book, especially these days. Or at least not one they rightly own.'

'Me neither. Make a note, we didn't ask him if he had a firearm, but he's not on the firearms register, I've checked.'

–

On their arrival at Peel Street Police Station, the great glass doors glided open. In Reception, Marty was dealing with an obnoxious 'customer', who was apparently late answering his bail. He lifted his head briefly, acknowledged their presence, and automatically pressed the button to allow them to enter the inner sanctum of the police station once the buzzer had sounded. Charley winked at the older man, and with a confident swagger marched through the door.

'Is his daughter back at work now?' Mike said, glancing at Marty through the glass partition.

'Kristine? Yes, light duties only. She's still in her wheel-chair, but most importantly, she's back in the saddle; something I never thought possible after the accident that killed Eddie.'

'You've been friends with Kristine forever, right?'

Charley nodded.

'Is it true that you both joined up at the same time?' he said.

'Same time, same passion. Horses.' The mention of horses, and the thought of her best friend Kristine and the hobby that they shared, caused a warm feeling to flush through Charley's veins. Instinctively her hand went to the golden horseshoe hanging from a chain around her neck. It felt warm and reassuring to her touch.

Charley stood on the first landing of the police station and looked down at Mike climbing the stairs, slowly, one step at a time. She would never tire of the view from this window which showed her the historic town buildings of Huddersfield, and the green rolling hills and valleys beyond. 'However, circumstances out of my control took me on a very different path to Kristine,' she said quietly. 'She's back working with the horses.'

'Things happen for a reason, so they say,' said Mike as he joined her.

'Yes, so they say. If I hadn't been sent on secondment to London, studied for my Inspector's exams, and got promotion to take up the position of head of CID here, then maybe we wouldn't have found out who was responsible for it,' she said turning to face him briefly, before pushing through the door to see a windowless corridor. They walked past the management offices with their closed doors in silence, their conversation on the subject clearly over.

Mike followed a hurrying Charley through the Incident Room into her office. 'I get the impression that won't be our only visit to Raglan's estate agency.'

'I'm sure you're right. It'd be nice to find something to get under his skin so we could rattle his cage. Let's face it, his going to the house to challenge the Dixons about the rent seems highly improbable. He's unlikely to intimidate anyone, let alone a couple of armed robbers. They'd eat him alive!'

'Unless he had something, or someone with him to intimidate, or frighten them?' suggested Mike.

'Or he was carrying a gun?'

Inside Charley's office there were papers and documents piled up on the SIO's desk ready for her signature. Charley gave priority relating to items that Forensics had examined; then there was a visit to the mortuary to arrange to see what else could be gleaned from the sets of human remains.

Charley was drawn to the formal report on the pagan dagger, and her instinct told her that it would be naive not to research more about the present-day local pagan following. Charley was well aware of the district's annual Imbolc Gaelic festival, which marked St Brigid's Day and the end of winter. The traditional event took place between the winter solstice and the spring equinox. When she was younger and had lived in the area, she had always enjoyed the community celebration, while being in awe of the fire-eaters and fire-dancers. The memory of being frightened by the sculptures when walking through the woods near the Standedge Tunnel made her smile. The festival embraced the turning of the year and celebrated the first stirrings of spring, and was imbued with the idea of growth and renewal.

When she had policed the event as a young uniformed officer, she had taken a different viewpoint. Issues concerning health and safety were paramount at the event. Charley was conditioned to be an unbeliever, primarily because of her job, unless evidence was ever to prove otherwise. However, as she had been brought up by folk-lorists, she also tried to keep an open mind, as she had read too much compelling evidence that could not be explained rationally.

The spell was broken by the arrival of a message on her screen, and her mind instantly switched to thoughts of Lily Pritchard, at St Anne's Church. She wondered what she might know of local pagan history. She was intrigued to know what the church records might reveal, but with her eye on the clock, and the mortuary to visit, she knew that that line of enquiry would have to wait. Whilst murder investigations required energy, drive, passion and determination, they also needed a vast amount of patience.

She hoped the examination of the bones and remnants of flesh that she was about to witness would reveal more to help them find the killers.

And although the victims had died years apart, Charley had no idea if they were related or not. The DNA analysis would confirm it either way.

Chapter 17

The post-mortem examination of the female skeleton confirmed much of what the police already knew. 'We're very lucky, Inspector, to have the skeletal remains intact.'

'Why's that?' said Charley, coffee mug in hand in the anteroom at the mortuary, as Professor Davis Chevelle prepared for the theatre.

'The osseous labyrinth inside the petrous temporal bone has higher amounts of endogenous DNA than any other skeletal element. A minimally invasive cranial-base drilling method, called C.B.D.M, will enable us to access this area of the temporal bone, from the basal region of a complete skull without, you'll be pleased to hear, causing damage to the anthropologically important cranial features.'

'Sounds costly. In simple terms, tell me if I'm wrong, but, am I right in thinking that you intend to drill a small hole carefully, at the rear of the skull?'

'Isn't everything costly these days, Inspector?!' replied the professor.

'HQ will no doubt be on to me about expenditure, especially in these times of cutbacks, but how can you put a price tag on a murder investigation?'

Annie was at Charley's side, glad she was distanced from the odour associated with the dissection of bodies by the walls and the pane of glass of the viewing room.

'There's a suggestion that there was some discussion about the woman having stabbed herself,' Charley said.

Professor Chevelle's eyes found hers. 'Certainly not. It's more likely that stabbing yourself in the chest would result in a small, moderately painful wound, minor blood loss, and possible infection, but that's all.'

Annie stood and demonstrated the action. 'Even if she used both hands, with force, like this?'

'It's actually incredibly difficult to kill yourself by stabbing yourself in the chest hard enough and accurately enough, against your pain and reflexes, to do any real damage. Unless of course you happened to drop dead from the shock, in which case you might succeed.'

'I guess even if it was possible, we'd have to ask ourselves who laid her out, and built the secondary wall to hide her remains, if it wasn't the murderer.' Annie turned to Charley. 'An accomplice, maybe?'

'If it was suicide there'd be no need for conceal-ment,' said Charley, 'so I think we can safely say she was murdered, but by whom and why, that's the question. Once we know who she is, then we might have possible suspects by association.'

'Find out how she lived, and we'll find out how she died?' concluded Annie.

'Exactly,' said Charley.

'I guess we can safely say that the murderer is dead by now too, judging by the estimated age of the corpse, so it would seem whoever the killer was, they lived their life without retribution,' suggested Annie.

'Maybe so, but it won't stop us discovering who it was. I want a clean slate on my record. Undetected murders don't look good on the CV.'

The second, male corpse offered more by way of evidence. Charley was hopefully that the teeth and metal plate screwed to the left tibia would lead to the early identification of the male. With gloved hands, the professor, fully dressed in protective clothing under the bright lights of his operation theatre was ready to make a start. CSI Neal Rylatt was at hand with his camera to take photographs as required. DC Ricky-Lee, exhibits officer, was in the viewing room with Charley and Annie waiting for exhibits to be passed to him via the internal drawer from the examination room. Chevelle peered over his face mask and briefly found Charley's face a few feet away behind the glass, where she stood with Annie, tentatively watching the dissection of the body through the viewing-room window. It might not suit some, but, similar to Annie, the isolation was far more agreeable to the Senior Investigative Officer today than being at the pathologist's side at the edge of the post-mortem table.

'Odontology will assist with the teeth,' Chevelle said, stepping back for a moment to allow Margery, the mortuary assistant, to remove the top of the dead man's skull.

Annie squirmed at the cracking sound the procedure made.

'Like taking the top off a boiled egg,' Charley said smiling, her focus keen, her voice eager with anticipation.

Examining the open skull at close quarters, Professor Chevelle raised his eyebrows, and drawled. 'Well now, Inspector, aren't you the lucky one?' Charley could feel herself holding her breath in anticipation, as the professor plunged a pair of long-nosed tweezers into the man's skull, and plucked out a bullet. 'Look, I've a present for you.'

At the shrill 'ping' of the bullet dropping into the tray beside him, Chevelle's gaze drifted away from the corpse to Charley's face once again, and when their eyes met he continued, 'Your starter for ten! I'm no firearms expert, but I'm sure they'll be able to tell you, quite quickly, what sort of weapon that was fired from.'

Charley's expression was one of pleasure, and some relief. The examination of the second victim was revealing positive lines of enquiry. DNA testing, without the need for extra, expensive procedures, would hopefully give them more.

Charley thanked Davis before leaving, who aired his suspicions that the female had died from a forceful stab wound to her chest, which would have entered her heart. The male corpse had died from a gunshot wound to his head, and the bullet recovered from within, proved it. He was likely a victim of an execution. As Charley left, she couldn't help thinking that Chevelle was good, no, he was excellent!

Whatever had taken place, Charley now had confirmation that both killings had been premeditated and intentional.

'Strange how the actions after the murder were similar in both killings, though years apart,' said Annie thoughtfully, as they travelled back to the Incident Room together.

'What do you mean?' asked Charley.

'Well, after the murder, both bodies were hidden. The killer, I assume was hoping that they would never be found.'

'It keeps going around in my head, what could the motive be?' Charley said, as she steered her car into Peel Street Police Station's back yard.

On their arrival, the Incident Room was buzzing. More enquiries could now be set in motion, and there was plenty to discuss; all relevant information would be imparted to the wider team at the debrief.

'I want an urgent enquiry setting up with the ballistics experts,' Charley told Wilkie Connor. 'I want to know what sort of weapon the bullet came from, and I want to know if that type of weapon was known to be linked to any other crimes. I'm sure they'll treat it as a priority, but just in case, give them a gentle reminder. I don't want to hear about their workload, we're all busy. We have an armed murderer out and about and who's to say that they won't strike again soon.'

The afternoon was drawing in as she debriefed the team. When a suspect was traced for the death of the male victim, she was mindful that a team armed with weapons would be required to effect the arrest. It would be a serious mistake to use unarmed officers, thereby potentially putting lives at risk.

'Risk Assessment is a ball-ache, but a necessity,' Charley told Annie. 'Life on the street is dangerous, possibly more dangerous in the UK than ever before, and ignoring the warning signs and neglecting to take remedial action is not an option in my book,' she said. 'My priority is the protection of the public, and you lot.'

Charley then updated Divisional Commander Stokes with the mortuary's findings. His concern was about the cost of the investigation. 'Just make sure you get all the funding you can from Headquarters, Charley. I don't want to bankrupt the Division.'

His concerns were duly noted. 'There's no need to panic yet,' she told him. 'It's early days.'

Stokes looked at the running costs, and grimaced. 'Any suspects yet?'

'No, we don't even know who our victims are yet, but once we do, I expect things to move quickly.'

'Good, keep me posted.'

Back in the Incident Room, she had a question for her team. 'That metal on the man's broken bones?'

Mike responded immediately, 'An urgent enquiry has been made at the local hospitals.'

'The DNA that Chevelle took from the male is already on its way for checks by Forensics,' said Ricky-Lee.

Annie looked downcast. 'Sadly, the identification of the female isn't going to be as straightforward.'

Charley saw tired eyes, set in tired faces around the table. 'What we must remember is the detective's mantra: *clear the ground beneath your feet before extending the parameters on the search field*. We're doing all we can, and I want that to be how it remains throughout. Whilst we carry on with new lines of enquiry, I want the intelligence cell to look at every crime that the Dixons ever committed, including the ones that they are still wanted for. After all, the pair lived at Crownest within the time parameters that have been suggested by the post-mortem of the male corpse.'

Charley turned to Annie. 'Get on to the cold-case team again, will you? I want to know from Ben and Terry exactly what sort of weapons the Dixons are known to use. I also want to know if the previous investigations included Ballistics to assist in linking the crimes known to have been committed by the pair, and I want to see those reports.'

The attending officers took notes and their heads nodded in compliance.

What Charley desperately needed to do was to place the gun that had fired the bullet into the man's skull in the hands of the killer, whoever that may be.

The Dixons remained the priority. To put them in, or out, of the enquiry was her aim sooner rather than later. Their criminal record, and the fact they had lived at Crownest, made them prime suspects to the crime.

As the team went back to their desks, Charley returned to her office. The day wasn't over yet. She wondered if, when the Dixons were traced, they would have weapons on them. Her next thought, as she sat at her computer screen with her fingers hovering over the keyboard, was that no weapons had been found at the house, nor had any ammunition been recovered, other than the bullet in the victim's skull.

She uploaded the Dixon's file, to see if there were any weapons seized on their last arrest. She paused, waiting for the results, and when they came, she felt the sinking feeling she associated with disappointment – the recorded data told her nothing.

Perhaps the pair had lured the male to the house to kill him? If so, why? Perhaps Mr Raglan should think himself lucky than he wasn't one of their victims, too. Her mind raced, with so many questions, possibilities, ideas running through her head. She knew that sleep would be hard to come by that night. Copies of the full intelligence file on the Dixons had been added to the Incident Room suspect database. It would make good bedtime reading, if she didn't get chance before she left the office.

Murder enquiries are essentially about eliminating people, so she couldn't be limited in her thinking. Her instincts told her that the culprit had to be someone who knew of the tunnel behind the fireplace. Therefore it made sense that it had to be an occupant, or someone who knew Crownest well. After all, as Joe Greenwood, the owner of Nevermore had told her, there was no mention of the tunnel shown on the original plans for the property, so it had to be someone with inside information.

Her concentration was so deep that when Annie knocked on her office door Charley jumped.

'Ben and Terry are off today,' she said.

Charley threw her head back and ran her splayed fingers through her hair. 'Isn't that always the case? Days off are days wasted!'

'They are,' Annie grinned. 'However, Tattie has it on good authority from their team lead that no weapons have ever been recovered at, or after, any of the Dixon's arrests.'

The SIO's head dropped, her eyes lit up. 'I want copies of the files which show what witnesses have said.'

'Yes, ma'am,' said Annie.

'I want to know what type of ammunition, shell casings and so on, have been recovered at the scene of the crimes.'

Annie smiled. 'The Dixons are reported to have matching handguns.'

Charley nodded. 'I'd believe anything where those two are concerned.'

Annie tilted the notepad in her hand to allow her to read the notes she had made and highlighted. 'The bullet casings recovered from their previous crime scenes are nine millimetre.'

Charley frowned. 'That's a common calibre with most types of handgun.'

'Apparently so, and handguns are the weapon of choice for criminals these days, with a lot adapted from imitations, or conversions of original weapons, I'm told.'

'Just as lethal, Annie. I'll give Ballistics a ring, and give them the heads-up on what we see as a possible link. I want to know what their timescale is. The bullet from the skull should be with them shortly.'

'Perhaps then we'll get some answers,' said Annie.

'We can live in hope,' Charley smiled as she turned to the telephone. 'Come on, pick up. I'm not going to hang up. Surely you don't wear ear protectors all the time at Ballistics!'

Chapter 18

Ballistics could confirm two things. The shell casing had arrived, and on initial visual examination, the expert declared it nine millimetre. She would have to wait for further insights. Frustrated and demoralised with the process because it appeared this was all she was getting for now, Charley dropped the telephone receiver dramatically onto its cradle. She was more than aware that the necessity to carry out the desired tests meant she was at the mercy of the specialists' workload, yet again, and it galled her. Patience was a virtue, she reminded herself with gritted teeth.

In the briefing room, on sharing the news, the dip in moral was tangible.

Looking around the room, Annie saw demotivated faces. 'On the positive, we know that our male victim was killed with a single gunshot,' Annie said in a weak attempt to lighten the mood.

Tattie hovered on the periphery of those gathered at the briefing. Her movements somehow exasperated Annie's momentary hiatus. Annie forced a smile. She hated people hanging around, it reminded her of the convent where the nuns constantly hovered in the background. Annie's rational self began to fight with her deep-seated emotions, as they always did when she remembered her brother's suicide, the result of his abuse at the hands of the priests, at school. It was the reason she had become a copper, to try to do her utmost to try to stop man's inhumanity to fellow man, or at least make sure the guilty paid the price for their crime. She would never ever understand how her mother could still justify her religious faith given what had happened.

'Why didn't the bastards take a leaf out of Judas's book and kill themselves?' Annie had screamed at her mother.

She had watched those of the cloth who had been found guilty leave the courtroom, those cruel, sadistic people whom Ash, her brother, had trusted and obeyed. Ash had been a good kid, but he'd never got over the abuse he had suffered at their hands, which resulted in his suicide. She conceded that mass suicide of his abusers would be yet another selfish act, for if they threw themselves on their swords it was their belief that it would redeem them from their crimes, and Annie was glad that wouldn't be allowed to happen.

Cheeks flushed, her voice cracked, she came back to the present-day meeting, and continued, 'we also know that the preferred weapon of the murderer was a handgun.'

Charley glanced over her, concerned. Annie looked particularly peaky. Was she expecting too much from the youngster who had relocated from the city as a uniformed officer? She had then been catapulted into Peel Street CID because the dinosaurs in the hierarchy, who liked their old style of rural policing, didn't know what to do with Annie's vibrant, go-get-'em personality. Charley, on the other hand, liked Annie, and rejoiced in the young detective's inquisitiveness, especially if Charley's own enthusiasm was waning. She felt a little fed up now, most probably due to the head cold that was threatening to take hold, and the fact that she had just been informed by

Wilkie Connor that a local expert in the field of paganism who they had tracked down looked like a non-starter.

'I hear on the grapevine that you're having trouble finding someone who knows a bit about heathens?' said Winnie following the briefing, as she counted drops of eucalyptus into a bowl of steaming hot water which she then placed on the edge of Charley's desk.

Charley looked into Winnie's kind eyes, but she couldn't help wishing it was her mum who was the one administering the TLC to her.

'It's okay, something'll come up,' she said, sliding the bowl to one side so she could get to her computer keyboard. She looked at Winnie rebelliously, 'and I haven't got the time or the inclination for that sort of malarkey!'

Charley sniffled ungratefully into a tissue Winnie offered her. The bright lights of the computer screen hurt her eyes, and the pain in her head made her nauseous. When the stabbing pain came, it made her flinch as if from an electric shock. She shut her eyes momentarily and cried out loud. Immediately her hands went to her head.

'Hmm… Well, that's a matter of opinion,' Winnie said as if to herself, and after watching the young woman struggle, her voice rose. 'Charley Mann, you're as stubborn as a mule. Just for once will you bloody well do as you're told! Put the towel over your head, like a tent, and breathe in. It'll make you feel a whole lot better.'

Too tired to argue, Charley moved the bowl closer and inhaled the aromatic odour, before she began to cough incessantly. 'Well, I wonder who I take after?' Charley gasped when she caught her breath.

'Point taken,' Winnie said, with a slight cock of her head as she thought of Charley's Dad, Jack, her childhood sweetheart, the love of her life who, at seventeen, had stubbornly decided that if she went away to college, whilst he stayed home lumbered with looking after the family farm, then they were finished.

Then, when Winnie returned home from her adventures, it was to be greeted with the news that Ada, Charley's mum, was found to be expecting, and given the old-fashioned ways of the family a shotgun wedding was planned. The rest, Winnie had told Charley, was history. One thing you could say about Jack, he never turned his back on his responsibilities. Which had only made Winnie love him more, even it had been from a distance for the rest of her life.

Charley's spluttering broke Winnie's reverie. 'Do you know someone, a pagan specialist, I mean?' she asked, with more than a little desperation in her voice audible from her position under the towel.

Clutching the duster in her hand tightly, Winnie polished the corner of Charley's desk with vigour. She smiled. 'Not quite, but I'm sure if I asked my old friend Josie Cartwright, she'd be able to help you.'

Charley swiftly lifted the corner of the towel. 'The writer, author, historian Josie Cartwright is *your* friend, really?'

–

From the main road Josie Cartwright's house was too far away, and too small to appear as more than a black smudge on the opposite hillside. Winnie's directions were to follow the path of a chain of electricity pylons, which swung precariously in the wind, across the bleak valley from one hillside to the next.

A broken five-bar gate leant against a toppled, moss-peppered dry-stone wall. It led Charley, Annie and Winnie down a single uneven farm track which took her to the door of a quaint old cottage overlooking a cobbled courtyard. It was impossible to see what the other surrounding buildings would have once been, as they had already been absorbed back into the landscape.

There were the markings of a flower garden and a vegetable garden which were very obviously lovingly worked by its owner. Charley stood at the cottage door and raised her hand towards the knocker, but before she placed her hand on it, the door was opened by a slight, stooped, white-haired old lady who held a crocheted blue shawl together between her thumb and the first finger of her arthritic left hand.

As soon as she saw Winnie through her watery blue eyes, her smile widened, her arms flew open, and she embraced her friend warmly. Winnie, full of excitement and joy, scuttled ahead of them down the higgledy-piggledy, narrow corridor with doors leading off into other rooms. 'That sloping floor'll show you whether you have a small inner ear canal,' she called to the younger women, and then abruptly vanished through a door under a small twisted staircase.

'Whatever does she mean?' whispered Annie over her shoulder to Charley. But before Charley got chance to tell her it was probably a reference to a person's balance, Josie ushered the detectives into a cosy room with a blazing fire in the iron grate of an old stone fireplace.

The two elderly ladies came together in the lounge, to share a moment of giggling, just like children. 'When we were younger, we used to tell our friends that this crooked little house was haunted,' said Winnie.

'Stop frightening the lasses,' said Josie with a shy, gentle shake of her head. 'Truth be known, she's never grown up that one,' she whispered.

'Why would I want to grow up?' said Winnie aghast.

A magnifying glass sat on a low coffee table, next to several pairs of discarded spectacles, and a heap of books stood in front of Josie's comfy chair.

There was a whistling from the kitchen. 'Kettle's boiled,' Winnie said, cheerily, clearing spaces at the table to one side of the room. It was covered with a large plastic floral tablecloth, the very latest fashion, 1960s-style.

Annie looked about her. 'Oh, this place is just... awesome,' she said to Josie. Reaching out tenderly she touched the wooden beams, and stained glass with her fingertips. 'I absolutely adore old things, and the dustier the better!'

Charley gave Annie a nudge. What was she thinking of?

Annie wasn't paying any attention to Charley; she was already meeting Josie's eyes and blushing. 'I'm so sorry! I didn't intend to be rude.'

Josie laughed out loud, and, when she laughed she looked years younger. She liked Annie. She liked old things too.

When Winnie returned from the kitchen, she was carrying a tray of hot drinks, and a much-coveted plate of homemade biscuits. With a proud nod towards Josie, Winnie carried on. 'She bakes all her own bread, cakes and biscuits, y'know, and makes her own jam and pickles. She also grows her vegetables and flowers, and at one time she'd have wrung the necks of those chickens in the coop. Puts me to shame, she does.'

Annie awkwardly took from the tray a small bone-china cup which rattled upon its saucer. The look on her face told the others she was terrified of breaking it.

Winnie chuckled at the young detective's grimace, 'It's not as delicate as you think.'

'Indeed, it's made from cattle bone,' Josie said, sitting down opposite Annie with a groan, and a moan about her ailing bones.

Annie took a sideways glance at Charley. Her expression turned quickly to one of suspicion. She looked from one woman to another, finally settling on Winnie's face. 'You're winding me up, right?'

'No, no, I promise you. It's true,' Josie said. 'That's why it's called bone china.'

The older ladies exchanged local news for a while, but the lighthearted atmosphere soon shifted as Charley explained the reason for their visit. It soon became apparent to Charley that without Winnie's interaction, Josie Cartwright would not be talking to them, nor to anyone else about Crownest. When Charley started to share with Josie the information regarding the discovery of the bodies and the reason that she needed her help, the old lady paled, her eyes clouded over and her questioning eyes fell upon Winnie. With lips slightly parted she took a deep breath. 'I'm sorry, I can't talk about it,' she said. 'Not even for you, Win.'

Winnie reached for Josie's hands and, with great gentleness, she sandwiched them between hers. 'Hear her out. It's okay, you can trust Charley. She's Jack's girl. You remember Jack Mann?'

Puzzled, and slightly disorientated it appeared, Josie's look remained suspicious. Winnie nodded her head reassuringly. 'It's time…'

Chapter 19

'The official records show the Alderman family resided at Crownest for many years, as you are probably more than aware. However, what you might not know is that Agnes, the mother of the present sexton of St Anne's Church, was the woman locals sought for bringing babies into this world, and for laying out the dead.'

The news about the old midwife was nothing new to Charley, but the next bit of information that Josie shared made her ears prick up.

'Seth's wife, Lucinda Alderman, it is rumoured, was with child when she was bundled off to Australia to a place of safety with her friend Catherine, her sister-in-law, by Father Michael O'Doherty, the then-priest at St Anne's.

'At the loss of his wife and heir, Seth was said to be beside himself with grief and he took his own life. There couldn't be a more poignant place for his death other than at the door of the tunnel that he'd insisted be bricked up in order to save his wife returning to Crownest and falling victim to his increasingly dark moods, caused by his drink and drug dependency.

'Again, owing to the distance of time, the paper trail goes cold, and we know nothing more, for sure, about what happened to Lucinda and her child, or to Catherine Alderman. I guess Catherine may have married and taken her husband's name, and Lucinda might have done the same, and remarried in Australia.' Josie was silent for a few minutes, appearing to collect her thoughts.

Eager to hear more, Charley urged her on.

'So what more do we know about Agnes, Lily Pritchard's mother? How does she come into the tale?'

'Only that she was a bit of a rebel. And a local oddity.'

'Like mother, like daughter,' she whispered to Winnie.

'She was?' said Charley, 'In what way?'

'Oh, it is said that she flatly refused to follow the religious ways of her husband, a devout Catholic, who married the young girl solely to keep her out of the poor house, thereby forsaking his calling to become a priest. And, would you believe, she then rewarded him by refusing to join him in his faith and worship. Against his will, and after several failed attempts to keep Agnes away from other men, she formed a meaningful relationship with the local blacksmith, Atherton. She was caught lying with him and he was banished from the village. A couple of days later he was found dead. The official recording of his death tells us of a tragic accident.'

'That sounds mighty suspicious,' stated Annie.

'One might think so, yes. Apparently he was kicked in the head by a horse he was shoeing, on farmland owned by the church. However, his demise, for obvious reasons, didn't sit comfortably with some of the village folk who said he was far too experienced for that to have happened. That said, so embarrassed by his wife's behaviour, but unwilling to disown her, Agnes's husband, Walter Pritchard became increasingly tormented by his religious beliefs and some said, by his possible role in Atherton's untimely demise. It appears that the church and its ways became a sort of prison for Walter. He was found collapsed at the altar in St Anne's Church, soon after

Atherton's accident, stone-cold dead. Heart failure some said, a broken heart said others.'

At the chiming of the clock, Josie stirred and looked at her watch. 'Now, you must have better things to do than listen to the ramblings of an old woman.'

Charley shook her head. 'No, not at all, I for one could listen to you all day. Tell me about the priest who helped Lucinda and Catherine, Father Michael O'Doherty.'

'Michael was a wonderful man, but I suspect he spent most of his latter years praying for guidance, owing to the other colourful characters around him.'

Winnie looked puzzled. 'Well, yes, I guess he must 'ave either been naive or stupid not to know what was happening around him.'

Josie's mouth rose at one corner. 'Quite the Miss Marple, Win! It is said that Connor O'Doherty, his nephew, was thick as thieves with Seth Alderman. The church, along with the Alderman's wealth and support, dictated what the villagers could do. Rumour has it that after Father Michael O'Doherty's death, it seemed a natural thing for next in line Connor O'Doherty to be ordained as the head of St Anne's Church, which was then said to be more alive by night than day.' Josie frowned. 'Have you spoken to Lily Pritchard?'

Charley's eyebrows rose. 'Only briefly, but there was nothing mentioned about Father Connor...'

Josie leaned forward, as if to share a secret. 'Ask her about the candle she held for him, back then.'

'You were friends with Lily back then?' asked Charley.

'We were the best of friends, back then... But, that was a long, long time ago. Another lifetime it seems.'

'You wouldn't know where we could get hold of any photographs of the people we are talking about? It always helps to have visuals.'

Josie's drawn, thoughtful face told Charley that she was beginning to tire. 'I recall Lily showing me her treasure trove once. It was an old tin box, and, let me tell you, to a seven-year-old, it was veritable treasure. She said it belonged to Father Connor. She allowed me a peek inside. There were heaps of pictures, old black-and-white photographs – not very interesting to someone expecting precious metals, and jewels.' Josie smiled, then her face suddenly clouded over. 'Although on the dark side, I understand now that Connor had a taste for voyeurism, and he encouraged Agnes, Lily's mother, to take lovers and then spied on her exploits. I heard Agnes slept with at least two dozen men, but it was all to please the priest, with his unusual tastes in – or rather, looking *into* – the bedroom. However, with an adult's understanding, Lily may have destroyed the indecent images of course. Who would want to taint the memory of their mother and the local priest?'

The light was fading, but no one appeared to notice other than Winnie, who rose, without invitation to switch on the lamps, and returned in a zigzag path, back and forth to the window, where, with a familiarity, she pulled the curtains together and shut the night out.

'I presume that both the priests are buried in the grave-yard at St Anne's Church?' said Charley.

'Yes,' nodded Josie. 'The O'Doherty's graves are side by side; they have large headstones and Lily always kept them tidy. You shouldn't have any trouble locating them.'

Charley took out the evidence bag that contained the small ring they had discovered with the skeletal remains, and showed it to Josie.

Josie strained her eyes, in the dimmed light. 'Put on the big light will you, Win?' she said.

Annie chuckled. 'Big light! I love that Yorkshire expression.'

'Well that's what it is, the biggest light in the room, isn't it?' said Winnie. 'Don't make things more complicated than we need to, us Yorkshire folk.'

'It's a wedding ring.'

'A wedding ring? Why would a pagan wear a wedding ring? I thought they were non-believers?' said Annie.

'The ancient pagan Romans were more likely responsible for beginning the common use of engagement and wedding rings,' said Josie.

Annie's eyes were wide. 'Really?'

'They wore the ring on the fourth finger of the left hand because they believed that a vein from this finger, the vena amoris, runs directly to the heart,' said Josie.

With a serious face, Charley looked Josie in the eye. 'Do you think that it is possible that Seth banished Catherine to Australia because he was jealous of hers and Lucinda's relationship?' Then in a low voice she continued. 'Or do you think Catherine, or Lucinda, could be our corpse in the cellar?' Charley frowned, 'But if it is Lucinda, whatever happened to the child?'

The look on the old lady's face told Charley that nothing should be ruled out. 'Who knows… Seth was a very complex character. The depths of his emotions and feelings knew no bounds, or so we are led to believe. Who else would dig a tunnel with his bare hands? Then when he felt he was a danger to his wife, order the door to be bricked up so that he could do her no harm?'

'It doesn't sound like the actions of a man who is sound of mind, does it?' said Annie. 'It sounds more like the actions of a schizophrenic.'

'How'd you know about the tunnel?' said Charley to Josie.

'I played in it as a child with Lily. Hide and seek was great fun in that big house.' Josie paused. 'You see so much has been written, and more rumoured about the Aldermans and Crownest, that we simply don't know what is true and what is false, and probably never will.' Josie swallowed hard. 'What I do know from my research is that Agnes, the local midwife, was a pagan. She was a stunning woman, with the face of an angel in her youth I heard my father say, on more than one occasion.'

'Do you know if Agnes had any children, other than Lily? There would be no contraception available in those days and it seems strange if she was as sexually active as has been suggested, that her dalliances only resulted in one pregnancy.' said Annie.

There was a long pause in which Josie yawned, 'Oh, I don't know. I think that's something that you should ask Lily.'

'I think we should be going,' said Winnie after a few moments. She stood up and put a hand on Josie's shoulder. 'Enough is enough for one day, my dear friend, eh?'

Josie nodded her head in agreement, grateful it seemed, for the fact that Winnie knew her well. She was tired, very tired, and more than that, she felt emotionally drained.

–

The journey home was hazardous, as much to do with the meandering of the country roads, as to the darkness and rain which did not help on the unlit roads. The conditions did not allow Charley's concentration to drop enough to process the chat with Josie properly, never mind talk, so much of the chatter was between Winnie and Annie. When they dropped Winnie off outside her house, with a hug and a cheery 'see you tomorrow,' the car seemed very quiet for a while.

Annie was unusually quiet, as if in thought. 'Could our body in the cellar be Agnes, do you think?'

'But why would she be buried at Crownest, and surely Lily would know whether her mother had died or gone missing?'

'As well as being a midwife, Agnes also laid out the dead… It could be Catherine. Maybe she never did get to Australia?'

'But, if it was Catherine, then why would Lucinda be sent for safe-keeping by the kindly Father Michael to Australia to join her? He must have had contact with Catherine when she arrived in Australia to set up Lucinda's passage.'

'Oh, I don't know. We're going to have to keep an open mind. I'm going to send Mike with you to interview Lily tomorrow. We need to prepare an interview strategy. I'd like to know the time that St Anne's Church priests spent in the locality, and as much background information that is known about the church, and its inhabitants during the time of the Aldermans. We also need to inform Lily of our intention to see what lies beneath Seth's grave.'

'I was involved in an investigation dealing with paedophile priests,' said Annie after a while. Her voice was flat and unfeeling.

Charley's concentration on the wet road surface was such that she didn't see the tear that trickled down Annie's cheek. 'Child abuse is unpleasant. All children deserve to have a safe and happy childhood,' she replied.

'The priests had been touching young boys, and taking lewd pictures of them. Of course they denied everything, but eventually years later they were found guilty, and sentenced, and I hope they will never ever be released,' Annie said.

'Even now, it sometimes takes years for the perpetrators to be found guilty,' said Charley stealing a glance across at Annie, whose head was turned to look out the window.

'Yes, but not before Ashton Gloveria committed suicide.'

Charley turned and eyeballed Annie. 'You knew Ashton Gloveria? I was in the Old Bailey when the case was being heard...'

'He was my brother.'

'He was your brother? But, you're called Glov...?'

Chapter 20

It seemed to Charley that the Crownest murders had taken over her life, and engulfed her remit as the SIO, to the extent that she was forced to fight a growing sense of loneliness and vulnerability, as days turned into weeks, and still there was no sign of a resolution. The pressure from the hierarchy to get the cases solved owing to increasing costs and use of resources didn't help. At times she struggled to keep her composure. Her day-to-day functions were unaffected; the difficulty was caused by the disorientation brought on by the need for results and the number of unanswered questions. As she went over the evidence again, and visited the mortuary again, her sense of smell begged for something other than the stench of death, and to touch something other than through plastic gloves. Ultimately there was only one sense she could depend on, and one that she had become increasingly reliant on – her gut feeling.

Sitting quietly at her desk a week later, whilst the others were about their duties, Charley became aware of the hypnotic whisper of the wind swirling around the building. She closed her eyes and fancied she felt the breeze upon her face and hair. The urgent need to be in the saddle became overwhelming. Charley ached to feel the familiar vibration of horses' hooves thud upon the ground beneath her, and the gentle tug on reins slipping through her fingers as she galloped across the moors.

Anxiety rose from deep within. She simply had to get away.

Fleeing from the office, with her coat over her arm, a dismissive wave of her hand, and 'I'm on my mobile if you need me,' Charley's speedy exit was curtailed within a few steps of the CID office door, where she was confronted in the corridor by Ruth and Flora. Ruth smiled; a smile that suggested happiness. It was a fact that the typist and her guide dog had a formidable relationship, and Charley felt a pang of jealousy.

Charley concluded that everyone needed someone to go to at times like these.

–

Driving on the open road, where her mind was not required for any purpose other than to cruise, there was a moment when she came to realise that, although she had colleagues and acquaintances, she had very few friends; people she could confide in and trust implicitly. In fact apart from Kristine, her childhood friend, and fellow police officer, she had no one.

How she ended up at the stables, given the gloom that consumed her brain Charley had no idea, but she was glad she had. The farmhouse was deserted, so it was obvious to her that Kristine was at work, at the police station. In Charley's experience, shift work did not help relationships, although it appeared that people who worked in the emergency services needed to form a solid understanding amongst family and friends if their relationships were to have longevity.

On the positive side, Wilson, her favoured ex-police-horse at the yard, greeted her with a gentle grasp of his lips. Charley smiled, and scratched the bay's neck which Wilson stretched out, allowing him to shove his nose in her face to 'lip' her.

Playfully he laid his ears back and showed his teeth, his eyes as plain as the writing on the wall. 'Cupboard love mister,' she laughed. 'You're not after a kiss, you're looking for treats.'

Wilson nudged her several times before she reached deep inside her pocket and retrieved a packet of Polo mints. He showed her his equine happy face.

As Charley rode out of the stable yard along the single dirt track peppered with mud-holes, she felt an exhilarating sense of freedom. With a deep sense of trust for the horse, she allowed Wilson his head. For a short while they traversed the fringe of the copse, past the beech trees, continuing along the well-trodden path. She saw the trees thickening further, forming a tunnel, arching together to blot out the sky. The dense light was just enough to navigate the gloom.

Eventually, and not a minute too soon, they left the depressing, grey-brown behind them and welcomed the thinning of the trees which heralded the green lushness of the windswept Yorkshire moor ahead. Charley heard the wind in the distance hissing through the long grass, and it made her heart swell.

It appeared to her that Wilson had sensed her need for solitude, and he had decided to bring her here. He was sharp, alert and at the same time she felt he was in charge, and she thoroughly enjoyed the experience.

In her enthusiasm to break free, riding high onto the ridge of the moors to survey the domain, Charley leaned down over Wilson's neck and called for him to respond to the clenching of her thighs, to encourage his full speed ahead. As his trot turned to a canter, so a high snorting noise came from Wilson's flaring nostrils, and his excitement heightened hers, resulting in an overwhelming energy coursing through Charley's body. For the first time in a long time her mind was crystal clear. The incredible high gave her strength, resolve and freedom from the constraints recently placed on her by her mind and body. She felt more alive than she had in a while, but that brought with it the rawness of an open wound. Charley fancied she could feel Wilson's wordless feelings, primeval instincts, and his carefree spirit more acutely as they rode on. Soon her doubts and fears were stored neatly away, not erased, but in a place where accessing them required a conscious effort, and for that she was thankful.

Tightening Wilson's reins, she allowed him to continue at a gait that would cool him down, until at last they arrived back at the stable yard. Effortlessly she jumped down from the saddle and quickly removed it. Rubbing the bay down, she brushed him until her adrenaline wore off. Patting his neck she spoke soothingly as she buried her face in his mane, took a mint from her pocket, put it in the palm of her hand for him to take, and reluctantly said goodbye.

Having spent every emotion and ounce of anxiety she had unwittingly suppressed for some time, Charley was breathless and sweaty, but she felt good.

—

Charley's alarm clock brought her out of a deep sleep at six thirty the following morning. With one eye open she silenced it with the swipe of a flailing hand, and the clock tumbled to the floor. Both eyes instantly wide open, she caught a breath, and at the same time grabbed hold of her hot-chocolate mug that had been in its flight path. Holding the handle a little too tightly, she noticed her hand was shaking, and it reminded her of the strain her body had endured yesterday. With a groan, she threw back the covers and slid out of bed. Hobbling to the bathroom, she wished that she had paced herself – riding for so long, and so hard was not for the novice, or one who had not been in the saddle in a while. Biscuit crumbs on the floor felt like grit under the soles of her feet. Charley cringed.

She saw nothing to smile about in the bathroom mirror. A puffy, pale face looked back at her. She had gone to bed early, as well. 'What's happened to that fun-loving person?' she asked herself. Early nights, she decided, were not good for her!

Her sore muscles made getting dressed harder. She struggled into her dress, straining for the zip at the back; it was at times like these she wished she didn't live alone. Her determination to succeed however could be likened to her desire to keep the double murder enquiry's momentum going – she refused to give up.

A message in Annie's handwriting, from James Thomas, awaited her at the office: *Not a happy bunny! He wants to know when it's likely he can get on with the demolition at Crownest?*

Screwing the note tightly up in the palm of her hand, Charley aimed it at the bin until she realised that Annie stood, leaning on the door jamb, her expression questioning. 'Until such time as we know for certain that there is nothing else to find on the site JT Developments will not be allowed back on site,' Charley stated before she sat behind her desk. Annie sat opposite her.

Eyes down, flicking through the post, Charley continued, to reassure herself, 'It's still early days. The identities of the bodies are still unknown.'

Ricky-Lee tapped on the SIO's door waving a bag in his hand, like a white flag. 'Bacon, and egg, with tomato sauce; just as you like it,' he said. He was smiling broadly. Charley eyed him suspiciously. 'What've you done?'

Ricky-Lee looked crestfallen, 'Moi?'

Mike, close behind, pushed him further into the office. The sergeant's eyes questioned Annie, who with straight lips shook her head at him in little jerky movements.

'A win on the horses?' Charley was not ready to give up on her questioning.

Ricky-Lee lowered his eyes and slumped in a chair.

'Thank you,' she said. 'That's all I needed to know.'

Mike opened their meeting. 'The intelligence relating to baby-face Brad and Brittany Dixon reads like a horror story. They're ruthless, they're dangerous, they're still at large,' he said, handing the most recent picture of them around for the others to see. 'That big, evil-looking woman and her weasel of a husband have proved time and time again that they are loyal, but only to each other.'

The phone rang, and Charley picked up.

'Eira White from Forensics,' said the sharp, curt voice at the other end. Charley's eyes turned upwards, and rested on her colleagues' faces.

'Go on,' said Charley. A phone call from Forensics so early in the morning could only mean one thing – there was news.

'The dagger,' said Eira.

'What about the dagger?'

'We've found traces of human blood in the shaft.'

For a moment it felt like her heart had stopped beating. 'The victim's blood?' she said.

'Most probably, but whilst we were working on the DNA profile this brought up not just one blood type, but two. We will know which is the victim's when we can match that to the DNA from the skeletal bones. When that's confirmed then we can run the other through the national database to see if there are any hits.'

'That's great, it's just what we need this morning, something positive.'

No sooner had she replaced the phone, than it rang again. This time it was Ballistics. Liam told her that the 9-milimetre casing was confirmed to be from a semi-automatic pistol, a Baikal handgun, of Russian origin, the criminal's choice of weapon and one that was easily adapted from guns that were originally used for firing gas canisters, not bullets.

Charley's heart sank. 'Does that mean we're looking for a needle in a haystack?'

'No, not at all,' said Liam. 'The striation marks on the casing are tell-tale signs, like fingerprints, and will give us an indication as to whether the gun has been used previously. If it has, it's going to be on the database.'

Charley's spirits rose. The type of weapon was confirmed! Good news came in threes, and she wondered what the third would be?

'Ricky-Lee, I want you with me today,' said Charley. The detective frowned. His expression seemed to say, Why me? 'While Wilkie and Annie are visiting Lily Pritchard at St Anne's Church, I could do with a lift.'

'A lift?' he said. Putting a hand to his lower back, he pulled a face and groaned.

'I want to see if there is any way of getting inside Seth Alderman's grave to see what's inside.'

'By anything inside, I presume anything other than a coffin?'

'That's right! You've got a problem with that?' she asked.

Ricky-Lee shook his head 'No, no... not at all, boss. How do I do that?'

'Oh, I don't know. I'm sure all that time that you spend at the gym recently will have considerably strengthened those muscles of yours.'

Chapter 21

From where Charley and Ricky-Lee stood at the gate to the graveyard, they could see Lily Pritchard opening the door of her home, within the cluster of church buildings, to Annie and Wilkie. When the old wooden door closed with a judder, and Charley heard the latch drop, she beckoned Ricky-Lee to follow her. Carefully she negotiated the moss-covered gravestones, which, in the absence of a path, formed a slippery walkway to Seth Alderman's resting place. 'Tell me, what else do you think we might find in his grave?' Charley asked, in a hushed tone.

Hands in the pockets of his suit trousers, Ricky-Lee shrugged his shoulders. 'A skeleton?'

Charley turned sharply, 'No one likes a smart Alec!' Then she paused, one eyebrow raised at the detective, before she turned and walked on. 'That's the best you can come up with, is it?' she said, over her shoulder, 'a skeleton'? Her voice sounded flat and controlled, which was far from what she felt inside towards him.

At the perimeter of the gravestones, the two detectives stood in silence looking down at the exposed cracked limestone slabs that lay on top of displaced broken bricks. Ricky-Lee was the first to lift his head, and in doing so, scanned the rest of the graveyard through slitted eyes. He looked at his watch, delved into his jacket pocket, and pulled a single pill out, immediately throwing it to the back of his throat.

Charley could feel the tremble of rage creeping over her. 'Am I boring you DC Lee, because I can soon get you off the case, and back in uniform today, if you'd rather be elsewhere?'

Ricky-Lee jerked as though he had been electrocuted. 'No! 'Course not,' he said. Unable to meet her eyes, he made a half-hearted attempt at a laugh.

'Course not what?' she said crossly.

He hung his head, 'Course not, boss.'

Head down, he kicked the grass with the toe of his scuffed shoe. Suddenly a shaft of sunlight burst through the heavy, low-lying clouds and settled on Ricky-Lee's face. It showed Charley the dry flaky skin on his pink eyelids, the dark rings underneath his eyes, his chapped lips, and the cold sores at the corners of his mouth. His hands were shaking uncontrollably; all the signs told her that trouble was lurking around the corner.

For a moment or two it seemed as if time stood still. Eventually, he lifted his eyes to see her tight-lipped expression, and looked at her in an apologetic, heavy-eyed way. 'I don't know what you want me to say.'

'Well, it would be nice if you could at least offer me your thoughts on the job in hand, even if you don't want to tell me what's going on with you.'

Ricky-Lee's face broke out into a tired smile. His attention, it appeared, was secured for now.

Disarmed, Charley almost smiled back. 'Let's start again, shall we?' she said, more softly. 'We know that a tunnel from Crownest leads to this point in the graveyard, and it has been suggested by Josie that Seth Alderman dug this extension himself. Have you any thoughts as to why?'

Ricky-Lee frowned. For a moment he looked disconcerted. Then she saw a spark appear in his eyes. 'Maybe this plot was already chosen for him, and he made use of it by digging the secret passage to the outside, before it became the site of his grave?'

'Why would you build a second tunnel so near the first?'

'This exit is outside the church, the other inside,' Ricky-Lee said matter-of-factly. 'Perhaps it was built after the first was bricked up?'

'Smacks of desperation though.'

'Surprising what one does, if despairing enough,' he said, with feeling.

Charley swallowed hard and moved on quickly, desperate for Ricky-Lee not to lose his train of thought.

'OK,' she conceded. 'Maybe, for some unknown reason, he wanted to visit the graveyard, but didn't want anyone to know?' She paused to consider what that reason might be. 'I'm curious,' she said, looking down into the sunken grave. 'Why would the grave be sucked up into the ground so?'

His eyes told her that he was surprised that she'd remembered that he knew about such things.

'What?' she said, to his unspoken question. 'Why wouldn't I make use of your Master's degree?'

Touched, Ricky-Lee swiftly leaned in to touch the cold, flat side of the gravestone. 'Well, at a guess the roots from that tree are a contributory factor,' he said, nodding in the direction of the fallen tree near to the collapsed dry-stone perimeter wall.

'Meaning?' said Charley.

'Considering its location, in what must be one of the wettest parts of the graveyard, I think this is absolutely natural, in fact practically unavoidable, but something else strikes me here. Although this has happened to other graves in this graveyard, it's not quite as obvious. You see, when soil is replaced into a grave following the coffin going in, it will inevitably contain more air pockets than the compacted soil before evacuation, hence the drop when it settles.'

'Ah, but what you're saying is that in your experience, this grave is different from the others?'

'Well, no, not necessarily. I suggest that since the ground was excavated, it wasn't compacted with soil as well as the others when the burial had taken place, and it was filled back in.'

With rounded shoulders and hunched back, Ricky-Lee raked his damp fringe off his face. He looked at his watch again, and back at Charley.

'I knew it.' Charley cocked an eyebrow and her nostrils flared with rage, as she observed him. 'Tell me, the horses, the dogs, are they not thrilling enough for you these days? Maybe you're betting on land snails now?'

There was no mistaking the look in her eyes.

Colour rose in Ricky-Lee's face. 'Terrestrial pulmonate gastropod molluscs,' The words quietly rolled off his tongue.

Charley's rage flared higher. 'What the hell?'

Ricky-Lee's throat was parched, his mouth dry, and his hands shook uncontrollably. Sweat poured from his forehead and neck. 'Snails and slugs.'

'I know what they are. I'm a farmer's daughter for goodness' sake!' Momentarily Charley closed her eyes that stung with tears. 'How can you be so fucking smart one minute, and yet the next so fucking distracted? What the hell has happened to you?' she said. 'Look at you, you used to take pride in your appearance. Tell me, are you taking unprescribed drugs? I need to know!'

Ricky-Lee hesitated, and Charley thought he was about to talk to her. She listened expectantly.

'No, no, just over the counter, honest,' he said, taking a tablet container out of his pocket and rattling it in front, of her to show her the aspirin. 'I don't need help, I'll be fine.'

Charley didn't realise that she had been holding her breath until a sigh left her lips. 'Well, I beg to differ, but if you won't talk to me, I insist that you speak to a professional.'

Ricky-Lee shook his head repeatedly. 'Honestly, I'm fine, boss. I had a little bad luck that caused me a few sleepless nights, and I've a blinding headache today, but it'll be okay now, promise.'

Charley took a deep breath. 'If you say so. I know you don't want to go back into uniform, but a team is only as strong as Its weakest link, and I can't afford to carry you, so, if you have any doubts about staying in CID, or if you give me any more cause for concern, you will be on your way, pronto. Do you hear?'

Ricky-Lee reached out and touched Charley's arm. She flinched. He took a step back. 'I'm ok, I promise.'

The moment passed and Ricky-Lee continued as if nothing had happened, as he looked back at the grave, but now with renewed interest it seemed. He spoke confidently. 'I suggest, boss, that the appropriation of such a grave would not have been a reaffirmation of Seth Alderman's social prominence and his wealth,' he said.

'You don't?' said Charley. 'I wonder why he wasn't buried with the rest of the family?'

Ricky-Lee pursed his lips. 'Maybe the family tomb was full?'

'Or he chose not to be buried with the others?' said Charley.

'Or maybe those who buried him didn't want him to be buried with the rest of his family?'

Charley considered the fact. 'Possibly, and let's face it, there are enough reasons why not.' Charley couldn't conceal a smile. 'Of course, it could also be that those who buried him wanted the burial to be a statement about his failed relationship with the church – although he is in sacred soil – just. We know his wife, Lucinda, lived here with her parents before they were married.'

Ricky-Lee frowned. 'Didn't Seth commit suicide? Maybe that is why his body was distanced from his family's plot.' He paused.

Charley smiled to herself, this was the Ricky-Lee she knew; an intelligent man. It was clear he desperately needed a distraction from an addiction that she feared was about to drag him under, to destroy his life, if he let it. Charley was not going to let that happen, not on her shift.

'Well, we don't actually know it was suicide,' she said. 'Although, there is evidence of someone spending time at the bricked-up wall; etchings, names and depressive quotes, and scribblings. There are also piles of bottles that have been proved by Forensics to have contained alcohol and drugs.'

'He was known to be a drug-taking alcoholic,' Ricky-Lee stated. He stopped, and briefly looked at her like a child who had been severely reprimanded.

'What you mean is that he was an addict, and it's highly likely that the addiction ruined his life, and no doubt shortened it,' said Charley.

Ricky-Lee dropped to his haunches and started pulling away the loose bricks around the bottom edge of the grave. He pulled at the soggy, wet grass, which in turn revealed a sloppy mud mess underneath. Digging the mud out was not as hard as he expected. After a minute or two he looked up at Charley.

'I don't think we will find a skeleton in this grave because I don't think it is a grave at all. Here! Look! It's a step... and another!' he said. 'Soil would have been used to fill in the gaps and to restore the original to ground level, when it was filled in, hurriedly, I suggest by the amount of it.'

'By whom though, and after Seth's death or before it?' said Charley.

Ricky-Lee stopped for a moment. 'But, if Seth Alderman isn't buried here, then where is he buried?' asked Ricky-Lee.

Chapter 22

Delegation had never been easy for Charley, as a self-confessed control freak, but she had learnt, quite quickly, to be comfortable with it since attending a senior management course, where she had overheard an instructor shouting to another that empowerment was 'delegation' for grown-ups, and that if he didn't grow up pretty sharpish, he'd be off the course quicker than he could say Robert Peel!

Being in charge of murder enquiries wasn't just about catching the killer either, she had discovered. Seldom did people know that the process of actions taken, or not taken, by her officers throughout an investigation had to be documented in a personal log created by the SIO. Charley had quickly realised that her personal log was a godsend to her at any future trial, as the document acted as her Bible, showing in black and white all her actions and reasoning, timed, dated, and signed by her. It was also essential that all monies spent were accounted for. Every piece of paper relating to the enquiry required the signature of the Senior Investigating Officer to show that it had been read and authorised. As a result, Charley had also learned to speed-read pretty quickly because documents had to be turned around quickly for further work to be completed, or to be filed as a record.

Her signature had never changed over the years; her grandpa had told her that all her loops and swirls meant she was artistic, outgoing and people-orientated, apparently.

–

That evening's debrief brought about more welcome news for the team. There was a hit on the database for the firearm that had been used to kill the male victim at Crownest. It had been used at an armed robbery of a local convenience store a while ago, so the identical marks on the bullet casing that were retrieved at the scene told them.

'This is one of the incidents that Ben and Terry want to speak to the Dixons about. The suggestion is that the gun was discharged into the air, at the convenience shop robbery as opposed to being pointed at anyone,' said DS Mike Blake.

Reading the report, an icy shiver ran down Annie's spine. 'My God! According to this, if it hadn't been for the beamed ceiling, the shot could have killed someone upstairs!'

Mike nodded. 'Absolutely! Mr Chaudry's wife and children were in the flat above the shop when the robbery was taking place. But what we have now is Mr and Mrs Dixon back in the frame for the murder of our male, at Crownest,' he continued. There was a renewed energy in his tone. 'As we know, they're already being sought in connection with other cold-case robberies, but as yet, I can confirm again that no weapons have been recovered when the pair have been arrested previously. Therefore, it would appear they may still have access to them.'

After the meeting, Charley sat quietly, sipping coffee whilst searching the database for the file relating to the robbery. She stopped only when she found what she was looking for. Suddenly she was aware of the quickening of her heart. 'HD/674/' she read out loud, whilst writing the crime number down at the top of a clean page in her notebook.

Slowly, page by page, line by line, and word by word, she read the details of the incident report, to try to understand what had taken place – and if there were any other links to Crownest.

> Victim: Mr Waseem Chaudry.
> Age: 61 years old.
> No physical injuries, treated for shock at the scene by paramedics.

The information on the next screen saddened her. Four weeks after the robbery Mr Chaudry was found dead. The cause – heart-attack.

The family, she read, was convinced that the early death of the mild-mannered family man, who was well regarded by the local community as being upbeat, cheerful and charitable, was no doubt due to the violent robbery. Evidence-wise, sadly there was no proof that the shopkeeper's death could be attributed to the armed robbery.

Mr Chaudry also had a history of angina. She knew that cause of death was extremely important when it came to proving that the deceased had been murdered and that the death had not occurred because of some other contributory factor associated with illness.

Charley jumped to the next screen to read the details of the incident.

> Armed robbery: Chaudry's Convenience Store.

Incident address: 332, Manchester Road, on the A62 between Marsden and Slaithwaite.

Known facts:
Two masked people were involved in the robbery: one motorcyclist and one pillion passenger. Both had entered the store.

Both wore crash helmets with scarves around their faces. Two passers-by thought that one assailant was wearing a pig mask underneath the helmet.

They wore dark clothing, with gloves and leather jackets.

The motorcycle was a Kawasaki, and blue in colour.

The motorcyclist apparently made a lot of noise by revving the engine and was seen to drive off dangerously on the A62, in the direction of Manchester.

Charley was eager to read what evidence, if any, had been secured from the scene, and to see the CCTV footage attached to the crime file. She read on.

Traces of DNA (Mr Brad Dixon) have been found on the glass shop counter.

She then clicked on the video link. The CCTV footage showed her two people entering the convenience store wearing motorcycle gear, their faces concealed. Both held handguns. Raising their voices at Mr Chaudry, they ordered him to do as they bid: 'Open the till NOW!'

Mr Chaudry, hands in the air, appeared to freeze on the spot. That was until the smaller of the two robbers fired the handgun, pointing it towards the ceiling. They then leant towards the shopkeeper, and with a flick of the wrist, the barrel of their gun was under Mr Chaudry's chin. Seeing the whites of the victim's eyes, Charley took a deep breath and imagined she could feel his fear. It wasn't until the second robber stepped forward to hold their gun to Mr Chaudry's temple that he opened the till. The pair greedily grabbed wads of notes and stuffed them into backpacks, but still they were not satisfied, and demanded more. No doubt fearing for his life, Mr Chaudry reached below the counter and showed them a blue bank bag. It was in their haste to grab the bag that Charley saw one of the robbers flinch and jump backwards from the counter. 'Was this when, by exposing the skin between his glove and sleeve, Brad Dixon had left DNA for the police to find?' she considered.

Then the robbers were gone, the duration of the terrifying incident over within a matter of minutes.

Her attention on the screen was broken when DS Mike Blake tapped on Charley's office door. She beckoned him in.

Mike watched as the SIO puffed her cheeks and blew air through her loose lips. 'I think in a job like ours we get somehow desensitised to words. Reading a file, or hearing about a robbery, can't portray the violence, or the fear someone is subjected to,' she said. 'However, CCTV leaves you in no doubt as to how brutal this incident was. What a pair of bastards the Dixons are.'

'They definitely aren't amateurs. It's obvious from seeing that footage. They know what they want, and they know how to get it. The CCTV certainly suggests to me that they would go one step further and commit murder, if those threatened did not comply with their requests,' added Mike.

'I agree. We have to also consider that it might not have been the Dixons who used the gun that killed our man. Could it be a 'pool' weapon used by others or sold on? Hopefully not. On a positive note for the investigation, the weapon is possibly still in circulation. What we know for sure is that our murderer used the very same gun that was used to threaten and rob Mr Chaudry. Even though the Dixons were living in Crownest at the time the pathologist thinks our man died, supposedly from receiving a bullet from a gun that the Dixons have been known to use, we need to prove beyond doubt that it was one of them who used it to kill him. We'll run with the knowledge that it could be them, and that they may still have access to firearms when we locate them. To not do anything else would be madness.'

'Agreed. It seems probable they are involved, and like you say, we work on the presumption they are armed, until we know otherwise.'

'I'm sure we're right. It sounds simple doesn't it, find the weapon and then you'll find evidence to place it in the hands of the killer, but you and I know that is not the case.'

'On this occasion we need to assume, eh, boss?' said Mike, with a wink of an eye.

Charley nodded her head. 'Although we are working with known facts, we need the evidence to prove that we are heading in the right direction. It'll come. I'm certain of it,' said Charley, with a tight smile. 'At least now we will be able to take the lead in locating the pair. If a wanted poster for the Dixons isn't already in existence, then get one prepared for me to feed to the media, will you?'

'Ben and Terry thought that the pair had gone to Spain,' Mike smirked, 'or hoped they had, so they could take a trip to warmer climes. But they hadn't firm evidence that the pair had left the UK even, last time I spoke with them.'

'Exactly, and even if they'd absconded, as was suggested, the Spanish sell English newspapers.' Charley appeared thoughtful. 'We could involve Crimestoppers and offer a reward as an enticement for someone to tell us of the Dixons' whereabouts?'

Mike's tone was defeatist, but he nodded, 'There would have to be a substantial amount of cash incentive, to get anyone to grass on a pair of violent armed robbers.'

The investigation was continuing to bubble, and Charley was eager to keep the momentum going, and increase the pace of the enquiry again in the Incident Room.

An hour later ex-police officers from the cold-case team, Ben and Terry, sat opposite Charley and Mike in the SIO's office. Tattie was very vocal in her observation that Ricky-Lee was conspicuous by his absence in the CID office that day, and for some reason Charley found herself defending the detective constable.

'Ricky-Lee was with me at the graveyard earlier,' Charley said, before going on to enlighten the men as to the recent ballistic update regarding the murder, and the evidential link they now had between the firearm known to belong to the Dixons that was used in the robbery, and the bullet found in the skull of the male victim at Crownest.

'Also, just yesterday further evidence has come to light. The robberies that the pair were originally sought and sentenced for, have finally after all this time, been linked to the robbery at Mr Chaudry's Convenience Store,' added Ben.

Suddenly there was an air of expectancy in her office. 'Okay, so we know that the Dixons are connected beyond doubt, in some way, to all the incidents, even if we can't prove murder. What else have you got for me?'

'Not much, unfortunately. The pair of photos are being circulated this side of the channel and beyond as you know, and since we last saw you, we've been mostly visiting known acquaintances,' said Ben.

'I assume therefore that you haven't had much joy?'

'I'm sure you know the format. Most told us to 'do one!', ma'am, followed by the proverbial door slam. Even those who owed us a favour could only suggest they'd fled the country.'

'That's the advantage of working alone or with a reliable other, isn't it? No one to grass you up! Let's cut to the chase. You might have thought that the Dixons had gone abroad, even had it suggested by their known acquaintances that this might be the case, but we have no actual evidence, have we?'

'No,' Terry replied, with a shake of his head.

Charley turned her computer around to show the men the two pictures on the screen. 'Tell me this, do you know if these pictures are still a good likeness of the pair?'

Ben leaned forward, closer to the screen. 'As far as I'm aware,' said Ben. Charley looked at Terry to see a confirmatory nod. 'Since then, zilch! It's without doubt that they've gone to ground.'

'Okay,' said Charley. Her face was serious and there was authority in her voice. 'From here on, I will be taking charge of their pursuit. The pair are our prime suspects for the murder at Crownest now we have positively linked them to the firearm. My thought is to push these images out to the media now, with the pair first and foremost being wanted for robbery, but also for elimination from an unconnected murder investigation, given that they were the tenants at Crownest during the time under investigation.'

If Mike had been less taken with the fact that Ricky-Lee had just opened Charley's door and on seeing Ben and Terry had made a swift exit, he might have seen blank disappointment on the detectives' faces, no doubt at the thought of being taken off the case.

But Charley, facing them with her back to the door had seen the look on the men's faces. 'I'd like you to work alongside us,' she said. Her voice was positively upbeat. 'Your knowledge of the crimes that these two have committed in the past could prove very useful to us. However, be assured I expect professionalism from you both at all times. Now, tell me is there anything else that you think we need to know before you go?'

There was a decidedly brighter look in Ben's eyes as he turned to his colleague. 'Actually, there is something that we think is of interest, but our boss thought it wasn't worth pursuing.'

Charley tilted her head. 'I'm all ears.'

'Mr Chaudry's nephew, a man by the name of Faisal Hussain, came up from Birmingham for the funeral. Apparently, according to a family member, he's a would-be gangster, but a charmer, too, when it suits. We've done a check on him and he's got quite a few previous for drugs… but alarmingly there is a police marker on him for violence and for suspicion of carrying a firearm. He's not long been out of prison.'

'Mmm… I can understand why a nephew attending his uncle's funeral is not worthy of a visit to Birmingham, especially if he's into the drugs scene. Be like trying to find a needle in a haystack, and your focus would be on locating the offenders, but tell me, there must be more than meets the eye here for this man to be of interest to you two?'

'Well you see, Miss Finch, the girl at the local estate agent's in your murder case spoke of someone that would perhaps fit Hussain's description. Apparently someone had been enquiring after the Dixons, and became annoyed when she wouldn't confirm, or otherwise, that they were living at Crownest. According to her statement, it was Lily Pritchard at St Anne's Church who had suggested that the estate agent might be able to help the Dixons.'

'Glad you have been keeping up to speed,' remarked Charley.

'You've got to ask yourself why Faisal Hussain, if it was him, would be looking for the Dixons,' questioned Mike.

'We could only guess that he was going to confront the Dixons about the suggestion that they were involved in the robbery… By the way, have you been in touch with the Chaudry family recently?' asked Charley.

The men nodded. 'Yes, we are in contact with the family, mainly to reassure them that they haven't been forgotten and that we are still on the case. They're a nice family.'

Charley tapped her finger on her lips. 'That's good, that's good.' she said. 'Could you make it in your way to call on them and let them know that the Dixon's images are going to be circulated again for elimination purposes, in connection with the recent murders at Crownest. I don't want it to come as a shock for them to see the media coverage ramped up all of a sudden. If you'll do that, then I'll speak to Connie at the Press Office tomorrow; she's on days according to the rota. It'll be the evening crew on now. Only time will tell if the media can bring them to us.'

Chapter 23

'Those two might have more service in than you and me, but God they need a rocket up their arse,' Charley said to Mike about Ben and Terry, as she watched them leave the CID office in a sloth-like fashion. The SIO stood in the CID office with her hand on the back of Ricky-Lee's chair.

'You can't deny they managed to lift a few good collars in their day,' said Mike. 'They just need a bit of motivation and strong leadership.'

'Talking of which, where is he now?' Charley said.

Mike looked shifty. 'Ricky-Lee?'

Charley viewed Mike through suspicious eyes. 'I know that look, DS Blake. You can't pull the wool over my eyes.' She raised an eyebrow at his silence, and cocked her head. 'Well?'

Mike blushed, and as he did so he gave a little grimace. 'He's in the building somewhere. Or at least he was ten minutes ago,' he said.

Charley eyes were wide. 'How'd you know that?'

'I saw him through the window of your office when he came in. When he clocked Ben and Terry with us, he was out of the door like a cat on hot bricks.'

'You think there is still something going on there?'

Mike shrugged his shoulders. 'He promised me he'd stopped gambling.'

'Me too. You believe him?'

Again, Mike shrugged his shoulders.

'Well, I don't!' Charley scowled. 'You know some-thing, don't you? What is it that you're not telling me?'

Mike put his hands up. 'I know nothing!' he said in a bad French accent.

An involuntary groan escaped Charley's lips. 'Hmm, why don't I believe you?' Raising her eyes to the ceiling, she shooed him away with the wave of her hand. 'Go have a word with the surveillance team, and see what their diary is like for the next month or so, just in case we get a result on the whereabouts of the Dixons.'

Head down, Mike silently turned on his heels.

'Oh, and find knob-head will you, and let him know they're gone, and that I want to see him, pronto!'

At that very moment, Annie staggered into the CID office carrying a large cardboard box. Wilkie followed behind and held the door open for Mike. They nodded amiably to each other.

'You haven't seen Ricky-Lee on your travels, have you?' Mike said.

Wilkie shook his head. The SIO thought she saw a look of concern on his face before he turned, and spoke to Mike in a hushed tone.

Charley rushed to help Annie to put the heavy container down on the nearest surface to the door. Out of breath from exertion, once the box was safe, Annie linked her fingers at the end of stretched arms and cracked the bones in her hand to relieve the pain. Her face was illuminated with enthusiasm. 'Lily insisted we take them,' said Annie apologetically.

Wilkie's face showed he was feeling cynical. 'I am in no doubt that that lot of old paperwork will be about as useful as a glass hammer!'

'You don't know that,' said Annie, crossly, pulling her fingers so they clicked, one at a time.

'I do, and can you stop doing that?' he said wiping his hand over the leather bindings. 'They're clean, and dust free. Did you see a dust-free surface in her place?'

Annie scowled at her colleague.

With adrenalin rising, Charley ushered the fractious pair towards her office.

Wilkie sat opposite Charley, pointing sideways at Annie. 'I thought she could natter, but bloody hell, that Pritchard woman, she could talk the hind legs off a donkey!' Slowly he rose with a groan from the chair. 'Excuse me, I'll have to go for a leak.'

'Don't forget to wash your hands, and bring us back a drink will you?' Annie shouted after the retreating detective. An arm appeared behind his back and he showed her his middle finger. She smiled, slowly shaking her head, but her smile quickly turned into a frown when she looked at Charley. 'We haven't had a thing to eat or drink all day,' she said, nodding towards the paper carrier bag next to Wilkie's chair that held food from the bakery.

Charley frowned. 'That's not very hospitable of Ms Pritchard not to offer you a drink,' she said.

'Oh, no, it wasn't that. She offered us hot drinks, cold drinks, wine and God knows what else from those bottles on the shelf, while she drank that blood-red wine which she had a liking for the last time we were there, but...' Annie retched, 'you should have seen the inside of her mugs, and the dirt and grease on the glasses.'

'Had she got her electricity fixed?'

'Yes, thank goodness. There were no bare wires hanging from the plug on the kettle this visit.'

Annie seemed eager to share the news they brought from St Anne's Church. Wilkie Connor was only too pleased to let her talk, whilst he tucked into a sandwich stacked high with chicken and salad filling. Mayonnaise dripped onto his shirt, and he wiped it away with a quick flick of a licked fingertip.

'According to Lily, it depended on the priest at the time as to what records were kept at the church. All churches, including Roman Catholic churches keep their own records, though apparently very few found their way into the National Archives in 1837 and 1857 when the Registrar General called in the non-parochial registers as part of the process of establishing the new system of civil registration.' Annie snapped open her notebook. 'Let me give you some facts that Lily shared with me that might help us understand at least some of their thinking. The 1559 Act of Supremacy made the Protestant Church of England the nation's established church. Roman Catholic baptism, marriage and burial registers were collected together, as I said. But few Roman Catholic records registers were surrendered because, according to Lily, they contained records of illegal marriages between 1754 and 1837, and under the terms of Lord Hardwicke's Marriage Act, it was a legal requirement to be married in the Church of England. Which explains the lack of records at St Anne's, given it was a Roman Catholic church, don't you think? The records have likely been lost for years.'

'I guess so,' said Charley. 'A Catholic wouldn't perhaps agree to the Church of England's claims to be both Catholic and Reformed...'

'To be honest, what intrigued me most about interviewing Lily was not what we may, or may not, find in
words written down, but in the tales she tells. As gripping
as they are, whether they are true or not, I don't know.
Most people around the turn of the century couldn't
write, so the records that were kept were by the people
who could, and those would be the educated folk, who
were in the minority, weren't they? The papers that we
brought back today might authenticate some people's lives
by a formal civil registration, but not all the births, deaths
and marriages will be included, so, how do we know what
is fact or what's just folklore? I guess we don't—'

'Well, you don't have to be a genius to see that the old
hag is as mad as a box of frogs!' said Wilkie, through a
mouthful of pork pie. 'We can't take a thing she says as
gospel.'

Charley chuckled. 'We wouldn't take anyone's word
as gospel. You know that. We'd have to have irrefutable
evidence, and that's quite hard, when anyone who could
give us that evidence is believed to be dead and buried!
Go on, Annie.'

'We know from previous enquiries with Lily Pritchard,
that Jeremiah Alderman's children were said to be inces-
tuous, and that the stillborn of Catherine were thrown on
the fire by Lily's mother, Agnes. Those little ones will not
be registered in these books.'

'If the stories of the stillbirths being thrown on the fire
are true, of course,' said Wilkie.

'Lily told me that there is no doubt that Michael and
Connor O'Doherty would only record what they would
have wanted to be read in the future.'

'Or, maybe the priest wouldn't be told about the still-births in the parish, birthing being seen then as woman's work?'

'We'll never know the truth, because the truth may be so bizarre and unthinkable for us to comprehend, that these days we would automatically think something so macabre was a made-up story – and a thriller at that!'

Wilkie Connor reached to take a coffee mug from the tray on Charley's desk, and opening a bag of little cakes from the bakery bag. He offered them around, and added, 'Like I said 'afore, there is no doubt in my mind that what the Pritchard woman gave us will tell us nowt we don't already know.'

'Did the old woman have any further thoughts since our last visit as to who the skeleton at Crownest might be?' asked Charley.

'No, she reiterated what she had said before about Catherine and Lucinda; nothing new.' Annie blew out her cheeks, and shook her head. 'I can't believe there were so many people going to the other side of the world in them days!' she said.

'How could we prove that the corpse is Catherine, or Lucinda, without being able to get DNA from a descendant?' asked Annie.

'We can't,' said Wilkie. 'No dental records, no hospital records.'

'It's also a possibility that Agnes is the one entombed at Crownest,' said Charley.

'Killed by whom, and why?' said Wilkie.

Annie took a brown paper bag out of the carrier, laid it on her knee, and tore it open to reveal a slab of carrot cake. She took the icing-sugar carrot off the top and gently placed it on her tongue. 'I'd have thought there may have been a few who could have felt like killing her, her husband for one,' said Annie.

'Does Lily know what happened to her mother or where her grave is?'

Annie took another bite of her cake and spoke with a mouthful. 'Apparently not. She was a young girl when she was told that she had died, leaving her an orphan.'

'Lily did say, however, that if you were not a devout Catholic you wouldn't be allowed to be buried in the graveyard, so when death occurred you'd either be burnt, or buried in an unmarked grave in the surrounding countryside,' said Wilkie.

'That's a good enough reason as to why our lady, whoever she is, was entombed in the cellar at Crownest, isn't it?' said Charley.

Annie appeared thoughtful. 'It seems to me that she was much loved, by someone who tried their hardest to give her a pagan burial because he, or she, didn't want her to be buried in an unmarked grave.' She paused for a moment. 'Let's say it is Lucinda then. She is supposed to have gone to Australia, to be with Catherine. If she didn't arrive, wouldn't questions have been asked, and if she was pregnant, like we said before, where is the child?'

'Good question,' said Wilkie. 'We've had no luck with our enquiries into the immigration records on this, on the other side of the world. Whoever the woman is, she's got to be someone who had connections with the house,' said Wilkie.

Charley put her elbows on her desk, and bowing her head, she put her fingers to her brow. 'I said that,' said Charley. 'It's so infuriating that we have no surviving relatives of the Alderman family to be able to speak to! If only we were having this conversation when Adam, Felix's illegitimate son, was alive. There is no confirmation, so far, to say that Catherine set off for, or even arrived in Australia, other than what Lily and Josie tell us. We don't know if Catherine went on to have any children, who would presumably now live on the other side of the world, and we don't know officially if Lucinda was pregnant by Seth, and if she went on to give birth to a child, or if he or she is still living. Is it worth DNA-testing Lily, which would tell us if the corpse was Agnes, and therefore narrowing our suspects down?'

The CID door slammed into the metal filing cabinet twice, and all three lifted their heads to see through Charley's office window who had made such an entrance.

Charley took a deep breath as she watched Ricky-Lee slump into his chair, head in his hands. 'Go tell 'em to come in will you, Wilkie. I think we need to put our heads together, and now seems like as good a time as any.' Charley spoke through clenched teeth. 'I'm just in the mood to see what everyone can contribute.'

Chapter 24

Annie had put the last of the church papers back in the box and closed the lid. She wrapped her arms around her stomach, lowered her forehead onto her desk, and groaned. To her annoyance she felt the tears of disappointment burning behind her eyelids. She hated it too when Wilkie Connor was right.

Returning from their enquiries, the others filtered into the office, sharing raucous banter. Demoralised, Annie prayed that they had had more success than her. She looked up at the clock, then back at the cardboard box. How many hours had she lost sifting through the grubby documents, without any information forthcoming to move the enquiry forward? She felt sick.

Charley entered the CID office, her voice raised. 'Anything of interest?' she said to everyone and anyone in the room. 'Together for a debrief now, please!'

Annie picked up the piece of paper in front of her that contained her notes she had collated throughout the day. When it was her turn to speak, she tried to sound more upbeat than she felt. 'Just bits and bobs that confirm the Alderman family history from the church registers, but other than that there was nothing in the church records.'

Wilkie rolled his eyes. 'Well, what a surprise?' he said under his breath, in an I-told-you-so fashion.

The young detective's tears which were buried deep inside, began to surface, only to be quickly brought under control. Instead, Annie let out a deep sigh, and gave him a sideways glance of exasperation.

There was a pause. Charley turned towards Annie. 'Tell me more,' she said.

'The marriage of Jeremiah Alderman to Roselyn is registered. Michael O'Doherty performed the ceremony and their children's births and baptisms are also recorded. The church was, as we were told by Lily, the beneficiary of Jeremiah's great wealth at the time, which continued after he died, under Felix and Seth Alderman hence I guess the pot of gold that Lily refers to. Adam, Felix and Mary Shires' illegitimate son, was baptised at St Anne's, but not until he was a year old, which is when he was presumably brought into the Alderman fold. This can be authenticated by the date Mary Shire's death was registered, and the date that Felix was buried in the churchyard after he was hanged by his neck on the gallows, as we know he was supposedly responsible for murdering Mary.

'Adam was christened by the deacon of the parish at the time who was Walter Pritchard, Agnes's husband, and Lily's father. However, Adam's confirmation ceremony was conducted by the priest, Connor O'Doherty, some years later. There isn't a reason given for this.'

'I thought that a confirmation had to be administered by a bishop?' said Tattie, settling the tray of warm drinks down in the centre of the conference table. She sat. No one moved. She looked around at the other, and raised her eyebrows at their apathy. 'I'll be mother, shall I?' she said, standing, with a tut upon her lips.

Annie continued, 'It is normally. However, a priest, in this case Connor O'Doherty, would be legally able to perform the ceremony with the authority of the bishop, if my memory serves me right,' said Annie.

Wilkie eyed the young detective with surprise. 'How'd you know stuff like that?'

'It's surprising the stuff you pick up when you're schooled by nuns.'

'Not that it really matters to the enquiry, but is there anything that would lead us to believe that Connor was granted that authority?' asked Charley.

Annie shook her head again. 'Nope! Nothing to suggest or confirm that the authority was requested or given. Neither Lucinda's marriage to Seth, nor their child's birth, is registered. In fact, the registers are pretty scant after Father Michael O'Doherty died, so throughout Connor O'Doherty's term of office.'

'Well, what did you expect? We know that Connor was a bit of a would-be loose cannon. Pardon the pun.' Wilkie sniggered at his own joke which, by the look on the faces of those present, fell on deaf ears.

'We know from our enquiries that Lucinda was a pagan, so I wouldn't expect any record by association at the church, would you?' said Mike.

'The more I have read about Connor O'Doherty, the more I don't like the man. He appears to be nothing like his uncle, whose reputation and records appear to be all in order, and I do wonder if Walter Pritchard was a little afraid of him, for him to allow the priest to use Agnes for his own pleasure?' she said.

'Maybe the priest pulled rank,' suggested Ricky-Lee, 'because, after Rev Pritchard took the decision to marry Agnes, allegedly to save the young girl from the work-house, Connor would know that Walter could never achieve more than the rank of a deacon, giving him a direct line to the job of looking after the parish when his uncle Michael O'Doherty died.'

'Maybe Walter Pritchard never was er…' Wilkie looked as if he was considering his choice of words, 'interested in the fairer sex?'

'Yet he is Lily's father,' said Annie.

'Is he? Or could she be the result of any one of the number of liaisons that Agnes is reputed to have had outside the marriage?' said Charley.

'I had at least hoped to find Lucinda and Seth's child's birth mentioned somewhere, whether in the register, or in the records, but it's as if the child never existed.'

'Maybe it never did,' said Ricky-Lee. 'Perhaps Lucinda miscarried; then again, the young woman could have had a stillbirth.'

'Hmm, but both Lily and Josie told us the same story independently – that Lucinda had a child.' Charley turned to Annie. 'What did Lily have to say about the treasure trove of pictures and papers that Josie referred to?'

'She didn't. She brushed it off as Josie being fanciful.'

'Do you think Lily told you everything she knows?' said Charley.

'Did she 'eck,' said Wilkie chasing the crumbs of his sandwich around its plastic container before popping them into his mouth.

Annie looked quizzically at Wilkie. 'Can I just ask, is that your dinner or your tea?'

'Depends which part of the country you come from,' he said. Wilkie's smile was mischievous.

Charley pursed her lips. 'Perhaps now's the time to bring Lily Pritchard out of the comfort of her home and into the station to speak to her.'

Wilkie leaned forward with a smirk on his face, and menace in his eyes. 'Then, because she's a Bible basher, we'll have one on the table in the interview room. If we think she's telling porkies we can get her to swear on it.'

Charley pulled a face. 'That is not helpful or professional. If you've nothing productive to say, keep it shut!'

Wilkie mumbled something under his breath, something along the lines of, it was no different from a lie detector, no biggie.

Mike knew Charley well enough to know that when she turned to him, her expression would be one of frustration. 'For God's sake take the comedian with you, will you and go see Jonathan Raglan again. I want to know more about Waseem Chaudry's nephew's visit to the estate agents.'

Mike pushed his chair backwards and looked as if he was preparing to stand. 'More to the point, find out why Raglan didn't think to tell us about it, and the fact that the nephew, Faisal Hussain, had been enquiring about the whereabouts of the Dixons.'

Charley dismissed the group, but she raised her hand at Ricky-Lee. 'I'd like a word with you,' she said. 'My office, now!'

Chapter 25

Ricky-Lee saw DI Charley Mann sit down, as if in slow motion, on the swivel chair behind her impeccably tidy desk. She had a deep scowl etched on her face and, when she sat, her posture was stiff and unyielding. The detective closed the door slowly and quietly behind him, a gnawing beginning in the pit of his stomach.

'Why are you avoiding Ben and Terry?' Charley found herself clenching her teeth as she spoke.

Tension filled the air, and she waited for the officer to respond. Ricky-Lee moved to the edge of a chair, leaned forward and cleared his throat. He looked down at his interlocked fingers which he was wringing, in the space between his legs. After a few silent moments, he took a breath, and looked up to see black eyes, as sharp as granite, looking back at him. Charley's expression shocked him.

'DC Lewis, I know you're an intelligent man, so don't piss me about. What the hell is going on? I'm dealing with a double-murder enquiry and your behaviour is becoming a distraction that I can well do without. I thought we had an understanding after our talk in the graveyard, but it appears not.' She paused briefly. 'You've got one chance to tell me what's going on. Don't leave anything out, and don't lie to me,' she said. Charley's voice had a sharp edge to it that Ricky-Lee had never heard her use before, and it sent goosebumps down his spine.

Ricky-Lee's voice sounded shaky to his own ears. 'Boss, I'm sorry. I've been trying to avoid anybody or anything that has to do with gambling, not just them,' he said, quietly. 'The truth is, I can't be around gamblers. Not if I want to kick this addiction. That's why I walked out, when Mike saw me, rather than join you, and Ben and Terry.'

Charley put her elbows on the desk and clasped her hands together. 'Go on then, tell me about it. I'm listening,' she said.

Ricky-Lee took a long deep breath. 'It all started six years ago. I didn't think gambling would be a problem, not for me. I was working undercover; a big drugs case. The job required infiltration into the drugs gang. The fun part for me was the race meetings, a bit of light relief from the violent world I found myself involved in. At least, I thought it was fun at the time. We were given free hotel rooms, free meals, as much alcohol as we could drink, and the cartel provided the drugs and the girls. I was more than happy to people-watch, with the odd visit to the betting stand to authenticate the reason for being at a race meeting. I had to be one of them. I'm not much of a drinker and I was engaged to be married. Money was no object; we had wads of money to play with. It was like Monopoly money, it had no value to me whatsoever.' He gave a half-hearted laugh. 'They needed to get rid of their dirty money somehow, and believe me, it's true, money attracts money.' Ricky-Lee's eyes filled with tears, but swallowing hard somehow seemed to stem their flow. 'How stupid was I to think that I could do the same, after the job had finished, with no tip-offs from the professionals: the trainers, the stable hands, the jockeys who were all happy to help and take the backhanders. But I was hooked.'

'Why on earth has this addiction reared its ugly head now?'

Ricky-Lee shook his bowed head. 'Once a gambler, always a gambler, I suspect. You see, two years ago I couldn't stop myself driving to race meetings. My girl-friend, Beth, and I were buying a new house at the time and we needed as much money as we could get for the deposit. I became obsessed. I'd study the horse's form, weight, stamina, how well the jockey knew the horse, how good the trainer was, if he liked the racecourse, soft or hard ground, etcetera. I bought racing papers, books, and with the small amount of spare cash I had, I had a few mediocre wins. We put a deposit on a house. It was to be our forever home. A four-bedroomed house, at a price that was beyond our wildest dreams just a few months before. Beth was over the moon.'

At the mention of his fiancée's name, Ricky-Lee began sobbing as if his heart would break, with tears that blurred his vision, and no amount of furious blinking would stop them from escaping to run down his cheeks. He swiftly wiped them away with the back of his hand, but it was futile, as they kept falling.

Charley lent over and offered him a tissue, which he accepted gratefully. 'Your fiancée Beth, she knew you were gambling to get the money?'

Ricky-Lee shook his bowed head. 'No, I never had to lie, because she never asked. She knew I couldn't, and wouldn't, talk about my work, and so she never ques-tioned a new interest or hobby, and I explained it away as research, which was mostly true. You can't go into a life-and-death undercover situation unprepared, can you?'

Ricky-Lee sniffed, and held back his head to help stop the flow of tears. 'We were so, so happy. Then it all started to go wrong. I began to lose. I persuaded myself that it was just a little bad luck. I used credit cards to get more money, and then one day, on impulse, I stripped our savings. Would you believe I bet on the colours that a certain jockey was wearing?' Twiddling his thumbs, Ricky-Lee's words were no more than a whisper. 'When Beth found out, I'd lost everything. We had lost everything.' Ricky-Lee drew in a deep breath and looked her straight in the eye. 'Beth moved on. There was no going back for her. I couldn't bear living in the same place as her – hearing what she was getting up to was killing me… So, I asked for a transfer, anywhere, and there was a vacancy for a detective at Peel Street Police Station. It was supposed to be a new start for me.'

'Tough, but you haven't given up though, have you?'

'I had, boss, but there was no one to tempt me here. Gambling ruined my life once. I was determined that I wasn't going to let it happen again. Then when Ben and Terry started visiting the station from HQ, they brought the racing papers into the office, and I enjoyed their banter. I haven't made many friends up North – let's face it, the hours we work who would want a relationship with someone in CID? I found that talking about race meetings was something I could talk to them about, that I could join in with. It was obvious looking back, that I would be tempted, for how could I know so much about the sport and not have a flutter with them; it would have looked odd. We had a couple of wins, and then I got daily messages asking me what I fancied, in this race or that… but I've not only let myself down, now I have let you down, and I feel terrible.'

'Tell me, how are you funding your gambling?'

'The first few wins gave us the stake money to carry on for a while without it costing any of us anything. When it started to get out of hand, I called a halt to it. I've told them. I have. That's God's honest truth, that's why I'm avoiding them now.'

Charley looked serious. 'I have a problem with you. I want my staff focused on the murder enquiries. Not on what's going to win the bloody four o'clock at Haydock! I don't want any of my officers being distracted from the job in hand. Do I make myself clear?'

Ricky-Lee nodded emphatically. 'Crystal clear, boss. I'm sorry. I promise I never did let it interfere with any of my enquiries on this job, honestly I didn't.'

'Well, whatever you say, the *Racing Post* ended up on your desk and you studied it. I saw the evidence for myself, so tell me why I should believe you now? I've got to decide if I can trust you to do the job which you're paid to do, or do you need to be taken off this enquiry?'

'Please don't; the thought of that really scares me.' Ricky-Lee begged. 'I don't know what I'd do. The job, my colleagues, it's all I've got. I had a relapse, but never again, I promise. You can trust me. You know you can.'

Charley stared at the detective, shaking her head. 'Don't judge a book by its cover, but the first time I saw you I got the impression you were self-centred, what with your tanning and your designer clothes, but it's only now that I know you are. As your supervisor, I can't just take a cloth and wipe this sorry mess away. I am leading a team of people and am dusting, sweeping and mopping up their shit on a daily basis. Look at Wilkie; he's got a disabled wife who relies on him for everything. Do you hear him wailing on, woe is me? This is life.'

She thought that Ricky-Lee had the decency to look ashamed.

'Look at you, feeling all sorry for yourself, with not a single thought for your colleagues whom you are in danger of pulling down with you by your lack of attention to the job.'

Charley paused, and sighed. 'Okay,' she said. She took a moment and her expression softened as did her voice. 'This is what we'll do. I'll refer you for professional support. You'll accept. Deal?'

'Deal,' said Ricky-Lee. His sigh was one of relief and gratitude.

'If you need help, my door is always open. I've already fired warning shots across Ben and Terry's bows. After today it's in the past, but if you feel you're slipping again, then you speak to me, do you hear; my door is always open. You're safe for now. Don't let me down again, otherwise you know the consequences.'

'Thank you, boss, thank you. It means everything to me to get a second chance, everything.'

'Good, now get back to work, and that's all I want you to be doing in work's time, okay?'

Ricky-Lee got up to leave.

'And don't let me have to have this conversation with you again,' she said.

The detective turned with his hand on the door handle. 'You won't regret it boss, I promise.'

'Make sure I don't. Now get out of my office before I change my mind.'

Chapter 26

'Oh no, detective,' said Raglan's assistant, as she jumped up from behind her desk. 'You've literally just missed him.' Through the large front window young Miss Finch scanned the high street, as if she might still be able to locate and stop Mr Raglan in his tracks. 'Mr Thomas called in to take him somewhere.'

'Will he be long?' asked Mike.

Miss Finch paused, as if something had just occurred to her, and turned towards Mike with her mouth half open. She frowned, looking a little puzzled. 'Actually, he didn't say where he was going.' She raised her finger as if to remember. 'Just not to contact him, "Unless it is something very important",' she repeated, parrot-fashion. Colour rose in her cheeks, and she looked questioningly from one detective to the other. 'Is it urgent? Should I call him?' she said hurriedly. She took two quick steps to her desk, and picked up the phone.

Reaching out, Mike indicated for her to stop. 'No, that's okay. It's our fault. We should have rung ahead and made an appointment.'

Wilkie sat down on one of the ladder-back chairs in front of her desk. 'Perhaps you could help us instead?'

Mike wrinkled his nose. 'It would save us time, if you could?'

Miss Finch looked unsure.

Wilkie winked at the dark-haired girl. 'I think we all know that nothing much goes on around here that you don't know about. In fact, I daresay you run this place.'

Miss Finch giggled. 'Oh, I don't know about that. I will try and help you with your enquiries though, if I can,' she said, coyly.

Mike followed her lead and took a seat. 'As you are aware, for obvious reasons we have an interest in Crownest, but the previous tenants, the Dixons, are also of interest to us.'

The secretary nodded. 'Yes, so I understand.'

'We understand that a young Asian man came here asking about them. Do you remember him?'

Miss Finch's eyes flew open. 'Yes, I most certainly do, for a number of reasons. Firstly, he parked on the double yellow lines outside the shop in a royal blue cabriolet sports car, which just has to be one of my favourite cars in the whole wide world,' she said excitedly. 'I knew he wasn't from around here, otherwise he would have known the traffic wardens are dead keen.' She leaned closer and lowered her voice to a conspiratorial whisper. 'Secondly, his gear was super cool. He had a suit made from black velvet, jacket belted-in with a thick, studded silver belt. When he spoke to me, his voice soft, and it was hard not to stare at the chunky gold rings on his fingers. He asked me if he could speak to Mr Raglan.'

Miss Finch turned towards Mr Raglan's office door. 'Surprisingly, the boss told me to tell him he was too busy to see him.' She scowled. 'That's so unusual; Mr Raglan never turns anyone away. He likes the company. However, the man wouldn't take no for an answer, marched towards the boss's office, and although I protested, barged in and shut the door in my face.'

'What did you do then?' asked Mike.

'Put it this way… when I heard him shouting, I was frightened enough to get your card out of my bag, DS Blake.' She squinted her eyes and pinched her fingers close together. 'I was this close to making the call.'

'What was the man shouting about, do you know?'

'Like you, he wanted to know where the Dixons had gone, and Mr Raglan kept telling him he didn't know. The man obviously didn't believe him. Although the boss swore he didn't.'

'Then what happened?'

'Mr Raglan's office door flew open and I saw the man pointing a finger directly at him, in a threatening way.'

'Did he say anything else?' said Mike.

'He told Mr Raglan that if he found out he was lying he would be back. But most upsettingly, I saw his face when he said, "You don't know who you're dealing with". That man was angry, really angry. He stormed through this office and slammed the door behind him, so hard that he cracked that window. The glazier's supposed to be coming by to fix it. Mr Raglan is having the whole shop front triple-glazed. I've seen the quote, it's costing him a fortune.'

'Has the man been back since?' said Wilkie.

'No, not to my knowledge. Not whilst I've been here, and I'm here every day from nine to five, except Sundays.'

'Do you think that Mr Raglan does know where the Dixons have gone?' said Mike.

Miss Finch shook her head. 'No, well at least, I don't think so. I never met them, but Mr Raglan told me when 'the squatters', that's how he referred to them, had cleared off, and he's been a lot easier to work with since.'

'What do you mean by that?' said Mike.

'He's happier, calmer, less jumpy, y'know. He had seemed on edge before.'

'It looks like the Dixons have literally vanished into thin air. No one appears to know where they are,' said Mike.

Miss Finch looked downcast. 'I'm sorry, I wish I could do more to help.'

'Do you think you would be able to recognise the flashy gentleman visitor if you saw him again?'

'Oh yes, most definitely I would.'

The pair stood. 'Just one last thing.'

Miss Finch looked up, questioningly.

'Mr Raglan told me the last time I was here that he was going to try and get back from the bank the cheques written by the Dixons which had bounced. You don't happen to know if he's managed to do that, do you?'

Again Miss Finch looked puzzled. 'Cheques? How old school! We don't use cheques these days. I can't remember the last time I saw a cheque, we do everything by BACS transfer.'

'Thanks for your time, Miss Finch,' said Mike. 'Don't bother telling Mr Raglan about our visit, we'll catch him another time. You've have been very helpful.'

Miss Finch giggled, 'I have?'

'You have,' said Mike. 'However, it may be that we need a written statement from you, is that a problem?'

'Not at all! Like I said I'm here every day nine to five…'

'Except Sundays,' said Mike with a smile.

–

The Incident Room was a hive of activity when the pair returned; it was almost time for debrief, and since it was near to teatime, hunger had set in and a sugar rush was required. There was a scramble for Tattie's homemade cookies which she'd placed upon a plate to put in the centre of the table, and her reluctance to hand them over was a cause of banter amongst the team, who were succeeding in winding the office manager up. Seeing Charley Mann's office door closed, Mike set about inputting the new information he had gleaned from his conversation with Miss Finch into the database.

'Why would Raglan lie to us about the cheques, and not inform us of the visit from Faisal?' said Charley, when Mike updated her before the debrief. 'I want you to liaise with West Midlands Police and see what their intelligence can tell us about the bad boy. And get a current address for him, will you? We might just have to pay him a visit.'

Mike diligently noted the action.

'Then, when we get that information, I think we ought to invite Mr Raglan into the station, and see what he has to say when we tell him we know he has lied to us, as well as being sparing with information he does hold. He needs eliminating like the rest of them, but the more I hear about him, the more he is of interest to me.'

Wilkie's day was made because he managed to secure a cookie and a cup of tea. He chuckled. 'You don't like Raglan, do you boss?'

'A pet hate – lying – especially when there is no need. All we want is the truth for God's sake, which is the whole point of any investigation.'

Wilkie dunked the last of his biscuit and popped it in his mouth, 'Ah, well, no doubt you'll scare the shit out of him, boss.'

'That's my intention, although the old man must be tougher than we think.'

'How'd you mean?' said Wilkie.

'Well, Faisal didn't worry him enough to report his visit to us, did he? Although he might look a wimp, wimps in my experience can suddenly grow in stature. The big question for me is, was he involved in the murder of the unknown man we found behind the fireplace? One thing for sure is there is no way he would be strong enough to move the stone wall and fire basket himself. He would need an accomplice. Who could that be?' Charley turned to Annie, 'I want the financial investigation team looking at his finances, and get them to look at James Thomas's too, while you're at it.'

'Proving who didn't do it is just as important as proving who did,' said Ricky-Lee.

'Exactly. It's about time we made contact with Mr and Mrs Hayfield in Milford-On-Sea, and see what they can tell us about Crownest, and how the house came into their hands. I'm interested to know how Raglan came to market the property, and I'd like to see if their story fits in with what Mr Raglan would have us believe.'

'They're an elderly couple, by all accounts. It'll be a day trip for a couple of the team,' said Mike.

'Part of the reason why I haven't subjected them to a visit, until now. Milford is a six-hundred-mile round trip, and I'm not a hundred per cent that what they can tell us would be worth the time, nor the expense. However, needs must. We have to find out for ourselves what they have to say, we can't believe anything Raglan tells us any more, and whoever does go, remind them to remain professional. I don't want to see a selfie of anyone on a beach eating ice-cream, if they value their job.'

Wilkie chuckled. 'It's the middle of winter!'

'Nuff said,' replied Annie.

Charley unwrapped her evening meal at her desk, and stabbed a few chips with the simple wooden takeaway fork. Faisal's antecedent history and previous convictions made interesting reading.

A tap came at her door, it was Ricky-Lee. 'You'll get indigestion,' he said.

Charley relaxed back in her chair, and smiled. With the others gone for the night, and the lights dimmed, the office was quiet and calm, and it gave her a feeling of peace. 'Yeah, and I'll stink of fish fried in beef dripping. Ne'er mind,' she said, taking a deep breath. 'I'll content myself with a quick scrub with a flannel and then go out and stand in the wind for a while later.' All of a sudden, Charley felt a feeling of nostalgia come over her. 'My granny used to say that,' she said, quietly.

'She sounds a bit of a character, your granny,' said Ricky-Lee, mirroring her smile. 'I'll be off now, boss. I'll see you tomorrow.'

Charley watched him leave. She prayed she was doing right by him, and the others – the victims of the crimes they were investigating – by putting her faith in him. Charley emitted an unladylike burp, the acidic taste of partially-digested cod and chips welling up from her stomach. Thankfully, she knew from years of eating fast food, usually cold fast food, that indigestion never lasted long, but that didn't stop her feeling how she did. Legs tucked beneath her, she settled down and read on.

Chapter 27

Faisal Hussain, Charley read, was a career criminal. From quite a young age, the local criminal masterminds had his life mapped out, as his file showed her his quick succession up the ranks of the drug world. He was presently being investigated, believed to be one of the linchpins for a network which traded drugs from Birmingham to the Black Country, and to Oxford, London and Bristol. His drug-dealer customers were also believed to be acting as national co-ordinators, facilitating onward supply to other criminal gangs all over the UK. At thirty-two he was considered to be at the top of his tree on the West Midlands drug scene − far enough up the tree now to keep his hands clean. However, if evidence could be secured by the National Crime Agency whose radar he was under, he wouldn't stay clean for long. Warning red text markers highlighted *VIOLENT* and *KNOWN TO CARRY WEAPONS* on his personal file. It appeared he wasn't afraid to use them.

A few stretches in prison, notably for money laundering, possession of an offensive weapon and possession and supply of class A drugs, had resulted in a growing list of known associates.

It seemed Hussain had nothing to lose, living in the extreme luxury he was currently enjoying. He was in that world too deep to leave it alive.

However, if the corpse was involved with Hussain, there was no suggestion that he had ingested drugs, nor was there any evidence that the victim had been in possession of drugs when he was shot. That troubled Charley, because she knew that drugs, like rats, were never far from trouble, and you couldn't get more trouble than a murder. Keeping an open mind in order to glean from the intelligence only the facts which could connect Hussain to her enquiry, she knew she couldn't disregard him from her investigation, on the basis that he had links with firearms, coupled with the fact that he had been in the area within the timeframe that the experts had given her for the death of the male corpse.

If Mr Raglan wasn't fazed by Hussain and his threats, he should have been, Charley thought, having read his profile. She had known people shot for no more reason than looking at the likes of him in a way that they thought was disrespectful. Deaths that occurred by means of an execution-type killing were nothing new when rival gangs decided it was time to expand their turf or to deal with someone stepping out of line. Word of this style of death taking place would be enough to spread fear, and silence the would-be grass for good. Not always for fear of recrimination on themselves, but for the threat of death or torture of their family members, whom on most occasions were a much easier target.

Elbow on desk, chin in her hand, Charley spoke through clenched teeth. 'Who the hell was the male corpse? Why was the DNA result taking so long?'

Once again, Charley scanned the positive lines of enquiry. They had been lucky in as far as they had the teeth of the corpse, a metal plate used to mend a broken bone and DNA. 'If only we knew who the victim was,'

Charley thought again as she sat back in her chair and let out a deep sigh. She desperately wanted to pick up the phone and chase everyone, but she knew once they had information to impart she would be the first to know.

Instead, Charley picked up a pen and started to list possible links to the Dixons, James Thomas, Raglan and Faisal Hussain. She could find only one – Crownest. How else could these people be linked in another way? She shook her head. Mobile-phone analysis may shed light on her enquiry, but first she had to find relevant phone numbers, and she knew this information wouldn't be easy to come by, because some criminals used burner phones.

In the world that the likes of Faisal Hussain lived in, it didn't make good business sense to keep the same number for long.

Charley could only see one way forward, and that was to keep enquiries tight and focused, at least for now. The ground beneath the team's feet was still being cleared, which was necessary before they could change direction to follow up other possible lines of enquiry.

–

It was six o'clock in the morning, and still dark, when Charley set off for the police station the next day. As she stepped out of her door the icy wind was so strong it nearly took her breath away. Yet for once she was grateful for the cold air; it cleared her head of the nightmares that had plagued her all night. Now, she was left with a dull ache. There was a hard frost on the windscreen and on the ground. She breathed deeply to fill her lungs. 'Today will be a good day,' she told herself. Settling down in the driver's seat, her teeth chattering, she started the engine.

Mornings were Charley's favourite time of day. There was a period of stillness between the time the night birds and criminals went to bed, and the morning people got up. Usually at this time of day she felt calm, but today she felt agitated. The pain in her head spiked when her phone rang.

She dug her mobile out of her pocket with her gloved hand, but the shrill tones continued to pierce the inside of the car, as irritating to her as nails being scraped down a chalkboard. 'I'm not on-call,' she wanted to scream as she tore her glove off to answer the call. Suddenly, there was a loud crack as the phone slipped through her fingers and hit the floor. Charley swore under her breath. Now the screen was likely to be broken and the phone call might have been urgent. Annoyed with herself, she picked it up off the floor.

Head slumped against the car's headrest, she exhaled and released her hold on the phone. She closed her eyes, and clenched her jaw. When she opened her eyes, it seemed lighter. She looked down at the screen as it lit up and rang again. Putting the phone to her ear she looked across at the horizon to see the morning sun had broken free from the clouds.

'Charley, it's Eira from Forensics. Sorry for the early call, but I've some exciting news that I knew you'd want to know immediately.'

Charley felt her heart miss a beat. Her eyes were on two crows on the roof of her house. Their beady eyes were trained on the rubbish bin, they wouldn't miss an opportunity today, and neither would she. 'Go on,' she said.

'We've obtained a DNA profile link on your male found shot in the head at Crownest.'

Charley raised her chin to see her hooded eyes and pale cheeks in her rearview mirror instantly turn brighter and glowing. 'How sure are you that it is a match?' she said eagerly.

The SIO could hear the smile in Eira's voice, 'Oh don't worry, it's a match all right.'

'Thank you,' she whispered, on the back of a sigh of relief.

'It's my pleasure,' Eira chuckled. 'I don't know how he fits into your enquiry though.'

'Why? Have you run it though the database already? Who is it?'

'Yes, your deceased is one Faisal Hussain.'

Charley was silent.

'You okay? Charley, you're very quiet. Are you still there?'

'I wasn't expecting that. He's just come into the periphery of the enquiry.'

'Well, it's definitely him,' she said.

Charley slammed both hands on her dashboard. 'Result!' She shouted so loud that the crows in the trees took flight.

Chapter 28

Charley couldn't wait to get to the Incident Room, and as soon as she arrived she was reeling off instructions for enquiries that required urgent attention.

'I want the other identifying factors, the metal plate from Hussain's leg, and the enquiry into the teeth, to be continued,' she told the team at the morning briefing. 'They've been started so they may as well be concluded. They all add weight to the evidence.'

Ricky-Lee entered the office late to the sight of Tattie pouring tea into his favourite mug. Annie shuffled up to allow him to pull up a chair at the table. He puffed his chest out in an exaggerated manner. Annie tried her best not to stare at the overnight tan, and his muscles on show in his white short-sleeved shirt while he dug into his bag, from where a strong smell of bacon emanated. 'Can I tempt you to a sandwich? I got several from the shop,' he said, with a wide smile.

Wilkie looked at the Rich Tea finger between his finger and thumb, and slowly, but purposefully, put it back on the plate that Tattie was offering him. 'That does smell good, I suppose the biscuits can wait.' Tattie smirked.

Charley tucked into her sandwich, but her eyes showed suspicion. Ricky-Lee showed her a smile of perfectly white teeth. There was a twinkle in his eyes.

Wilkie let out a groan of appreciation. 'I think this is the best bacon sandwich I've ever had,' he said to Ricky-Lee.

'Do you think that Hussain had caught up with the Dixons'?' asked Annie.

'Looks like it, doesn't it?' said Wilkie. 'Why else would he end up dead, in a tunnel behind a fireplace, in a stranger's house?'

Annie pulled a face. 'Wonder if he had a gun with him to avenge his uncle's death when he found them?' she said.

Wilkie chuckled. 'Yeah, well it serves him bleedin' right if his plan went tits up, and he ended up the victim.'

Annie cocked an eyebrow. 'The Dixons were obviously faster on the draw that day.'

'Or had they been expecting Hussain?' said Mike.

Annie scowled. 'How come? As far as we're aware, he wasn't an associate, was he?'

Ricky-Lee rolled his eyes in her direction. 'He means someone gave them a tip-off.' Annie gave him a shove.

'Raglan?' said Mike.

Charley had listened to them before speaking.

'We're making assumptions,' said Charley, not sure whether she was talking about her assumption of why Ricky-Lee appeared to be on top of his game this morning, or about the enquiry. 'Where's the cabriolet, his mobile phone, and the rest of his personal property, including the gold rings Miss Finch talked about?'

'The Dixons were not the type to hang on to things, I would suggest,' said Wilkie. 'They'd be sold on before his body was cold.'

'Probably,' said Charley. 'Find out if the cabriolet was registered to Hussain. If so, the automatic number plate recognition system seems to be a good place to start finding out where he might have travelled, and when. Who knows what the Automatic Number Plate Recognition cameras will have picked up that would be useful to us?'

'Maybe we've found out the real reason why the Dixons left Crownest suddenly, and it's not the story that Raglan told us about his threatening them and their leaving. That was all bravado,' said Mike.

Charley picked up a pen, and threaded it through the fingers of her hand. 'I understand that Raglan doesn't appear to be a physical threat without a gun, but what doesn't sit right with me is that if the Dixons did the deed without anyone else to help them, how the hell would they know about the tunnel behind the fireplace?'

Ricky-Lee shrugged his shoulders. 'We know Hussain was shot with a weapon that the Dixons are known to have used before, because the gun has been linked to the previous armed robberies, but I've been thinking that to dispose of a body at the house they were renting was taking one hell of a risk, don't you think?'

'I agree, but they would have known that the house was about to be demolished, wouldn't they, so they might not have seen it as such a risk?' countered Mike.

'Was the house deliberately set on fire then, and if so by whom, because this would have triggered an early demolition for safety reasons?' said Annie.

Charley had been making notes throughout, so that all the lines of enquiries would be included on the database. 'I suggest we speak with the relevant family members about Faisal's death first, then I'll speak with Connie at the Press Office. Until we're ready, the media don't need to know that we have identified the male corpse,' she said. 'I also want a team led by Mike to go to Birmingham and speak with whoever Hussain lived with. His next of kin hope-fully,' Charley shook her head from side to side. 'That's if we can find an address for him. Then I want Raglan brought in prior to our sharing the I.D. of the victim to the public. That way it will give him less time to think about what he has planned to say should the body ever be identified. In addition to that I want the intelligence I requested on Raglan and James Thomas ASAP.'

Ricky-Lee caught up with Charley as she was about to go into her office.

'The reason I was late was that I called in for an update from the team we tasked with getting into Seth Alderman's grave. There was no body, no bones, nothing, just steps down into a grave-sized empty space. So perhaps, as we suspected, it was just an access to the tunnel, until the roof collapsed,' he said.

'Or, was it a meeting place,' said Charley, thoughtfully 'Well, at least we know there isn't another skeleton. That's a relief! But where is Seth Alderman's body laid to rest then?'

When Charley settled in her chair behind her desk, the detective hung about at the door.

Charley looked up after a moment or two. 'Was there something else?'

'No,' he said.

'Nice aftershave,' said Annie, as she passed him. Head turned, he walked out.

Annie stood in front of Charley's desk, paperwork in hand. She showed her lip to Charley. 'The gee-gees again, do you think?'

Charley shrugged her shoulders. 'I don't know, and I don't care. He's had the Scarborough warning, he's a grown man, the rest is up to him.'

'Scarborough warning?' enquired Annie.

The question brought a smile to Charley's face. 'I keep forgetting you're not from round here. There are a few ideas of where the saying comes from, but I like the one from the thirteenth century that talks about the implementation of the law back when the town's judicial privileges and immunities were confirmed by royal charters. The result was that offenders soon found themselves severely punished, and the town gallows were in constant use.'

Annie looked confused. 'I thought a Scarborough warning was a colleague that complained of symptoms of a bogus illness, the day before a particularly good weather forecast, and then when they didn't turn up for their shift the next day, they were said to be on Scarborough leave?'

'Really? Believe what you must, but I prefer to think of it as the Halifax gibbet-law, given that the gibbet was used on our doorstep.'

Annie pulled a face. 'You don't really mean it, do you? In terms of Ricky-Lee?'

'Oh, yes, I do! You get one chance in CID and he's already got his head on the block,' said Charley.

Chapter 29

Wilkie sat watching Annie. It was half past ten, and unusually for her, she was still at her desk. 'Isn't it about time you were off out, young 'un? You're not going to catch y'man inside, as they say.'

A complacent smile crossed the young detective's face, but she didn't look up from her typing. 'Why, Mr Dinosaur, didn't you know that the ease and influx of information sharing, invention of social networking, and the development of technology for telephones, has drastically changed the volume of information available now online, and the way we communicate since you last struck a bat?'

'Cheeky mare, I don't know what you mean,' the older detective said grumpily, as he drank the dregs of his coffee. It was cold. Wilkie pulled a face, but finished it anyway. Tattie turned from her audio-typing and he flashed her a smile, and lifted his cup. 'Time for another,' he mimed, but Tattie wasn't to be distracted.

Annie's mobile phone pinged. Wilkie frowned. He saw her lips turn up at the corners as she read the text. Immediately she pushed her chair back and stood up. Unspeaking, she looked extremely pleased with herself as she headed directly for Charley's office door. She knocked and the SIO beckoned her inside.

'The cabriolet Hussain was using. He bought, and paid for it in cash at a Northwood Garage, Birmingham,' Annie said. 'The salesman distinctly remembers that Hussain brought the money in a man's brown leather shoulder bag. Apparently, he had reported it to the police, as is his firm's procedure regarding cash purchases.'

'What's the number plate?' said Charley, pen poised.

'5. M.A.C.K. The number five on the private plate looks like a letter S, illegal, of course, but he's feeding his ego, because it reads "SMACK".'

Charley scoffed. 'Nothing like advertising the fact that you are into drugs, but, hey ho, makes it easier for us.'

Annie looked over Charley's shoulder to see Annie's clapped-out orange VW Beetle through the window, sitting out in the yard. 'My first thought when I see a young man driving around in a very expensive car, is, what proceeds of which crime paid for it?' said Annie.

'Being observant is what being a cop is all about. Proving that a lifestyle is funded by the proceeds of a crime however is not always that simple, as you're more than aware. Those kinda machines are the dealers' status symbols, don't forget. Car dealers are used to the likes of Faisal Hussain walking in with cash. How else are you going to get rid of excessive amounts of dosh, if you don't spend it on ridiculously expensive cars and jewellery, which are nice and visual but a sure way to get our unwanted attention.'

'Any news on the ANPR enquiry?' asked Annie.

'No, but it'll be interesting to see what they can come up with, and if there have been any sightings of the car since Hussain's murder.'

'It's hardly likely to be still being driven around though is it, unless it's on false plates?'

'Who knows?' said Charley. 'Time will tell. In the meantime, we will have to be patient.'

Annie strolled back to her desk, throwing Wilkie a cunning smile.

'I'd have got the information in the end,' said Wilkie.

'Course you would,' said Annie as she sat down, allowing herself to feel a little smug satisfaction.

–

The visit to Mr and Mrs Hayfield, who lived on the south coast, in the village of Milford-On-Sea, had proved fruitful, as Mike told the others when he and Ricky-Lee returned later that afternoon. Apparently, George and Dinah Hayfield had lived in their bungalow for forty-five years, and had only recently been able to buy it.

'It was very unexpected, that Di inherited the big house,' George told them. 'Di was in hospital, we'd been informed she wouldn't walk again, and we were wondering how we were going to manage. Then out of the blue, we received this letter from the solicitors, who informed us that her cousin Adam Alderman, had left her his fortune and Crownest in his will.'

'I didn't know about my mother's side of the family. Apparently, she never spoke about her past, not even to my father,' said Dinah, who still appeared unbelieving of the facts. 'I assumed that mother was an only child, I don't know why. She died in childbirth, having me.' Dinah paused to swallow a lump in her throat. There were tears in her eyes. 'I was told that my father had to work to live, and wasn't able to look after me, and so I was sent packing to England, to my father's parents who lived in Portsmouth for them to care for me. My father remarried, and sadly I never saw him again.'

'The solicitor, Mr Knowles, has since died,' said Mike, 'but the couple will be for ever in his debt, as they are sure that he persisted in his enquiries to trace Mrs Hayfield, the only known relative of Adam Alderman.'

'Where's Ricky-Lee?' asked Charley, looking round.

'I dropped him off to buy cakes for the debrief. He was insistent. He should be here any minute,' Mike said looking at his watch.

Charley appeared to be happy with the explanation and Tattie went to put the kettle on. 'Were they made aware of the history of the house?' Charley asked.

Mike nodded. 'Yes, that's why they decided to get rid of it as soon as possible. Well, you would, wouldn't you? Apparently, the money that Adam Alderman left them made them financially secure for life, so they weren't in any rush. It's all in the detailed statements we took.'

Annie looked confused. 'You mean they weren't desperate for cash, and that's why they decided to rent the house out to the Dixons without waiting for references?' she said.

Mike shook his head, 'No.'

'Then Raglan lied to us?'

'It would appear so.' Mike looked at his watch, then at the door, and he frowned. 'Where the hell has Ricky-Lee got to?'

'How come they chose Raglan to sell the house for them?' said Annie, eagerly.

'Mr Knowles, the deceased solicitor, gave them Raglan's details, and since Raglans were local estate agents of long standing, it seemed like a sensible thing to do, but...' Mike's eyes lit up, '...there's more. I was going to wait until Ricky-Lee got back, but would you believe that Raglan has been to see them?'

'You gotta be kidding me. Recently?'

'Yes, he took them pictures of the fire-damaged building from the first fire. He said he wanted to speak to them personally because he had bad news about the house. He told them that he had an acquaintance who had advised him that Crownest was now uninhabitable and their first plan of restoring the property was not an option. The property would have to be demolished, and quickly, as it was deemed unsafe. Should an accident happen prior to its demolition then the owner would be liable. Raglan didn't hide the fact that he had a friend who knew people who had ready money to buy the land for building purposes and had advised them to accept. Truth known, I think Raglan frightened them; they were really concerned about anyone being injured.'

Charley looked thoughtful a moment then shrugged. 'They left it in his capable hands, considering him to be an honourable man. What a complete bastard.'

'Yes, you're right there, they even offered to pay his travel expenses, but apparently, he declined. They told him as far as they were concerned, the money raised from the house was to be donated to charity, and although they were hopeful that the sale would raise as much as possible, they were realistic as to how much it would achieve.'

'How big of him to decline travel expenses! So, the last contact they had with Mr Raglan was, I presume, that he had managed to secure a sale,' said Charley.

Mike nodded. 'They're awaiting the transfer of money for the sale. Surprisingly, they've received nothing, yet.'

'They're knocking the house down now, so the sale must have gone through, surely?' said Annie.

'Exactly,' said Mike. 'A fact of which they were unaware of.'

'What did they think about the Dixons renting the property?'

'They had no idea! As far as they had been told by Raglan, like I said before, it was uninhabitable.'

Wilkie was aghast. 'Who has got the money then? If James Thomas has paid up? Would we assume it is with Raglan?'

Charley's mouth formed a perfect O. 'I'm so looking forward to the findings of the financial investigation team. That information will be invaluable to us in tracing the movement of money in and out of Raglan and Thomas's accounts.'

'What's also interesting was that the Hayfields told us that Mr Knowles had given them a copy of the Alderman family tree. The one he had used to trace Dinah,' said Mike.

As he passed the paperwork to Charley, the door flew open and in walked Ricky-Lee. The smell of his aftershave preceded him. His smile was as wide as the Cheshire Cat's.

'Where the hell have you been till this time?' called Mike. 'The tea will be cold.'

'Always complaining,' he said with a chuckle. 'I've bought you cream cakes, haven't I?' The detective walked towards the kitchenette and Annie stood up and followed.

'They're called buns round 'ere, cream buns,' she said. Ricky-Lee's shiny shoes squeaked on the lino floor when he turned suddenly to hand her the carrier bag. 'Hey, isn't this the same shop you get the bacon sarnies from, and those sandwiches?' she said, ripping open the cake boxes. 'Couldn't you have got them any nearer?'

'What's your problem?' Ricky-Lee said, handing her plates from the cupboard above the sink, 'and, for your information they're called bacon butties round 'ere.'

Annie shook her head, but her expression was questioning. 'Whatever,' she said looking up at him, but he was smiling warmly at her.

'What?' he said, with a glint in his eye. 'I buy you cream cakes, and you're moaning about where I've got them from?'

'Seems to me like you're visiting that place a lot lately, that's all…'

'A right little Ms Christie, aren't we? How about you shut your cake 'ole, as they say round 'ere, and enjoy?' Swiftly he carried the plates into the CID office.

Wilkie's eyes grew wide when he saw the size of the cream buns, and realised there was one for him. The room fell silent as they ate and considered the new information that Mike had given them.

Charley licked her cream-covered fingers, 'It feels good to be making some progress after what feels like such a long, hard, struggle,' she said.

She looked around her. The office was a monument to paperwork. Charley sighed in relief. 'The murder of Faisal is our focus, but I wonder what part, if any, Raglan played in it, or is he just driven by making money?'

Chapter 30

'Lily Pritchard has got to know more than she's telling,' said Annie, through a mouthful of sandwich that Ricky-Lee had insisted on fetching, despite Tattie's arguments. The morning sandwich run was her escape to the shops on work's time. 'Well, they did close the canteens down,' she said on a regular basis, 'besides, if everyone took time out to go for their sandwiches, then everyone would be out of the office for an hour, and work would soon grind to a halt.'

'I agree, but how are we going to get her to open up to us?' said Charley.

Annie signed deeply. 'Mmm... That is the question I keep asking myself.'

By the time they'd finished lunch they had acknowledged that, for now, the enquiry had raised more questions than they had answers for.

'It's only a phase, and you and I know that every investigation has its peaks and troughs,' Charley said, hoping she sounded more positive to her team than she felt. Things were moving forwards now and she was keen to notch them up a gear.

A call came into the Incident Room, via Crimestoppers. The anonymous male informed them of a sighting of the Dixons at a Primrose Pastures Holiday Park on the East coast, where the couple seemed to be living in a mobile home. Annie was bursting to share the news.

'That's it?' said Charley. 'Just a sighting?'

'Yes.' Annie's disappointment at Charley's reaction was obvious.

'How do we know it isn't a hoax?'

The younger detective looked troubled. 'Well, we don't.'

'Make some discreet enquires. I want to keep the element of surprise on our side for now. Take Ricky-Lee with you, book a caravan. After all, you're the most likely looking couple on our team, so you won't draw attention to yourselves.'

Annie stared at Charley aghast. 'You've got to be joking? You really want me to sleep alone, in a caravan, with him?' she said, tossing her head in the direction of the detective who she could see from Charley's office window, sitting at his desk. She pulled a face.

Charley shook her head. 'Unless you've someone else in mind?'

At that Annie laughed out loud, uncertain as to whether Charley was joking or not.

Charley's face was deadpan. 'We need to know if this information is right without revealing our hand, get my drift?'

'Yes, boss.'

'If it's confirmed that the Dixons are holed up there, I want you to get hold of any signed documentation that the Dixons have completed which may be available at the site. Anything from which we might get DNA, or fingerprints.' Without waiting for an answer the SIO bowed her head, then with pen to paper she wrote as she spoke. 'There will be a lot of red tape. We'll need the

North Yorkshire Chief Constable's authority to use armed officers in the county.'

'Are you going to tell Ricky-Lee, or am I?' said Annie.

Charley looked up at her and frowned. 'For God's sake, Annie, I'm not asking you to go to bed with him, I just want you to do some discreet enquiries and make observations together.'

'You seem to forget I was brought up by nuns, ma'am.'

Charley's lips turned up at both corners. 'Yes, and you, Milady, appear to use that card when it suits! This information could yet be a hoax, but we can't leave anything to chance.'

With just one thing on her mind, Annie walked out of Charley's office to find Ricky-Lee.

Charley was speaking to the financial investigations team, when Annie returned to the office later with her suitcase, but there wasn't anything more of note to tell the pair. With Annie and Ricky setting off to the coast, Charley decided she'd visit St Anne's Church to get some fresh air and wander around the graveyard alone, in order to think, before debrief.

The black-and-yellow police tape required by Health and Safety, and which advised caution, was placed around Seth Alderman's grave. It announced the would-be burial site to Charley from the slatted wooden gate. It was bitterly cold. She paused to catch her breath, and suddenly she felt the faint rays of the winter sun on her face and it brought her a moment of peace.

Charley stood for a moment or two at the grave, rolling her shoulders to get the blood flowing into her chilled bones. Surrounding her, lining the graveyard, were row upon row of grey-mottled, moss-covered fallen head-stones. Some of the graves were so tiny that they could only be the burial site of an infant, some large enough to house a whole family. Others told stories of a life lived, in brief messages, including quotes from religious texts, lines from poems, or verses composed especially for the deceased. Some depicted images of little creatures, such as Brownies, Elves, and Hobgoblins, and this made Charley smile. It reminded her of the Yorkshire folklore that her grandparents had shared with her about the Hob and his companions, it seemed the tales were destined to always be part of her life. Blue Birches, the shapeshifting hobgoblin who played harmless pranks in the home of a shoemaker and his wife, was her childhood favourite, and when she was asked to read *A Midsummer Night's Dream* for her English Literature exam, she was eager to meet Puck, one of the fairies who inhabited the forest and servant to the Fairy King, Oberon. Recalling the story now, Charley felt compelled to bend and pluck a wild flower. On lifting her eyes to the horizon, there was nothing as far as the eye could see but barren moorland and she thought that before cemeteries and churchyards existed, grave markers would be nothing more than piles of rock or wood, placed not far from the family home.

The sound of a rat scurrying across the stone plinth in front of her brought her back from her reverie. Charley dropped the flower in her hand as if she'd been stung. She shivered, and attempted to calm her racing heart. She berated herself. It wasn't the first rat she'd seen for good-ness' sake! However, rodents had always had the ability to shock and frighten her. Another rat, and another, disappeared down the hole that the CID had made an initial attempt to investigate. It had proved difficult to see what was underneath without removing the stone, which proved to be too heavy to lift without industrial equipment.

Charley took the torch from her pocket, knelt down and pointed it at the hole that the rats had disappeared down. There was a lot of scratching, scrambling and squeaking, and to her surprise she saw a circle of gleaming red sparks staring up at her. She jumped back and nearly lost her balance. Shocked, and feeling slightly foolish, she spun around to see if anyone had been watching, and as she did so two, tall, marble effigies at the far end of the graveyard, glistening in the sun, caught her eye. Slowly, and carefully, she walked as if transfixed, towards Michael O'Doherty's grave that was clearly connected to the one next to it, that of his nephew, Connor.

A flattened grass path led from the graves to the church. Sparkling clean marble, the grass around them was short and neat, a hand-tied posy at their base. Both full of fresh wild flowers, suggesting to the SIO that someone visited and tended the graves regularly.

These gigantic memorials were indeed a statement of the deceased's relationship with the established church.

Charley knelt to examine the flowers. There were no cards, or anything else that would suggest who had left them, yet they could not be more than a few days old.

An obvious starting point of call was Lily Pritchard, and if it wasn't her who'd left the gift of flowers, then maybe she'd know of a regular visitor to the graves who might have.

Having taken pictures of the graves and the flowers on her mobile phone, Charley was just about to leave when a rotund robin made an entrance behind her, singing a bittersweet song. The plump bird with a bright orange-red breast, face, throat and cheeks, walked boldly towards her along the overhanging branch of an overgrown tree. Charley took a step towards the little bird. 'I wish I knew what you're telling me,' she said, sadly.

–

Back at the Incident Room, Charley contemplated who to bring into the station first: Lily Pritchard or Mr Raglan.

'I've been thinking,' she said to Mike. 'The indications suggest that Lily Pritchard is tending to the priests' graves. Instead of inviting her down to the station, perhaps we should make her an unannounced visit to ask her? We may find confirmation in her rooms; maybe she has flowers on display, like the ones on the graves? More importantly, I'd like to check to see whose pictures she has on display.'

Wilkie raised an eyebrow. 'Sounds like proper detective work to me, boss. But looking after graves is part of her job, surely?'

Charley shook her head slowly as though she was unsure about her answer. 'It is, but she's singled two out. Why would she do that? The rest of the graveyard is, let's face it, a wilderness.'

'There is a difference between devotion and infatuation, isn't there?' said Mike. 'A blindness to infatuation that makes people see what they want to see.'

'Perhaps because of that, they would know they could trust her with anything,' said Charley. 'Tell you what, unless we get diverted by information coming in from Annie and Ricky-Lee, we'll go and see her tomorrow, shall we?'

Chapter 31

Unobserved, Annie smoothly parked her old orange Beetle under a large oak tree, less than fifty metres from what would become known as the Dixons' mobile home, which was perched on the cliff top, away from the static caravans. The detectives heard strange noises coming from beyond the thick privet hedge that separated them from the parked car. There was a sweet smell of pine trees in the air, and the sea could be heard intermittently, crashing against the rocks. As she watched, Ricky-Lee uncurled himself from the worn leather bucket seat, clutching a paper bag with a sandwich inside. Suddenly a flying squirrel appeared from nowhere and ripped it from his clutches and the fright made him throw himself to the ground.

'What the fuck?' he shouted, seeing both the squirrel and his sandwich shoot up a tree. Annie laughed out loud as Ricky-Lee disappeared from view as he hit the ground. When he got up, his hair was dishevelled, and his expression told her he wasn't amused.

'Serves you right for not eating it earlier,' she said. 'I thought you said you were starving. Was it the argument with the girl at the counter that put you off it?'

'No,' he said, like a sulky teenager. 'Mind your own.'

'Probably people feed the squirrels whilst they are staying at their caravans, so they are used to humans.'

Annie cupped her hand to her ear as she heard another strange noise. 'I guess we shouldn't go knocking, whilst the caravan's rocking,' she said in a sing-song voice, trying not to laugh as she watched Ricky-Lee compose himself.

'It sounds more like someone's getting strangled to me,' he said, brushing the soil from the knees of his jeans. 'Best close your ears, it's not our problem. We're just a courting couple wanting to rent a caravan, remember?'

Annie paused, and frowned. 'Shouldn't we at least go and investigate?'

Ricky-Lee nodded his head in the direction of the garden chalet which was located at the bottom side of the picnic area. The new, handmade sign indicated that the ramshackle wooden building was the booking office and information centre. 'If it makes you feel any better, you can mention it to the receptionist.'

An ancient-looking, large battered banner tied to the fence with frayed rope, displayed the caravan park's name, and the two detectives followed the arrows down the driveway.

'At least we know we're at the right place,' said Annie, with a chuckle.

Ricky-Lee took his phone out of his pocket, looked at the screen, and put it back.

'How many times are you going to check your phone?' Annie snapped. 'Is there something you're not telling me, I am your girlfriend, after all.'

However, before he could answer with one of his usual cryptic comments, Annie spotted an Alsatian dog tethered to a picnic table. The rope was wound so tightly round the table legs, that he looked as if he was in danger of choking. Running to the dog's aid, she immediately went down on her haunches beside him. Whispering comforting words in a soothing voice, she tried to free the animal, but his head was too near the ground with the knot tight on his tether. The dog's nostrils flared, the whites of his eyes showed. Annie turned to Ricky-Lee, her eyes pleading for help.

Ricky-Lee instantly dropped to his knees. 'Let's untangle you, mate,' he said softly, taking over from Annie who was struggling with the knot. The dog looked up at his rescuers with red, watery, frightened eyes, but he was losing consciousness. Once Ricky-Lee had untied the dog, he continued to stroke its soft head, and eventually the animal stood on shaky legs, which enabled Annie to pat under his belly. She cringed when she felt his ribs. Her pained eyes went from patches of missing hair on his legs, back to Ricky's face.

'Hopefully, the owner has only left him here for a few minutes,' he said.

Annie took a picture of the dog on her mobile phone. 'This is disgraceful!' she muttered, angrily. With her hand under the dog's jaw, she smiled, and promised she'd return with food and water.

To the left of the reception chalet was a large house. The downstairs windows had bars on, and the gate was secured with a thick metal chain.

Annie knocked at the chalet door, and noticed several pairs of mud-splashed wellington boots lay where they had been hurriedly discarded. When no one came to the door she tried the handle, and it slowly opened. 'Hello' she said, to announce her arrival. The smell hit her like a punch in the stomach, a rancid mixture of stale sweat and urine. She turned and looked over her shoulder to see Ricky-Lee watching her, from where he sat with his new-found friend by the picnic table. She pinched her nose tightly with two fingers. He acknowledged her with a nod of his head. He appeared relaxed, as though he was taking in the scenery. However, she knew otherwise. He was on alert, she could tell by the way his eyes were actively scanning the area and Annie had an overwhelming feeling that she was safe with him.

Inside the chalet, Annie observed her surroundings. Instead of a bright, neat, clean office space to greet her, with a desk, computer and a display of brochures for nearby attractions that she would have anticipated at a holiday caravan site, she was presented with a messy, dark living space. In the far corner was a large faded, moth-eaten armchair. Next to the armchair was an aged heater. An old-fashioned boxed TV set stood on spindly wooden legs in the opposite corner. A pile of well-thumbed magazines, and several mugs with mould at various stages growth inside them, sat upon an upturned blue, plastic crate, which served as a table. Annie took a moment to examine the pictures on the walls. Then she saw the hunting photographs and small taxidermy animals. Her stomach turned.

A dragging noise preceded a shuffling, followed by a loud bang when the door was flung wide against the wall. A lady, dressed in a long black dress, stood in the doorway. On her feet she wore flat Jesus sandals, with worn ankle socks that had holes where her big toes peeped through. Her uncombed, salt-and-pepper hair had been dragged back, and tied in a long plait with an elastic band at the back of her head. She observed Annie from behind spectacles that she pushed up by the bent frame with grubby fingers.

'The likes of you don't want to stop 'ere,' she said in a thick Yorkshire accent.

'Oh, we do, we really do,' said Annie. Taken aback, Annie protested a little too loudly. She shot a surprised look at Ricky-Lee over her shoulder, but instead of coming to her aid, as she had expected him to, he continued to observe from the picnic bench.

The lady looked from Annie's right hand, where her interest in Annie obviously lay. She clicked her tongue in disapproval. 'You're not married, are you?' she said.

Annie swallowed a giggle. 'With respect, I don't think that's any of your business,' she said, again feeling much stronger for having Ricky-Lee's presence nearby.

'You didn't expect someone like me to 'ave morals, did you?' The woman held up a small, chubby hand and flapped it up and down. She sat down heavily in the chair. 'Go away!' she said. 'I've met your kind 'afore and we don't want the likes of you 'ere.'

'Are you mad?' said Annie slowly, in one long exhaled breath. 'You can't afford to turn paying customers away, not at this time of year, surely?'

The woman raised her eyes to the ceiling, and averted her gaze with the air of a person who was not for changing her mind. 'Don't tell me what I can and cannot do, young lady. I choose who I want to stay here, and I told you 'afore, I don't want the likes of *you*!'

Annie could hear someone outside hurrying towards the building, calling out, but she couldn't quite make it out the words for the sound of a motorbike's engine.

The Alsatian dog greeted the young man with an open mouth, and a lolling tongue, combined with a ferociously wagging tail. The man put two shiny dog bowls down on the ground, and ruffled the Alsatian's head. Words were exchanged with Ricky-Lee. Annie was too far away to hear, but the conversation looked amicable. Ricky-Lee pointed to the chalet, and the young man put out his hand in a friendly wave, before moving towards the door. 'I'll catch you later,' he called over his shoulder to Ricky-Lee, 'Thank you.'

'There you are, Gran!' said the young man as he stepped inside. He looked and sounded relieved. 'I only left her for two minutes to get Bruno some food and water,' he said, by way of an explanation, 'but, then when I looked round the kitchen, she'd vanished.' Walking slowly and carefully around the crate he put his hand on the chair arm, and gently put the other under the old lady's armpit, encouraging her to get up. 'Why don't you go and find mum, she'll get you a nice cup of tea and a Kit Kat,' he said. The old woman smiled up at him adoringly, did as she was told, and got up from the chair. She then turned to Annie and scowled, 'Harlot,' she growled, and then she was gone.

The young man turned to Annie. 'I'm so sorry,' he said.

Annie laughed. 'Oh, don't worry, I've been called worse, believe me.'

'You see my grandfather died very recently. She's got vascular dementia, and so has Bruno, his dog, and now they're both pining for him. We're doing our best, but this park was Gran and Grandfather's life, and he wouldn't let anyone interfere. Not even me to see to his ailing dog. As result, none of us know what the hell we are doing now. I'm Sean Dean, by the way,' he said, holding out his hand for Annie to shake. His hands were warm and soft, the hands of a healer, not of a manual worker, 'but you're not here to hear about our family troubles, are you?' he said nodding towards Ricky-Lee outside. 'Ricky-Lee briefed me about your visit,' Sean said as he pulled his mobile phone out of the back pocket of his jeans. 'How can I help?' he said.

Annie produced her warrant card. 'I don't know what he told you, but we believe that you could have suspects staying on your site who we want to interview about murder.'

'My God, really?' He pulled a face, and groaned. 'That's all we need.'

'Yes,' said Annie. 'We have information that tells us that the Dixons are here, and may have been for some time.'

Silently, Sean scrolled through the database on his phone. 'I'm sorry,' he said, after a few minutes, 'none of our residents go by that name.' He saw Annie's questioning look. 'We're trying to update things, it's proving to be a slow process. Maxine, my sister put the historical information on yesterday.' Again he scrolled through the database. All of a sudden, his face lit up. 'Hold on, we had a Mr and Mrs Dickinson staying here last season.' His face fell. 'Don't suppose one of your suspects has mobility requirements though, do they?'

Annie wrinkled her nose, then shook her head. The young man looked crestfallen.

'Take a look at this photograph,' said Annie, 'and see if you recognise anyone. It's a distinct possibility that they haven't registered in their own names.'

Annie produce a photograph of the Dixons from a buff folder in her bag.

Sean frowned. 'I'd have hoped my grandfather would have checked their details before allowing them to park up on the site,' he looked sad for a moment, 'but, we know he had a lot on his mind at the end. I haven't met all the residents, so I may not be able to help you.'

Turning the photograph around to face Sean, Annie saw a flicker of recognition in his countenance. He studied the picture with his vivid blue eyes, then looked back at her face.

'I know them, but they're not called Dixon, that's Bill and Babs Bennett. They're renting a pitch and they've paid a year in advance.' Sean opened a map of the site and pointed to the location of their pitch. 'They have a large American-style motorhome, and they've got a motorbike, which they use for getting about.'

'Do they go out often?' asked Annie.

'Not often, but when they do, they're often away for a few days at a time. In fact you've just missed them.'

Annie looked confused.

'The motorbike you heard, that was them. I waved to them on my way back here. To be fair they've been no trouble to us.' Sean's lips turned upwards in a faint smile. 'I do know Gran has a distinct dislike of them because, according to her, they won the money that they paid for their pitch off Grandfather – on the same night they arrived. Once a gambler always a gambler, eh?'

–

Sean led the detectives to the house. With Bruno at Ricky-Lee's feet in the kitchen, and none the worse for his bad experience, the officers spoke to Sean, and then Maureen, his mother, who agreed that they would co-operate fully with the Police. The owners swore that they would not say anything to anyone, and contact the officers when the Dixons returned.

'In the meantime, can you show us the location of the motorhome?' asked Ricky-Lee.

And once they had securely recorded the registered details of the Dixons' vehicles, the detectives followed Sean around the park.

On the way, Annie pointed to several caravans that she thought would have a good view of the motorhome, in which they could set up surveillance equipment. 'Any of them empty?' she asked.

'One five seven is the gardener's. He uses it when he's working on site, but he's on holiday for the next couple of weeks.'

'Could we use it?'

'Yes, of course, but could I ask a favour? If you intend to arrest them, is there any chance you could do it off the site? I hate to ask, but it would hardly be good for business, would it?'

'We'll ask the boss,' said Annie.

'My mother and I would be much obliged.'

Annie took a calling card from her coat pocket. 'If I give you my personal contact details, will you call me when they get back?'

Sean nodded his head eagerly. 'Of course I will. It would be my absolute pleasure.'

Annie smiled broadly. 'Thank you. Someone from surveillance will be in touch.'

'If I give you my personal contact details, will you call me...' Ricky-Lee mocked Annie on their return journey.

Annie looked coy. 'He was rather cute though, wasn't he?'

Ricky-Lee's voice sounded deeper than usual. 'I'm not sure we can trust him,' he said.

'Bit late now.' She paused. 'We told him everything.'

'You mean you told him everything.'

'He said you'd briefed him! What was I to think?'

'I told him we wanted to rent a caravan!'

'There was no point in staying over if it wasn't necessary,' she said. 'Anyway, I think he's sound.'

'Famous last words,' Ricky-Lee scoffed.

Annie looked in her rearview mirror, put the car into second gear, and put her foot down, to give her enough power to pass the lorry. Her face was set. 'I like him. He seemed genuinely nice,' she said, a few moments later, after settling back in the inside lane.

The Beetle was holding its own on the M62, and for that she was grateful. Ricky-Lee was used to comfort, and her car, like the owner, she was reminded, was never quite up to his standards. Well, tough! For most of the two-hour journey Ricky-Lee had slept. 'Do you think they're still at it?' he said, when he woke with a jerk.

Annie fleetingly turned to him. 'Robbery?' she asked.

He nodded his head, took his phone out of his pocket and looked at the screen.

'In my experience, leopards never really change their spots, so I guess so,' she replied.

Ricky-Lee flinched.

Annie looked pensive, and appeared unaware of his reaction. 'Now we have the vehicles' registration numbers we can enter them into the number-plate recognition system, and if we're lucky, we might get sightings of the vehicles' movements. We'll need to flag up the users of the motorhome as having access to weapons as a warning.'

Ricky-Lee yawned. 'There might be historical number-plate recognition data recorded that could also be useful to us.'

–

Charley ushered Annie and Ricky-Lee into her office, and closed the door behind them when they returned, surprised, as she hadn't expected them to travel to the coast and back in a day.

'That's very interesting,' she said, when the detectives updated her. 'The cold-case team have no reference to their living in a mobile home. I can quite understand Mr Dean not wanting them to be arrested on site if we can avoid it. Nor do we want a lot of people hanging about on the site for surveillance.'

'Sean... Mr Dean promised to contact me when the Dixons return to the site,' Annie said.

Charley cocked an eyebrow at Annie. 'Sean, is it?' Colour rose in Annie's cheeks. 'I take it we can trust him to do the right thing?'

'He seemed like a genuine guy.'

Ricky-Lee sighed. He got to his feet. 'I'll go put the kettle on, shall I?'

Charley nodded. 'I'll liaise with a firearms tactical advisor for advice. He won't like it when I tell him there could be a motorcycle involved.'

'Sean said that we could use the gardener's caravan for surveillance if required. I told him that if we needed to they would be in touch,' said Annie.

Charley clapped her hands together. 'Well done, you two. Now, all I need from you is your written report, and then we can get that information on the system.'

Ricky-Lee looked at his watch. 'Tonight? It's late.'

Charley nodded. 'Unless you have something else more pressing? It is important everyone knows the vehicles which armed robbers are using, it may just save someone's life.'

Chapter 32

Firearms Tactical Advisor, Acting Chief Inspector Tim Watson was not convinced that they could pull off a raid on the Dixon's mobile home, purely because of the close proximity of the other residents.

'There is no doubt I'd rather contain them at Primrose Pastures, but the safety of the public has to be our priority. If the Dixons open fire, we could have a major problem on our hands.'

'Then we are looking at a mobile stop?'

Tim pulled a face. 'The mobile stop of a motorbike isn't easy in an intercepted road block, and the last thing we want is a game of cat-and-mouse on a public road, but, don't worry, that's my domain. Inspector Steve Reynolds from North Yorkshire and I will plan for every scenario. What do we say, fail to plan, plan to fail, it was one of Detective Inspector Jack Dylan's favourite sayings,' said Tim. 'He was our boss, back in the day. Have you two met?'

'No, but his reputation of being a hard-nosed detective precedes him.' Charley grimaced.

'Hard, but fair. He's saved my skin on a number of times,' he replied as a knock came at the door, and Charley sat back in her chair, nodding her thanks to Tattie for the coffee and biscuits she'd brought in on a tray.

'Do you know what would be music to my ears right now?' Tim said when she'd gone. 'Confirmation of a time of day when the pair use a particular route to a known destination.'

'They known to carry weapons. So it's highly likely they'll be in possession of firearms when they're stopped,' said Charley. She picked up the plate and offered him a biscuit. Tim accepted one and bit into it with pleasure.

'What a treat,' he said. 'Homemade cookies?'

Charley nodded. 'You're privileged,' she said, 'and lucky that DC Wilkie Connor is out with DS Mike Blake, otherwise they'd normally be long gone by this time of day.'

Tim sat back in his chair, smiled and looked nostalgic for a moment. 'Wilkie Connor. That name's a blast from the past; he was one of the best firearms officers that I've ever worked alongside.'

Charley was genuinely surprised. 'He was?'

'He certainly was. Highly commended by the Chief Constable and judges alike for his bravery was Wilkie.' Tim frowned, and sighed. 'It was a sad day for us when he had to step down from our team, but his wife's needs had to come first.'

A slight tap on the door announced the arrival of Tattie again. Charley cocked her head inquisitively at the administrator, who leaned over the desk to pass her the morning mail. Seeing that the plate was empty, she picked it up to take it away. Tim took her hand as she passed him on her way to the door. She looked down at him, and smiled. 'Don't I know you from somewhere?' he said.

Tattie's smile was broad. Tim continued, 'May I say those cookies are the best I've ever tasted. Are you married?'

It seemed for a moment, that the administrator was struck dumb. Her eyes met Charley's, who was incredulous of what she had just heard, and waited with bated breath for Tattie's response. A blush rose in Tattie's cheeks, and she raised her hand to pat her nest of frizzy hair. Her slightly parted lips showed her recently applied lipstick smeared on her buck teeth. She giggled at Tim. 'Visit again,' she said, 'and I'll bake another batch, just for you.' Tim jumped up and opened the door for her in a gentlemanly way.

Charley shook her head, a smile not far from her lips when Tim sat back down. 'You are incorrigible,' she said. 'God help those who had the job of supervising you when you and Wilkie worked together.'

Tim winked an eye. He leaned forward as if to share a secret. 'Back in the old days, Wilkie and I never wrote a single statement, because the lovely admin ladies were more than happy to write statements up from our notebooks,' he chuckled. 'Yeah,' he said. 'They sure were the good old days.'

Charley moaned, 'Well if that smile was anything to go by, you've made her day.'

Tim's interest turned to the morning mail. 'Anything of interest that I should know about?'

Charley thumbed through the papers in front of her. She shook her head. 'Nothing of great interest to either of us. Just the ivory tower sending out more Home Office guidelines.'

For a moment Tim was silent. 'It's unlikely that the Dixons will give themselves up easily, especially if they have weapons, and/or drugs with them.'

'The background we have on them both is firearms-related,' Charley said solemnly. 'Although they have discharged firearms we have no intel that they have fired directly at anyone. However, they do need to be neutralised as quickly as possible.'

'Don't worry. The armed team will deal with whatever arises on the day. If they put up any resistance, they won't mess about. The safety of the public and the team is of paramount importance. You understand what I'm saying?'

Charley nodded her head.

'Am I right in thinking that the Dixons don't know we're onto them yet?'

'There's nothing to suggest they're spooked, but, you know as well as I do that as soon as they get a whiff of a copper, they'll be off like a shot.'

'How much time do I have?'

Charley puckered her lips. 'We know from a Mr Sean Dean on the site, that the couple regularly go away for a couple of days at a time, and apparently they left yesterday, mid-morning. What their intended destination is, or what they are doing there, and for how long, we have no idea.'

Charley followed Tim to the office door, to see a wink and a wave pass between him and Tattie.

'Aww... What a lovely man,' Tattie smiled across at Charley, from her desk next to the window. Then her smile turned to a frown. 'I wish this lot 'ere were as appreciative.'

Charley turned and put her hands together in silent prayer. *Thank you, God! The last thing I needed was a complaint bordering on sexual harassment from her.*

Charley could feel her adrenaline building as her thoughts switched back to the case. Taking any armed criminal off the streets was a result, but the Dixons' arrest would make decent inroads into the murder of Faisal Hussain.

With the hope that the Dixons would soon be in the traps, Charley was adamant that the operational plan would be completed soon, and the team briefed as quickly as possible. Then all they had to do was wait for the tip-off that the Dixons were back on the caravan site, so that the teams could enact their plan and await for the Dixons' next trip.

Charley sat at her desk, quietly running over what the investigation had revealed so far. Charley picked up a pen, and pulled a sheet of paper from her printer. She started to make notes.

1. Dixons housed – Primrose Pastures Holiday Caravan Park.
2. Personal data about the Dixons gained from Primrose Pastures has enabled ongoing cell-site analysis for mobile phone.

Patience was not one of Charley's virtues, but it was one that was required of an SIO. She got up to go and make herself a coffee. In passing, Tattie warned her, 'This operation is going to be costly.'

'Ah, but money well spent,' said Charley. 'I have every faith in Tim.'

'Oh, absolutely,' Tattie smiled.

Annie stood at the kitchen door and nodded her head at the administrator. 'What's up with her, has she been drinking?' she mouthed.

Charley tittered. 'Never before has Ms Tate not given me grief over the cost of an operation. I'm a very happy bunny,' she said.

There were no calls by lunchtime to say the Dixons had returned to Primrose Pastures. With the arrival in the office of Mike and Wilkie, the team were going over the intelligence about the Dixons. Annie Glover was sitting at her desk, quietly researching any undetected robberies in the North Yorkshire area to see if the suspect criteria matched the Dixons.

'Maybe the heat got too much for them? Maybe they decided it was time to retire from a life of crime,' she said, when nothing was forthcoming in the immediate area.

Charley shook her head. 'No, I'm not buying it. Look further afield. These guys are cute, they won't shit on their own doorstep again, not so soon.'

–

With the team updated on the Dixons enquiry, Charley and Mike set off to visit Lily. It was 2.30 p.m. in the afternoon. Lily, as Charley wanted her to be, was surprised to see them.

'Is everything all right?' she said, licking her lips as if her mouth were too dry as she answered the back door of the church.

Lily stepped back to let them in, her speech was rapid, and Charley wondered if she was nervous. If so, why?

'Please sit down,' Lily said, gathering papers that were strewn around the room, and stuffing them haphazardly into carrier bags. Cleaning up was not a pastime that Charley had learnt to associate with Lily Pritchard, so she wondered what was the rush.

'Do you want a drink?'

Charley and Mike politely declined. Lily poured herself a large glass of blood-red wine from the decanter on the table, next to her chair, then she sat. Charley eyed her closely.

A picture of Father Connor O'Doherty had been left out on the table. Charley recognised his picture from the intelligence report on the board in the office.

'You knew Father Michael O'Doherty, too didn't you?' said Charley, pointing at the photograph.

Lily nodded. Charley wondered what she was thinking. 'He was an old man when I was a girl. I knew his nephew much better,' she said, with a fleeting glance at the photo.

'Uh-huh, well, we have lots of loose ends that need tying up in relation to the murder investigations at Crownest, and with your knowledge of the church and the people associated with it, we thought you might be able to help us solve a few of them,' continued Charley.

'In fact we don't know anyone who knows the place like you do,' said Mike, with a broad smile.

Lily appeared flattered. 'I'll try my best, but the old grey matter isn't as sharp as it used to be,' she said with a half-laugh.

'One of the things that cropped up during our invest-igations is suggestion that he was a sexual deviant,' said Charley.

Lily looked taken aback by the statement and crossed her arms tightly around her, in a defensive pose, which told Charley to tread carefully.

'We understand that Connor was a voyeur. We are led to believe that he took photographs of women, and that he prostituted out at least one woman to fulfil his needs.'

The old woman took a sip of her drink without taking her eyes off the SIO. From her body language, Lily was not happy with the way the conversation was going, but Charley need to press on.

'None of us, I suggest is without sin,' she said quietly. 'Father Connor was protective and sensitive to the requirements of his flock. He wasn't sexually promiscuous, if that's what you are saying. Although, my mother did tell me that he was obsessed with her, and she did say that she would do anything for him.'

'We are not here to judge, but we have to investigate rumours and speculation, to see if there is any truth in them. We have been told that you are in possession of lewd, or artistic, depending on your viewpoint, pictures which belonged to Father Connor O'Doherty. Is this true?'

Lily shivered, her body stiffened, her eyes watered. 'Josie Cartwright,' she said. 'You've been talking to Josie Cartwright. She never could keep a secret that one.'

'We are not trying to discredit the Reverend, we just need to understand what happened back then, and if there were secrets we need to know about them.'

Chapter 33

'Can you confirm that Father Connor's box of photographs still exists?' said Charley, in a matter-of-fact manner. 'What we are trying to establish is whether these pictures could be connected to the murder of the woman that we discovered in the cellar at Crownest.'

Lily kept her facial expression so impassive that her emotions were unfathomable.

Charley turned to Mike, which was the indication for him to continue the questioning, in the hope that he could get Lily to open up to them.

Sympathetically, he leaned towards the frail woman. 'We are investigating a murder that occurred many years ago.' Mike's voice was soft and reassuring. He repeated their line of questioning. 'We are not investigating the taking of the photographs to discredit Father Connor O'Doherty as you might think,' he said, 'but what we are trying to establish is, could these photographs be of assistance to us in identifying the murder victim buried in the cellar?'

Still the old lady's face was unreadable.

'This is really important. If the pictures can't help us then that is the end of this line of enquiry. Do you understand?' asked Mike.

At that moment, Charley saw the sun shine through the stained-glass window at an angle that transformed the adjacent wall into a colourful mosaic.

Oblivious to what Charley was looking at, Mike carried on. 'You see sometimes Lily, through misguided loyalty, people do things that they think might help someone, but in fact it just creates more problems. Does that make sense?'

The room was silent, warm and peaceful. Light turned to darkness when a cloud covered the sun. But the next ray of sunshine, stronger than the last, put the cut-crystal glass vase containing a posy of wild flowers into the pool of light. She counted five; primrose, spear thistle, red campion that was actually bright pink, snowdrops and bee orchid.

Lily's cloudy eyes followed Charley's gaze. 'I assure you I'm not being obstructive. You see, my family and I… we are indebted to Father Michael, who found a way for my father to take my mother into the church instead of the workhouse… and to Father Connor also—' Lily faltered here, '—as what you don't understand, is that later on in life I found out that he was my father by birth.'

'How?' said Mike.

'When Walter, my father, was dying, I was the one who nursed him. When he needed a blood transfusion, I gladly offered mine. But my mother denied me the chance to help him. I screamed and shouted, as I couldn't understand why she would do that.' Lily's face twisted in pain. 'In the end she had no choice but to tell me that it was because she knew it would be futile, because there was no blood connection.'

Charley absorbed the information and picked up on her enquiries. 'But when you saw Connor's photographs, even as a young child you must have suspected that there was something wrong about them?' Charley said. 'Why else would they be hidden? Do you think you didn't tell anyone about them in order to protect Father Connor, or for fear that your home life, as you knew it, would be changed for ever?'

Lily put her hand to her forehead. 'I don't know. I was a young girl. I came across the photographs by accident. Father Connor had sent me to fetch the copy of the precious Saint John's Bible. I felt honoured, and quite nervous. Whilst doing so I must have inadvertently triggered a lever in the sacristy, which opened the secret cupboard. I must have been gone a long time because Father Connor came looking for me, and that's when he caught me looking at the photographs. He made me swear on the Holy Bible that I wouldn't tell, and then he took the box from me, and gave me the Bible as a present. He told me I was his very special girl, and I deserved a gift for my birthday.'

'Do you remember anything else that happened that day?'

'It was a hot, sunny summer's day. He said I could invite all my friends around to my party. He took us down to the stream, and Mum made sandwiches, and jelly. We swam, and played in the garden, until our wet clothes dried and the sun went down. Father Connor loved taking photographs.'

'Did he take photographs that day?'

Lily nodded, 'Yes.'

'Even though he made you swear on the Bible, you did tell someone about the photographs though, didn't you?'

'Josephine… my playmate and the person that I thought of as a sister for a while. We told each other everything. That's why when you told me you knew about the photographs, I knew it had to be her that had told you.'

'Are you still in touch with Josie?'

Lily looked sad. 'No, not long after my eighth birthday party, she vanished. I know it sounds odd, but I was told she had been adopted, and that was that! There were no goodbyes and she was never mentioned again.'

Charley looked surprised. 'Did you ask to see her?'

'Yes, but I was told her new mummy and daddy wouldn't allow it. I remember thinking that if God loved us, why had he done this to us both?'

'Yet you haven't tried to contact her since? Especially now that she is back in the area.'

Lily shook her head. 'I know where she lives, but it is only recently that her adopted father died. I read in the papers he was a hundred years old. Truth is, I didn't feel it was ever the right time to intrude.'

'Do the photographs still exist, Lily?'

The old lady hesitated for a moment. It seemed that her words were caught in her throat. After a few moments, she nodded.

'Can you show us where they are?'

Choked by emotion, Lily's voice wobbled. 'They're still where I found them.'

Charley frowned. Her questioning eyes found Mike's. 'We've searched, haven't we?'

Lily cleared her throat, inviting the detectives to look at her. 'Yes, but there are many secret hiding places in this house of God.' She sensed Charley's frustration. 'Please, don't blame your officers, this is nobody's fault but mine.' Lily stood up, and shuffled towards the door leading into the church. Before she disappeared into a shaft of light, she beckoned them to follow.

The old tin box was easily found. With gloved hands Charley took it from Lily. Tentatively she opened the lid, and fleetingly she looked at a photograph or two inside.

'Do you know any of the people in these photographs?' asked Charley.

Lily closed her eyes, her chin dropped to her chest. 'Yes,' she whispered. 'Father Connor showed me my mother.'

'Now, is there anything else that you can tell us that may shed light upon the skeleton of the female that was discovered at Crownest? Anything else that you are withholding?'

'No,' she said. 'I'd swear on mother's grave, if she had one.'

Charley looked at her questioningly.

'It's a long story. She was cremated, and her ashes were spread up on the hills, free, where she wanted to be.'

–

Back at the office, the detectives took the photographs out of their exhibit envelope with gloved hands. Charley and Mike watched, as each photograph was painstakingly fingerprinted by the CSI, and swabbed for DNA. Each picture was placed in separate see-through exhibits bags and given an exhibit number.

'There is no doubt in my mind that these photographs were taken by a voyeur,' said Charley as she looked down at the Incident Room table where the tagged photographs had been spread out.

With tears in her eyes, Annie tried to look brave. 'Those poor youngsters,' she said looking from one to another.

Mike studied one picture closely. 'Can you pass me the magnifying glass? The one we got the boss as a joke?'

Wilkie moved to open his desk drawer and handed over the glass. 'Getting a bit serious aren't we, Sherlock?'

Annie and Charley moved behind Mike to look over his shoulder. 'That young girl, she looks familiar.'

'Lily? Josie? They all look the same to me.'

'I can't understand why she wouldn't have destroyed these when Connor died,' said Annie.

Annie was subdued. 'She's probably been brought up to think that this sort of thing was normal, and because of the enquiries she is having to revisit her past. She is probably having to come to terms with the fact that the person that she had thought of as her father, was not related to her at all; her mother was prostituted out by her real father, who was the man she looked up to, and a priest to boot. Not only that, by speaking to us, she has had to expose him as a voyeur.'

Silently, Mike lifted and studied photograph after photograph as the others looked on. 'Do you think we've discovered an historic pedophile ring? It was, presumably, unchallenged at the time and maybe interference was dealt with by death?' said Mike.

'You think that it's a possibility that the female corpse we found was a consequence of Father Connor's debauchery?' said Wilkie. 'God forbid what happened to him then when he received the judgement at the pearly gates!'

'I wonder if there is anything buried in the priest's grave that might help us?' said Wilkie.

'Such as a body… or two?' said Mike.

'Exactly,' said Wilkie. He turned to Charley with questioning eyes.

'There'd be outrage if we exhumed a priest.'

'I know that, but it's not going to stop you, if it's needed to solve a murder, is it? Let's face it, it wouldn't be the first time someone has used an existing grave to hide a body, would it?' said Wilkie.

'Hold that thought,' Charley replied, 'but, before we do we'll lean on Lily Pritchard a bit more. I think now she's started to revisit her past, there'll be more forthcoming. For the moment, let's wait and see if there are any fingerprints or DNA on the exhibits, and if so, where that leads us.'

–

Charley's mind was drawn back to the Dixons. A couple of officers from the surveillance team were now on site at Primrose Pastures and had taken up position in the caravan that had been offered to them. This took all responsibility away from Sean Dean at the caravan site to inform the police of the Dixons' return.

The last sighting of the Dixons' motorhome tracked through the automatic number-plate recognition system was on the A64 on the day that the couple had booked into the site. However, in respect of their motorbike, there had been numerous hits, and the team had spent time trawling through the data to see if there was a repeat trip to one place. A common trip for the Dixons appeared to be on the A166, to and from The Tradesman's Cafe, a well-known meeting place for bikers and also renowned for a good breakfast.

According to the surveillance team supervisor, a planned moving stop on the Dixon's bike was feasible along this particular stretch of road. An isolated area, it offered no risk of interference in the operation, accidental or deliberate, from pedestrians or the public.

As she could feel the tension start to build again in the case, Charley liaised with Tim Watson on the phone regarding the firearms operation. 'Is there any point on the A166 that can be identified in advance?' Charley asked, wanting to know as much as she could about the details.

'The Tactical Pursuit and Containment supervisor will call it on the day,' he told Charley. 'Steve Reynolds is the TPAC lead on this operation, and he has a great deal of experience in managing and terminating police pursuits. I've been involved with many of those with him. His forte is stopping fleeing vehicles, including rolling roadblocks, use of spike strips, and his 'box and stop' containment method is a joy to see. Don't worry, we're ready. All's well, ma'am.'

However, Charley *did* worry, because this part of the operation was out of her hands. It had to be delegated to those who confronted armed criminals on a daily basis as this was their area of expertise. But thankfully things were moving at pace and she felt upbeat at the progress.

Tattie stood at Charley's door until she had finished her call, 'The financial investigation team have sent you an update, so I've printed it off for you to read.' She handed over some paperwork to her boss.

The report identified irregularities in the business accounts of Mr Raglan.

'The devious bastard has been money laundering, there is no other explanation!' she exclaimed to Mike as she handed him the summary to be included on the database ten or so minutes later.

Mike pulled up a chair. 'So, in light of this, what's our next move?'

'Raglan's dug his own grave, hasn't he? We will have enough to charge him with something at the end of the day, and his long-standing family business will close when he's dealt with, that's for sure. One person I am still curious about is James Thomas. Nothing has been flagged up for him. Yet I have a strange feeling that he might be part of a much larger, more sophisticated network.'

'Could it be that the Dixons have turned their hand to drug dealing for money, as opposed to armed robberies, and that our players, such as Faisal, Thomas and Raglan know each other better than we think, because of that connection?' said Mike.

'It's a possibility. Let's chase up the cell-site analysis and see if they can enlighten us with any connections via the Dixons' mobiles. You liaise with the drugs team, and I'll liaise with the National Crime Agency. The last thing we want to do if there is an ongoing opera-tion that we are unaware of, is to blow any undercover officers' identity who may be involved, or highlight a police informant's role. Once we get the update, and can confirm no ongoing interest elsewhere, we will strike as soon as we're ready.' Charley's eyes were bright. 'Don't you just love it when a job starts to come together?'

Chapter 34

Charley lay in bed, her thoughts chasing through her mind. The minutes passed, and she tossed and turned, but still she could not fall asleep.

'If you turn a stone over you never know what you might find,' Grandpa had told her, usually before revealing a toad or a newt to startle her. The thought made her smile. What else was to be expected turning over a house built of stone?

Raising herself on one elbow, Charley leaned over to the bedside table in the dark, and with fumbling fingers, found her notebook. But where was her pen? She sighed and flopped back onto her pillows, doing her best to hold on to her patience. Getting angry was not going to magic up a pen into her hand to enable her to transfer the thoughts in her head on to paper, so that she could sleep.

She heard the clock strike three. Charley must have then drifted off to sleep, but she slept fitfully as her dreams woke her repeatedly. She was scared by fragmented images of tormented souls fleeing through Crownest's large, rusty iron gates, as they begged her to listen to their stories and to catch their murderers. 'God does not hold grudges. God decided it was time for her to leave this Earth,' wailed a man nearby, who was dressed in the farmers' clothing of yesteryear, throwing dead bodies, wrapped up in soiled rags tied up with string, into his cart. Where had he appeared from?

Next was an appearance by her grandpa, 'Grandpa,' Charley cried out.

'Trust in God to show you the way,' the old man said, as a warm feeling filled her body, and Charley awoke abruptly to find a pen at her fingertips, and her notebook containing her previous night's thoughts. She looked at the paper, as she hadn't been aware of making the notes or of taking the pen from her bedside table during the night, but she must have done:

> *Possibility of the Dixons having past history of drugs/dealing?*
>
> *Crownest burnt intentionally, whilst being used to grow cannabis plants – intense lighting – hydroponics – cause of fire?*

Whilst reading the almost illegible scrawl below, she questioned her state of mind. The scribbled words made little sense. *Where is she?* was one of the last things she had written in capital letters. *Who should I be looking for?* Anxiety gripped her. Was there another body secreted in the house?

'No!' Charley put her head in her hands, 'Stop!'

Tossing her notebook on the bed, she calmly tried to convince herself that it was nothing more than the ramblings of an overactive mind. 'I will let the evidence speak for itself,' she said. Saying the words out loud felt good. If the Dixons had been using Crownest as a cannabis factory there would have been evidential residue, which there wasn't, and there would have been the well-known smell in the air, which she knew there hadn't been from her first visit to the site.

–

At the Incident Room the morning meeting was eventful. The strategy for the Dixons' arrest was agreed between the two police forces in West Yorkshire and North Yorkshire, and the operational order signed off accordingly by the hierarchy. Things were beginning to move; Charley just wanted the Dixons to do the same.

'The Police Search Advisor and her team have been notified to search the mobile home, to see what evidence we can find after the suspects' arrest,' said Wilkie.

'When the Dixons' have been apprehended I want them to be brought here, to Huddersfield cells. There will be no talking to either of them, but please make notes of anything they say en route. When you arrive, I want them to remain separate at all times, so that they don't have a chance to speak to each other.

Not knowing when the operation would take place, but understanding that it could be imminent, brought about a tension in the office, whilst the day job continued. The atmosphere was electric with expectation. The net was closing in.

After the meeting Charley pulled Mike to one side. 'If I shoot off, I'll be on my way to Wetherby Police Station, with Tim Watson, for a rendezvous with North Yorkshire Firearms Inspector, Steve Reynolds. From there, the three of us will be driven to Primrose Pastures, Filey in the command vehicle. My mobile phone will be on silent.'

Half an hour later Charley was sat with Tattie, in the SIO's office. Charley had been adamant that no one was to disturb them under any circumstances as Tattie desperately needed to obtain signatures on documents that were for the Charley's immediate attention.

Her mobile phone rang. Without introduction, the observation supervisor spoke. 'The blue Kawasaki motorbike registered to the Dixons has pulled up alongside their mobile home, ma'am. There are two people on board, both wearing identical black leathers and helmets. We are unable to ascertain which is Brad, and which Brittany, at this time. The pair are having a good look around them. A large holdall is being taken from the rear pannier. They are now making their way to the mobile home.'

'I'm on my way,' Charley said. To Tattie's surprise she jumped to her feet, threw on her jacket, picked up her bag and bid her goodbye in a matter of seconds.

'Mike, it's started. I'm on my way.'

–

As she sat inside Tim's car Charley caught her breath. Game on, she tried to control the adrenaline racing through her veins. Any firearms operation was dangerous for all involved.

'Doggy bag?' said Tim. One hand on the wheel, he passed Charley a brown paper bag before setting off, meanwhile finishing the half-eaten sandwich hanging from his mouth. 'We don't know when we are going to eat again, so I thought I'd grab us some food to eat on the way. It'll take us approx an hour and fifteen minutes to get to York at this time of day.'

Charley took off her coat, tossed it into the back of the car, and rolled up her sleeves. Taking the bottle of cold water from the paper bag, she drank thirstily. When she finished, she gasped for air, wiping the sweat from her brow with her forearm.

'Not hungry?' asked Tim, watching her place the bag on the floor between her feet.

Charley rested against the headrest and shook her head from side to side.

He looked concerned. 'You okay? Your face looks as if you've run a marathon.'

The rush of adrenaline had subsided, and Charley suddenly felt drained. 'I'm good,' she said, with a deep sigh and a sideways smile.

Tim enthusiastically continued to air some of the aspects of the operation. 'Steve is waiting for us in Enterprise. Enterprise!' he laughed. 'Sounds like something out of a space movie doesn't it, not a make-do transit van. I wonder who named it?'

Charley raised her eyebrows. 'I guess some wanker they pay to sit on his arse all day, procrastinating.'

Tim continued as if he hadn't heard. 'Sounds like the Dixons might have bedded down. Might 'ave had a long drive. For how long is anyone's guess. Doesn't help me, not knowing how long to keep this present team in a state of readiness, before replacing them. They can't be on high alert for too long.'

Charley watched the two Firearms Tactical Team advisors greet each other. It was apparent that the two were well-acquainted, having been together on incidents and courses over the years, judging by the tales they told about each other, many of them humorous. Despite Steve being slightly built, he had powerful shoulders. She was relieved that the pair had restored her good spirits, because being driven on the northbound A1 in a windowless tin can, which acted as her temporary mobile office, was certainly not a comfortable experience. As they neared the location, her buoyant feelings gave way to tension, and the hour's journey in Enterprise became even less enjoyable as the three concentrated on their upcoming roles in the imminent operation. Waiting for the off was an anxious time. They had to hope that their preparations would cover all eventualities.

Suddenly, the voice of a member of the observation team came over the dedicated radio channel. Instantly all banter stopped dead, and there was silence. Holding their breath, they listened intently.

'It looks like we may have an off. Two bikers in black leathers with backpacks, at the motorbike now. Repeating two bikers in black leathers believed to be targets one and two at the motorbike now.'

All members of the team listening to the channel heard the news. The Dixons were on the move.

The next message came with a heightened edge to the officer's tone. 'We have an off, off, towards exit of the site. Keeping within the requested speed restrictions of five miles an hour at this time.'

Charley concentrated hard, glad that the officer with 'eyeball' repeated for clarity and changes in direction.

'We are presuming that the rider is Brad, and Brittany is the passenger. According to intelligence gleaned from the campsite, Brittany had only ever been seen as the pillion passenger,' said Steve.

'At the exit of the campsite we now have a left, left onto the A165 heading north towards Scarborough, speed is a steady fifty miles an hour.'

The plain-clothes surveillance unit who were following at a distance, took over the running commentary as they had 'eyeball'. The motorbike continued north, onto the A615. It wasn't long before they were taking a right turn onto A64 towards York.

Charley's heartbeat had increased dramatically, and she expected her colleagues' had too. It didn't matter how many times she had been in this situation, when the targets were armed, and lives were at risk, it always affected her the same.

The update from the unmarked car following came minutes later. 'Speed increased to seventy, seven zero, still heading in the direction of York on the A614.'

'I'm confident they're heading to the repeated location that's showed up on ANPR,' said Steve.

'The Tradesman's Cafe,' said Tim.

'Breakfast or a drop?' said Charley. 'Or both. Let's hope we're right, because that's what we anticipated and planned for.'

'At their speed it won't be long now before they reach the location of the intended intercept,' said Steve. 'What works best from experience, is choosing a point on the road where our temporary traffic lights bring the traffic into a single lane. Road blocks are ready to move into place front and behind the suspect, so that the only vehicles on this stretch of road will be the motorbike and the armed police unit. Nothing, and no one else.'

'An off-road bike and rider is now in place at the rear of the surveillance, ready to be called forward if required, just in case they go where the four-by-fours can't,' confirmed Tim, in line with their earlier discussions.

'Where's the helicopter?' asked Charley, seeking the 'eye in the sky' above.

'Not available; we will have to work with what we have,' said Tim.

Steve nodded.

Silence was once again observed.

'Targets now approaching temporary traffic lights at location of intercept. Targets now approaching temporary traffic lights at location of intercept. Targets slowing down as they approach red light, targets slowing down at red light.'

Charley found it difficult not being inside one of the pursuit cars with visible contact, but she knew from the radio commentary exactly what was happening. She found herself holding her breath. It was almost time to act.

The commentary started again, almost immediately.

'Target not stopping at red light. Repeat target not stopping at red light. They have continued through the red light. We are in pursuit.'

The distance through the traffic lights was short, but the route took a right-hand bend which resulted in the drivers not being able to see what was ahead of them.

'Strike! Strike!' ordered Steve.

Armed response vehicles now sped forwards at both sides of the traffic lights, blocking the road in front and behind the target's vehicle.

'The bike has broadsided. The bike has broadsided!' The engine could be heard revving.

'Armed challenges now being made.'

'Armed police! You on the motorbike, turn off the engine and step off the machine!'

'They're not thinking they can escape, are they?' asked Charley.

More police units were now in position, physically blocking any possible exit.

The challenges were still being made and getting no response.

'Target is still revving engine. A passenger has dismounted, taking steps away from the bike. Passenger now kneeling on one knee.' The running commentary continued.

'Put your hands above your head,' came the shout loud and clear, along with the continuous instructions to the rider to turn off the engine.

'Passenger not complying. Handgun produced, held in both hands, rested on knee. Three shots fired!' was the relay, as came the noise of the weapon being discharged.

Chapter 35

The police returned the gunfire, and the shooter slumped to the ground. As still as a snake, watchful and unseeing at the same time, Charley prayed.

'One target neutralised,' were the next impassive words by the commentator.

The passenger lay motionless, spread-eagled on the tarmac. The police had blocked the rider's path in both directions as their shouted warnings went unheeded.

'Rider, turn off the engine, and dismount with your hands above your head,' was the command from the armed officers, as they moved forwards from the cover of their vehicles.

'The rider remains on the bike, revving the engine, looking for a way out,' said the observer.

Within a fraction of a second, Charley heard the motorbike's high-revving engine.

'Rider attempting to go off-road. Off-road police rider in pursuit.'

The Kawasaki engine reached its peak, Charley could hear, and she could sense the power of it.

Charley could feel, not see, the bike in mid-air, the wheels spinning. The engine was noisily whining, as the rider instinctively throttled back. She closed her eyes and cringed, imagining the inevitable impact on the turf.

The commentator gave an immediate update, with his controlled breaths coming in short, sharp gasps. 'Target has lost control!' he cried. 'Now he's off the bike in a ditch, motionless.'

Armed officers pointed their weapons directly at the body that was face down in the dirt, twisted in pain.

'Target two neutralised. First aid to both suspects, paramedics required immediately. Weapon of suspect secured.'

Emergency life-saving treatment was quickly given to the shooter, while the team were waiting for the paramedics. 'Two bullets to the chest, one to the cheek. Person confirmed as the female partner,' reported the observer.

'That'll do,' Tim said out loud, as he readjusted his sitting position.

Meanwhile, the other suspect, who was identified as Brad Dixon, was quickly hoisted to his feet and arrested, his sore and bloodied hands handcuffed together behind his back. The bike, rocking and thrusting on the ground, was finally silenced.

The sound of the paramedics' siren could be heard, wailing louder and louder, as the ambulance approached the scene, from the nearby service-station car park, where they had been waiting on standby, for the call to move forward.

Within minutes of their arrival, they had pronounced Brittany Dixon dead at the scene.

The silence in the command vehicle was broken as it also moved at speed.

Tim Watson's face was grave. 'Have you had many dealings with the Independent Office for Police Conduct, because I suspect that's where this case is going.'

Charley nodded. 'I worked in the Met for a few years, and was involved in several incidents that were referred to the IOPC, as the police watchdog.'

'Everything was being videoed and recorded, so my main concern is that we allowed three shots to be fired before the target was neutralised, that could have been three dead police officers... thankfully none were hurt, but everything will come out in the debrief,' Tim said.

An investigation, on top of an investigation was not something Charley looked forward to, but the positive side was that the incident was in the domain of the North Yorkshire Police, which meant that it was one less investigation that she would have to take charge of, leaving her to continue with the murder investigation. It was an excellent piece of police work, and the inevitable confrontation was one that was always around the corner for violent assailants such as the Dixons.

The door of Enterprise was opened, and Charley could hear voices coming from outside, all demanding attention from the command team. Just then the uniformed duty inspector pulled up alongside in a marked car; he was the person with whom it was her job to liaise. He was the officer who would ensure the road was kept closed in both directions and that the scene was preserved whilst a homicide investigation commenced, but Charley knew already that the outcome would be a lawful killing. She felt for the officers who had discharged their weapons. Whilst the team constantly practiced for armed confrontations like this, they never wanted to have to use firearms.

'The on-duty Assistant Chief Constables from both forces have been informed of the fatal shooting,' he told Charley. 'Professional Standards have been called out as part of the ongoing investigation.'

'Once they arrive, I'll be off,' said Charley. 'Can you ensure that you get duty statements from everyone involved? The IOPC watchdog will need them, but we'll also need copies ASAP, please, for our Incident Room, as the suspects are wanted on suspicion of robbery and murder.'

Steve Reynolds overheard her request. 'Tim and I will deal with the surveillance and firearms officers' statements,' he said, pulling Charley to one side. 'I've just been informed that two of the assailant's shots hit the police car. We're bloody lucky there were no further casualties.'

Charley felt her stomach turn; she let out a long low breath. 'Once Dixon has been checked over, I'll arrange for him to be taken straight to the cells at Peel Street, and of course, he'll have to be told that his wife is dead, if he isn't already aware.'

Steve nodded his head towards the crumpled body of the woman, whose body remained where she'd died. 'As if it isn't obvious.'

Charley looked about her. Her usual SIO role, taken over by the North Yorkshire Police SIO Detective Superintendent Barlow and his second-in-command, Detective Inspector Walker, left her as the spectator. There was much activity. She could see the inner and outer scene cordons being identified, and the area taped off by experienced officers. The damaged police vehicle remained *in situ*, the bullets to the passenger side door, just below the window, a reminder of how lucky the officers had been.

Three shots had been fired in response by the firearms officers, all of which had hit their target, the shooter Brittany Dixon. Brad Dixon had been left with superficial injuries which had been attended to by paramedics. Charley wondered did Brad also have a gun on his person?

'Dixon's quite subdued,' said the duty inspector.

'Most likely in shock,' replied Charley, 'but, I can't say I've much sympathy. It's the risk you take when you point at gun at someone. Now he knows what it feels like to be on the receiving end,' she said. 'Brittany had enough warnings to put her weapon down, but she chose not to.'

Charley waved, as she climbed into the marked car to be taken to Wetherby Police Station for the debrief. She knew from past experience firing weapons, that most had hair triggers, three shots fired in the blink of an eye. The time she had spent training at the police firing range had been an eye-opener. The array of weapons she had fired included a sawn-off shotgun and a Second World War machine gun, which was capable of firing seventy-five rounds in seconds. It showed her the impact of different firearms and their capability – something that had stayed with her through her career.

'Debrief in about an hour?' Steve Reynolds shouted.

Charley felt her shoulders relax in relief as she rode in the rear of the police car. There was plenty to talk to Brad Dixon about in an interview, but she was eager to know if the gun Brittany Dixon had fired, which for now was part of the investigation into her death, was a Russian Baikal semi-automatic pistol, and importantly, if it was the same gun which had killed Faisal Hussain and had been used in the Chaudry shop robbery. She turned to look out of the window, to see the calming fields passing by in a haze of flat green-and-brown landscape. Her thoughts turned again to the firearms officers – the firearms team was under constant demand due to their specialist role, and they were forever being tested. No one wanted to kill another human being, but if that was what was asked of them, then they were highly trained to do just what they had done today. Primarily though, she knew what had yet to be discussed, and it was a concern to her, Steve and Tim as the advisors on the scene. Why had they let Brittany Dixon fire any shots at all? Charley, despite her questioning, had nothing but praise for the men and women who put themselves at risk, on a daily basis, in front of someone who was armed.

–

'The gun that was used today has been identified as a Heckler and Koch pistol,' said Steve Reynolds.

Charley was sitting beside Steve and Tim, at the front of the team. She turned to see his face. 'No, that can't be!' Charley desperately wanted to shout – not a Baikal? Instead she swallowed hard, and continued to take notes, in silence.

On arrival back at the Incident Room at Peel Street, Mike Blake was the first to greet her. He followed her through CID and into her office, carrying two mugs of coffee. It was dark outside.

'One survivor, one dead. We were lucky no police got hurt. Have you heard an update from Tim?'

Mike shook his head. 'No, but I assume he will be the West Yorkshire Police officer liaison with North Yorkshire force from now on?'

Charley nodded. 'Which will allow us to concentrate on Brad Dixon, now we've got him in the traps. North Yorkshire will deal with the drug seizure, and at some stage will want to speak to Brad Dixon about supplying drugs, but our murder enquiry will take priority.'

'You'll be pleased to hear that Dixon is booked in, looking somewhat sorry for himself, according to Percy Shaw, on-duty Custody Sergeant.'

'Well, his wife has just been shot dead, and he's facing a long time in prison. I guess he's had better days. I'm sure he'll want to see his wife's body at some stage, but he must remain in handcuffs.'

'The gun, it wasn't the one that killed Faisal Hussain, I understand?'

Charley shook her head. 'Sadly, no. It makes you wonder if it still exists.' She took a deep breath. 'Just minor details, have faith, as what do I always tell you, Mike?'

'The evidence will always speak for itself.'

—

Charley was in the custody suite stood before ex-army commander Percy Shaw in the cell area. 'All okay?' she asked the old-timer.

'Dixon had two possessions on him. Two thousand pounds in cash, folded in wads of one-hundred-pound notes, and the other a key, which he says is for his mobile home. It's been recorded as an exhibit and taken by the search team.'

'Bet they'll be chomping at the bit to get on with the search, I know I would.'

The sergeant's shirt, Charley noticed, bulged a little too tightly across his belly. His hooded blue eyes looked nostalgic for a moment. 'Those were the days ma'am, when we went out and searched our 'scns,' he said. The old man's grin was toothy, and wide, under his thick, grey moustache which sat beneath his button mushroom nose, completely hiding his top lip. However, the absence of his top lip was completely compensated for by his bulbous bottom lip, which was set in a slightly perpetual pout.

Did the fact that Charley didn't feel more emotionally upset about the fact that Brittany Dixon had been shot dead mean she was growing insensitive, she wondered. Or was her contained mood down to the overwhelming feeling of relief she felt given that the threat had been neutralised quickly and no one else had been killed, mainly due to the dedication and the professionalism of the officers involved? The operation had undeniably been a success.

Back in the Incident Room, updates were coming in quick and fast. No more firearms had been found, yet the search of the Dixon mobile home continued. Numerous items had been seized, along with the motorhome itself, which had monetary value and would be ultimately dealt with under the Proceeds of Crime Act.

Annie sat at the table with Wilkie looking expectantly at Charley's door, waiting for the debrief. 'Brittany Dixon had some balls to kneel in the road, and take careful aim at the cops,' she said.

'Balls?' gasped Wilkie. 'Stupidity more like.'

Wilkie and Annie exchanged a duelling stare. 'Or maybe she relished the fact that she and Brad were destined to die in an ambush, just like Bonny and Clyde?' Annie paused. 'I wish they'd found the Baikal weapon, which would have undeniably given us a lever with Brad Dixon.'

Charley's mobile rang as she stepped out of her office. She stopped, listened intently for a moment or two. Her face lit up. She walked a few more steps towards them. Her eyes went to the ceiling. 'Thank you, God,' she whispered. 'Love you big time.'

Annie's eyes searched Charley's face.

Eyes shining, smile wide, Annie's superior carefully put her phone down on the table in front of her.

'Guess what? Taped under the bonnet of the motorhome was a Baikal semi-automatic pistol,' she said, excitedly.

'Crafty bastards,' said Wilkie.

Chapter 36

'Pretend you're sitting on the coast of Santorini, not at your desk,' Winnie said, reaching into her tartan trolley bag. Without Winnie's help the meal run would not have been done, leaving those who hadn't brought sustenance with them from home, with none. Winnie put Charley's sandwich down carefully in front of her.

Instinctively Charley grabbed her cold, bony hand, and rubbed it hard to increase the circulation. 'What would we do without you?' she said, meaningfully.

Winnie squeezed her fingers as tight as her arthritis would let her, before wheeling the trolley out into the CID office to hand out the food supplies to the others. 'I'm glad to be useful, but it's always nice to be appreciated, thank you,' she said, with feeling. Charley watched her through the window that looked into the CID office. Winnie must have sensed her watching her as she turned and gave Charley one of her warm, comforting smiles. Charley picked up a tomato, and nibbled it between her teeth. Winnie's smile had never changed in all the years Charley had known her, and she wondered if that was what her father had first fallen in love with, all those years ago. The thought came to her that Winnie could quite easily have been her mother.

Winnie popped her head around Charley's office door before she left. 'I'm off to Josie's this afternoon to order some jams and pickles, if you want some,' she said. 'Let me have your order before I clock off at half past two.'

Wilkie sat at her elbow and sank his teeth into his well-filled teacake. 'Part-timer!' he mumbled.

'There's nothing wrong with my hearing, you cheeky bugger,' Winnie replied, giving him one of her throaty laughs. 'I've been here since half past six cleaning up after you mucktubs.'

Ricky-Lee was quiet, as he studied his lunch as if it was a great work of art.

'Yes, it's a sandwich: salad and meat, or cheese, placed on or between slices of bread,' joked Annie.

'The sandwich was named after John Montagu, fourth Earl of Sandwich,' Ricky-Lee said.

'Everybody knows that,' she said.

'Ah, but I bet you didn't know that the third of November is National Sandwich Day?'

'That's relevant, because…?'

Ricky-Lee looked at Annie with a surprised expression, even though he wasn't really surprised.

'Since when have you been interested in a sandwich, other than it fills your cake 'ole, and it stops you talking bullshit for a couple of minutes?' Wilkie slurred, around a mouthful of sausage roll.

Warm gravy spilled down Annie's chin, and she quickly caught the running liquid in a napkin. 'Since he copped off with the girl in the sandwich shop.' The meat pie garbled her words.

Ricky-Lee turned his head to face her. 'No comment,' he chuckled, but Charley noticed the twinkle in his eye.

'Don't speak with your mouth full, Annie,' snapped Tattie, with a scowl. 'It's not very ladylike.' Wilkie's mouth dropped open. 'What, young Molly Fisk? No way! She's got legs up to her armpits. You lucky bastard,' he said, much to Ricky-Lee's amusement.

Annie's eyes were slitted. 'Beauty is in the eye of the beholder. What do you say, Tattie?'

'My mother always said the way to a man's heart is through his stomach. I guess she wasn't wrong. In fact I'm betting on it,' she said, with a wink.

Annie giggled. 'Tattie, you little minx, you've kept that quiet, haven't you?'

Working lunches were not ideal, but this enquiry demanded it, as major enquiries often did. And a decent lunch was often what the team needed to bond together, as enquiries regularly took them on different paths out of the office, and the briefings and debriefs were more formal affairs, with others from different departments taking part. With Dixon's custody time clock ticking, the afternoon was to be used for collating information against Dixon, pulling all the facts together, and obtaining links with Crownest in preparation for his first interview.

'Brad Dixon is with his solicitor,' Charley told them, 'but I know, looking at the work we have to do, it is highly unlikely we'll get to speak to him before tomorrow.'

Her duty statement about the shooting in North Yorkshire had been completed, and at the same time, she had requested that the head of West Yorkshire CID thank North Yorkshire for their professionalism and support in the joint operation. Tim Watson was to call to see her, to collect her statement, and she toyed with the idea of letting Tattie know that the firearms tactical advisor would soon be returning, but decided she would wait until the end of the working day. Tattie was required to concentrate on her work, and not to sit day-dreaming, repainting her lips and checking her hair was in place, or to rush off home to make cookies while there was still a mountain of work to get through.

The few watched the rest gathering in the Incident Room. 'Just because we've made an arrest doesn't mean our enquiries are complete, far from it,' Charley said at the briefing. 'The pressure is on, and for those who haven't worked on a major incident before, the initial detention period of twenty-four hours will pass in a flash. When you take into consideration Dixon's rights for rest periods, toilet breaks, exercise and meal times, there is little time left for interviewing him. I know it is tough to have him rule our next few days but, in my experience, it is best to keep him sweet and on our side, as it will give us the results in the shortest possible time, and that's best for us all in the end.'

'Will you be asking Divisional Commander Stokes for the twelve-hour extension afterwards?' asked Annie.

'Without a doubt, owing to the amount we've got to talk to him about. I'm expecting to be going to the Magistrates' Court to request that they grant us the extra thirty-six-hour detention, too. Unless Dixon rolls over at the first interview, of course.' Charley allowed herself a brief smile at the thought.

Instinctively she looked up at the clock above the door, making a mental note to keep her eye on Dixon's custody clock, as she was required to attend the Magistrates' Court within the last hour of the extended twelve-hour detention as granted by the Divisional Commander, should they not have enough evidence to charge the suspect. However, if the results from other agencies, such as Forensics, came back very quickly she might not need the extra time.

Charley put her hands together on the table, as if in prayer. 'His detention clock started when he arrived in the cells. You need to be made aware that Dixon has not admitted to the historical armed robbery offence at Manchester Road, which is our holding charge for him. He's not going to be bailed, which is a good thing. Theoretically, we have enough evidence to charge him with the offence, but I'd like to know more about the murder of Faisal Hussain before I do, in an interview, if possible. I'm hoping Dixon might talk to us. Having said that, he has just witnessed his wife and partner-in-crime shot dead in front of him. That won't, I suggest, encourage him to talk to us, and I daresay his brief from his solicitor will advise him to make no comment, but we're used to that, and it won't deter us from putting questions to him, and giving him the opportunity to reply. Admissions are always helpful, but as we know, not always necessary. We have a lot to do, so let's get to it,' she said as she gathered her notes in front of her, and rose from her seat. 'Mike, Annie, can I see you in my office now, please, to talk about interview strategies, and,' she turned to Ben and Terry from the cold-case team, 'I want you two to interview him for the armed robberies.' Charley raised her brows. 'I bet Brad Dixon has never felt as popular. Will he enjoy all the attention, who knows?'

'The drugs team and National Crime Agency have been given his details, so I imagine they will want to speak to him as well with regard to drug distribution at some stage,' said Mike.

'Of course, but we have priority, so let's use the time we have with him wisely.'

–

Charley consulted her computer in her warm office. It was raining outside, heavily and noisily, and the sky was full of dark, thunderous clouds. The overhead light was on, and it lit up her office as if it was daylight. 'I'll be watching the interviews via a video link,' she said to Mike and Annie. 'I want to see first-hand what Dixon's body language tells me. Both of you are tier five trained advisors, you know as well as I do that we can't expect much from this interview, but it'll go one of two ways: he'll either throw his hands in the air and talk for England, knowing that he's bang to rights, or, he'll clam up like a shell and we won't get as much as a peep out of him.' Charley leaned towards them. 'I'd particularly like to establish a link to confirm Dixon's relationship with Raglan and Thomas. We already know that Brad Dixon was charged with burglary at Raglan's Estate Agency some years ago, but surely that can't be the only connection, can it?'

'Maybe we'll find their contact details on the Dixons' mobile phones which have been seized?' said Annie.

Charley crossed her fingers in front of them. 'Let's hope so.'

'Have we any new information on Thomas's financial situation and the money laundering?' asked Mike.

Charley shook her head. 'No, I've seen nothing as yet. However, for the interviews, just focus on getting relevant information that will help us find out who killed Faisal Hussain,' she said. 'I have a gut feeling that Raglan, Thomas, or one of the Dixons did.'

Walking at a brisk pace, the interviewing officers' footsteps could be heard echoing in the otherwise empty corridor that lead to the interview suite, under the gaze of the CCTV cameras. Their faces were set and determined.

Dixon's solicitor, Frank Maddock had arrived back at the police station, Charley had seen him pull up in the car park from her office window, at the rear of the police station. She was in the wrong job, she mused, as she admired his Audi Quattro.

Nursing her mug of coffee, Charley relaxed back in her chair, and put her feet up on her desk, her eyes flicking from the interview strategy notes she'd worked on with Annie and Mike, to glancing at the monitor ready for their arrival.

All was still and quiet in the interview room, empty of everything apart from a table and chairs that were screwed to the floor. It looked like something out of a scene in a soap opera, she thought. The SIO waited, and after a few moments she put down the file, unable to concentrate on the written word. Suddenly the heavy door opened. Annie entered, followed by Dixon in prisoner's overalls, his solicitor, and lastly, DS Mike Blake, who closed the door behind them. Dixon was facing Mike, and the suspect was sat in the perfect chair for Charley to watch his every move. He looked pale, unsure of himself, even nervous, until he looked up at the camera, where he knew someone would be watching. A satisfied gleam appeared in his eyes. The shock of seeing it hit her, and she had the strongest urge to slap his smarmy face.

Mr Maddock, a local solicitor, was a thin, bald man, dressed in a crew neck grey jumper under his dark suit. His hair was flattened to his head, and he carried a mac over his arm and an umbrella in his hand. In his other hand he held a briefcase. He sat alongside his client, opposite Annie. Calmly and professionally, Mike, after the necessary introductions for recording purposes, outlined the circumstances surrounding the discovery of the body of

Faisal Hussain at Crownest, following the recent Dixons' residence there.

'No comment,' Dixon replied repeatedly to Mike's questions, even though at this early interview stage, the detective sergeant was only asking the prisoner about his lifestyle. This didn't bode well for the controversial questions to come later.

Dixon's responses to Annie's questions were also negative, consistent, and predictable, but Charley was pleased to see that the interviewing officers weren't intimidated by Dixon, or by his demeanour. In fact it appeared to her that with every question put to Dixon, they managed to secure a positive, rhythmic interviewing technique and were comfortable with the agreed strategic approach.

–

'Early days,' Charley assured them when they came out of the interview.

'Let's face it we didn't really expect him to roll over, did we?'

Charley was upbeat. 'Wait until we get around to disclosing the recovery of the gun that was taped under his motorhome's bonnet,' she enthused. 'We haven't disclosed yet that we have found his fingerprints all over the duct tape used either, which connects him nicely to the weapon. Remember, we are still waiting for DNA results and a response from Ballistics. Once that's dropped on his toes, I'd expect a much different response from him.'

Charley felt an ache in her stomach as she left for home late that night. She wanted the results that were outstanding to come in so badly. If they didn't arrive the next day, then she would have no choice but to let Ben and Terry interview Dixon for the historical robberies, and charge him with the ones that they could prove. That would enable her to put Dixon before the courts for a three-day lie down in the police cells, which would enable the necessary interviews for the murder of Faisal Hussain to take place. By then she was hopeful that the results they were eagerly awaiting would be in.

There could be an advantage to this strategy, Charley thought, as she drove along the dark, wet roads that led over the Marsden moors, because by the time Dixon had been charged to appear before the courts for the robberies and could see the evidence stacking against him, he might accept his fate, roll over, and tell her officers about his relationship with Raglan and Thomas. Also, the National Crime Agency would be snapping at his heels by this time due to his alleged drug dealing. The seized mobile phones would ultimately assist in tying all the information together, but time was of the essence for Charley.

–

With no results forthcoming, thirty-six hours later, Brad Dixon was placed before the Court, charged with armed robbery. The prosecution told the Magistrates that this was merely a holding charge, as he was under arrest for more serious crimes. He was duly remanded to police cells for a further thirty-six hours. Time was now pressing and Charley and her team began to feel the pressure.

The morning after Dixon was in court, they received the call they had all been waiting for from the ballistics expert. It confirmed, without doubt, that the Baikal semi-automatic weapon recovered from beneath the bonnet of the motorhome, was the murder weapon used to kill Faisal Hussain. This added enormous weight to the evidence mounting against Dixon. Only Brad Dixon's fingerprints were found on the tape used to secure the gun beneath the bonnet of the vehicle. A further bonus was a later call from Forensics who had identified Dixon's DNA on the weapon.

'Thank you Eira,' Charley said as she took the call. 'I owe you a drink when this is all over.'

Charley bounced out of her office, on a high. 'It's not often we get that much evidence at a crime scene,' she said, taking a large ginger cookie out of the tin and munching it. She looked around. There was someone missing. 'Where's Ricky-Lee?' she asked.

'Day off,' said Tattie. 'Are they okay? I made some of those for Tim…'

'Mmm… delicious,' she replied. 'Who approved that leave then?'

'DS Blake,' said Tattie. 'Do you really think they're okay? I wondered if I'd put a tad too much ginger in them.'

Annie opened her desk. Her eyes were downcast. 'I think you need to know something, boss,' she said, handing Charley a newspaper, marked up for racing day.

Charley put her head in her hands, 'Where did you find it?'

'In the office bin, by the door,' Annie said, glumly.

Wilkie shook his head. 'No, it can't be his. He's stopped, he swore to me it was finished! He wouldn't lie to me.'

'I hope not,' Charley snapped. 'For his sake, and ours.' The SIO tried to smile, but it didn't reach her eyes. 'Let's not jump to conclusions; we're having a positive day, so let's keep it that way.'

Charley got up, walked back to her office and slammed the door.

'Ouch,' said Annie.

Charley took two steps inside before she turned and flung her door open again. 'Find out if there is anyone else's DNA on the gun, will you, and if so, do they know whose it is? I can't understand why Dixon didn't get rid of it after the murder, and why, if it is his weapon, he didn't have it with him that day we arrested him. Brittany was armed.'

'Him saying Brittany killed Faisal would be the easy option under the circumstances,' suggested Mike.

'He'd be there with her though,' added Annie, 'and would he really grass on his dead wife?'

'Of course, he would! However, he's dead in the water whatever he says, isn't he?' said Wilkie.

Charley turned to Mike. 'Did you give Ricky-Lee the day off?'

Mike nodded. 'He said it was either that or his love life was history.'

'Well, let's hope she's allergic to horses! In the meantime, I want you to ensure we are crossing all the Ts and dotting the Is on this case,' snapped Charley as she marched back into her office.

–

It was Dixon's final day in the police cells, before going back to court to be remanded to prison until his trial. Charley stood at Mike's desk.

'Let's interview him one last time and give him a final opportunity to speak to us,' she said.

'I think you're flogging a dead horse meself,' said Wilkie.

'That's what Ricky-Lee's been doing, not us. We've nothing to lose and everything to gain. We'll give Dixon one last chance.'

'That's one determined lady,' said Wilkie, in her wake.

Chapter 37

Having made the required evidence disclosures to Dixon's solicitor, Frank Maddock, and given him time to discuss them with his client, the CID team were now ready for the next interview. Dixon's solicitor looked pale and tired. Four days of toing and froing to the police station at all times of day and night, in the rain, wind and cold, had obviously been draining for the older man. Although he knew his client was involved, he was unsure as to what extent, based on the little Dixon had confided in him.

Mike made a start by outlining the background of the discovery of the body during the demolition.

'Brad, we know you and your wife rented Crownest for a while from Raglan's Estate Agents. They tell us that the cheques you signed in payment, bounced, is that correct?'

Charley watching on the monitor in her office was interested to see Dixon lift his eyes to look at Mike.

Mike's reaction to seeing the corners of Dixon's lips turn upwards into a smile was quick. 'You're smiling. So, is it true?'

Frank Maddock dropped his pen, and as he picked it up, he looked up towards his client, his expression one of surprise at his interaction with the detective sergeant.

'Do I look like someone who uses a cheque book?' Dixon sniggered.

'Mr Raglan also says that you were warned of imminent eviction, but you left without settling the debt? Is that true?' asked Mike, eager not to lose the connection he'd made.

It appeared that once Dixon had started sniggering he could not stop.

'You're obviously finding something amusing. Is there something that you want to share with us?'

'No,' he said. Eyes down, Dixon brushed his thighs with the palms of his hands on his prisoner's suit. He slowly shook his head.

'Mr Raglan is talking to us, he's telling us his story, so if that's not correct, then tell us. I mean, in your younger days you did burgle his offices, so he's not exactly going to do you any favours, is he?'

Dixon's dark, steely eyes stared across at Mike. Was the suspect trying to weigh Mike up or intimidate him, Charley wondered from her vantage point as an observer. If it was the latter, it wouldn't work.

'If Brittany was here, I'm sure she'd be telling you to sort it,' Mike suggested sensitively. 'You know she would.'

Dixon's face twisted, angrily. 'Well, she isn't! You lot fucking made sure of that. You killed her.' For a moment the officer and suspect shared an uneasy glance.

'Brittany did shoot first, Brad,' Mike continued. Charley leant forward to watch the footage carefully. Was that a tear that the prisoner brushed away, at the mention of his wife's name? Could that be the way to break him?

Dixon raised a shoulder and dropped it just as quickly. With eyes downcast, he twiddled his bony hands in his lap.

'I'm sorry for Brittany, but she was always going to go out in a blaze of glory, wasn't she? A shoot-out with the police. Let's face it, she'd have loved that, wouldn't she?'

Mike stopped talking to allow Dixon to take in what he had said. When Brad didn't react, he continued. 'You knew her better than anyone. What happened could have happened on more than one occasion over the last few years, what with you two being so active. How long had you known about the secret passageway between the house and the church?'

A deep frown appeared on Dixon's brow.

'You do know about it, don't you?'

Dixon's silence, and his expression, suggested to Charley that perhaps he wasn't aware of the tunnel, and that puzzled her, as how else would Hussain's body have been dumped there? Or was this what Dixon wanted them to believe?

'Look, I understand Faisal Hussain came to Crownest to sort things out, perhaps looking for revenge for his uncle's death from heart failure sometime after *your* robbery of his shop. Mr Hussain's body was found at Crownest having been shot in the head with *your* gun – the Baikal pistol which we found concealed under the bonnet of *your* mobile home. We know it's your gun because your DNA and prints are all over it. We are also aware that you have discharged this weapon at previous robberies that you are known to have committed. Everything points to you as the killer of Mr Hussain. To emphasise again, as your solicitor has already informed you, your gun's specifications are a ballistic match for Faisal Hussain's execution. We are here to give you the opportunity to speak to us, to explain why that was necessary.'

Dixon remained silent. With cold, hard eyes, he glared at Mike again, and his fists clenched, while the tightening of his facial muscles showed a rhythmic twitch in his jaw.

'Obviously you don't want to talk to us, so let's terminate the interview, and save everyone's time,' Mike barked, looking across at Annie. She nodded agreement and stood; she had remained silent throughout to allow the rapport developing between the men to continue.

Once they had stopped the recording device, Annie and Mike left the interview room quickly, but Mr Maddock and Brad Dixon remained. The detectives had only been back in the Incident Room for a short time when the office phone rang.

Mike was still shuffling into his suit jacket when he came to Charley's door. 'Boss, according to his solicitor, Dixon states he wants to speak to us,' he said, a broad smile on his face.

'Go for it, let's hear what he has to say.'

'Déjà vu,' Mike said, watching Annie close the door of the interview room behind her as she slid into the seat opposite Dixon's solicitor. Frustrating as it was, the necessary procedures of starting the camera and stating who was present had to be followed before the interview could start.

'Now, what was it you wanted to say to us?' Mike asked.

Dixon was slumped in his chair, elbow on the desk, fist to his cheek. 'I didn't kill him,' he mumbled, 'Neither did Britt.'

There was a long pause. Dixon sat back in his chair, and sighed heavily. His eyes lifted and found Mike's face. Charley watched Mike and Annie wait patiently, using silence in the hope that Brad Dixon would continue.

In the SIO's head she counted the beats, the extra silent seconds that might make the difference to Dixon continuing or not.

'I admit it was my gun, okay,' he said eventually, 'but it wasn't me who killed him.'

Mike spoke with some finality in his voice. 'I'm sorry, if that's all you've got to say, it's not enough. You need to tell us who else was there, and explain what happened if you want us to believe what you are now telling us is the truth, because the evidence we have already disclosed to you suggests otherwise.'

Slowly, Dixon turned towards Frank Maddock, who nodded in agreement.

'The first thing you need to know is that Raglan is a drug addict. He's a regular user of cocaine, which he snorts. It gives him the tremors, but he won't stop. He let us live in the house for free, as long as he got his sherbert.' Dixon gave a little nod. He stopped. Waited, it seemed for a reaction, but when he got none from the two detectives, he continued.

'Anyways, Thomas, the money man, says he wants a meet with us with regard to moving us on. He told Raggy to tell us that he would make it worth our while. Raggy arranged it, a meet at Crownest, to do a deal. That night, we're sat having a chat, doing a bit of haggling on a figure we'd accept to see us out of the house without any bother. Raggy was fucking spaced out. He was sat with this stupid grin on his face that I really wanted to wipe off, when suddenly this Asian guy crashed through the front door. At first I thought Raglan or Thomas had set us up; I thought the guy was one of your lot coming for us, but soon I realised that wasn't the case. The next minute this guy has me grabbed in a headlock, and he has a gun pointing up my fucking nostril.'

'What happened then?' asked Mike.

'He's threatening to kill me; it's summat about his uncle dying because me and Britt robbed his shop...' Dixon shrugged his shoulders. 'I couldn't deny it, we might have done. But, what I did know was that we hadn't killed anybody. Then, out of the corner of my eye, I see Raggy reach down the side of the chair he was sitting in and put his hand into my backpack. He pulled out my gun, the one you have, and then, bang, the gun goes off, and I realise I'm still standing, he hasn't hit me, but he has hit the other guy, who drops like a stone at my feet.'

'Are you suggesting that it was an accident?' asked Annie.

Dixon sniggered. 'Put it this way, it was obvious that Raggy had never held a fucking gun 'afore, love. But he probably saved my life.'

Annie's head was to the side and she showed Dixon a blank expression.

'Do you expect us to believe that?'

Dixon shrugged his shoulders. 'That's up to you. I don't really care, but that's what happened.'

'What happened next?' asked Mike.

'Thomas started screaming, and shouting at Raggy, telling him he's killed him and that he didn't want anything to do with it.'

'What then? I presume that you checked to see if the man was alive?'

'I didn't need to. He had a bloody great hole in his head. Britt took over. She slapped Raggy round the face to bring him out of his stupor. Amazing how quick he recovered. But it took us into the early hours to get his body into the hole behind that fucking great fireplace that Raggy knew about. Britt drove his car to his office, and I stood and watched Raggy clear out his safe. We agreed to take the dead man's gun. Then me and Britt, we left, taking the dead man's car with us. The least Raggy could do was pay us for our silence.' Dixon's eyes flashed wide. 'Then would you believe it. We found out that the fucking gun that the guy had on him was an imitation!'

'Where is the vehicle now?' asked Mike.

'Sold it to some car ringers who I know, but I won't name 'em. Got a few quid, and with Raggy's payout, we bought the motorhome and fucked off out of the country till we'd spent up.'

'How much did Raglan pay you?' Annie asked.

'Not enough.'

'Where's Faisal's gun?' Mike probed.

'At the bottom of the deep blue sea,' Dixon replied, in a smug way.

'How's that?' said Mike.

Dixon grinned. 'It sort of fell off over the side of the ferry.'

'Why did you do that when you could have sold it?'

'I told you, it was imitation, and we didn't want someone finding it and linking it to us.'

'Really? I don't believe you. Faisal Hussain is known for carrying a real firearm, and let's face it, he's not going to come after an armed robber with an imitation weapon, is he?' pushed Mike.

Dixon's stare was threatening. 'Prove otherwise,' he said.

'Have you spoken to either Raglan or Thomas since you've been back in the country?' Mike continued, in the hope he would carry on talking.

Dixon shook his head. 'No, why would I?'

'Tell me, I'd be interested to know why you didn't dump the gun we found under the bonnet of the motorhome in the sea, too?'

Brad looked puzzled. 'Because it's mine,' he said.

'Just one last question,' Mike said. 'Why now? Why tell us now after all the denials?'

'Me and Brit were better off on our own. We should have known not to get involved with anyone else. Your boss reminds me of her. She were fucking bossy, too. You were right, when you said before that Brittany would have wanted me to sort it, she would have, and I have now.'

–

'What he's told us is plausible,' said Mike, over his shoulder to Annie who was following him down the corridor to the Incident Room, where Charley was waiting for them.

Charley was smiling. 'Well done,' she said. 'It'll be interesting to hear what Raglan and Thomas say now,' she said. 'Seems to me that Thomas's drug dealing, and Raglan's drug habit involved them in a pointless murder, and it has now secured their downfall. Dixon was right about one thing, the Dixons were better when they worked alone.'

'I think Raglan's ancestors will be turning in their graves if they could see what happened to their business in the hands of their successor. If you think about it, an estate agency is not a bad guise for a money-laundering operation though, is it?' said Annie. 'With the price of houses, who'd question large amounts of money going in and out of the accounts?'

'So, now let's focus on James Thomas and Jonathon Raglan's arrest strategy...'

Chapter 38

The confirmation that Brad Dixon's DNA was the only DNA on the Baikal gun didn't help the credibility of the story he had told in the final interview. Charley felt a little disappointed, she had been hoping for a connection to Raglan, but after all, it didn't mean conclusively that Raglan hadn't touched it.

She scratched her head, her frustrations were palpable to the team. 'We have evidence to arrest Raglan, but we don't have any evidence to charge him.'

'No, I guess the word of a convicted criminal who is trying to get out of a murder charge doesn't quite—' said Annie.

Charley threw her hands in the air, 'It doesn't make sense that Dixon has practically rolled over for everything we put to him, and yet not the murder itself. Don't you think if he'd have done it, he would have confessed? What has he got to lose?'

'Raglan's drug addiction has got him involved with the wrong kind, no doubt about it, and they've used and abused him by getting him to launder the money perhaps; maybe it's payback for something else that we don't know about?' said Annie.

'What?' said Mike. 'Having interviewed Dixon, we both know he's going away for a long time, but he's not that fucked up that he doesn't know if he fired a gun and killed Hussain or not. He doesn't say he was injecting or had been snorting drugs, so we presume he was quite normal, whatever normal is.'

'He's admitted being involved in the murder of Faisal Hussain, and our objective is to put those responsible for Hussain's murder before the courts to be dealt with. I want Dixon charged with murder,' said Charley. 'Even if his story is true, he still assisted an offender by concealment of the body, and the disposal of evidence, and he can still be tried and indicted as a principal. Crown Prosecution might go for a joint enterprise charge, if we're lucky. Whether he co-operates with the National Crime Agency about the drugs, or not, is up to him, and not of any concern to our investigation.'

There was no mistaking Brad Dixon's screams and struggles as he was dragged out of his cell to face the charge. Charley leaned her head back on the cold stone wall of the stairwell to the lower floor, where the cells were. 'I told you who did it. Why don't you morons listen? I'm not fucking guilty!' he shouted at the Custody Sergeant Percy Shaw. Charley watched as he was taken back to his cell.

–

The old building had now been flattened to the ground, and as she approached Crownest, Charley was shocked to see how much the landscape had opened up to show views of the town and surrounding countryside. An old four-wheeled-drive red pick-up truck with a broken number plate filled with stone was at the old gateway to the house. The police officer in her stopped to watch an old man, with some young children helping him, throw more stones in the van. She drove slowly forwards. Finn, the young Irish worker she'd met previously, came into view, kicking the hard ground around a small fire that was burning the last of the debris. She stopped the car alongside him and got out.

The old man looked at the smartly dressed lady who wore an official badge on her lapel, with fear and suspicion etched on his face. He called the children over to him. 'It's the copper I told you about, Da,' Finn shouted. 'She's cool!'

Nevertheless, the old man ushered the kids into the van. 'I haven't done anything wrong, missus, honest I haven't,' he said in his strong Irish accent 'You ask our Finn. He's asked his gaffer if I could 'ave this stone. He's a good lad, our Finn, he looks after his da,' and without so much as a by-your-leave, he climbed into the driving seat and Charley watched him drive off as fast as the vehicle would allow him. Billowing smoke poured out of the exhaust. The van coughed and spluttered as it disappeared over the hill to the valley below.

'Shit scared of you lot, is mi' Da,' Finn laughed. 'He's had his collar felt so many times for wrongdoing, when in fact he was just in the wrong place at the wrong time. Swears he's framed.'

Charley laughed. 'A little bit of fear never harmed anyone, my dad used to say.'

'Exactly, but he never seems to learn! I can't count how many times a copper has brought him home drunk rather than put him in a cell, much to mi Ma's horror.'

'I'll bet she probably refuses to open the door, told 'em to take him back, and bring him back sober? Am I right?'

Finn chuckled. 'That sounds about right.'

Charley glanced down at the fire. 'Tell me there aren't bones in there, are there?'

'No,' he laughed. 'The demolition team have gone, and we're moving on to a new site on Monday. I'm just cleaning up the last bits of rubbish,' Finn looked around him. 'I can't say I'm sorry to see the back of this job,' he said.

Charley scanned the site. 'Is the boss around?'

Finn nodded in the direction of a portacabin, just in time to see Joe Greenwood coming out of his office. Joe raised his hand in Charley's direction and headed briskly towards her, and had started a conversation with her long before he reached her. 'The foundations will be in and the outer shells up before you know it, once the builders start. Any news on the identity of the bodies?'

'We're getting there slowly; it's surprising what you can get from fragments of bone. Thank you for calling it in,' she said sincerely. 'I know it caused you a lot of sleepless nights, and aggro, but you did the right thing. You'll be pleased to know we have one person charged with murder, and a couple of others yet to speak to, so keep watching the news.'

Joe sighed deeply. 'Yes, well, in the end they are each somebody's relative, and whoever they are, they deserve a proper burial.' All of a sudden his eyes lit up. 'While you're here, give me a minute, I've got something for you.'

'Really? Did one of team leave something behind?'

When Joe returned from inside the cabin, he was carrying something wrapped in a dirty old piece of hessian cloth. He was out of breath from rushing. 'A present,' he said unwrapping it. A dark oak wood sign, the size of a letterbox, had the words 'Crownest' carved into it.

Charley was touched. 'Young Finn 'ere saved it from the fire,' he said. 'We thought maybe you'd like it.'

'Thank you,' she said taking hold of the sign. 'I'll keep it in the Incident Room. Have you seen any more of James Thomas? Happier these days now the buildings down, I'm sure?'

'No, I haven't. Rumour has it that he's sold the land to another builder. That's how he makes his money apparently, buying and selling.' Joe raised an eyebrow. 'I understand he has his fingers in a lot of pies.'

—

On arrival back at the station, Charley immediately headed for the movable boards in the Incident Room, which held the pictures of those involved in the case, important facts and dates. These boards acted as a visual aid of vital information which was readily available for all the team members.

'I want to discuss the arrest of Jonathan Raglan, for murder and money laundering,' she said to Mike. She was thoughtful for a moment. 'Whilst we're at it, let's get James Thomas locked up at the same time, then there's no chance of their contacting each other, if they have something to hide.'

'I wonder whose arse will drop out first?' said Wilkie.

Mike didn't take long to consider the question. 'If what Dixon told us is true, I think Thomas will sing like a canary.'

'No doubt they'll have already heard through the media about Brittany's death, what with the headlines, and also about Brad's arrest,' said Ricky-Lee.

'Yes, and who knows, that might make them feel safer,' asked Charley.

'Both their addresses have already been assessed for the lock-up and the searching thereafter, boss,' Wilkie told her. 'Jonathan Raglan's home is a bungalow, run down, no kerbside appeal, easily accessible. He isn't married, nor does he have a live-in partner that we are aware of, so I don't expect to find anyone else at the address. In contrast, James Thomas lives in a very large, new, detached house in the corner of a small cul-de-sac of four houses. It has a private driveway accessed by electric gates. The distance between their houses is approximately twenty-five miles.'

'We need to make sure we have the ability to open those gates. I don't want us stuck outside – that would be embarrassing,' she added.

'It's already sorted, boss.'

'Of course it is, what else would I expect from a cop with so many commendations?' she said with a wink, as she walked away. 'You are one dark horse, DC Wilkie Connor.'

Wilkie sounded puzzled. 'Who's been talking about me?' he called. Swivelling around on his office chair, he looked for a guilty face or two, but there were none.

Tattie scurried into her office the minute Charley sat down at her desk, with a pile of letters that she had typed for the SIO to sign. 'I hope you don't mind, but I gave Tim your statement about the shooting, that was on your desk. He came to pick it up this morning while you were out.' Charley smiled, and with her head down, she scribbled her signature on one letter, after another. 'What did he think of the cookies?'

'He ate them all, and he promised he'd be back to see me for more,' she said, gliding out of the office, as if on a cloud, with a smile on her face.

'I'll bet,' Charley muttered as Annie walked in.

'Say it again,' said the young DC, as she stood at the side of Charley's desk, two cups in her hand.

Charley slowly shook her head. 'Oh, nothing,' she said. 'Are we ready for the briefing tonight?'

Annie nodded her head enthusiastically, passed Charley her mug of coffee, and sat down. 'Can I just go over a few points in the operational arrest strategy with you?' She lowered her voice. 'Wilkie has tasked me with it and I don't want to disappoint.'

It was Charley's turn to nod her head. Sitting back in her chair, she sipped the hot drink. 'Go ahead, I was just about to make notes.'

Annie sat on the edge of her chair. 'Each team will include officers from the financial investigation unit. They are already aware over at FIU.' She looked up at Charley for a nod of approval. 'Their expertise will be useful for advice in the money-laundering aspect.'

'Good point,' said Charley.

'Two POLSA search teams are arranged, one for each address. Sniffer dogs for drugs, money and firearms will be joining us.'

'Great. The dogs will be sure to find anything much quicker than we could.' Charley looked thoughtful. 'For the interview with James Thomas, I want to be firm, but fair. Being arrested will be devastating for him hopefully. He has no previous convictions at all, as far as we know.'

Annie busily noted Charley's requests, to add them to the document to be circulated to the teams involved.

'Or maybe he's never been caught,' suggested Annie.

'True. We will need a back-up team of officers searching Raglan's address to get the keys for the estate agency premises at the same time. This will save their having to force the door.'

Charley spoke her suggestions out loud, and Annie was finding it hard to keep up with her. How she wished, at that moment, that she had listened to the nuns, who had insisted that shorthand would be useful to her one day.

'I also want both Raglan and Thomas to be brought to our custody suite, where they can be booked in, and placed in a cell until the interview teams are ready to speak to them,' Charley concluded, much to Annie's relief.

–

Charley opened the briefing. An air of anticipation filled each corner of the room which was packed with officers, all eager to hear what the head of CID had to say.

'These briefings are always an anxious time for everyone, as we all want the operation to go to plan in order to achieve the best results. However, I am hoping when you leave this meeting you will be confident of your role, so much so that you will get a good night's sleep, and we can move off swiftly tomorrow morning at six-fifteen, without the need for any further discussions, unless they are urgent.'

Ben and Terry sat beside each other. Charley watched intently, to see how Ricky-Lee reacted in their presence, but at no time did the detective rise to their banter. He even joined in confidently, she was pleased to note. Sometimes, she had learnt it was better to do nothing when she was angry, as she had been with Ricky-Lee; it was obvious to her now that he was working through his issues in his own way, in his own time, and she felt proud of him.

'Have you an update on the robbery at Mr Chaudry's shop?' Mike asked the pair from the cold-case team.

'Yes, we've talked to Brad Dixon following your inter-view with him, and liaised with Mr Chaudry's close relatives to inform them that Brad Dixon has been charged with the robbery at the store, as well as the murder of Mr Hussain,' said Ben.

Charley continued with the brief. It was important at this stage that everyone understood the links in the case. 'Brittany Dixon was shot dead by armed officers after she open fire on them. At the same time, her husband who was unarmed, was arrested. These two had been wanted for outstanding cases of armed robbery. Brad Dixon has now been with charged with the cold-case offences. One of these offences of armed robbery was where a gun was discharged. This was at an off-licence, where six weeks later, the owner who had confronted the Dixons, died of a heart attack. Faisal Hussain was his nephew, and was searching for the Dixons because of this, we presume for some sort of retribution. Hussain was by no means an angel. A drug dealer who carried a weapon. His weapon has not been recovered. His was the body we discovered behind the fireplace at Crownest and he had been fatally shot in the head. The weapon causing this fatality was discovered taped under the bonnet of the Dixons' motorhome. We know the rest. Brad Dixon says in interview it was Raglan who pulled the trigger, not him, and then all of them, including James Thomas hid his body. He tells us also that Raglan is addicted to cocaine, and that he launders money in connection to drugs and property through the estate agency. Dixon states that he paid no rent for Crownest because he kept Raglan supplied with his preferred drug, as that was the deal. After what happened with Hussain, Dixon sold the car to someone he doesn't wish to tell us about, and threw Hussain's gun into the sea. He claims the piece was an imitation, which intelligence suggests is highly unlikely.

That's it so far, in a nutshell. Our aim tomorrow is to arrest both remaining targets, Thomas and Raglan, and search their homes, and other related premieres, to secure evidence against them both prior to subsequent interviews.

Exhausted, but fitful, sleep didn't come easy that night for Charley.

—

At six-fifteen the following morning, the convoy set off. When they left the confines of the vault of the police station, which doubled-up as a garage where some of the vehicles had been parked overnight, it was pitch black outside. Charley could tell the team were excited at the prospect of closing the case. The arrest stage was the icing on the cake to any investigation.

Charley headed to the Control Room so she could listen in to both arrests simultaneously, and be available for any enquiries or decisions that needed to be made quickly. It also gave an overview as to what was happening at each address.

'Penny for them?' said Tattie when Charley sat down next to her. She handed her a mug of coffee.

'I hate being here, and not there in the thick of it,' she said. Charley was aware that her own adrenalin levels were as high as that of the team. 'I love to see the reaction on their faces when they're surprised by an officer waking them up.'

'Well, look on the bright side, they'll all be wearing body cams so you can watch it later,' said Tattie, nonchalantly.

There were three boxes of biscuits piled up on the chair to her side. Tattie gave one to Charley. 'Here, have this,' she said.

Charley chuckled. 'Oh, no, I couldn't. I know there is someone more important that you'd like to give them to.'

Tattie shook her head. 'No, there isn't. I overheard Ben and Terry talking last night…' Her voice lowered to a whisper. 'Did you know Tim is divorcing his *fourth* wife?' She shuffled her crossed arms under her ample bosom. 'He'll be looking for someone to look after him, but that's not me. It's the last time I'll be baking him biscuits; I'm not about to become his fifth!'

Charley tittered despite her anxiety. 'Obviously he's one of life's charmers, Tattie.'

'He'll be doing it without my biscuits; I've got the measure of him. I know what rules him and it's not his head, or stomach!'

The teams were now on the road heading to the addresses of their separate targets. Charley stood and walked backwards and forwards, waiting for one of the team on the ground to break the silence.

'Target One, James Thomas, arrested,' came the welcome news over the radio.

Chapter 39

The minutes seemed like hours to Charley since she'd heard of the first arrest over the dedicated radio channel. She wanted to know and hear more. It was like wearing a blindfold. She schooled herself to be patient and fought to remain calm. She thought of previous raids to distract herself during the lull in action: the sound of colleagues, wearing boots with steel-toed caps rushing up the stairs in front and behind her, pounded in her head, and at the same time threatened to deafen her, 'On the floor! On the floor! Let me see your hands! Get down!' came the shouts of her colleagues. Charley knew the drill well. She tried hard to shake her head clear, and tried to concentrate on the present, when suddenly the radio silence broke.

'Target Two, Raglan, under arrest, and being removed from the premises, ma'am.'

Further information was passed to the Control Room. 'He appears to be under the influence of drugs. Team Two deployed, with keys, for work premises on the high street, the estate agency.'

Charley imagined the scene. Those arrested being escorted to the waiting marked police vehicles to be transported to the cells, the hand of the police officer being placed on top of the prisoners' heads as they climbed carefully, with their hands cuffed behind their backs, into the rear of the car. 'Mind your head, we don't want you to hurt yourself, do we?' she would say.

As the prisoners left, Charley could visualise the search teams going in to the designated site, each one of the specialist team chomping at the bit to start emptying drawers and cupboards, searching for anything that could connect the prisoner to the crime, to help secure a conviction. At the thought, Charley's fists clenched around the handle of her empty mug so tightly that her knuckles turned white. It was a waiting game for her, a waiting game to see what was recovered from the premises.

–

Charley walked down the police station steps alone. From one floor to the next, she didn't see a soul, until she reached the basement level and the custody suite. At the secure gated access, she called for the door release, and waited patiently for the CCTV camera pointing at the door to be checked. On entry she was met by single line of closed doors that lined each side of the empty, brightly lit corridor. Two doors had been left open. Inside she saw a toilet without a seat, and a wooden bed base with a thin plastic mattress on top. Charley shuddered. A windowless room with a locked door was her worst nightmare.

As she made herself comfortable in the back office in the custody suite which was situated directly behind the custody desk, Charley planned to watch the prisoners being brought before the Custody Sergeant Percy Shaw. Here they would be booked in at the desk and asked to hand in their personal property.

'Place them as far apart as you can, will you?' she had asked the custody staff. She didn't want to give Thomas or Raglan any opportunity to speak to each other, by shouting down the corridor in the cell area. Though she thought it wouldn't harm to let them each know that the other had been apprehended.

When the buzzer announced the arrival of a prisoner at the back door, it made her jump, such was her concentration on the file she was reading. James Thomas appeared through the door. The arrogance that he had displayed at Crownest was gone, as anticipated. His grey, puffy face looked bewildered, he was shaking and extremely upset. When it came to having his personal property taken from him, he asked, very politely, if the officers would be careful with his sovereign ring, which meant a lot to him.

'Do you understand why you have been arrested?' said the Custody Sergeant.

Thomas replied, 'I do, but it wasn't me.'

The Custody Sergeant was typing up his comments onto the computer. 'Oh, I wish I had a penny for every time someone told me that,' she said, when she turned to face him. Her forced smile quickly dropped from her lips. 'Cell twelve,' she said to Ricky-Lee. 'Take him away.'

As James Thomas turned, Charley stood, and walked towards him. 'We will be speaking to you soon, but in the meantime you will need to talk to your solicitor,' she said.

The backdoor buzzer sounded again, noisily. Ricky-Lee began ushering Thomas down the corridor to his cell, as Jonathan Raglan was brought in, bleary-eyed. He was clearly agitated, struggling, and kept shrugging off Mike's steadying hand from his elbow as they reached the desk.

'This is preposterous! Heads will roll!' Raglan roared at the Custody Sergeant. 'I know the Chief Constable!'

'Coincidentally, I do too.' Charley chuckled. Quickly her face turned serious. 'I couldn't begin to imagine how many times I hear that in a day, either. Do you understand why you've been arrested, Mr Raglan?'

Raglan stood at the desk, as still as he was able to manage whilst under the influence of drugs. 'Get me Duke Coggins, my solicitor!' he said. 'He'll sort this out, and you'll be grovelling at my feet with an apology, before this day is out,' he said, with a quivering voice.

Raglan's attitude was no different from what she remembered.

'Cell two,' Percy Shaw said. 'Take him away.'

By late afternoon, the officers had started to return to the police station with bags of exhibits from the different sites of investigation. By the time the majority of the team were back in the Incident Room office, it was time for the debrief where they would share the information from each address, and find out what evidence had been seized.

With a silent room, full of tired bodies, the debrief began.

'Let's start with James Thomas, shall we?' asked Charley.

'Twenty grand has been recovered from a holdall, found behind a panel in the house, thanks to police dog Oscar,' reported the dog handler.

'Yes, and we've discovered a load of paperwork; we're working through it with the financial team, who will scrutinise it to see if it is relevant,' said Ricky-Lee.

'No evidence of drugs?' asked Charley.

Ricky-Lee shook his head. 'No, clean as a whistle.'

'Anything from his car?' asked Charley.

Again, Ricky-Lee shook his head. 'Nope.'

'I suppose we haven't found a firearm?'

'No, boss, but the firearms sniffer dog is presently searching the building, so there's still hope.'

'Target Two?' Charley asked Mike.

'Jonathan Raglan was asleep on his settee, fully clothed, when we entered the property. There was a fruit bowl on the coffee table beside him that contained several wraps of cocaine. Apart from being, shall we say, three sheets to the wind, he was otherwise co-operative. We've recovered items of a financial nature from a set of locked drawers in bedroom two, and at the estate agency, we've also recovered five grand in cash.'

'Owing to the amount of paperwork we have recovered, I can say from the off that this is going to take us quite some time to get through, but as soon as we find any discrepancies, you'll be the first to know,' said Martin Jones, the leader of the Financial Investigations Unit.

'Let's get all the exhibits booked in, and then we can assess what we have to work with.' Charley was eager to move forward. 'I'll speak with the National Crime Agency regarding the cocaine seizure to see if Jonathan Raglan's name features in any of their known distribution chains. It would be easy to go off at a tangent here, but we have to remain focused on our objective, which is to convict the murderers of Faisal Hussain. One thing to remember, from the time the prisoners were booked in, is that their custody clocks are now ticking and we will need to start speaking to them as soon as we possibly can.' Charley turned to Mike. 'An initial interview this evening would be good.'

At the close of the team briefing, Charley's mobile phone demanded her attention, and she shared the contents of the text with the team. 'Jonathan Raglan has been medically examined and is pronounced fit for interview.' She looked up from the screen. 'That's good. DC Ricky-Lee, DC Annie Glover, if he's been fed and watered, first interview please, and I think we'll leave James Thomas until a bit later, make him sweat a little longer, what do you say, Mike?'

Mike followed Charley back to her office. 'You're not really coming into the interview, are you?'

'Why? I want to get under his skin just as much as you do. It's the best part of the job.'

'Because, The Police and Criminal Evidence Act says it's oppressive for your rank to interview a prisoner; you know that, the solicitor knows that. He might try to get the interview thrown out in court, and then we may lose anything he might disclose...'

Charley considered his remark. 'Oppressive? Moi, oppressive?' She laughed in mock horror. 'I don't know about that.'

'Well you do scare the shit out of that lot in there,' he said, nodding in the direction of the CID office.

'My dad used to say that a little bit of fear never did anyone any harm and I tend to agree with him. There's something though about James Thomas that doesn't sit right, and it's annoying me, because I don't know what it is.'

Mike looked puzzled. 'What do you mean?'

'I get this feeling that he likes to be thought of as Mister Clean, generous towards charitable causes et cetera, but I think he knows exactly what he is doing It's as if inwardly he's at home on a stage, and he enjoys the limelight.' Charley paused for a moment or two in thought. 'In brief, he's a devious bastard whom I don't trust. According to Dixon there were five people in that room when Faisal was shot dead. We know that four out of the five were involved with drugs. He might not be a user, Mike, but he's amongst it, which suggests to me perhaps he injects cash into the distribution. That's what I'm thinking...'

'He's a gibbering wreck at the moment, by all accounts.'

'That's how he wants us to see him. If he's innocent and he's nothing to hide, why should he be a "gibbering wreck"?' Frustration was written all over her face. 'Okay! You're right! I won't interview him. Take Wilkie in with you. I'll be watching on the monitor.'

An hour and a half later, Ricky-Lee Lewis and Annie Glover had spoken with Jonathan Raglan, and were in Charley's office with the result. Charley, fresh from her strategy meeting with Mike, was eager to hear what was said.

'We threw everything at him and his arse well and truly fell out! He's been crying, and he says he didn't kill anyone. Though he did think that he himself was going to be killed. He admitted to being a drug addict, and he even confirmed to us the name of his supplier, which as we thought, turned out to be the Dixons.'

'He never questioned what you were saying?' Charley interrupted.

'No, and his solicitor was as good as gold. He just let him talk and talk, which makes a change.'

'What did he say when you informed him that Brad Dixon told us that Faisal Hussain's firearm was an imitation?' Charley was keen to know more.

'Nothing, as far as he was concerned it was the real thing.'

'What about Faisal's body?'

'Raglan admits to helping hide the body.'

'Who does he say fired the gun?'

'He didn't, but he did confirm that there were two guns. The old man's head was bobbing all over the place, his tick appears to get worse when he's put under pressure or panicking. Having said that, for his age, and considering all his drug problems, he's still a wily old bastard. He knows what he's doing.'

'His solicitor told us that his client wanted to make a written statement about everything, including the drugs money going through the business account, the Crownest house sale, and Faisal's death, so we've left them to it,' said Annie.

Charley took a deep breath. 'That's going to make some interesting reading. I'll look forward to it. Tell me,' she said. 'Do you believe he'll tell us the truth?'

Ricky-Lee and Annie shook their heads in unison. 'No,' said Ricky-Lee. 'He's up to his neck in it, and blames anyone and everyone rather than himself for the situation he's found himself in.'

Annie lifted her shoulders and yawned. It had been a long day. 'It's only the first interview, of course.'

Charley smiled. 'You wouldn't want to buy a house from him then?'

'He comes across as dodgier than a car salesman,' Annie said, 'and car salesmen are well dodgy!'

'Not all of them, Annie,' Charley chuckled.

—

Soon after, Charley had her eyes glued to her monitor whilst Mike and Wilkie sat in another interview room in the cell area. The door was open as they waited for James Thomas and his solicitor to arrive.

Formalities over, Mike took the lead in the interview.

'You've met my boss, Detective Inspector Charley Mann, before Mr James, at the site of Crownest, when you were told that enquiries were being made into the discovery of two skeletons inside that building, and you were also made aware that enquiries were being made into how those people came to meet their deaths. We know you are aware, as your solicitor has been informed, that the remains of the body behind the fireplace have been identified as one Faisal Hussain. We also know his death was caused by a shot in the back of the head, and the weapon that was used has been recovered. I think it's fair to tell you that, Brad Dixon, who was allegedly renting the property at Crownest, has been arrested, as has Mr Raglan of Raglan Estate Agency. Investigations are all to do with ascertaining the truth about what took place, so with that in mind, this is why you are here. But, before we talk about that, tell us a little about yourself,' said Mike.

Charley could see, by the expression on Thomas's face, that this opening line of questioning was most unexpected.

Chapter 40

James Thomas pulled himself to the front of his seat – he was sweating profusely even though they were in an air-conditioned room. 'What do you want to know?'

Charley leaned back in her chair in her office as she watched the interview on screen. She felt almost relaxed, there was no rush.

'Whatever you want to tell us.' Mikes responded.

'I'm a businessman,' he said.

'Hobbies?' asked Mike.

'I like the finer things in life, fine dining, the theatre, my cars, but my passion is amateur dramatics.'

'What is your business exactly?' prompted Wilkie.

'I'm an entrepreneur.'

'What exactly is an "entrepreneur"?' asked Wilkie.

'An entrepreneur is someone who operates a business, or businesses, taking on greater than normal financial risks.'

'That could be anyone who starts up a new business?'

James Thomas nodded. 'I suppose so, yes.'

'What do you actually buy and sell?'

'If I see something where I think there's a profit to be made, then I'll invest in it or buy it outright. Whatever that might be.'

'Like Crownest?' said Mike.

James nodded. 'Yes, but like I said, I don't just deal in property, or land. I buy and sell anything that I think might be profitable, that's why I called the business JT Developments, as it covers a multitude of investments.'

'Then, you're telling us that you are driven by money?'

'I used to be.' Thomas paused. 'You see I was brought up on a council estate in a strong working-class family. As it happened, we were classed as rich because we had glass in our windows. It wasn't easy for my parents. I've worked hard to get where I am today.'

Mr Thomas appeared to be happy talking about himself. 'Where would you say that is?' Mike probed a little harder.

'I have my own house, and I am financially stable, which enables me to invest and support charitable causes.'

'My officers tell me that you lived in Rome for a while. Is travelling something that you like to do?' the detective continued.

Thomas shrugged his shoulders. 'If the mood takes me. I don't have anyone to answer to but myself.'

'You live alone?' said Mike.

James smiled. 'You know I do.'

'Never met the right person or through choice?'

'In my early twenties I went to Rome to become a priest, something I had trained for, but although I had a terrific time, I met someone.' James swallowed hard. 'It was unexpected, and traumatic, and my life took a very different road from the one I had planned, and I guess you could say that from then on, my disillusion with the wider world began.'

'You fell in love, he let you down?'

James looked at him with surprise. 'How did you know that?'

'Call it intuition, but, let me assure you, I have no issue with your sexuality.'

James smiled, a genuine smile. 'Well, let's just say, from that time I have carried with me a sense of rejection and unfulfillment which often comes to the fore in bouts of low mood or when things are not going to plan.'

'So you have a temper?'

James nodded his head. 'As your boss saw first-hand at Crownest that day. I just get frustrated.'

'When did you first meet Jonathan Raglan?' asked Mike.

'A few years ago. I have quite a portfolio of properties which I have acquired from him over the last few years, and now he contacts me if he has been to value property which he thinks might be of interest to me.'

'Okay, so we have determined from our little chat that you are an intelligent, generous man. What is your involvement with Crownest?'

James Thomas turned his head sideways to look at his solicitor, who nodded his head for him to continue.

'Crownest is probably the worst investment I have ever made. It was sold to me by Raglan as an undesirable property whilst it stood, but with the promise that when it was demolished, it would leave prime land for development. He assured me that plans would be passed by the council to build several prestigious detached houses. Offers were invited for the sale of it, and I subsequently put an offer in which was immediately accepted. Plans were drawn up for the development, at my expense I might add, and planning permission was put in to the council. Then out of the blue, Raglan informed me that the sellers had accepted a higher offer from another buyer, which I was obviously very upset about because I thought

I had already completed on the property. The approved planning permission for the new houses came back several days later, so when Raglan rang me to say that Crownest had come back on the market, I immediately put my offer back on the table, to have it accepted again. In the meantime, the Dixons had already moved in, temporarily I was told... As you can imagine I wasn't very pleased about this because we couldn't immediately start the demolition... and, you know the rest.'

'We've heard other people's versions of what happened on the night of Faisal Hussain's murder, but we'd like to hear yours,' said Mike.

'Raglan told me that the couple renting were reluctant to leave the property. He said that, knowing the couple, if I was willing to offer them a monetary incentive, he was sure they would depart. Delays for me meant losing money, so I wasn't against this idea. It turned out that when I arrived at Crownest, Jonathan Raglan was already there. He was acting very strangely. However, the couple, introduced to me as Brad and Brittany Dixon were hard to strike a bargain with, and in the end, Raglan offered to go halves with me for the price they were demanding. I remember thinking at that point that he didn't look great, but he hadn't looked well in recent months... although he remained a shrewd businessman nevertheless.'

'Had you met the couple, the Dixons, before that night?' interrupted Mike.

James nodded. 'Yes, I saw them briefly when I went to the address previously with Joe Greenwood, the owner, to discuss the house demolition.' Suddenly, James's eyes grew large and round. 'Anyway, the time I went to discuss the Dixons' departure, the next thing I knew was that a big, angry-looking Asian guy had burst into the hallway brandishing a gun, and before anyone could do or say anything, this guy had Brad Dixon's head in a headlock, and was pointing the gun to it and threatening to kill him.'

Mike and Wilkie remained silent.

James Thomas took a clean, neatly folded handkerchief out of his suit pocket, and held it to his cheek, then he mopped his forehead, before putting it back in his pocket. 'I was absolutely terrified. The whole thing was just surreal, like something out of a play. Next thing I heard was a gun going off, and I saw the stranger fall to the floor. I turned to look at Mr Raglan, and he was holding the gun that was pointed in the direction of Brad Dixon. I didn't know what to do. I panicked. I can recall Mr Dixon saying the man was dead. After that, it all seemed slightly crazy. Mr Dixon told me that I had to keep quiet about what I'd witnessed, or else—' Thomas put his hand over his face. '—his nose was pressed against mine,' he said. Thomas's hand shook. 'Mr Raglan appeared to be in shock. I promised them that I wouldn't say a word if they let me leave. Under duress, and in fear for my life, I helped to hide the body, after which I hastily left. I remember my heart was beating so hard against my ribcage that when I got into my car and had locked the doors, I was trembling so badly that I couldn't put the key in the ignition.'

'How did the others appear to be immediately after the shooting?'

James considered the question. 'That's just it, when I think back, they were all quite calm, matter of fact. A man had just been shot in front of their eyes, and they didn't really bat an eyelid. They appeared to be only concerned about being caught.'

'Did you want the building to be demolished as soon as possible to get rid of the body on their behalf? Is that why it was set alight?' continued Mike.

'No, not at all! I had enough on my plate trying to carry on and act normal after what I had witnessed. I could only surmise, when the bodies were found in the house, that one of them was the stranger I had seen shot dead that night. I did want Crownest to be demolished for one thing, and one thing only, and that was to get the job done, so that the builders could start.'

'If you want us to believe that this is the truth, tell me, why didn't you come forward before now? You had time before the human remains were discovered, and plenty of time since,' said Mike.

'God's honest truth? I was petrified that they would kill me. I still am.'

'You've heard of Crimestoppers haven't you?' said Mike.

Thomas nodded.

Wilkie's eyes became suspicious. 'Why didn't you make an anonymous call?'

James hand flew to his mouth. 'Why didn't I think about that? Although... now I am thinking about it, I was the only person who knew about the shooting, other than Jonathan Raglan and the Dixons, so it wouldn't have been hard for them to work out who the grass was, would it?'

'Are you involved in the drugs scene, in any way?' asked Mike.

James shook his head vehemently. 'No, no, never. You've searched my house by now, I guess,' he smiled wanly. 'Give me a test, right here and now if you want.'

'I didn't ask if you were a user. I asked if you had any dealings with drugs. You grew up on an estate, you know how to handle yourself, you're a self-made man, you come across as being astute and intelligent, so what puzzles me is why you would be dealing with someone like Raglan, who's presently acting irrationally. And let's not forget, through him you've met a pair of armed robbers who are wanted by the police, and a murder has taken place while you are in their company. How do you think all that looks to us?'

'What I've told you is the truth.'

'Then why don't I believe you?' Mike said. 'I don't deny you have a business buying and selling different investments, but I also believe that you have been dabbling with the selling and distribution of drugs, which you know is a global money-making business, and from which you can make a substantial profit.'

'My client is not under arrest in relation to any drug charges, and I must object to this line of questioning,' interjected Mr Kane, Thomas's solicitor. James Thomas's face was unreadable.

Mike was quick to answer back. 'You can object all you want, but we know that the Dixons and Raglan were involved in the drugs scene and in money-laundering, so the question is relevant for us to understand whether your client has been using his entrepreneurial skills in the drugs world.'

James Thomas broke the silence. 'Sergeant, let me assure you that is not the case. Have you found anything in my home or my car to suggest otherwise?' Mike and Wilkie remained silent.

'No is the answer, because I know you won't,' James said with some finality.

'You'll be telling me next that the Mafia are God-fearing individuals. I think it is time to terminate this interview to give you some time to reflect,' said Mike collating his paperwork from the table in front of him.

Mr Kane followed Mike out of the interview room. 'I suggest that maybe my client is willing to make a statement, if he isn't charged with any offence.'

'I'm far from satisfied that your client was simply on the periphery. Even if he wasn't the one that pulled the trigger, he knew what went on and assisted the others, and you know as well as I do that for assisting offenders he can be tried and indicted as a principal,' Mike told him, letting him know there were going to be no deals. Mike saw the solicitor's jaw drop. He turned and briskly walked away.

It was the end of a shift, and the corridor was noisy with the banter of officers and support staff leaving the building as the officers made their way back up the stairs to CID.

'You enjoyed that, didn't you?' Wilkie said, when he eventually caught up with Mike outside the Incident Room. As the pair walked into the office, Charley was waiting to greet them.

'Nice work,' she said. 'I don't think I've ever seen that pompous prig so docile.' She walked behind them, a hand on each of their shoulders. 'I'll be giving his details to the National Crime Agency. He's as guilty as the others. I'm sure of it.'

Wilkie sat at his desk and Charley and Mike walked towards Charley's office. Annie put down the phone. 'Boss,' she shouted. Both detectives turned. 'The team searching Thomas's car... they've found a key and fob in the sun visor. It relates to a locker at the theatre.'

Chapter 41

Ricky-Lee pulled his chair beside Wilkie's desk. He handed him a brown paper bag, tied with an elastic band.

Annie was sat at her desk opposite them, quietly reading Raglan's statement.

'I'd 'ave put money on Thomas's arse dropping out...' Ricky-Lee said thoughtfully.

'Good job you didn't,' said Wilkie. 'Raglan's just made a statement basically canonising JT. The boss told us she wants Thomas charging.'

'Makes me wonder who Raglan is more frightened of, Dixon or Thomas?'

Wilkie peeked into the bag full of assorted broken biscuits and smacked his smiling lips together. 'I'm glad you're not knocking a lass off that works in't ironmongers,' he said. 'Put t'kettle on.'

Ricky-Lee stood up, and collected the others' cups from their desks. 'There's no way Thomas is clean.'

'According to Raglan, he's cleaner than a duck's fart.'

Annie glanced over her computer screen, 'Slippery as an eel, more like,' she muttered. 'I wonder what Mike and the boss will find in the locker?'

'What's Raglan actually said in his statement?' said Ricky-Lee.

'He blames his drug addiction, which he says started as medicinal,' said Annie.

'Of course,' said Ricky-Lee.

'He actually talks about Thomas rather fondly,' said Annie.

Wilkie sat at his desk opposite Annie, screwing up his face. 'We know he's not as green as he's cabbage-looking though, as our lass says.'

'He knows more about James Thomas's business ventures than he's letting on,' said Annie.

Wilkie nodded his head. 'He knows which side his bread is buttered, that's for sure, and when to keep his gob shut.'

'What's interesting is that he talks about the night of the shooting in his statement, but in his first interview he declines to tell us who shot Hussain. He says that he was sitting in an armchair, when Brittany Dixon indicated to him that there was a gun in the rucksack, by his side. At the time, Hussain had a gun to Brad Dixon's head apparently, and he was threatening him, eyeball to eyeball. Raglan admits to retrieving the gun to pass to Brittany, at her request apparently, but says that whilst he was doing so the gun went off. He also admits the Dixons paid the rent by supplying him with drugs for his personal use.'

–

It was some time before Charley and Mike appeared back in the Incident Room from their investigation at the local theatre. Bags of exhibits filled Mike's arms. 'We had to wait for Neal Rylatt to photograph the contents of the locker *in situ*,' said Mike, laying the exhibits on Annie's desk.

'A handgun,' said Annie.

'A *loaded* handgun,' said Charley.

The young detective looked up at Charley questioningly, 'Hussain's, do you think?'

Charley shrugged her shoulders. 'Either way, we need to arrest Thomas now for possession of a firearm, and he needs interviewing again. Annie, call his solicitor will you. Let's get things moving.'

Charley sat down next to Wilkie.

'What're you thinking happened, boss?' he said.

'I think that the four of them somehow disarmed Hussain, and held him on the floor whilst they put a bullet in his head. Like the pathologist said, it was an execution, not an accident, as Raglan claims in his statement. But we may never know for certain who actually pulled the trigger.'

'I'm glad I'm not eligible for jury duty. This murder enquiry is going to be a nightmare for each and every one of them,' said Annie.

Charley gave her a tight smile. 'Unless of course, the Crown Prosecution suggest that this was without doubt, a case of joint enterprise. Which would mean we charge them all with murder and in the evidence show that they were all complicit with what went on.'

'But Dixon's defence team are sure to try and confuse the jury by playing out the different possible scenarios, emphasising that they must be absolutely sure what happened on the evidence that is put before them in court, in order to make the decision for the verdict,' added Wilkie.

'That would be nothing new for the defence, Wilkie, but the prosecution would lay out everything before them and make it simple for them to understand. But remember, it's our job to put the evidence, and the offender, before the courts. Occasionally jurors get it wrong but that's very rare. I think they'll convict them of the murder.

–

There was a notable change in Raglan in his final interview with Annie and Ricky which had been set up to talk about the content of his written statement. The estate agent was trembling with such vigour that the interview had to be suspended shortly after it had started.

'We will have to accept that we have got all we are going to get from Raglan,' Charley later told the team at debrief.

Once the debrief was finished, Charley headed to update Chief Superintendent Stokes before returning to her own office seeing a chance for a moment or two of silence. She leaned her head back on her office chair headrest with her eyes closed. She was tired; her eyes were aching. She was waiting for the Crown Prosecution Service to call her when Mike and Wilkie walked into her office. Their rowdy entrance startled her.

'We have good news and bad news, boss, which would you like first?' asked an eager Wilkie.

Charley covered her mouth with her hand to suppress a yawn. 'Start with the bad, then at least things can only get better.'

'Raglan collapsed in his cell,'

'He has?'

'When you were in the meeting with the Divisional Commander.'

'And?'

'He was taken to hospital but they turned him around, after checking his vital signs. They put the episode down to possible withdrawal. He's been given medication for the custody staff to administer until such time as he goes to prison.'

'And the good news, Mike?'

'Thomas's interview about the discovery of the firearm, ma'am. On being told he was also under arrest for possession of a firearm and ammunition, I thought he was going to collapse, but he somehow gathered his composure, and remained silent throughout our questioning. He certainly didn't expect us to find it.'

'I think Mr Thomas is going to realise very quickly that he is now in a very different world. He knows he has slipped up, now the inevitable will begin to sink in, namely that he is going to be locked up for perhaps a long time.' Charley looked up at the clock above her door. 'We're running out of time on those custody clocks – let's get James Thomas charged with murder, and the remand files ready for Court tomorrow morning. CPS haven't responded to me, so I've made the decision and I'll give them a courtesy call to let them know the brief details of them attending the Magistrates Court tomorrow for a remand in custody.'

Mike closed the door behind him as he left Charley's office, just as her phone began to ring. She picked it up.

'DI John Harris, National Crime Agency,' said the man at the other end of the line. 'Sorry for the delay, we've had a live incident to deal with. How can I help you with your enquiry? I heard you've been trying to get hold of me.'

'DI Charley Mann, Peel Street, CID. I've just sent you information about a man called James Thomas which I think may be of interest to you.'

'Thank you,' he said. 'Funnily enough, that name has cropped up on the periphery in regards to drug distribution recently where firearms have been involved.'

'Do you also know the name of Faisal Hussain? He is the victim in one of our local murder enquiries,' probed Charley.

'Indeed, I do!' DI Harris seemed surprised. 'I for one won't lose any sleep over his demise. As they say, he lived by the sword, and he died by the sword, or in his case, the gun.'

'It's being suggested to us that a weapon Hussain was carrying was imitation. Is that likely from the intelligence you have? We haven't recovered an imitation firearm, but recently we have recovered a firearm during the searches of premises of one of the suspects.'

DI Harris laughed out loud. 'The likes of Faisal Hussain carry a toy gun? Christ, no, absolutely not! Even the idea would make him a laughing stock. I suggest someone is shovelling you a load of bullshit, like they do. He'd have been taken out years ago by the opposition if he carried imitation firearms.'

'Exactly my thoughts; that's all I needed to know,' Charley said. 'I'll get our intelligence cell to send you our current info on Hussain's murder, and the details of those charged, along with further details of the recently recovered weapon I mentioned, once Forensics and Ballistics get back to me.'

'Yeah, that would be good.'

Charley's next call was to the Crown Prosecution Service who apologised for not returning her call earlier. She informed them that the custody clock was against her, and couldn't delay charging the men any longer, explaining that they had now been charged with murder, and Thomas with possession of a firearm and ammunition. The relationship between the police and the CPS was about assessing the evidence independently for the Crown Prosecution Service. The last thing anyone wanted was to have to withdraw a charge of murder, or be reprimanded at a later trial, by the judge, if there was insufficient evidence. Charley outlined the evidence against the offenders and the CPS were in full agreement with her decision to charge. The SIO breathed a sigh of relief, although she had never been in doubt about the substantial evidence in the case.

She then sat for a moment reflecting on the enquiry so far. A derelict house had revealed the remains of two humans. As a result, they now had one armed robber shot dead by the police, three people charged with murder and related offences, and two firearms had been removed from circulation. Who would believe that all this had come from her stopping on a whim at Crownest that cold frosty morning?

Her mind quickly wandered to thinking about why James Thomas would keep a firearm in his locker; could it be the one that was missing, the one that belonged to Hussain? Hopeful Forensics would be able to confirm this, and it would negate some of Brad Dixon's story of how things had happened and the supposed disposal of the imitation weapon in the sea.

Her phone rang, breaking her train of thought.

'Charley, Tim Watson, Firearms Tac Advisor.'

'Please tell me we haven't another job running at the moment, Tim?' Charley heard the desperation in her voice, and wondered if Tim did, too.

Tim chuckled. 'Keep calm, it's just a heads-up about the independent enquiry into the shooting of Brittany

Dixon. The outcome has confirmed that she was killed lawfully. Obviously, this won't be in the public domain for at least another week, but I thought you'd like to know immediately.'

'Yes, thanks Tim, that's great news for all concerned. Although we were never in doubt, it is nice to have that conclusion endorsed by an independent enquiry.'

As Charley put the phone down, she knew with satisfaction that the incident was closed with a positive result. There were lots of loose ends to tie up; Forensics were still due to get back to her, and there was a vast amount of paperwork to be done, but one murder was in her view now solved, even though there were a few loose ends to tie up.

Charley's thoughts turned to the female skeleton in the cellar and the baffling mystery of her death. She looked out of her window at the darkening skies. The office felt stifling to her. Rain and thunder threatened. She needed air. She stood and put on her coat.

'Where you off?' Mike said as she walked through the office. 'Want some company?'

Charley stood at the side of his desk. 'No, I just need to clear my head,' she said. 'I'm off out for a drive round. I'll have my phone with me.'

'You're going to the church, aren't you?'

Charley nodded. 'You read my mind,' she smiled. 'More than likely. Then I will head for home. I'll see you tomorrow.'

–

Charley sat quietly in her car. She may never find out the truth, or know the harrowing experiences of the Yorkshire folk of yesteryear who had lived in Crownest, for she knew that the official records and history books back then were written by those who could write. However, being a Yorkshire lass, she wouldn't give up. 'if you hit a brick wall get under, over, or through it,' is what Jack, her Dad would tell her. 'Don't let anything stop you moving *forward*. Where there's a will, there's a way.'

Was Charley intrigued by how the mysterious skeleton had been murdered and the way she was hidden, or was her fascination due to the skeleton's age and Charley's love of history? Maybe it was even because of the tales her granny had told her. She didn't know, but she was driven by a wish to solve the mystery, and she was not going to be satisfied with resolving half of the mysteries that Crownest had uncovered. Murder is the supreme test for any detective, and this present case was just that.

Charley drove on. Most of the enquiries had been historic, but she was suddenly aware that she had forgotten the golden rule: to clear the ground beneath her feet. It didn't matter how many times she revisited the church, as long as she got a result in the end. Whilst Lily had answered questions in a reasonable and satisfying way, there was a lot of information that she had been vague about, and it was easy to be deliberately vague after so much time, Charley realised.

A slight wind was blowing the overgrown branches of a few trees edging the moors, making them scrape slowly across the roof of the car. The dark clouds had cleared and had not remained static in the valley, as they so often did. Charley stepped out into the middle of open pasture, surrounded by primroses, snowdrops, spear thistle, bee orchid to name but a few winter flowers.

The afternoon had been forecast as pleasant on the radio but the weather had turned cold, and Charley pulled her coat around her to stop the breeze from chilling her bones. Immediately as she stepped into the graveyard, she noticed the quietness of her surroundings, with no bird-song. It was such a shame that the majority of graves were neglected and overgrown, apart from the posies placed on selected graves. She wondered if that was because the occupants of the graves no longer had living relatives, or if the relatives no longer visited their ancestors' resting place. It seemed sad. The church door was locked.

Charley wandered from one grave to another, reading the gravestones as best she could. She did not really know what she was looking for, but she was aware that should she be seen by another, she would have been thought of as odd or perhaps having lost the plot.

Cold, she returned to the car, and telephoned Mike Blake. 'Mike, tomorrow once we have got Hussain's killers' remand hearing over, let's arrange to pick Lily Pritchard up and bring her in. I think we're due another word with her, at the police station this time. I can't put my finger on it, but I have this nagging feeling that she has secrets still to share, and before you say anything, I know I'm jumping from one murder to the other, but it's something we need to do.'

Chapter 42

'Catherine Alderman didn't emigrate to Australia, Lily, like you would have us believe, did she? Please be truthful,' asked Charley.

In the stark white space of the police interview room, Lily could do nothing but look about her in awe, squinting as she did so at the brightness of the lights. She appeared puzzled by how the interview chairs were screwed to the floor. Annie had placed hot drinks on the table between her and the detectives. Charley's tone of voice, and the harsh surroundings, seemed to intimidate the old lady. The look in her bewildered eyes reminded the SIO of a rabbit caught in car headlights. Yet, hard though it was, this approach was necessary.

Softly, Charley continued. 'Lily, are those Catherine's remains that we found in the cellar at Crownest?' Charley had gone out on a limb, and with her heart in her mouth, she waited for the reaction.

After a moment or two Lily dropped her gaze, looked for a moment at the gnarled hands that lay knotted together in her lap, and then she began slowly shaking her head. 'No,' she said, in a hushed tone when she lifted her head. Tears were in her eyes, and as she stared at Charley, one or two spilled over, and rolled down her cheeks. 'You've got it all wrong,' she slurred. 'That's not the story that my mother, Agnes, told me on her deathbed, and I've no reason to doubt her words.'

Charley took a sharp breath. 'What did she tell you?' She spoke quietly hoping Lily would carry on.

'She told me that she wanted me to know everything before she died, so that if they came asking, I could tell them the truth. But I promised her, on the Bible, that I wouldn't tell another living soul apart from them.'

Charley frowned. 'Tell who, Lily, tell them what? Why can't you tell us?'

'I can't, because you're not *them*,' she said, angrily.

'I'm not who? Who is it that you're referring to as "them"?'

'Those whom God didn't lift a finger against to help prevent it from happening. My faith has been put to the test. It was the least I could do to find them, and tell them the truth, but I didn't.' Lily's gaze lingered on Charley's face for a moment or two. Suddenly, she took a deep intake of breath, and leaned forward conspiratorially. 'One thing I can tell you is that Catherine did go to Australia, and she had a daughter. I don't know what happened to her daughter, but Agnes believed that when Catherine died, the girl was brought back to England, to be looked after by Catherine's husband's parents. I should have gone looking for her, and I didn't. God let her down, and I let her down, and I can't forgive myself.'

Charley could see how distressed Lily was, but she needed to carry on in her questioning. 'What happened in the past is not your fault, nor is it God's. Can't you see that His love saved you for a much greater purpose, Lily, to do these things now if you can, and also find a proper resting place for the poor woman who was killed and buried in the cellar? You were young, it was wrong for the elders to put this on you. Is it true that Seth sent his sister, Catherine away?' asked Charley.

Lily nodded, through her sobs. 'Yes, according to my mother, Agnes, Lucinda looked up to Catherine as an older friend and confidante, and chose to continue to confide in her after she married Seth. Seth didn't approve of his sister interfering in the couple's marital affairs.'

'There must have been a trigger though, for such drastic action?' said Charley.

'You are very perceptive,' Lily gave Charley a watery smile. 'Lucinda, I was told, became pregnant quite quickly after the couple married, and as Seth's dependency on drugs and drink continued to grow throughout her pregnancy, it brought with it dark, low moods and violent rages, which he took out on his wife and sister. Catherine witnessed the shouting and some of the abuse endured by his young, pregnant wife, until apparently one day, fearing for Lucinda's and the baby's life, she decided it could not continue any longer. In one of Seth's more lucid moments, Agnes told me he had agreed to Catherine's suggestion that the tunnel between the house and the church be bricked up, and the gates to the house locked, to stop his visiting the church where Lucinda was taken for her safety, to be looked after by her parents. Lucinda pined for Seth, and he did for her, but she knew she had to stay away, at least until the baby was born. It was said that she would sit at the bricked-up doorway, on the cold stone slabs, talking to her husband long into the night. He could be heard by others, wailing like an animal in pain, begging her to come to him, but she resisted. Most nights Catherine would cover her brother's sleeping body on the dirt floor in the tunnel, as he was too heavy for her to lift back into the house.

'In his poor state of mind, Seth is said to have blamed everyone else for the situation he had found himself in, and grew to believe that if Catherine, whom he believed was Lucinda's captor, was not around, then his wife would come back to him. Unknown to anyone, he arranged for his sister to be kidnapped and sent as far away as possible, and whilst waiting for his plan to come to fruition he began digging an alternative secret tunnel, for in his deranged state, he thought that Lucinda was being kept prisoner and he need to rescue her. Once he started, Seth became as obsessed about the tunnel as he was about everything else. He bragged to the couple of servants left about it, claiming that the speed with which it was being dug was down to help from the Hobgoblin. He was, as you can imagine, a laughing stock, but they egged him on because he paid them well, for the privilege of their company. Relentlessly, he carried on digging until he was nothing more than a skeleton himself. He didn't eat, neither did he sleep much, because the compulsion forced him to continue digging, day after day, night after night, until he had built a lengthy underground tunnel which led into the graveyard... to his elected burial plot. He worked mostly by candlelight. When Catherine went away, he supposedly continued to beg Lucinda to see him, Agnes told me. However, she did not dare, not because she didn't want to, but because of the threat to her unborn baby, whom she loved above all. Then rumour has it, that Lucinda fled the church one night after the baby was born, and never returned. Agnes believed that Lucinda finally gave in and went to be with him. Not long afterwards, Seth was found dead, it is said by young Adam. There is no mention of his burial in the church records; it was thought that the exit of the tunnel must have been turned into his grave by the people who worked for him, such was their commitment to Adam. So disliked was he by those at the church that he wasn't bestowed the proper burial, in the ground that was rightfully bought for his final resting place, and as you know, his body has never been found.'

'And Lucinda was never seen again either, you said?' asked Charley.

Lily was quiet. Head down, she dabbed her cheeks. The interview room took on a feeling of peace and serenity. Charley did not know what had just happened, but something had.

'What became of the baby?' asked Charley.

'I can't… I really can't tell you any more,' Lily said, with some finality, and Charley could tell by her expression that her word on the Bible was her bond.

There was a knock at the door, and Mike opened it slowly. 'Is everything okay in here; can I get anyone anything?' he asked.

Lily stood. 'I have to go, can I go…?' she said.

'Can we give you a lift home?' Charley's eyes flashed from Lily to Mike, and he nodded reassuringly.

'No, but thank you,' she said, softly. 'I've something extremely important that I need to do first.'

–

Charley sat alone in her office for a while, her thoughts on the skeletal remains of the body in the cellar, wondering how she would prove an identity with no living relative to provide DNA. Her mobile phone rang, and it sounded extra loud, as if alerting her to an emergency.

'DI Charley Mann,' she said, brusquely.

'Help me, Charley! Please, help me!'

'Winnie? Is that you?'

'I'm at Josephine's house, the door was open, and she's lying on the hallway floor, there's blood, and broken glass.'

Charley headed for the door. 'I'm on my way. Have you rung for the ambulance?'

Winnie was sobbing.

'I'll ring them. Winnie, go outside.'

'What?' she cried.

'Go outside, and stay outside, do you hear me?'

Charley rushed towards Wilkie's desk. 'Where's the fire?' he asked.

'Let Mike know we might have a job on,' she said, edging her way to the door as she spoke. 'I'll get back to you asap. Annie!' she called, 'Where's Ricky-Lee?'

Annie looked up from her computer and shrugged her shoulders. 'I don't know.'

'Find him now! If he's at the bookies, he's a dead man walking. I want you both at Josephine's cottage now!'

Charley ran down the steps of the police station two at a time. 'I need a uniform car blue-lighting its way to Bramble Cottage, Cow Lane, Marsden,' she said to the Control Room operator on her phone as she explained en route what Winnie had told her.

Charley drove at speed. She was concerned not only for Josephine, but for Winnie, too. Unusually for her, she sounded her car horn aggressively, and flashed the car's lights at anyone or anything that was in her way. She could hear sirens in the distance behind her, and somehow the sound comforted her, and she hoped that the women at Bramble Cottage could hear them approaching, too.

Charley created a swirl of dust as she screeched to a halt outside the old cottage. Running down the path she could see Winnie, shaking uncontrollably, tears running down her cheeks; she looked frantic, helpless, old and frail.

Charley grabbed hold of her and held her tight. 'It's okay,' Charley said, like a mother comforting a child. 'I'm here now, and can you hear the sirens? Help is on the way. Are you okay?' she said, watching as the paramedics' car rocked from side to side as it made its way down the unmade stony road towards them.

'I'm okay. Please Charley, go see to Josephine. She's not good.' Charley approached the door to the cottage quickly but cautiously. Inside she could see Josie on her back, her right leg twisted beneath her. As Winnie had reported, there was indeed broken glass and blood splashes on the wall, and on the floor nearby. On her haunches, the SIO checked Josephine for a pulse. It was faint, but there was no doubting she was still alive. She motioned for the paramedics to join her and put in another call, 'Can you get hold of Neal Rylatt, CSI supervisor?' she said to the Control Operator. 'I need him at the Cow Lane scene.'

While the paramedics worked on helping Josie, an ambulance arrived. Charley sat with Winnie in her car. She bent over and took the old woman's hand in hers. 'She's alive,' she said. 'We'll follow them to the hospital.'

Seeing Annie's car arrive at the cottage, with Ricky-Lee in the passenger seat, Charley gave Winnie a bottle of water. 'Here,' she said. 'Sip this. I won't be a minute.'

Ricky-Lee looked shifty. 'I won't ask you where you've been, but be assured I will find out,' his boss whispered in his ear, as he got out of the car.

Charley turned to Annie as they walked towards the cottage, 'I guess Control will have filled you in. CSI is on the way. We don't know what happened, so I am treating it as a crime scene. Make sure they swab the blood, and get glass samples, will you?'

'Do you think someone tried to stop her talking to us?' Annie said, straining to see the scene from the doorway.

'I don't know, but until we do, we will treat it as suspicious.' Charley's eyes were drawn to a posy of flowers on the floor, by the coat stand.

Annie followed the SIO's eyes. 'Is that one of Lily's?' she said.

'Have it photographed and seized,' said Charley. 'I'm taking Winnie to the hospital to have her checked out. Are you okay with everything here? I'll contact Mike to join you.'

'I'll take her, if that helps?' said Annie.

Charley looked over her shoulder at the old lady waiting in her car, and her heartstrings pulled her chest tight. 'No, no, this is something I need to do,' she said.

Ricky-Lee was speaking to a paramedic, as they put Josephine's neck in a brace, and fitted an oxygen mask over her face before she was lifted into the back of the ambulance.

'Tell me,' said Charley, 'Where did you find him?' as she nodded over to Ricky-Lee.

Annie smiled. 'Not where you think. If he had been there, I'd have decked him for you. Nevertheless, love's young dream was where he shouldn't have been while he was on duty… letting his trousers rule his head!'

Chapter 43

Charley flashed her warrant card at the receptionist in A&E and explained the situation. Winnie's breathing was erratic, her lips pale, her skin clammy to the touch.

'I'm fine,' Winnie protested.

'Humour me; I want someone to check you over. She's had one of these turns before...' Charley told the receptionist.

A nurse ushered them into a cubicle and pulled on the curtain.

'Considering the shock you've just had, your symptoms are only natural,' said the doctor, in a calming, kindly voice as he examined the old lady. When he'd finished he turned round to face Charley. 'Everything thing seems okay, but I suggest you take her for a cup of tea and a bite to eat in the cafeteria, and I'll let the nurse know where you are, so she can send someone to update you on her friend's condition.'

Charley offered Winnie her arm, and she accepted it gratefully. 'My head feels like I've been on a bender,' she said, as they walked at a slow pace down the hospital corridor.

'What are you like?' Charley replied, feeling Winnie's hand sweating in the crook of her arm. 'I can't imagine you on a bender!'

Winnie stopped to get her breath. 'You young 'uns think you have the monopoly on the good times. Thankfully no one can take away my memories.'

Charley looked down at the smaller woman at her side, and squeezed her hand, knowing Winnie was thinking of Charley's dad, Jack.

'Josie was an orphan, you know. She told me that she had been left on the steps of St Anne's Church as a baby. How anyone could do that I'll never know. She came to my school when she was adopted. We've been the best of friends for over sixty years.'

Winnie sat in the cafe, staring blankly at the untouched toast and pot of jam on her plate, when Charley put down the phone to Mike whom she'd rung to update.

'An orphan, you said?'

'Yes, and no wonder she took a tumble, her head was full of talk of her adoption when I saw her last. It has weighed heavily on her mind lately,' Winnie said.

'Why now I wonder?' said Charley.

Winnie shrugged her shoulders. 'I don't think she ever got over finding her adoption papers in her father's documents when he died suddenly. It affected her that much she put everything on hold, even her work, to concentrate on her personal search to find her real parents' identities, but even with her vast experience of historical archives and research, she found nothing. I know it was her greatest wish to find out her origins before she died.' Winnie sighed. 'Now it might be too late.' A lone tear ran slowly down her cheek, which she brushed aside.

The news from the neurosurgeon concerning Josie's condition was not good. Hearing it from the specialist nurse seemed to make Winnie's sorrow a little easier to bear. The cafeteria was almost deserted, and the nurse thought about moving her to a private office, but it was less formal here, and Charley considered it was all right to talk to Winnie where she was sitting.

'Your friend is very poorly,' nurse said, when she sat at the table beside her. She held Winnie's shaking hand, as she delivered the devastating news that an operation was not an option. 'All we can do is make her comfortable as we can, and ensure that she isn't in any pain.'

'Is she going to die?' Winnie asked, aware of what the answer would be.

'That I can't tell you, but what I do know is that she is in good hands. The best, in fact.'

Winnie's eyes were hollows in her face. 'Can I see her? There isn't anyone else.' Her question was more of a plea.

The nurse looked up at Charley to see her reaction. She responded by briefly closing her eyes and nodding her head. At that moment, she was filled with admiration for the nurse: so gentle, so sympathetic, so kind. Nursing indeed was a vocation.

'I shouldn't really,' she said, 'family only, but come with me, I'll see what I can do.'

Charley held back the tears as she looked at Winnie broken by the news of her childhood friend and wondered how it was that a heart that had held a lifetime of love didn't break.

With the nurse by her side, Charley stood outside in the corridor and watched as Winnie talked to her sleeping friend. They saw Winnie cry, then laugh through her tears, and all the time she held on tightly to her friend's hand, which lay upon the crisp white bed sheet.

Charley leaned towards the nurse. 'Do you think Josie can hear her?' she whispered.

The nurse swallowed hard. 'I know she can,' she said, putting an arm around Charley's shoulder and squeezing her tightly. 'This will be a great comfort for them both.'

'You have a way with words, a proper angel,' Charley said.

'Me, an angel?' the nurse chuckled. 'My mum might not agree with you... I understand that Josie hadn't seen a doctor in the last month?' she then asked, seeking confirmation.

Charley shook her head. 'I wouldn't know.'

'When she passes, we won't be able to release the body straightaway. There will have to be a post-mortem,' she said to Charley. 'Local pathologist, but, as you know, if they discover any issues it will be stopped, and a Home Office pathologist called.'

Charley nodded her understanding. 'Don't worry, I'll tell Winnie, she'll understand.'

As the nurse walked away for a moment to speak to the staff nurse in charge, Charley went to kneel by her friend's side. Charley reached for her hand and Winnie held it tight.

After a while the two stood as the nurse had signalled that it was time to leave, but as they turned to do so, the alarm monitors around Josie's bedside starting bleeping loudly. The nurse and staff nurse were quickly alongside them, and Charley and Winnie were ushered outside. They turned the monitors off, and continued to check Josie's vital signs.

'She's gone, hasn't she?' Winnie wept.

Charley comforted her.

'I'm so pleased I was able to say goodbye,' Winnie sobbed.

The next day Charley stood on the step of Winnie's house and knocked at the door. She was glad she could give her the findings of the post-mortem, which showed that there were no extenuating circumstances in her friend's accident. It appeared that Josie had slipped on the bottom stone step, and in doing so, had fractured her skull badly and become unconscious. It was an injury from which she could never have recovered.

–

On the day of the funeral, Winnie checked herself in the mirror for the tenth time. Black gloves in her hand, she wore black shoes on her feet. Funerals were sad affairs. She looked out of her lounge front window, to see Charley arriving.

'You know what makes me really sad,' she said, when Charley asked her how she was feeling. 'I hate to think that Josie will go to her grave never knowing who her mother and father were. If there is one wish that I could have granted her, it was that she knew the answer to that.'

The service at St Anne's Church was quiet and moving. It had been Josie's wish to be buried in the graveyard, where she felt she belonged.

Following the service, and back in her office, Charley sat for a moment with her thoughts. Her black wool hat coat hung behind her door. She felt drained. Mike Blake put his head around the door, before walking in. 'They're already taking deposits for the new detached houses in the grounds of the old Crownest estate,' he said. 'Do you fancy one?'

Charley shook her head. 'Let's hope the occupants have better luck, and more happiness than those who lived on the land in the past,' she replied. Her voice was flat. She sat up in her chair and turned her head to the computer screen.

Mike sat down opposite her. He was smiling.

'What've you got to smile about?' Charley said.

'I have news, I had a call from Eira at Forensics whilst you were out. We can rule out Catherine as the body in the cellar.'

'How come?' she said.

'According to her, the comparison of the DNA taken from Mrs Dinah Hayfield, the lady who inherited Crownest from her cousin, Adam Alderman, shows that the skeleton in the cellar is definitely not Catherine,' he said. 'They know that because there is no family DNA match between Catherine's daughter, and the skeletal remains.'

Charley took a deep breath. 'Well,' she said. 'I guess we're going to have to accept that the body in the cellar still remains a mystery.'

'Feel sad?' Mike asked.

'A little, I hate being beaten.' Charley wrinkled her nose. 'On another note, do you think the posy that was retrieved from the floor in Josie's house was made by Lily? It does seem remarkably similar to the one in her home, and the ones that Lily leaves on the graves at St Anne's.'

'I wonder if that's where Lily was going when she left here? To see her childhood pal, after feeling unable to contact her whilst her adoptive father was alive? But why would she?'

'We'll go visit her in a while. Ask her about the posy, just for peace of mind.'

359

Sunlight was streaming through the stained glass window, directly onto the photograph of Lucinda Alderman that Lily Pritchard held in her hand. She stroked the pagan necklace, the one that the detectives had shown her, taken from the Crownest skeleton, that was hanging around Lucinda's neck in the picture. In her lap, Lucinda was cradling a young baby. Lily stroked her finger over the photograph. She felt glad that Josie had got to see the photograph of her mother before she died. After a moment or two, Lily carefully slid the photograph back behind the picture of Father Michael O'Doherty, before she put the frame back on the table where it belonged. On reflection, was the true reason that she had not sought out Josie for all these years actually not Josie's adoptive parents fault, but in fact her misplaced loyalty to her birth father Connor? Because by speaking to Lily about the past, had she feared it would open a can of worms for the church and her own family?

Lily had finally made peace with her old childhood playmate, the one who had questioned her beloved Connor's inappropriate acts, and the pictures he took. Who'd have guessed that Lily would be the last person who Josie would see? She was glad she had told Josie what Agnes had told her – at least Josie could rest in peace knowing who her parents were. She prayed to God that Lucinda, Josie's mother, was waiting for her daughter in heaven.

–

Charley sat still for a while whilst she was on the telephone to Eira from Forensics.

She had written down what Eira had told her, but Charley kept reading it back several times to take in the enormity of it.

The blood found on the knife that had killed the female skeleton held familial DNA to that of Dinah Hayfield. Acting on instinct Charley instructed a DNA test for Josie to also find a match.

'We knew that it was likely that Lucinda was Josie's mother but to have it confirmed by DNA that Seth Alderman was her father is just incredible?' gasped Charley.

'In all my career, I have never seen such a fascinating catalogue of events unfold,' Eira said, 'I'd run the skeleton's DNA through our database so many times without a hit, that I literally could not believe it when Josie's DNA turned out to be a match!'

'You're a legend!' Charley said, 'That's two drinks I owe you.'

'I'm just glad to be of assistance.' Charley could tell Eira's smile was wide by the tone of her voice, and she was as pleased for Dinah who had found out about her Alderman roots, as well as coming inheritance, and Winnie who had realised a dream for her friend to see a photograph of her mother before she died. It was just a shame that Josie would never know her true parentage.

A lump rose in Charley's throat as she tried to imagine the unimaginable – not knowing her parents or her grand-parents. The thought made the blood run cold through her veins. Another thought struck her. Could it have been Lucinda who placed her daughter, Josie, on the steps of St Anne's Church, knowing that her parents would look after the baby? Even though Lucinda had decided to go back to Seth, she may not have been sure it was safe to take the baby. Did the occupants of the collective church buildings know all along that the child was not an orphan, but Lucinda and Seth's child? Had they tried, in good faith, to protect her from the Aldermans' curse?

Ricky-Lee tapped on her door. Charley invited him in, but before he entered, he glanced over his shoulder, and the SIO looked through her window into the CID office where the rest of the team were egging him on.

'I heard you wanted to see me, and I think I need to clear the air, boss,' Ricky-Lee said, head bowed. 'I was out of order, visiting Molly when I should have been working,' he said. 'I apologise. I totally understand if you want to send me back into uniform, but I really want to stay.'

Charley leaned back in her chair, hands in her lap. 'How often have you heard the saying that the next phone call, or enquiry, could detect a crime?' Charley said.

Ricky-Lee's expression turned from downcast to bewilderment. 'Pardon?' he said.

'Would you say that a bit of luck was often the key to solving a crime?'

'As well as hard work,' he replied.

Charley sat up, and picked up the phone. 'Tell Mike I need to speak to him, will you?'

Ricky-Lee turned and swiftly walked to the door.

'Oh, and Ricky-Lee,' she said. Hand on the door handle he turned. 'Don't forget I'm watching your every move; you are walking a very thin line.' The phone was answered at the other end. 'Winnie,' the detective constable heard her say as he left the room, 'Can I come round, say in twenty minutes?'

All this time, Charley mused, Lily had known the secret that Josie had yearned for, if only Lily had sought her out and made amends for a childish mistake. It wasn't the fault of either of them that Josie was taken away, and they were denied contact. Most probably the decision to have her adopted was to protect Josie from Connor O'Doherty, after her grandparents had died.

When Charley arrived at Winnie's house, she was surprised to see Lily Pritchard sitting in an armchair drinking tea out of a china cup. There were cookies on the sidetable. 'A gift from Tattie,' Winnie said nodding at the sweet treats. There were tears in Winnie's eyes, but a sense of peace too. Winnie reached for Charley's hand. 'She knew, Charley, she knew... Josie knew, Lily went to see her before she died.'

'I know, you took her a posy of winter flowers, didn't you? I understand now, Josie was one of "them" that you spoke of, wasn't she?' said Charley.

Lily nodded. 'The other was Dinah Hayfield, Catherine's daughter, who I am going to speak to,' she said. 'I'm sorry Inspector, that I didn't tell you the whole truth, but I never lied to you. I swore on the Bible not to tell, but after our meeting at the police station, I knew I had to put things right, even if I were to be struck by lightning for breaking my promise. You've saved me a journey, I was coming to see you. I understand that you'll need a further statement from me.'

Charley smile was kind. 'There's no rush, I appreciate how hard this is for you.'

—

Charley sat in her car and inhaled deeply. She could, after all these weeks, feel her body relaxing. Murder investigations were exhausting. 'There is nothing stranger than fact,' her grandpa would say, and once again, that saying had proved to be true. Her only hope was that now Crownest had been demolished, all the demons had been put to rest, and God forbid that there would be the proverbial phoenix rising out of the ashes…

The sound of her phone ringing made her sit up as she set off back to the office.

'Where are you, boss?'

'Heading back to the office. I'll be there in a few minutes.'

With that Mike made to hang up, 'I'll speak with you then.'

When she arrived back at the station, Mike was waiting for her in the corridor to the CID office. He followed Charley into her office. 'You'd better sit down, boss.'

'Don't tell me we have another body?'

'No,' he smiled, taking his seat opposite her. 'It's good news. Hussain's DNA wasn't on the gun found in Thomas's locker. Apparently the gun had been wiped, but his DNA was on the bullets in the weapon.'

Charley's face was aglow. 'That's brilliant news!'

Mike was eager to tell her more. 'Ballistics say that the weapon we found is linked to a shooting in Birmingham. The victim lived, but suffered life-changing injuries.'

Charley made a fist. 'I just knew there was more to this.'

'Well, James Thomas might not have come to the attention of the police before, but he certainly has now. A number of police officers are lining up to speak to him about their enquires. He is clearly linked to Hussain and the drug organisation. But, I still wonder why he kept the weapon, especially in his locker?'

'Maybe to use again?' suggested Mike.

'Yeah, maybe… Perhaps we will never know, like we will never know exactly what happened that fateful night at Crownest?'

As he was leaving, Mike turned. 'The team are wondering if we should have a bit of a celebratory drink tonight?'

'It seems like a good idea. Everyone has worked hard on this double murder, but unlike the general public believe, a case isn't over for us when we apprehend and charge a criminal – there are still the files to be prepared.'

All of a sudden there was a lot of noise in the main office, then there was laughter. Charley followed Mike to the doorway.

Annie was the centre of attention. 'As I drove past the university, this twat wearing hoodie ran straight into the road like a bloody greyhound. I just missed him, the fucking dickhead.'

The young detective stopped as soon as she realised that Charley Mann was stood at her office door watching, and listening to her outburst.

'Sorry, boss. I've just had the scariest moment since I started driving. The idiot didn't stop at all. He never even looked at me. He'd been up to no good, you can bet on that.' Annie put her arms out to show Charley her trembling hands. 'I need a drink,' Annie said, sitting down.

Charley laughed and nodded once. It was indeed time for that well-deserved drink. The present enquiry was far from over, but Charley knew there would only be a limited amount of time before she got the next ultimate-adrenaline-inducing call; 'Boss, we've a body…'

Acknowledgements

Our special thanks to our publishers, Michael Bhaskar, Kit Nevile and everyone at Canelo for their hard work and commitment to making this Detective Inspector Charley Mann novel the best it can possibly be.

To our literary agent David H. Headley at DHH Literary Agency, who 'found us' and continues to support us, believes in us as writers, and is as passionate about our storytelling as we are about writing him stories.

To David's PA Emily Glenister – always at the end of the phone with a cheery voice, and the boss's ear!

To Elizabeth Woabank for her detailed job on the edit.

Thanks also to Gemma Beckwith, Judith Kay and Pamela McNulty whose contribution to *Condemned* we are very grateful for.

We couldn't have done it without you!